WHEN PELE STIRS

WHEN PELE STIRS

A Volcanic Tale of Hawai'i, Hemp, and High-Jinks

Wendell A. Duffield

iUniverse, Inc.
New York Lincoln Shanghai

When Pele Stirs
A Volcanic Tale of Hawai'i, Hemp, and High-Jinks

All Rights Reserved © 2003 by Wendell A. Duffield

No part of this book may be reproduced or transmitted in any form or by any means, graphic, electronic, or mechanical, including photocopying, recording, taping, or by any information storage retrieval system, without the written permission of the publisher.

iUniverse, Inc.

For information address:
iUniverse, Inc.
2021 Pine Lake Road, Suite 100
Lincoln, NE 68512
www.iuniverse.com

With a few obvious exceptions, the events described in this book are fictitious…but well within the realm of possibility. Though named places are real, characters (other than Leland Stanford his wife and son, Stephen Greenleaf, John McPhee, and the Davids Johnston and Packard) are products of my imagination.

Should any disciple of Pele be offended by my descriptions of that marvelous goddess, I assure you that I hold Pele in the highest esteem. I mean no disrespect. Though mostly lurking in the background of the action, She is the book's protagonist in the most complimentary sense of this word.

Diacritical marks follow current Hawaiian-language usage as closely as possible.

ISBN: 0-595-30224-6

Printed in the United States of America

For the science teachers of the Flagstaff Unified School District. While we were hot-footing it across active lava flows, cavorting in the surf at the Big Island's green-sand beach, and trekking across Kīlauea's wide and barren west flank, I was concocting the plot for this novel.

On The Front Cover: "A vaporously ethereal upper-torso likeness of Pele watches as lava-tube nostrils bleed white-hot molten rock into the evening surf along the south coast of the Big Island."

Pattern indicates parts of the Big Island covered by new lava since the first arrival of Polynesians

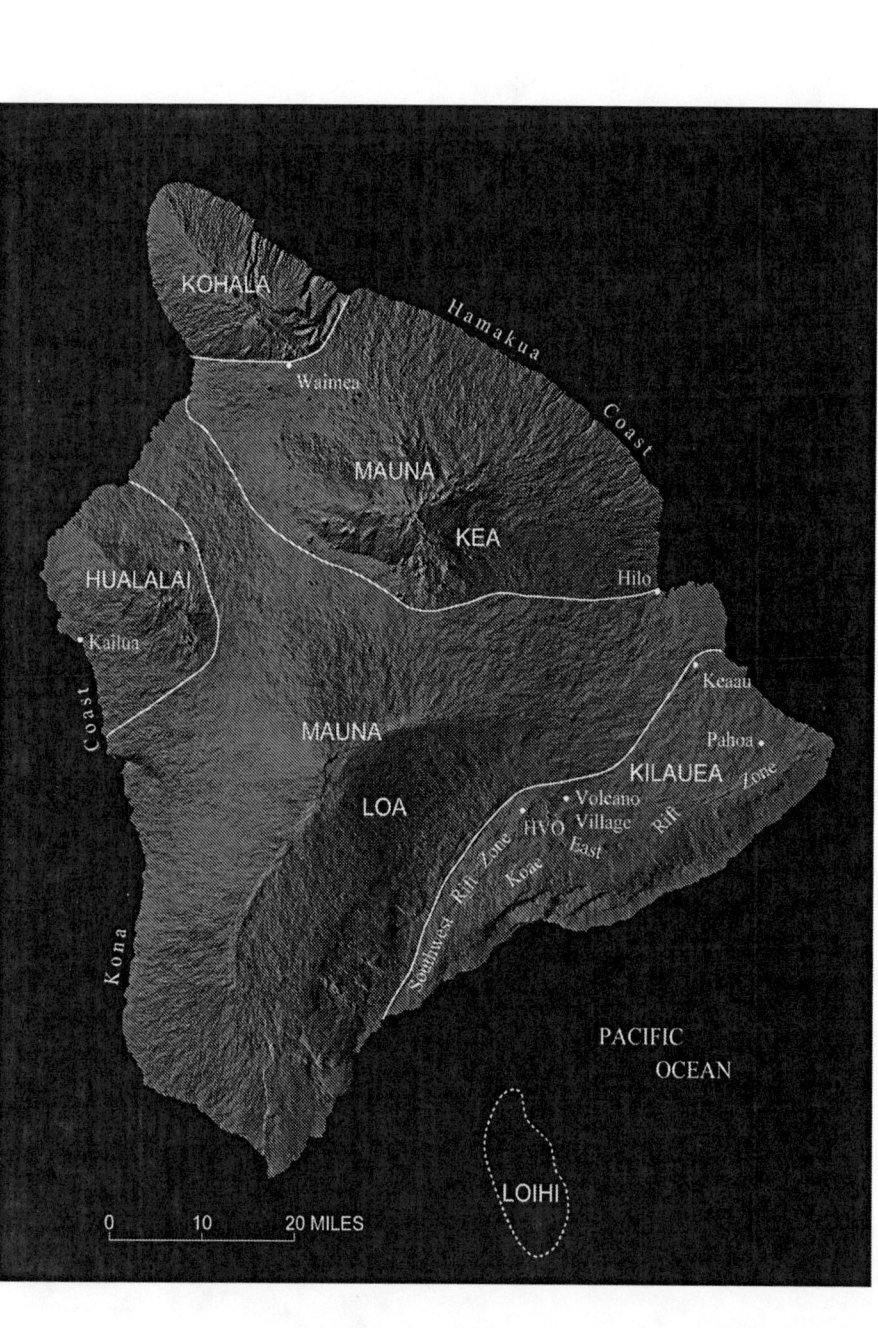

Contents

Part I	The Early 1970s
Chapter 1	A LAVA FLOW THREATENS HILO 3
Chapter 2	FUTILE HUMAN INTERVENTION 13
Chapter 3	PELE INTERCEDES 23

Part II	A Few Years Later
Chapter 4	PELE SHAKES HER VOLCANO HOME 29
Chapter 5	GEOLOGIST TALKS TO PELE 31
Chapter 6	POT-HEAD HEAVEN IN A PAKALŌLŌ PATCH 35
Chapter 7	SPOILED RICH BOY'S EPIPHANY 40
Chapter 8	HAY-SEED TEEN DISCOVERS BEER AND REEFERS.. 50
Chapter 9	GEOLOGISTS VERSUS RESTLESS VOLCANO 56
Chapter 10	HAY-SEED TEEN DISCOVERS HEAVEN AND VALERIE... 63
Chapter 11	BEN, THE EARTHQUAKE MAN 75
Chapter 12	RICH BOY'S EPIPHANY II 88
Chapter 13	HAK, THE HAWAIIAN HOOD 97
Chapter 14	AN INCREASINGLY RESTLESS VOLCANO 102
Chapter 15	POLICE VERSUS PAKALŌLŌ...................... 112
Chapter 16	AN INVENTORY PROBLEM 116

Chapter 17	A SWINGING ADVENTURE IN A WEBBED-ROPE SCROTUM	120
Chapter 18	A BONUS FOR ROTARIAN HAK	127
Chapter 19	LET THE SURVEY BEGIN	136
Chapter 20	THE LAVA TUBE WAREHOUSE	139
Chapter 21	LET THE SURVEY CONTINUE	150
Chapter 22	PAKALŌLŌ IN STORAGE	154
Chapter 23	THE CONVICT CHARADE	159
Chapter 24	BUREAUCRATIC B.S.	163
Chapter 25	BEN FINDS A BULGE	168
Chapter 26	A COMPUTER FINDS BEN'S BULGE	170
Chapter 27	IT'S HAPPENED BEFORE	175
Chapter 28	THE BULGE HISSES STEAM	178
Chapter 29	HAK MEETS OFFICER J. D. PICKETT	181
Chapter 30	A TWENTY-FIVE WATT BULB	188
Chapter 31	TWO WEEKS 'TIL CHRISTMAS	192
Chapter 32	THE FATAL BUG	194
Chapter 33	MESSAGES FROM MAGMA	196
Chapter 34	CODE ORANGE ALERT	199
Chapter 35	STEADY AS SHE GOES	203
Chapter 36	CODE RED ON CHRISTMAS EVE	206
Chapter 37	THE LAVA TUBE SCUFFLE	208
Chapter 38	ERUPTION!!	212
Chapter 39	A SQUEEZE BOX PLAYS A DEADLY TUNE	214
Chapter 40	IT'S LAVA AT FIRST SIGHT	217
Chapter 41	RANGER RITA HOLDS FORTH	221
Chapter 42	A CARBONATED FAREWELL FLING	226
Chapter 43	WHERE'S OLD JD?	233
Chapter 44	ERUPTION MARCHES EAST	236
Chapter 45	HIPPIES IN HARM'S WAY	239
Chapter 46	THE GIRL OF HIS DREAMS	242

Chapter 47	ERUPTION BACKTRACKS WEST	248
Chapter 48	JD FRIES AND HAK DIES	251
Chapter 49	THE WATER HAMMER HYPOTHESIS	256
Chapter 50	WEDDING PLANS	260
Chapter 51	ALL QUIET ON THE VOLCANO FRONT	267
Chapter 52	PELE MAKES PLANS	270
EPILOGUE		273

GLOSSARY OF HAWAIIAN WORDS *277*

ACKNOWLEDGMENTS

The book has benefited from the time and talents of several friends. Those who have helped in ways that they may remember are Dolores Biggerstaff, Suzanne Bratcher, Pam Dreher, Louella Holter, Claude Jaupart, Jean Jung, David Hill, Bob Mark, Helene Massol, Peter McGuigan, Greer Price, Sue Priest and Linda Stratton.

PART I

The Early 1970s

CHAPTER 1

A LAVA FLOW THREATENS HILO

Superficially, it was just another serene summer Saturday in Hilo, a city of several thousand people on the east shore of Hawai'i's Big Island smack dab in the middle of the Pacific Ocean. Last night's mid-July rain had freshened the town's carpet and canopy of tropical vegetation. Plants looked alive enough to frolic across the landscape, if only roots were legs.

Rain or no rain, every pandanus tree had surely taken another step or two last night on its leg-shaped exposed roots...unless local folklore was mistaken. Several checkers-playing Oriental octogenarians, once again monopolizing "their" benches along the seashore, would certainly work pandanus promenades into a daily ritual of discussing Hilo's happenings.

Huge puffy white clouds drifted lazily in from the ocean, passing high above these gossiping gray-bearded fixtures. By late morning, trade winds would sweep together a nearly continuous blanket of clouds, banking them against the massive buttress of an east-facing slope on 13,000-foot-tall Mauna Loa Volcano, Hilo's landward backdrop.

Still bathed by tropical sunshine, Hilo sat nestled under the passing clouds. Other than a couple of concrete-and-steel multistory hotels along the waterfront, most city architecture consisted of uniformly tired-looking two- and single-story wood boxes, whose original colors-assuming they had ever been painted-were largely hidden beneath a veneer of dark gray mildew. City streets were narrow asphalt strips applied over hard black basalt lava flows, which had long ago spilled down the side of Mauna Loa in innumerable overlapping volcanic ribbons.

Pacific waves lapped incessantly at the shore, slowly creating beaches by pounding basalt boulders to cobbles and cobbles to seemingly infinite grains of black sand. With two nearby volcanoes (Mauna Loa and Kīlauea) that might erupt most any time, the longevity of a growing beach was limited. Time and again, lava had flowed down these mountains into the ocean, instantaneously reconfiguring shorelines and burying beaches that had been centuries in the making. Change was the norm on these active volcanoes, and the Big Island had seen plenty. More was sure to come.

Moving south along the shoreline presently fronting Hilo, the coast turned abruptly to the east, at about mid-town, where the most recent contribution to the lava-flow foundation of the city had spilled into the sea. This bight of opportunity allowed early city planners to easily create a protected harbor and bay by building a single long breakwater, in the shape of a gracefully curving finger, anchored partway along the east-trending shore.

An onshore breeze was wafting across that breakwater and Hilo Bay, providing enough wind to caress the streets of the city with evaporative cooling, a welcome counterbalance to persistent human perspiration. Sweating was a way of life in Hilo's high humidity baked in tropical sunshine.

A few lone local window shoppers—appropriately and comfortably dressed in shorts, loose-fitting shirts, and flip-flop sandals—meandered along city streets. Without the jabber of conversations, the only sound was the soulful slap-slap-slap of those rubber sandals against the cracked and mildewed concrete of sidewalks. The abundant rains that brought this musty, ugly, and unwanted mildew also freely washed trash from sidewalks and gutters with a frequency that many cities would envy.

Most of the business part of Hilo lacked machine traffic today. Absence of the usual noise of poorly muffled cars, trucks, and motorbikes was a welcome change to the occasional listlessly drifting window gawker. In noise or silence, life on the Big Island jewel was never rushed, on weekdays or even during holiday shopping sprees. Weekends, of course, were strictly devoted to recreation, rather than to business.

For as long as locals could remember, "It's no big deal" had been the Big Island's motto. And everyone in Hilo lived out this motto…that is, everyone except naive newcomers recently moved in from the mainland and the few tourists who had somehow strayed from the Kona coast…the drier and almost always sunny western side of the island, the side with the only decent swimming beaches.

Suddenly, what sounded like a big deal slapped Saturday right across the face.

At exactly ten o'clock, sirens customarily used to warn of an approaching tidal wave (the tsunami of technical lingo) shattered Hilo's serenity. These trumpet-shaped yellow metal monsters, mounted atop posts along the waterfront, blared out their high-decibel announcement across the city. Only the totally deaf could have missed the ear-piercing drone. At 10:10, the noise stopped.

Oddly, though, citizens did not flee to tsunami-safe high ground in response to the shrill warning. Hilo's lethargic pace of life simply continued, uninterrupted. Everyone in town knew in advance what today's ten-minute signal meant, and it had nothing to do with water in the form of a giant killer wave.

Earlier that week, the City Fathers had instructed citizens to react to the siren blast, if indeed it should occur, according to where their house was located. For those whose place was near the ocean, the drill was to continue to live out the no-big-deal motto. For those with homes sitting on higher ground, partway up the slopes of Mauna Loa, the marching orders were drastically different.

The threat today was volcanic, not aquatic. The siren-borne message announced that a lava flow, originating high on Mauna Loa, would soon enter the uppermost fringes of residential Hilo. An earlier agreed-upon community strategy called for all residents living up-slope of 'Ōla'a Flume Road to now abandon their homes.

That road more or less traced out a contour at two thousand feet of elevation across the mountainside; a couple dozen homes were located higher up. The City Fathers reasoned that if a first phase of evacuation impacted only these few homes, the rest of the community would feel a minimum of concern. And, of course, the hope...and hope is all it was, since no one knew when an eruption might stop...was that the eruption *would* stop in time to avoid the need for further evacuation, at lower elevations.

Within an hour of the warning, the streets of Hilo began to buzz with activity, as obedient citizens played out their assigned roles. First, a lone car appeared, entering town on Highway 20, better known as Saddle Road. Soon, sporadic traffic morphed into a steady though brief procession of heavily and hastily loaded vehicles. The rising-and-falling din of auto traffic muffled the rhythmic slap-slap sound of sandals on sidewalks.

At the waterfront along Hilo Bay, most drivers turned left and headed north, across the Wailuku River Bridge to the safety of family and friends living atop wave-cut cliffs along the Hāmākua Coast. Others turned south, onto Highway 11 toward safe havens in Keaʻau and Pāhoa.

While this exodus exuded a sense of urgency, the laid-back sparse commerce of the downtown business district stayed unresponsive to the noisy siren warning. Ditto for activity in a nearby seaside park. Two entirely different populations seemed to exist, without interacting.

Lookers and a few buyers crowded an outdoor arts-and-crafts market along a broad grassy strip of park adjacent to the shore of Hilo Bay. A mountainous cache of umbrellas and tarps was on hand to protect valuable objects, should tropical rain suddenly drop from the over-passing clouds.

In another part of the park, well-conditioned young men played soccer as though nothing else mattered. In deference to Hilo's hot and humid climate, they wore shorts, shoes, and nothing else. Sweat nonetheless soaked their clothes and dripped from wet skin quickly and abundantly. In countermeasure, the occasional errant kick sent a ball into the surf, which provided a compelling, though trumped up, reason for players to enjoy a ball-rescuing dip in the sea. Even a casual observer could see that most errant kicks were not accidental.

Nearby, bikini-clad women, young enough to still be publicly proud of their taut elastic skin, stretched out on brightly colored towels. They were fine tuning already remarkable tans. A cyclic change from supine to prone positions created the appearance of pieces of tasty flesh on slowly rotating skewers. Unfastened bikini tops were properly though loosely positioned during supine time. Face up or down, all bodies were parallel, lined up to optimize the tanning efficiency of incoming solar rays. As stunningly eye-pleasing examples of mixed Polynesian, Oriental, and Caucasian heritage, these young women were swimsuit calendar beauties.

The soccer and sunbathing groups pretended to be unaware of each other, in one of those juvenile standoffish mating rituals. But the unmistakable musky emanations from male and female hormones working overtime mingled in gusts of shared breezes, stimulating the nostrils of both genders and belying the appearance of disinterest. Not surprisingly, some errant soccer balls sailed landward, into that sea of nubile female flesh, rather than into the salt water of the Pacific.

In another part of the park, generationally removed from antics of the mating game, middle-aged mothers, whose ample bodies were covered with tent-like muumuus, chased after children hard at play on the soft mat of clothes-staining grass. Meanwhile, inert overweight husbands and fathers chugged beer beneath the shade-giving fronds of a coconut tree. They chain smoked and woofed down junk food, while dissecting the intricacies of this and that professional sport. These men looked as though even vicarious sporting activity could be life threatening. They had been through the soccer phase of their lives long ago; ditto for their wives and tanning.

These relaxed citizens of Hilo ignored the brief evacuation procession of overloaded vehicles, peeling off north and south on the bay-front road bordering the park. Evacuation was complete by noon. The neighborhood above ʻŌlaʻa Flume Road was silent save for the sounds of birds, mongooses, and feral pigs drifting away from an unidentified though threatening something that seemed to be approaching from uphill.

Sluggish but potentially dangerous lava was still advancing so slowly toward the core housing areas and business district that people there could continue normal daily routines…for the time being. Some residents were old enough to have been through a similar, and successful, drill in 1942. For a while, that lava flow had seemed *so* threatening to the city. But then it stagnated at 2,500 feet elevation, a good seven miles outside the Hilo of the 1940s. With that experience under their belts, the concept of "It's no big deal" worked for these old-timers today.

Right now, though, a pesky fiery finger was pushing against a flaming Hicks Home, somewhere above ʻŌlaʻa Flume Road…a metaphorical "line in the sand" between man and volcano. Over the years, many a disappointed homeowner had learned the expensive way that the flimsy single-wall construction of the Hicks version of family housing can barely withstand the force of a moderate tropical wind, to say nothing about the force, heat, and fury of 2000-degree rock-forming lava. The battle line itself would disappear after several of these homes in harm's way had been destroyed.

Minutes after phase-one evacuation was complete and the first few abandoned homes were being engulfed in flames, the city's mayor and the minister of civil defense were taking turns shouting at the Scientist-in-Charge of the Hawaiian Volcano Observatory (HVO). Their stand-up-and-stare meeting was in the mayor's office, near a civic center famous for its gigantic, ancient banyan tree.

Mayor Shinta, a bald overweight politician known to be more concerned about the content and quantity of his next meal than the safety of citizens, was red-faced with emotion. Even his normally white bald pate was now flushed. Bulging bluish veins running up a flabby neck looked ready to burst. Soft pink-and-pudgy fingers, tipped with the long pointed shapes of professionally manicured nails, fanned the air in futile attempts to add emphasis to words. He wore a pale green seersucker suit, over an open-necked aloha shirt. Reflective, almost mirror sheen, white patent leather shoes protruded awkwardly from trouser legs inches too short. His shrill voice enhanced an overall lack-of-leadership image. His election had been the result of no-big-deal voter apathy.

"My god, Jackson, what kind of ivory tower operation do you run up there on your sacred Kīlauea Volcano? You're supposed to provide us with warnings about all our Big Island volcanoes, not just Kīlauea. But instead, what's happened!!?? Let me remind you!"

In seemingly involuntary motion, Shinta raised his right foot and nervously polished the already-shiny toe of his right shoe on the back of his left pant leg.

"First, you give us no inkling that an eruption of Mauna Loa is about to hit, in spite of all the fancy scientific doodads and highly trained staff at your disposal. And then, your basket of ideas about how to deal with this hot monster seems pretty damned empty. Bruddah, I don't know why the feds waste tax dollars on your HVO operation if you can't supply the warnings our community needs, here in the shadow of this giant volcano."

Shinta finished this tirade while wagging his right index finger in Jackson's face, a guitar-pick-sized fingernail nearly slicing Jackson's nose. Without losing balance, he buffed the toe of his left shoe across the back of his right pant leg. This kind of corporeal coordination for such a non-athletic man reflected considerable practice at the one-legged shoe-shining dance.

"I hope you remember that I put my reputation on the line for you last year, spending most of my political chits with the Hawaiian congressional delegation. I lobbied hard for an increase in your operating budget."

Jackson took a deep breath, gritted his teeth behind closed lips, slowly blinked his eyes once, and remained exceedingly calm. It wasn't his fault that Mauna Loa was acting up. No one, no matter how brilliant, and no organization, no matter how well funded and staffed, could control a volcano. Extensive university training, followed by years of field experience, had taught him that the best one could do is learn what and where the hazards are, make recommendations for mitigating procedures, and then live with whatever the politicians decided was acceptable risk in their land-use planning legislation. This was the weakest part of the process…getting the politicians to adopt land-use plans that recognized the compelling forces of nature over the self-serving ones of money-hungry real estate developers.

Like so many politicians, Shinta wanted simple answers to complex questions. And had this shallow self-centered joke of a mayor already forgotten that his precious chits resulted in zero new funding for HVO?

Before Jackson could remind Shinta of these truths, Frank "Fuzzy" Chee, of civil defense, jumped in. Chee was short, slender, and of obvious oriental descent, from his wide oval eyes to dainty feet. The nickname Fuzzy had followed him since early adulthood and was coined in reference to an unkempt goatee that decorated his chin. Those who claimed to know a bit about this rather inscrutable man said that Chee refused to comb his beard with anything other than his fingers. As a result, his chin was both skuzzy and fuzzy. Hard-to-identify foreign objects were known to fall from this tangled growth, sometimes at socially awkward moments during his official duties. News media painstakingly detailed such events, sometimes completely omitting (forgetting?) the original assigned story line. Chee's voice was firm but soft, with a singsongy lilt.

"You know, sir, your lack of a timely warning that Mauna Loa was about to erupt makes all of us in positions of authority look pretty foolish, to say nothing about putting our good citizens at risk."

Jackson found himself trying to identify a tune that would closely fit the cadence and words of Chee's message. The message itself was so predictable that Jackson ignored it.

As Chee spoke, he combed his beard with the fingers of his left hand. The first two strokes, timed to coincide with his spoken phrases, were continuous and smooth. A barely noticeable finger-comb catch during the third pass bespoke of a hairy snag.

Jackson watched as a small object fell from the tip of Chee's third finger at the bottom of that stroke. Pretending to stare downward in deep thought about the eruption, Jackson saw a living something scurry into a narrow opening between baseboard and hardwood flooring. He made a mental note to (anonymously) send this man some strong shampoo, with detailed how-to-use instructions. He also fantasized about the day when retirement would free him from having to deal with Hilo's bizarre and eclectic cast of politicians. It seemed he needed to be more a psychiatrist than scientist to deal with these folks.

"Maybe it's time to break camp up there at HVO and save the taxpayers millions of dollars in apparently useless volcano watching. How many years of research does it take before you can give us alerts?"

The ensuing silence indicated an end to the pontifical complaints. Jackson's mind was attempting to fit Chee's last words to the tune of "The answer my friend is blowing in the wind"…and with enough success to prompt a subtle grin.

He was also reminding himself that this wasn't the first time worried politicians had berated him. Nor would it be the last. This part of his job, as the leader of HVO, came with the territory. Still, having let them vent, it was now once again time for him to remind these politicos of a few facts.

Jackson took another deep breath and stood erect, squarely in front of the whiners, positioned to stare them down. Though in his early 60s, he was still physically fit from a life of studying volcanoes on foot in the field, rather than from books read in the soft comfort of an office chair. A rich, almost chocolaty tan and the emerging hint of sun-induced wrinkles across his forehead and forearms testified to years of outdoor work. A firmly muscled body, six-foot-five stature, and even low voice exuded strength and authority. He wore his usual uniform of faded blue jeans, a favorite off-white Filipino polo barong shirt, and sturdy walking shoes. He looked like a well conditioned out-of-uniform Marine, with moderately long hair. He alone of this trio had remained calm throughout the discussion, even when his detractor's voices were raised.

"First of all, gentlemen, remember that it wasn't my decision to build the city of Hilo exactly in harm's way of the largest and one of the world's most active volcanoes. It's only because your city government keeps approving building permits for ground higher and higher on Mauna Loa that any homes are being damaged right now.

"Number two: Yes, we have sophisticated equipment and the best trained volcano-observatory staff in the world at HVO. We're damned proud of this. But how the hell are we supposed to adequately study this huge beast called Mauna Loa when most of the mountain is so remote and inaccessible that it takes forever on foot or lots of unaffordable helicopter time to get there? We do everything possible within our budget and staffing."

Jackson was holding out his right hand clenched into an I-mean-business fist, coated with an invisible film of velvet. For additional emphasis, he extended one more finger with each point he made, aiming the digits at the appropriate antagonist. Three fingers now wagged back and forth between Shinta and Chee.

"I'm sick and tired of hearing about a 'lack of timely warning' that this eruption was about to start. You guys give that bitch a rest, okay! We all know why the HVO network of instruments failed to record telltale earthquake tremors that occurred during those last couple of nights before eruption began. If we'd known about those obvious precursors to eruption, we'd have warned you. But once again, politics screwed up science. You politicians know how that can happen, don't you. Surely you remember *why* we missed those red-flag warnings of impending eruption!"

Shinta and Chee nodded in grudging embarrassed agreement.

"So, don't criticize my crew for simply trying to be conscientious civil servants. Take that problem up with your Washington D.C. congressmen, if you need more explanation."

Shinta and Chee stayed silent and attentive…now looking cowed. Jackson was firmly in charge of the conversation.

"Number four: From the first appearance of live lava up there on Mauna Loa, I've kept both of you briefed daily, if not hourly, about every detail of how the eruption was developing, as best I knew the situation. There's never been a hidden agenda here, so don't complain about lack of current information."

All fingers of both hands were now extended.

"And finally, gentlemen, the lava flow that right now is burning and burying the homes of some of your good citizens has been marching slowly but steadily down toward Hilo for the past two weeks. Keep in mind that during all this time, we've tried every available technique to avert what's happening. What more can anyone do?! There's no magical lava valve that we can turn off, you know. So, let's just all calm down and try to find some common ground on how to deal with what this eruption might yet throw at us."

The three men looked at each other and gave sighs of relief that signaled an end to histrionic face saving. It was time to figure out how to save lives and property, instead.

In attempts at relaxation, Shinta tried, unsuccessfully, to crack his knuckles. Failure was undoubtedly the result of overly thick masses of fleshy padding around joints. He kept going through the silent motions, anyway.

Chee returned to stroking his goatee, as Shinta began another shoeshine shuffle.

Jackson simply stood Marine ramrod straight and continued talking.

"The good news is that your tsunami-warning sirens successfully triggered the first wave of evacuation. I congratulate you on such obedient citizens."

Jackson then turned away. Followed by Shinta and Chee, he walked toward a map of the Big Island, taped to the office wall. The sheet was about three feet on a side, and was one of the topographic charts made by the U.S. Geological Survey, the parent organization of HVO. The map featured five obvious mountains, from Kohala in the north to Kīlauea at the south. These marked the tops of the Big Island's volcanoes.

A deformed-bullseye pattern of concentric brown contour lines, labeled with their elevations, defined the shape of Mauna Loa, whose long gentle east side sloped from an elevation of more than 13,000 feet to sea level at Hilo. What the map didn't show was the additional 15,000 feet of volcano hidden beneath the waters of the ocean. The locals, though, were well aware that this monstrous 28,000-foot mountain is the largest volcano in the world. They understood that it was damned big and equally powerful, when in an eruptive mood.

Someone had penciled in a thin finger-shaped area on that part of the map, starting high on the slope, near the 10,000-foot elevation contour. The finger was colored bright orange, to mimic the hue of the active lava flow it represented. This colorful digit extended squarely across contour lines in a path pointing directly toward the city.

Someone had written the month, day, and hour at successively lower elevations along the finger to indicate where the front of advancing lava had been at various times since eruption had begun. Jackson studied this pattern and pursed his lips in thought. Shinta and Chee watched the thinking giant in silence.

"Now look, we only have five deaths attributable to the eruption…so far…and those are through no fault of ours. We know how fast the lava has been moving downslope and roughly where it's headed. What we *don't* know is when the eruption may stop. So, I suggest we try to figure out when a stage-two evacuation may be needed, assuming eruption will continue. We need to get the word out to the public about how we'll signal that next decision point."

As Shinta and Chee watched, Jackson stripped the map from the wall, carried it to a large table, and began the task of projecting the speed and direction of lava advancing toward Hilo.

CHAPTER 2

FUTILE HUMAN INTERVENTION

Eruption began on a Sunday morning when most people were at their chosen place of worship. At about the same time that church-going supplicants were asking a variety of gods for a favor or two, a half-mile-long fissure, pointed toward Hilo, opened high on Mauna Loa and started to gush molten rock. This hot ooze quickly formed into a one-hundred-foot wide river of lava, also headed toward Hilo. Presumably, these events were not in answer to prayer.

At first, though, the fiery river advancing down the mountain was an exciting and welcome sight to the local population. Such a colorful performance of raw natural power hadn't been visible from Hilo since 1942. And what was there to worry about, with the lava front at least twenty-five miles from town and advancing ever so slowly?

From a lifetime of living with their active volcanoes, locals knew that the lava flowing down Mauna Loa was not a fast and vicious killer. Many of these people had played safely along the edges of moving lava more than once, at both Kīlauea and Mauna Loa. They knew that a person would almost have to throw himself in harm's way to get burned or buried.

Yes, the buildings of Hilo might be completely burned and buried…eventually, if eruption lasted long enough. But the odds of this happening were miniscule. If people practiced mere common sense, perhaps spiced with a tiny bit of luck, the lava flow would claim no human victims and very little human property.

Meanwhile, the new eruption was an economic boon to local merchants. Tourists, who usually would have spent their entire vacation on the sunny-and-dry Kona side of the Big Island, flooded Hilo with their presence and money.

When weather permitted, buzzing aluminum insects of commerce filled the skies. In only a few days' time, air-tour companies were pocketing what would normally be months of income. With no set rules of engagement for over-flights, other than obvious procedures to avoid mid-air collisions, pilots were treating tourists to truly unique perspectives of eruption in action. Single- and twin-engine, fixed-wing aircraft cruised back and forth over the flowing orange river in relatively high flight paths. At lower levels, the more-maneuverable helicopters offered customers incredibly close-up viewing.

Unfortunately, on day three of the eruption a helicopter pilot tried to show his passengers the lava river a bit too close. While he hovered about two hundred feet above the two-thousand-degree molten rock, so the clicking cameras of his human payload could capture extraordinary images, a violent updraft suddenly lifted his chopper another two hundred feet. Turbulent air then flipped the machine over, and an equally strong downdraft thrust it, main-rotor first, into the river.

The spinning rotor immediately snapped off, on contacting thick and viscid lava. Next, the tail assembly swung wildly into the bank of the lava river, impacting with enough force to be bent back snugly against the main cabin. The resulting compact aluminum package began to float downstream. Surprisingly, the jet fuel of a nearly full tank simply evaporated rather than burning, in spite of being heated to the temperature of molten steel.

Neither pilot nor his four passengers, a vacationing French family, had much time to comprehend or react to their twisted and sizzling fate. The pilot did manage to transmit a panicky and terse last message, though, received by other aircraft in the area: "Holy camel dung!"

The pilot of a sister helicopter, hovering nearby, watched in disbelief. He had the presence of mind to broadcast a running commentary of unfolding events to the control tower at Hilo's airport. His observations became the basis of an official account, during later investigation into the accident.

"Hilo tower, this is helicopter zero niner alpha. Hilo tower, this is helicopter zero niner alpha."

A relaxed, almost bored-sounding voice responded. "Zero niner alpha, this is Hilo tower. Go ahead."

"I'm up here over the lava river. And…well…a sister chopper's down! A chopper's crashed into that lava river!"

Brief silence reflected initial shock of the radio operator at the tower. Then…"Keep talking, zero niner. We're going to tape this for the record."

"It's Ollie Stargel's machine…zero seven zulu. He and his load are goners for sure."

The radio operator at Hilo could hear an emotional catch in the pilot's voice, with the comment about "goners." The airwaves again went silent. "Keep talking zero niner alpha. We need the information."

"I…I think Ollie got caught up in strong turbulence. He was thrown up, and then back down…upside down…My god! Now his machine is gettin' bent into a ball…I'm guessin' from the push of lava and bangin' against the solid levees of the river."

"Okay, zero niner. I know this is tough, but keep talking. The FAA folks will want as much info as possible. This could be a tough accident for them to reconstruct."

The pilot's voice came back strong and steady.

"Bizzzzarre! Now it's floatin' along and bein' coated with black rock. Lava must be platin' out against the cool aluminum skin. This weird-lookin' package is bobbin' up and down…bouncin' and tumblin' with the flow. I've gotta tell ya the damned thing looks like one of those French sweets, a giant bonbon, a great big chocolate-colored goodie, headin' for Hilo."

This unique piece of imitation rock candy soon completely disappeared beneath lava. There was nothing more to report. The buried chopper and its human cargo were never found.

The entire episode, from updraft to candy coating to disappearance, was captured on movie film by one of the passengers in zero niner alpha. That footage brought its owner a handsome price in the following frenzy of media-bidding competition.

Major news networks had a good time with the story. Most tried to balance a proper degree of sympathy and reverence for the pilot and his Parisian passengers against the unusual and colorful sides of the tale. Reporters who dared to be a little tasteless gave the word *bonbon* its properly nasal French accent.

Back on the Big Island, lesson learned, future chopper flights stayed well above turbulent air. At ground level, jeep tours up Saddle Road from Hilo got folks close enough for great viewing with binoculars. Tripod-mounted cameras with phallic telephoto lenses captured publishable images. With nearly non-stop Kodak, Fuji, and Agfa moments from the air and on the ground, photo shops had no trouble selling their film at temporarily inflated prices.

Diners who wanted to be mesmerized by the eerie orange glow of molten rock reflected from the bottoms of clouds booked the outdoor dining rooms of hotels and restaurants every evening. The ooohs and aaahs of satisfied observers increased in number and volume with each round of mai tais consumed in comfortable surroundings.

Except for the helicopter mishap, fun and profit were being had in abundance by all.

However, ten days into the eruption, when the river of lava showed no hint of drying up and its leading-edge snout had descended to within three miles of Hilo's uppermost residential areas, public delight turned to official concern. That's when Jackson and Hilo politicians activated plans for lava diversion. Jackson had devised a two-pronged attack.

The U.S. Air Force began the war against lava with carefully orchestrated bombing runs. Their objective was to breach the rubbly rocky levees that had built up along the cool margins of the lava river. Jackson knew that holes in levees might divert flow from the long main channel aimed straight toward Hilo. If bombing could disperse the advancing lava into a broad front, Hilo would gain precious additional time before possible inundation.

At the request of Hawai'i's influential U.S. senators, pilots and their armed jet aircraft flew in from Hickam Air Force Base on O'ahu. Given the military's omnipresent desire for new and unusual targets to practice on, even a request from Mayor Shinta would have received a resounding yes. Captains Whittaker, Brubaker, and Jones, all experienced veterans of the Vietnam War, were assigned the lava-river duty. And they had a ball.

Each plane carried two heat-seeking missiles, mounted on the underside of the wings. These evil-looking messengers of destruction would challenge a powerful force of nature.

The pilots carried out their mission at dawn of day eleven, before cloud buildup might obscure the target. The FAA canceled all Big Island commercial airline flights that morning. Tourist flights, too, were put on hold for reasons of simple safety. No one wanted other aircraft in the same sky with missile-armed jets on the prowl and prepared to fire.

Hilo Airport served as a temporary Air Force command post. All three armed-and-ready jets were airborne by sunrise, circling clockwise lazily in formation two thousand feet above the Pacific, about thirty miles east of Hilo.

Public broadcasts of radio conversation between pilot and ground control provided colorful listening.

"Whittaker to ground control. I'm going in for a recon pass, to size up my target."

"Roger."

Whittaker broke from the pattern and headed west toward Hilo. He approached the island barely faster than stall speed, a few hundred feet above the deck and off to one side of the lava river. He wanted a clear long look at the target. He pulled back on the joystick just enough for his plane to follow the gently upward profile of Mauna Loa.

"Whoa! Look at that long orange restless finger, pointing straight down at Hilo. Hey, that shape kinda reminds me of my right hand's middle digit. I'll bet the volcano is sending a special and not-too-subtle message to the city."

"That's enough editorializing, Captain. The good folks of Hilo have plenty to worry about, without believing that Mauna Loa is flipping them the bird."

"Wilco. Aaaah, this mission should be a piece of cake. My target doesn't take evasive action, and it doesn't fire back. Man, what a treat after 'Nam. And if a heat-seeking missile can't find an oversized 2000-degree enemy, the U.S. Air Force is in deep excrement. Okay, I'm going back around and fire my first shot."

"Roger."

Whittaker pulled up and turned to the north, over Mauna Kea. He continued in a broad arc, out to sea east of Hilo where Brubaker and Jones were still circling, and then came around sharply to a west heading, lined up with the lava river. In an instant he was over Hilo, closing fast on his target.

"Ground control, I'm going for a mid-elevation hit…something around 5000 feet. Let's hope the missile doesn't decide to seek heat too soon."

"Roger, Captain Whittaker. Cleared for firing."

Whittaker's first missile hit the target squarely, creating a gaping breach in the lava-river's south levee. With another go-around, his second missile was equally effective, as were those of Jones and Brubaker, who followed in reverse alphabetical succession.

The mission was a complete success in terms of blasting away north and south levee walls at six spots between elevations of 5000 and 7000 feet, high above any inhabited areas. New streamlets formed off to the sides as lava spilled through the gaps. Within minutes, the flow of lava in the main channel slowed noticeably. When this news hit the public airwaves, the entire city sighed in relief.

Unfortunately, within a couple of hours, as pilots, ground crews, Jackson, politicians, and the press were still celebrating a job well done, the combination of gravity's constant tug and the shape of the mountainside pulled all six new streamlets back into the course of the main channel. An observation recon flight radioed this news back to Hilo. The entire expensive missile-run caper had bought only a few hours' delay in the advancing front of the lava river as it reached ever closer to Hilo.

Being a realist, experienced with the seemingly fickle behavior of volcanoes, Jackson was not surprised to learn about the futility of their aerial bombing. He huddled with Shinta and Chee.

"Gentlemen, it's time to put plan B into action. This time the agents of lava diversion will be giant earth-moving machines."

There weren't many rigs of this sort on the Big Island, and most of them were on the Kona Coast, where they were kept busy gouging and leveling land for new subdivisions, condo complexes, and hotels. But within twelve hours after the call for help, a dozen D-9 behemoths were working along 'Ōla'a Flume Road, pushing up a twenty-five-foot-tall barrier designed to deflect the advancing front of the lava river away from downtown Hilo.

Jackson's plan B called for a two-mile-long barrier ridge, or one as long as time permitted them to build. The upslope end would be at about 2000-feet in elevation, and the ridgeline would extend out to the northeast. They were back in the mayor's office. Shinta and Chee were feeling left out of the planning process.

"Come here, gentlemen. Look at this map of Hilo. Fewer houses stand in harm's way if we can divert lava to the northeast, rather than to the southeast. And even more homes can be saved if we can coax the lava across Hilo's abandoned golf course and beyond, into these large lava tubes, the Kaūmana Caves. This would at least put the destructively fiery stuff back underground…even if only temporarily. Filling those tubes would destroy a tourist attraction, but saving a few houses is far more important. Besides, between the two of them, Kīlauea and Mauna Loa seem to create new lava tubes every few years."

Shinta and Chee agreed with Jackson's reasoning. All present nodded approval of plan B. Shinta and Chee immediately got on the phone to Kona owners of heavy equipment.

Barrier construction began about noon on the day of stage-one evacuation, two weeks into the eruption. The sound and sight of straining diesel engines spewing plumes of sooty exhaust were heard and seen from Hilo and beyond.

That same day, the advancing front of lava encountered its first human-made obstacle…two miles upslope from where the big cats were pushing up piles of rock and soil into a ridgeline. By this time, stage-one evacuation was complete.

A sea-moss-green boxy house on three-foot stilts burst into flames triggered by heat radiated from lava still ten feet distant. Five minutes later the house was a pile of ashy residue. In another minute, ash and home site disappeared beneath glistening new lava. No one saw this happen, but it surely did.

As the lava river slowly yet inexorably advanced beyond its first "kill", the owners of some houses in harm's way sneaked back into the disappearing neighborhood. They came armed with cameras. They were fervently driven on a critical family mission. The Hilo rumor mill claimed that photographic evidence of a house bursting into flames before actually being touched by lava would justify a claim against fire insurance. If flames came after contact, though, conflagration was considered an act of god, not covered by insurance. Flames just before or after contact was a fine point, perhaps, but one that seemed worth some effort to document on the part of a homeowner whose entire material wealth was in his house.

In spite of laudable intentions motivated by financial self-preservation of their families, two of the home-owning photographers died due to inexperience with searing hot lava, carelessness, and just plain stupidity.

Frank Gomez was one of those who sneaked back into the evacuated and off-limits area. According to his mother, his wife, and even his five children, Frank had never been known for an adequate abundance of active gray matter. Once again he proved this to be true, this time by being stupid enough to use a full five-hundred-gallon propane tank as a shield between him and intense heat radiated by the advancing lava. Lava was only a few feet away when Frank captured the photographic evidence he wanted. His heat shield was working fine. But he lingered a minute too long, mesmerized by his house being engulfed in flames. Then, all of the calories being absorbed by the tank, instead of Frank, pressurized the contained propane beyond the breaking point of its now hot-and-weak steel container. The ensuing explosion and instantaneous fireball pretty much vaporized Frank. Days later, a human jawbone was discovered in the branch of a bush about a hundred yards from the home site. Matches with dental records, most especially the presence of deformed molars and a lack of wisdom teeth, confirmed that this was part of Frank…all that was ever found.

Once it was safe to return, his ever-fun-loving family remembered mentally challenged Frank with an epitaph carved in new basalt covering the home site: "At this place, we lost our friend Frank, whose lack of wisdom (teeth) was blown away with the tank."

Homeowner and would-be photographer Jimmy Chang became the victim of a bursting steam pressure cooker. His small house sat in a tiny clearing hacked out of dense lush rainforest vegetation. Like Frank, Jimmy got the photographic evidence he needed to collect his fire insurance. But suddenly, all the moisture in the water-saturated tropical plants and their roots underfoot was converted to a powerful steam explosion, triggered by heat from the encroaching lava. Jimmy disappeared with the explosion.

The steam burst unceremoniously tossed his fleshy rag doll of a body onto the fiery river. He was almost certainly dead before contact with lava, where his body simply floated along like limbs of driftwood. Bones and a little flesh that survived their hot journey were mostly engulfed by lava. Parts of his body were discovered a mile downstream from the home site once the eruption stopped. A barely recognizable corpse was embedded supine within the top of the lava flow.

After the news media broadcast the demise of these two concerned homeowners, the thoughts of others who had considered gathering evidence for the insurance company turned to preservation of human life, instead.

Two days and ten burned-and-buried houses later, lava met diversion barrier. The D-9 crew had managed to complete the entire two miles of this rocky ridge.

At first contact, success seemed at hand. As lava mushed into the obstruction, the leading edge of hot oozing molten rock hissed and clunked and grudgingly turned left, following the ridgeline direction. Flow continued at its slow steady pace, headed for the site of the now-defunct Hilo Country Club Golf Course. The Kaūmana lava caves were the following targeted place in line for plan B, should eruption persist long enough.

Jackson, Shinta, and Chee were among a clutch of officials present to see what would happen. They stood atop the barrier and cheered loudly and spontaneously when the lava river was deflected to the north. Scientists, politicians, and uniformed military men alike temporarily trashed normal decorum. Like excited teenagers, they jumped in glee and shared high fives all around.

Still uneasy with what he saw, though, Jackson knew that at best they were simply buying additional time before more evacuations were needed…even if the barrier held. He was also remembering that similar barriers had not been able to redirect the paths of lava flows during earlier attempts to do so in Hawai'i, and at other volcanic places, too, like Iceland and Italy. Why should today's barrier be any more effective than those failures? Because of this gnawing uncertainty, Jackson's level of enthusiasm during the spate of high fives and cheers had been less than soaring.

So, as the others babbled and partied on, he kept close watch on the downhill side of the barrier…manning the volcano equivalent of a forest fire lookout tower.

What none (not even Jackson) in the group had been able to see, as surface lava turned north, was that the molten stuff at the *bed* of its fiery river was burrowing slowly under the barrier, physically lifting the obstacle like a cork on water. And sure enough, within thirty minutes, this offensive submarining lava peeked out at the base of the downhill side of the barrier, like the head of an unwanted gopher surfacing in a vegetable garden, half-eaten bright-orange carrot in its mouth.

Jackson saw the orange lava emerge. He knew that a substantial river of molten rock would soon be headed straight for dense residential housing and the business district of Hilo. The rest of the VIPs were still celebrating their apparent success, oblivious to what was happening a mere three stories beneath their feet. Jackson cleared his throat at a volume sure to attract attention. Heads wearing puzzled expressions turned toward him.

"I hate to be the party pooper for all you happy folks, but look down for the bad news." He pointed to direct their attention toward lava oozing out at the downhill base of the barrier.

From their perch atop the ridge, Shinta, Chee and the others stared in disbelief. Jackson shrugged the shrug of one in the know. He was remembering the tired cliché about beauty being only skin deep, as he glanced from the barrier-diverted northbound surface of the lava river to the directly downhill and east-bound stuff oozing out beneath the barrier.

Suddenly realizing that they were riding a pile of loose rock floating on flowing lava, all but Jackson scrambled off the barrier to solid ground. Jackson followed at his own measured pace. He, Shinta, and Chee regrouped at the mayor's office to finalize plans for a stage-two evacuation, which would be put into effect early the next day, signaled by another ten-minute blast from the tsunami-warning sirens.

The situation looked grim. Bombs and barrier had failed. Lava was advancing toward the heart and soul of the city. A silent funk filled the mayor's office. In frustration, Shinta and Chee regressed to their shoe-shining and beard-combing exercises. Only Jackson was calm and rational enough to speak. "Okay, gentlemen. It's time to rethink our battle plan. Our Maginot line may be leaky, but we shouldn't give up yet."

Though sounding and appearing outwardly as strong and in control as usual, Jackson felt awash with a sense of helplessness. During the early part of his career, he had studied many explosive volcanoes around the Pacific ring-of-fire, before coming to HVO. Now, once again, he was reminded that even though Hawaiian lava flows rarely kill people, the horrendous and lingering uncertainty of how long and how far a flow might extend creates major-league anxiety, angst, and grief for people with property positioned in harm's way. By contrast, he was familiar with the death and destruction caused by a fast-moving volcanic hurricane of hot rocks riding in a stinky soup of fetid fumes, something geologists call a pyroclastic flow. This type of demise was instantaneous, leaving no time to worry about what may or may not happen.

He wasn't sure which type of volcano encounter he would choose, if he had to…a long life with ulcers and haunting recurring dreams, or a shorter happier life lived to the hilt until pyroclastic death. But he was downright certain that an ever increasing number of people would become victims of volcanoes, slowly or quickly, simply because more and more folks were choosing to be neighbors of the Mauna Loas, Krakataus, and Popocatépetls of the world.

Well, here in Hilo they would have to put a stage-two evacuation into action, and hope that Mauna Loa would soon tire of erupting. Jackson continued his soul searching.

"I don't know why I think of volcanoes as living creatures, when all of my schooling tells me that they are inanimate objects, subject to behavior according to the laws of science."

Inanimate object or not, he silently pleaded with Mauna Loa, the world's largest volcano, to spare Hilo. Then, he snapped back to being the rational scientist. "Gentlemen, here's what I suggest as our next maneuver."

CHAPTER 3

PELE INTERCEDES

As scientists and politicians worked late into that night developing a spectrum of evacuation scenarios, including one for total annihilation of the city, a group of adult native Hawaiians gathered at a home near Rainbow Falls Park, not far from the lava river.

They numbered ten. They were robust bronze-skinned men. Generous mats of rather coarse black hair covered their heads. They moved slowly and deliberately, organizing themselves and what looked to be mostly foodstuff. They spoke in low solemn unhurried voices, projecting confidence and a sense of mission. They wore traditional ceremonial garb…including colorful loincloths, robes, and ornamented helmets. A few carried long warrior-like spears, decorated for an event other than war. Their thickly callused feet needed no shoes.

The person addressed as Kahuna was clearly their leader. The others responded quickly to his suggestions and requests. They loaded their gear and themselves into a van. They drove as close as possible to the advancing lava, and then walked until they were within several feet of this hot tongue. There, in the darkness of night illuminated only by the glowing lava surface, they recited chants in their native Hawaiian language. Between chants, they laid offerings near the front of the lava.

A mix of traditional and contemporary gifts included fresh ʻahi wrapped in ti leaves, a bouquet of wild orchids, a branch broken from an ʻōhiʻa tree so recently that its bright red lehua flowers looked vibrantly fresh, ʻōhelo berries filling the half shell of a coconut, a bunch of bananas, three bottles of gin, and a scatterings of coins, mostly quarters of U.S. currency.

For their final incantation, sung in a strong vibrant voice charged with meaning and emotion, the ten men linked arms and faced the source of the lava river, high on Mauna Loa. Kahuna led the choir. He chanted a short simple line.

"E ola mau, e Pele e!" (Long life to you, Pele).

The others repeated the message. "E ola mau, e Pele e!"

After several more rounds, with a wave of his hand Kahuna signaled an end to the ritual. By then, new lava had covered all the offerings, an indication that the object of their ceremony accepted these gifts.

Satisfied, Kahuna gave one last silent salute to Mauna Loa, his arms raised and fully extended toward the mountain. Then, he and his followers dispersed toward their homes. Tomorrow, they would be wearing blue-collar attire at their rather mundane jobs in the Hilo workforce.

As they turned to walk away, sixteen days of continuous lava outpouring from high on Mauna Loa ceased. It was as though something, or someone, simply zipped shut that half-mile-long gash, which had been bleeding copious lava. Without a steady source of new molten rock, the twenty-five-mile-long fiery river cooled and froze to glistening black basalt by midnight.

Eruption was over, finished, all pau.

The final scorecard read, Mauna Loa: 15 houses and 7 humans. Hilo: Once again fortunate enough to have dodged major disaster.

Early that morning, exhausted scientists and politicians woke to good news. Jackson, Shinta, and Chee had slept in the mayor's office. No stage-two evacuation would be needed. The city could begin to heal.

When asked by Shinta and Chee, Jackson had no scientific explanation for why the eruption stopped overnight. He also admitted that he couldn't be sure that another eruption wouldn't start soon.

"Truth be told, gentlemen, I don't know why the eruption stopped last night. I *can* say that the source of magma dried up, but that only describes what's happened, not why. The more I study these beasts, the more I believe volcanoes have minds of their own. They also seem to like to tease those of us who spend our lives trying to understand them.

"For all I know, eruption might start again soon…later today, tomorrow, or next week. The pattern of the historical record, though, argues for several years if not a decade or more of quiet before Mauna Loa stages its next lava attack on Hilo. Let's hope that pattern is repeated."

Jackson spun around to return to his HVO office atop Kīlauea. He offered one last comment as he walked through the office door.

"I promise you a heightened level of volcano monitoring by my HVO team."

Had Jackson looked back, he would have seen the heads of politicians shaking back and forth in disbelief.

PART II

A Few Years Later

CHAPTER 4

PELE SHAKES HER VOLCANO HOME

She rolled slowly over, onto her back. A broad smile of self-satisfaction decorated her face. She was comfortable in her warm and familiar fluid-filled bed, deep within the subterranean roots of Halemaʻumaʻu Crater. The fluid sloshed with her role, enough to create a noticeable tremor throughout her home.

While moving, She made a special effort to muss her flowing red hair as little as possible. She wouldn't be herself without perfectly coiffed hair, and it was such a chore to comb out, once tangled. When properly cared for, which was most of the time, that lovely mane extended well below her waist.

Comfortably repositioned, She yawned and stretched simultaneously, lifting her coverings into an up-domed mass as She extended her arms. She vigorously rubbed the gritty accumulation of a long sleep from the corners of her eyes, causing her bed and entire volcano home to shake and quiver.

When her vision had cleared sufficiently, She glanced at the timekeeper beside her bed. "Ummmh, so it's already the autumn of 1982. How long have I been sleeping? Six years? Maybe as long as nine? Perhaps I should consider getting up and visiting some of my old haunts."

She yawned and stretched anew, and then rolled back onto her stomach, once again taking care of her hair. She closed her eyes against the warm liquid pillow.

"There's no need to hurry, I suppose. What's a few more weeks or months measured against several years. I really should get up and do something before the end of the year, though. I've always wanted 1982 to be an active time in my neighborhood."

As She drifted back toward the unconsciousness of sleep, thoughts of changing homes crossed her mind. After all, She'd been living in this same house for how long? Four millennia? Or was it much, much longer?

Still, She found her present abode extremely comfortable. And She had such a steady stream of friendly visitors to Halema'uma'u and other parts of Kīlauea that loneliness was never a problem. Yes, there were always a few cranks in the crowd, a few undesirables in the neighborhood. But She had her ways of dealing with them, wherever She might be living.

So, what to do, if anything, about a change in housing? She had recently learned of a lovely new edifice under construction, just a short journey to the south. Perhaps She would check that place out next year.

Meanwhile, She would continue to give Mauna Loa a rest and dream about plans for a hot-time party that She would soon host at Kīlauea. Shaking her coverings one last time, She slipped back to sleep.

CHAPTER 5

GEOLOGIST TALKS TO PELE

Nine o'clock that same day. A Monday morning in November of 1982. It was the beginning of a new workweek at the Hawaiian Volcano Observatory, perched along the western rim of Kīlauea Volcano. A tropical sun was shining warmly and brightly, while a chilly trade wind blew huge billowing clouds in from the east.

Andy Clark...alone, pensive, and puzzled...sipped industrial-strength Kona coffee as he stood facing a row of six slowly rotating cylindrical instruments, each about the size of a two-gallon can. Small pens, one attached to each instrument, were tracing thin black lines on paper charts that covered the moving surfaces, ready to record any unusual shaking of the earth. Most of the time, the pens produced straight lines, around and around each cylinder, hour after hour, day after day, testimony to a fairly tranquil earth, even here on a volcano. Just now, though, all six were slapping back and forth, tracing out identical-looking wave-shaped patterns that reminded Andy of ripples on the surface of a stone-splashed pond.

"Holy shit!" he muttered to himself, alternately looking down at the pens and then up through a window behind them to see if Kīlauea was erupting. He saw nothing unusual...just ever-present wisps of steam rising from the hot crater floor.

"What are you up to, Pele? What are you trying to tell me with your shuddering and shaking, making these pens twitch back and forth? Are you just shivering in the early morning chill? Is your stomach upset with a bloat of new magma? Is something else bothering you?"

The Pele of Andy's one-sided conversation had nothing to do with a world-class soccer player from Brazil. Andy was addressing a goddess, not a mere mortal.

Pele…the ancient Hawaiian goddess of volcanoes, whose home was right there through the window in front of him, deep within Halema'uma'u Crater.

Pele…revered and worshipped by modern Hawaiians, even though She has been discredited by Christian missionaries who first came to Hawai'i with their brand of religion in the early 1800s.

Pele…whose facial profile and long flowing red hair seem to appear in the swirling fiery fume clouds of every eruption.

Pele…the antithesis of the scientific method, yet still respected and discussed by most university-trained volcanologists…including Andy.

Andy rubbed weekend sleep from his eyes, took another sip of coffee, and continued to watch the bank of instruments. The pens quieted down a bit, briefly, and then slapped back and forth again, creating even wider tracings. Andy appeared hypnotized by what he was seeing.

"There you go again, you enigmatic female. What are you trying to tell me, anyway?"

Andy had a history of sometimes being slow to properly understand his female companions. Pele, though, was a special case. Frequently, She seemed to control the volcano, which meant She interfered with Andy's pursuit of pushing back the frontiers of science.

The pens continued to chart out their wavy tracks for several minutes. Then, just as quickly and silently as the pen-traced waves had first rippled across the chart, straight-line traces reappeared. Andy was not only confused, he was becoming frustrated.

"Jesus, Pele, give me a break. Either keep on shuddering and shaking, or be still. No schizophrenia today, please. I'm still exhausted from my weekend frolics with the ladies of Kona."

As a volcanologist trained beyond the tenets of pure science, Andy realized that all people who live with active volcanoes create supernatural beings as a way to communicate with and perhaps occasionally placate such a powerful force of nature. Earlier, as a geology student, he had learned that the Icelanders have their Surtur, the Tolai of New Guinea their Kaia, and the Japanese their Oni. So, he was not surprised that Pele had been one of several deities central to Hawaiian culture and religion, ever since the first arrival of Polynesian sailors to Hawaiian shores nearly sixteen hundred years ago.

He was familiar with current oral tradition, passed across centuries of telling and retelling, that Pele's first Hawaiian home had been on the island of Niʻihau at the northwest end of the chain of Hawaiian islands. As the story goes, She subsequently moved southeastward, island by island, always residing in an active volcano, and was now comfortably ensconced in Halemaʻumaʻu Crater at Kīlauea, right there in front of him.

He smiled inwardly as he reminded himself that twentieth-century scientists (including some of his former university professors), armed with state-of-the-art high-tech instruments, claim to have discovered that the islands are sequentially younger from northwest to southeast, dismissing or ignoring the long-standing oral tradition. But the fact that tradition had it right all along, bolstered by the knowledge that science had not yet learned all, or perhaps even most, of the secrets of Hawaiʻi's volcanoes, made Andy and like-thinking open-minded professional colleagues respect the power of Pele. She was the X factor in trying to understand Kīlauea's behavior.

Pele's appeal to the current native population was so strong that not even decades of emotional preaching and teaching by Christian missionaries had removed her from the scene, in spite of mass conversions to the new religion. Each year Andy watched with growing interest as Pele's followers dressed in traditional costumes and performed ceremonies of respect and recognition at her home in Halemaʻumaʻu. Chants and rituals were performed at the rim of the crater. Gifts of food, drink, and flowers were offered in profusion. Pele continued to be widely known and respected throughout Hawaiʻi with good reason. After all, the volcano hadn't gone away. Those nineteenth-century missionaries had simply introduced a new and seemingly less pertinent brand of religion.

Any personage, real or spiritual, that can produce flows of molten rock with the temperature of liquid pig iron should be respected. As true believers know (and Andy sometimes believed), Pele does so at her whim, whether in play or in teaching a lesson to humankind or one of their "lesser" gods. Pele has the power to destroy and to create. She buries and burns everything in the path of her lava flows. She adds new land to Hawaiʻi wherever her flows enter the sea. And She is restless; Pele's volcano home is the site of frequent eruptions. Records show that, during the twentieth century alone, rarely a year passed without at least one outpouring of lava.

Andy and other geologists usually characterize Kīlauea as the world's most active volcano. Oh sure, a fervently patriotic and cantankerously argumentative Italian or Frenchman might claim that his country is home to the world's most active volcano. But whether Kīlauea's rank is first, second, or even third matters little to those who have seen their homes and other worldly possessions go up in Pele's flames. Many have watched in helpless awe as their material possessions vanished before them. Could Pele be planning more destruction for today?

Andy began to relax, as flat traces continued to appear on the instruments. But given its shaky start, he wondered if the rest of the day would be quiet at HVO, or another gut-wrenching time of trying to understand Kīlauea well enough to warn the public of impending eruption.

"If my beer-and-sex-filled weekends at Kona don't eventually corrode my stomach lining and parts of other body organs, Pele alone might give me ulcers."

CHAPTER 6

POT-HEAD HEAVEN IN A PAKALŌLŌ PATCH

About twenty miles away, on that same Monday morning, Josh sat partway up to take another hit on his half-smoked joint. He then settled back into his cocoon-like hammock. He stared straight ahead, up into deep-blue sky decorated with puffy clouds that looked like giant balls of cotton, and inhaled slowly. As he continued to breathe, smoke fumes not absorbed by his lungs drifted lazily from his nostrils. He sighed in contentment and slid deeper into his cannabis-induced reverie.

Josh and his female partner, Valerie, were at "home" in a remote and isolated clearing they had hacked out of Kīlauea's rainforest, partway down the east flank of the mountain. Though the geologic setting was unknown to them, their clearing was exactly astride Kīlauea's east rift zone, a thirty-mile-long seaward-tapering ridge that had built up from innumerable past eruptions. This ridge would certainly build further with future eruptions.

From their platform drifting through the troposphere, astronauts described the rift zone as a huge finger, pointing eastward from the top of the volcano. For the better part of the past two decades, the part of the finger where Josh and Valerie resided had been spared the searing burn that accompanies eruption. Home seemed to be a safe haven for them and anyone else in their neighborhood.

Josh had no idea who owned the land where he and Valerie were living. For all he knew, it could be state forest, privately owned, or even within Hawai'i

Volcanoes National Park. Ownership didn't really matter, at least in Josh's gallery of values, because the spot was so remote that no one ever visited them from the comfort of what other people considered to be civilization. Josh rationalized his land grab as a legal homestead. He had cleared the land with his own hands, and he was raising a crop. Never mind that it was *Cannabis sativa*, and therefore illegal. Didn't all the effort qualify him for squatter's rights and a hassle-free life?

The splat of a couple of large raindrops on his belly reminded Josh that the annual rainfall on this part of Kīlauea was about two hundred inches. Today looked to be pretty dry, though. Clouds were scattered and moving westward quickly.

But with so much moisture spread out over the year and such warm tropical sunshine, unwanted vegetation seemed to grow nearly as fast as Josh and Valerie were able to keep it hacked back. So hack, hack, and hack they did, leaving large trees as a shade canopy and camouflage from snooping aircraft of the law. Their reward was a relatively clear forest floor used exclusively as a garden for marijuana plants, just enough to support their smoking habit and to produce a little additional product for bartering. Weather was conducive to year-round gardening.

At their hideaway elevation of about fifteen hundred feet above the nearby Pacific Ocean, clothing was an optional item. It wasn't needed for warmth or modesty. They chose to be naked at home, most of the time, to elevate their body comfort (no sweaty clothes sticking to skin) while reducing the cost and labor of living (no stinking pesky clothes to launder).

A crude pole-supported roof of corrugated green plastic sheltered them from the frequent and abundant rains. Runoff provided potable water, stored in a green plastic barrel at the downslope edge of the roof. With so much rain, that barrel was almost always overflowing with sweet fresh water.

Green was an integral and critical part of a camouflage design. Even their hammocks were woven from green plastic rope. They were determined to keep their homestead invisible to the airborne eyes of the law.

They collected food to fuel their bodies from the surrounding fertile rainforest. They knew how and where to search out productive oases sprinkled across the Puna District, as the politicians labeled this part of the Big Island. Abundant banana, papaya, guava, coconut, mango, and pohā were free for the picking, so long as they didn't come from an obviously cultivated field. For occasional variety and something a bit more substantial, Josh and Valerie walked into the nearby village of Pāhoa. There, carefully selected friends traded beans, meat, and the like for a bag of pakalōlō, the Hawaiian word for marijuana.

Even an occasional island-brewed beer was available to Josh and Valerie, surreptitiously exchanged, brown bag for brown bag, out the back door of the Puna Pool Hall. All in all, an adequately balanced diet was available, with no legal tender involved. The two maintained a healthy, quiet, and serene existence.

Josh rolled over on his stomach, holding the joint in his outstretched right hand. "Hey, Val. How're ya doing? It's a pretty mellow day, huh?"

Valerie was in deep sleep, in her own pakalōlō trance. Josh would have to entertain himself. He slowly focused his eyes straight downward, where a cockroach was fighting its way through grass-covered ground. Josh was sure the insect would get to wherever it was headed. Hell, insects probably would inherit the earth, once humans procreated and polluted themselves out of existence.

In high school, Josh had read a book about fossils. It said insects have been around in one form or another for millions of years. Though his fundamentalist parents were sure that the earth was only about four thousand years old, Josh believed what that book said. He also believed his teacher's follow-up point.

"Insects are much more adaptable than people. And they don't poison the land with gobs of chemical fertilizers."

As a former farmer, Josh knew all about saturating soil with fertilizers, used to squeeze fast and abundant growth out of plants. He had often thought about how tiring it must be for plants to have to live that way!

The cockroach disappeared into dense vegetation, legs pumping.

Following another hit from his joint, threaded up through the webbing of the hammock, Josh watched a mongoose scurry into the clearing. Seeing the hammocks and their human cargo, it stopped abruptly and hurried toward the protective cover of dense fern growth on the other side of the pakalōlō patch. This bushy-tailed mammal squealed at Josh when it passed near the green plastic sling, as though the human was the intruder. Actually, both were intruders on the indigenous Hawaiian scene.

Given an increasingly dismal record of care taking since humans had discovered the islands centuries earlier, one could only conclude that people were intent on reducing what had been a pristine island paradise to just another polluted and degraded population center. The mongoose was an instructive example of such human stupidity and lack of foresight. Josh had learned the story while reading in preparation for the trip that had brought him to Hawai'i.

Decades ago, these furry feisty beasts had been imported to reduce, if not eradicate, the island's rat population (also introduced by people). However, those who designed the rodent-control program failed to recognize that a rat is out doing its damage at night, while the mongoose is soundly asleep. The two species coexist and proliferate quite nicely, thank you, passing in the bedroom hallway at dawn and dusk.

As he lay in a state of self-induced suspended animation, Josh knew he need not worry about the crushing embrace of a tropical constrictor coiling itself around the hammock. Hawai'i was free of such cold-blooded serpents. When the island chain originated, as a bunch of volcanic links that had grown up from the ocean floor, the new land lacked snakes and most every other living thing at the moment of emergence. Then, by some minor miracle, people had not (yet!) introduced snakes, or even rabies onto the island paradise, in spite of centuries of human visitations. Those rats and mongeese (or was it mongooses?), though, were a different matter.

And pigs! So many damned feral pigs running rampant in the rainforest were another human screw up. Unless he and Valerie happened to be home at the right time, a pig or two could wreak havoc on weeks of pakalōlō growth. Judging by their increased squealing and a bit of staggering, those cursed creatures even got a free and apparently enjoyable high in the process of digesting the leafy weed. It didn't seem fair to Josh. Besides, he had a very personal and deeply ingrained history of pig hatred, developed during his teenage farm-boy years.

He rotated slowly over onto his back again, feeling secure that nothing harmful would disturb his hammock rest. He could handle a pig if one showed up.

The rainforest was totally silent, save for the pleasing soft sounds caused by a gentle trade wind breeze fanning the leaves of surrounding ferns and 'ōhi'a trees. Valerie was still asleep in her nearby hammock, letting the day drift away without a care in the world.

Josh sighed and hummed a few lines of "Yellow Submarine," followed by his rendition of "Don't Bogart that Joint." His ability to carry a tune was questionable. But the words were the important part for him, anyway.

One more tug on his dwindling joint. Ahhh. Then he pinched out the ember, popped the roach into his mouth and swallowed. The ultimate practice of waste not, want not.

Josh was content. Life was mellow. Life was excellent. Life was perfect. It had not always been so.

CHAPTER 7

SPOILED RICH BOY'S EPIPHANY

Andy continued to stare at the lines being written on the six earthquake charts. Each paper-covered cylinder was about sixteen inches long and twelve inches in diameter. All cylinders rotated at the same constant speed, on a single horizontal axial shaft driven by a small electric motor. A pen was attached to a metal frame over each instrument in such a way that it traced a fine black line as the paper moved beneath it. Simultaneously, each pen moved left-to-right along the length of its cylinder ever so slowly, driven by the spiral path of a worm gear.

Each instrument produced a full day's record of pen tracing on a single piece of paper. Every morning at seven, a technician removed the written-on paper and replaced it with a clean sheet. He then carried the records down the hall to an expert who could read meaning into the nonsensical-looking tracings. This routine occurred each and every day of the year, just as it had for the past three decades and would as far into the future as people chose to keep track of earth shakes and shudders at Kīlauea.

The six instruments, called seismographs in technical jargon, were mounted on a table-like stand in front of a long window. A housewife may have seen this as a chorus-line adaptation of special rolling pins. To a geologist, these seismographs were the so-called black boxes of science, instruments that help push back the frontiers of volcano research.

Through the window, just inches away, the morning's first wave of tourists glanced at Andy, and the instruments, as they ambled past the Hawaiian Volcano Observatory building. These visitors were headed for a nearby rock ledge from which they could see into Kīlauea Caldera, a two-mile-wide and three-hundred-foot-deep volcanic crater…a giant circular hole in the ground. A few stopped at the window, looked, and gesticulated in reaction to the developing pen tracings.

Anyone able to read meaning into a facial expression might have wondered if that geologist on the other side of the glass was worried about the volcano or something more mundane, like the rainstorm that appeared to be approaching rapidly from the east. Either way, Andy looked a bit unsettled.

The tourists were there to enjoy Hawai'i Volcanoes National Park, a fabulous place where even the most skittish of phobia-prone people can stroll safely all over an active volcano. In the grand tradition of human nature, once man walked on the moon back in 1969 and brought back pictures and pieces of that stark, pitted, and cratered lunarscape, an ever-increasing number of farmers, housewives, students, lawyers, and CEOs alike longed for a similarly exciting experience. After all, their tax dollars had paid for the moonwalks. So why shouldn't they get to do something to produce an equal surge of adrenaline in return?

Visitors to the park quickly discovered that walking across the cratered, vegetation-free, hot and sterile surface of an active volcano is a pretty realistic substitute for a moon stroll. Well-informed tourists knew that America's astronauts had trained at Kīlauea in preparation for setting off to the moon. These folks got the extra emotional rush of literally following in an astronaut's footsteps, albeit earth-bound footsteps.

Andy noticed that today's visitors included the usual assortment of sizes, shapes, ages, races, and body coverings. Tour groups tended to move about in compact swarms, no one wanting to stray so far from the pack that a departing bus might be missed. Mildly distraught parents chased after scurrying children. Lone adults stayed somewhat aloof, while most young couples looked and behaved recently married, or at least on a one-way path apparently headed in that direction. A few elderly folks shuffled by, aided by canes, walkers, and friends. Though the window glass muffled sound somewhat, Andy recognized conversations in French, German, and Japanese as well as English.

Many of today's crowd had obviously come straight up from the Big Island's coastal attractions. These folks were dressed in sandals, shorts, and bathing suits. As a nearly lifelong admirer of a well-shaped female body, Andy paid special attention to the bikini-clad visitors. Myriads of tiny goose bumps decorated almost all exposed skin at the cool four-thousand-foot elevation of Kīlauea Caldera, especially in the early morning. The centers of those bikini tops stretched across even larger intriguingly shaped chill-hardened protrusions. Whatever the degree of body covering, everyone wore at least one article of garishly patterned and colored clothing, in the tradition of Hawaiian aloha attire.

Andy had ogled the daily procession of tourists many times before. And he would do so in the future. Though not part of official job duties, a favorite and often-practiced pastime of the entire HVO staff was tourist watching, while pretending to be deep in thought over the lineup of seismographs there by the window. From their side of the glass, tourists saw scientists concentrating on new information being written on the paper-covered drums. On the other side of that glazing, gazing scientists saw a lot more than science in action. Today, Andy's attentions were actually on the instruments…in part.

In the morbid though common spirit shared by spectators at Caesar's Roman Coliseum on down to twentieth-century fans at sporting arenas, a steady stream of visitors traveled to the park each year in hopes of seeing violence…volcanic rather than human in this setting. On occasion, visual volcanic violence might include the spectacle of gaping fissures opening across park roads, perhaps trapping a tour bus. Then, fiery lava might spray two thousand feet into the sky, fall back to earth, and feed a lava flow that would cascade down steep mountain slopes on its way to the Pacific Ocean. There, an unsuspecting fish or two might be instantly boiled. Such an adrenalin-generating experience would take place over a background of earthquake-shaking ground.

Today, however, the volcano's caldera was quiet and clear, save for the ever-present wisps of steam. Because incandescent rock lay just a few feet below the surface, moisture from the most recent rainfall was boiling back into the atmosphere. Invisible, yet potentially dangerous sulfurous fumes were also part of the caldera's atmospheric mix. This pungent and wicked brew, which smelled like rotten eggs, came with all active volcanoes. The acrid odor was rising mostly from Halemaʻumaʻu, a quarter-mile-wide and two-hundred-foot-deep pit indenting the floor of the caldera. All of the stinking air dispersed to the west, on the wings of trade winds.

Between peeks at the seismograph pens tracing out their message, Andy surreptitiously searched for attractive young ladies among today's milling crowd. But no lingering sexy bodies were to be seen. Instead, everyone kept on the move. Today's trade winds were too weak to rapidly sweep away the bad air. The raspy sound of fume-induced coughing carried through the window glass.

In calm weather, the air in Kīlauea Caldera could be more hazardous to human health than that of Los Angeles, Houston, or Mexico City on pollution-alert days. Warned of this invisible risk, by both National Park Service signs and their own sudden fits of coughing, visitors tended to minimize their time in the caldera. But fumes seemed to be part of the moon-inspired volcano adventure. Bad volcanic air had to be experienced, if only briefly, so tourist tales told at home later around today's equivalent of the old pickle barrel would impress the listener sufficiently.

Andy harbored no moon-inspired romance about the volcano's sulfurous exhalations. He had had more than enough of this putrid volcanic vapor since coming to Hawai'i, because his job forced him to work in the stuff all too often. Along with his coworkers, it was Andy's job to try to learn about Kīlauea Volcano's behavior, and to understand it well enough to be able to warn people, like those tourists just an arm's length away, when, how, and where they should get out of harm's way. This demanded time spent in a variety of volcanic stews. Besides, he also knew that the moon has no fumes, no atmosphere whatsoever.

From the day it was established in 1912 by a brilliant but crusty old college professor, Thomas Augustus Jaggar II, the observatory's main task had been one of hazard recognition and appropriate warnings to the nearby public. In the grand intellectually snobbish tradition, Jaggar had adopted a Latin motto (Andy sometimes wondered what language ancient Romans used for their lofty sounding mottos…Greek? Sanskrit?) for HVO, "Ne plus haustae aut obrutae urbes" (No more burned or buried cities). He had steadfastly pursued this lofty aim, right up to his retirement in 1940.

When national park status came to Kīlauea in 1916, the observatory task took on added urgency, simply because more and more people were at risk as annual visitations increased.

As Andy and all of those HVO employees before him realized, the challenge laid out by Jaggar was unfinished. Many brilliant minds had been applied to the task along the way, but Kīlauea kept springing surprises just about the time a geologist thought he understood her. For some perverse reason, one question answered often introduced several additional questions in need of answers, creating a spiral of frustration without visible end. Kīlauea could be downright coy with the geologists who probed, measured, and observed her. But was it Kīlauea who was coy, or that goddess in residence…Pele?

Today was one of those "be coy" days, at least in Andy's mind. He continued to stare at the seismographs and puzzle over the pen tracings being recorded.

Each seismograph was connected electronically to its own distant seismometer, somewhere out there on the slopes of Kīlauea. Six seismographs paired with six seismometers, which were distributed here and there across the body of the volcano. Together, graph and meter produced a seismogram, that pen-traced paper chart of the volcano's quaking and shaking, whenever Kīlauea was being restless. Each three-part seismo-jargon set of equipment…'meter, 'graph, and 'gram…was the bread-and-butter tool of Ben, Andy's colleague who specialized in studying earthquakes for the observatory team.

When tranquil, Kīlauea produced a straight-line chart, and that was the normal situation. This allowed Andy and others at HVO to relax a bit on the job. The instruments also recorded powerful earthquakes from other parts of planet Earth, but these were easily identified as Kīlauean "foreigners"…just as foreign as the lovely French-speaking lady now looking at Andy from the other side of the window.

Many attractive female tourists were known to stare back at Andy through that big window. California born and raised, he had a shock of wavy sun-bleached blond hair. He stood a generous six feet tall. His eyes were so deep blue that they seemed unreal. Envious male contemporaries claimed that he wore tinted contact lenses, even though his unaided vision was 20/20 perfect.

Whatever the blueness resulted from, the opposite sex found it magnetic. Trite though it seemed, he was the flame that attracted those beautiful metaphorical moths. It didn't hurt his attraction quotient that at twenty-six he still possessed the muscular athletic body of his undergraduate years. Andy looked a lot like a perfectly proportioned Greek god, although the only Greek in his background was of college fraternity origins.

Even before his squeaky young teenage voice had dropped to a mellifluous baritone, he had always admired the anatomy of the opposite sex and craved female companionship. In character, then, he couldn't help but conjure up a mental image of swaying hula-dance hips when the seismograph pens swung back and forth in their steady rhythm there before him.

Books Andy had read in preparation for coming to HVO mentioned that Pele and her sister Hiiaka were pretty good hula dancers. But mostly those books talked about how Pele belched forth incredibly hot molten rock in fiery eruptions when she saw fit to do so.

Still, according to the seismic tremor, her volcano home there in Halemaʻumaʻu, straight outside the observatory window behind the seismographs, had been shaking in hula fashion just minutes ago. Fortunately, for Andy and tourists alike, this shaking was so gentle that only a very sensitive instrument could feel and record the motion.

Vigorous shaking could create public panic. Just as the gentle and friendly hip tremor of a hula dancer sometimes crescendoed into a gyrating frenzy of emotion, so too a mild volcano tremor might lead to increasingly violent earth shaking…the classic old calm before the storm. Andy and his HVO coworkers were expected to anticipate and even predict this possibility.

He sighed and gazed out the window at an unusually active and attractive set of tourist hips swaying by. He hoped that Pele wasn't being as mind-numbingly seductive as the Hawaiian hula dancers who so mesmerized him last weekend at the Kona Kāne Hotel. He knew that he needed a clear and analytical mind to understand Kīlauea. His rational side discounted the idea that Pele, or any other supernatural power, might be the cause of the recent volcano tremors at Kīlauea. Such an idea was contrary to the scientific method, and his entire career, once it had finally got underway, had been founded on this method. Still…

Andrew Randolph Clark had been born and raised on the peninsula of the Bay Area, about midway between San Francisco and San Jose. He was the third generation on the paternal side of his family to attend nearby Stanford University.

Andy's grandfather had majored in liberal arts at Stanford and went on to the gentlemanly agrarian pursuit of raising apricots. Most of the peninsula had been fruit orchards before the massive influx of people who reasoned that a salubrious Mediterranean climate should be enjoyed by them rather than trees, and before the phrase "Silicon Valley" became international code for **the center** of cutting-edge research and production in computer software and hardware.

His father had majored in business and subsequently became wealthy brokering the sale and resale of real estate as the peninsula changed from the open farm land that Leland Stanford had known into a bustling and crowded series of back-to-back suburbs. Just what these communities were suburbs of was no longer clear, for San Jose had quickly grown to nearly equal San Francisco in both land area and population.

All three generations of Clarks grew up and lived in the same comfortable yet modest house on an acre of rolling terrain in Los Altos Hills. Grandfather

Clark had several additional acres on which his apricot trees flourished. Then, when the next head-of-household took charge, Andy's father sold all but the acre on which the house sat. He realized he probably could buy the entire world's fruit output for any given year with the proceeds.

By the time Andy came along, the Clark neighborhood was nearly saturated with one-acre lots, the legal minimum for Los Altos Hills. Only the very wealthy, like the Clark's neighbor, computer and electronics wizard David Packard, could afford multi-acre spreads.

Being surrounded by an abundance of the kinds of fine material things that the Packards and their ilk could afford…even those relatively poor folk like the Clarks on one-acre lots were doing okay…Andy understood that he was living in a privileged and upscale manner. He was well prepared to comfortably slip into the aristocratic Stanford mold, where loads of undergraduate fun could be had by all but the most studious. Campus more nearly resembled a fabulous national park than a bastion of higher education.

His first two years on "the farm," a name that hearkens back to the days when it was indeed Leland Stanford's farm, were a blur of fast cars, beer-soaked fraternity parties, and multiple willing girlfriends. Andy, through his father's generosity, could afford these bacchanalian adventures.

Before the end of his first semester, Andy lost his virginity to a spicy Hispanic classmate from San Jose. Bingo! This was something that he had tried, but failed to accomplish the previous year as a party-loving senior at nearby Gunn High. He had had plenty of female friends in high school, but none of those relationships had come to a proper climax. After his inaugural night with Felicia, he guessed that those "lost" earlier years were worth the wait—his high school friends had been so immature and inexperienced, by comparison. Soon, Felicia was only one filly in a stable of active athletic lovers.

Off campus, beer, burgers and fries at a nearby Menlo Park hangout called the Oasis were de rigueur for frat boys and their Stanford dollies. The owner of the "O" provided free and unlimited salted-in-the-shell peanuts as appetizers, entrees, and desserts, with the stipulation that shells be thrown on the floor. Apparently the price, taste, crunching sound underfoot, and messy look were attractive to frat boys. A salt-induced increase in thirst for more beer was certainly attractive to the owner.

When the guys wanted a male-bonding night of quiet beer drinking, they congregated at the Alley, a small and quiet bar just off University Avenue in Palo Alto, and stayed 'til closing time.

Party mania at Stanford was fine for several months, but with increasing frequency Andy felt that something was missing, even in the afterglow of daily fun and frolic. While most of his classmates seemed content to continue the life of beery haze, studying just enough to pass through the required academic hoops, Andy suffered a gnawing in his craw that he guessed might originate from his off-scale high IQ and above-average curiosity, rather than an alcohol-induced acid stomach. His thirst went beyond lust for liquid, and it was not being satisfied.

As the end of his second year approached, the three Bs (beer, bonfires, and babes) just weren't enough any more. A fourth B had entered his life. He was bored. He wanted to do something meaningful, not knowing for sure what that word meant for him. Then, with absolutely no planning on his part, a near-religious epiphany that eliminated the gnawing came in the form of TV news one beery night at the Oasis.

He and his friends were drinking their way into final exams. Andy was in a particularly cheerful and receptive mood. On his way to the "O", he and Crystal, his babe for the night, had stopped at the Stanford mausoleum just off Palm Drive and discovered that one of this grand structure's broad steps was an exciting, though a bit too firm, couch for making love. Part of the thrill was wondering what the stern-and-matronly Jane Stanford would think, if only she knew!? Traditional student rumor claimed that her son, Leland Jr., would have almost died for the opportunity to put any lovemaking couch to use.

The date was May 18, 1980, a Sunday. In spite of high background noise from the usual boisterous "O" crowd, including the crunch of peanut shells underfoot, the volume of a lone voice coming from a large-screen TV suspended behind the bar demanded attention.

~~~~~~~~~~~~~~~~~~~~~~~~

"Today, a long-dormant volcano reawakened" intoned an announcer seated before a photo backdrop of a towering cloud of volcanic ash "with an unanticipated degree of fury. Following two hundred years of quiescence, Mount St. Helens, near Vancouver, Washington, blasted away nearly half of herself, leaving a huge north-facing amphitheater-shaped crater where a four-thousand-foot-tall cone-shaped mountain once stood.

"The eruption was not entirely a surprise. During the past two months, volcano experts on loan from the Hawaiian Volcano Observatory, working with other U.S. Geological Survey geologists and university colleagues, had taken the pulse of the mountain sufficiently well to forecast an eruption for some time in May. What was a surprise, though, was the release of volcanic explosiveness out the *side* of the mountain, rather than in the more usual straight-up direction."

Then came the part of the TV story that grabbed Andy's attention and squeezed dry his beer-soaked inner core. He even (temporarily) forgot that Crystal's right hand was gently stroking his inner thigh under the table.

"From his observation post some six miles from the volcano, USGS geologist David Johnston was in the informative yet unfortunate position of actually seeing the onset of eruption as the entire north side of the mountain broke loose and hurtled toward him. His last words, radioed back to the command post in Vancouver, were simply 'Vancouver, Vancouver, this is it!' Johnston apparently was swept away and buried by a volcanic hurricane that then surged over his position."

A playback recording of Johnston's actual voice followed.

Without a change in voice inflection or cadence, the announcer continued with a summary of the past week's Nasdaq performance, a topic of great interest to Bay Area residents because this market was largely driven, mostly upward, by business growth and success in Silicon Valley.

~~~~~~~~~~~~~~~~~~~~~

Andy heard nothing of the market news. He was left speechless, sobered and totally captivated by the human part of the volcano story. Johnston's voice had projected objectivity unimaginable considering the exposed position he had occupied at his observation post. This geologist obviously loved his work, loved his part in trying to understand the behavior of something as powerful as an explosive volcano. His last words even seemed to indicate that he had been prepared to pay the supreme price on the job. This was someone and something unusual and special, not just another day at the…you-name-it pedestrian situation.

Andy suddenly realized that he wanted to be a part of this kind of captivating career, rather than follow the path of money-chasing that most residents of Silicon Valley pursued. He now knew what could, and he hoped would replace the three Bs, although he certainly hoped that a chaste life was not a requirement for becoming a volcano expert. He was once again aware of Crystal's ministrations. Bonfires could be replaced by volcanic heat, and such intense heat would require at least some thirst-slaking beer. Maybe he could have it all!

He and Crystal discussed this possibility as they exercised another of Andy's favorite love couches, a raft floating in Stanford's Lake Lagunita, on the way back to student housing.

Inspired by David Johnston's professionalism, grace under fire and calm message, the very next day Andy declared geology as his major, left the fraternity life, and worked his way into becoming an academic-award winning student during his final two Stanford years.

Upon graduation with honors, Andy was a card-carrying geologic expert in rock mechanics, in understanding how volcanoes can bend, break, slip, and slide. His Silicon Valley roots made powerful computers a natural tool for analyzing the deformation of rocks, and now he was applying his talents to that living, breathing volcano called Kīlauea as a full-fledged employee of the U.S. Geological Survey.

By serendipitous happenstance, the USGS had been searching for someone to replace one of HVO's retiring geologists just as Andy was in a serious job-hunt mode. Given Andy's training, the match seemed made in heaven, for both parties.

CHAPTER 8

HAY-SEED TEEN DISCOVERS BEER AND REEFERS

Though content beyond measurement during his waking hours, the sleeping Josh now tossed in his hammock and emitted the low guttural moans of a disturbed person. His subconscious was once again reliving disturbing earlier episodes of his life. Those earlier experiences had been so deeply etched into his psyche that he had not yet succeeded in completely shedding this unwanted emotional baggage. Simply put, the rub was fun-versus-fundamental.

His parents were so extreme in their Christian fundamentalist approach to life that younger Josh had often felt that his life was incomplete, his personality stifled, even as a naive pre-teen boy. Once he had experienced part of "the other side" of life, though, during his high school years, he began to think for himself, even if he dared not articulate or act out his emerging beliefs at home.

He liked to compare this mental evolution with a lesson learned in senior physics class. As Mr. Hermes had liked to explain: "Pay attention, students. Vatch carefully and maybe you vill understand vhy the perfect pendulum swings as far to the left as to the right. It's all about gravity and the virtual lack of friction between pendulum and the air it svings through." Their lab experiment came close enough to perfect conditions to convince the students that their teacher wasn't kidding.

Now, with the passage of time in his Hawaiian retreat, Josh found that he remembered less and less of his youthful family life that he had lived way out there on the painful right. He was pretty sure that those family memories (there had been plenty of friction involved, but that was now history, gone from his life) would be completely erased if and when his pendulum hit its full-left position. Since setting up housekeeping with Valerie nearly two years ago, haunting family dreams visited him less and less frequently. He felt in full left swing.

❦   ❦   ❦

Joshua Oscar Brown had been born and raised on the mainland, in upper Midwest farm country. He was the son of Amos, a highly respected and solid citizen known throughout northeastern Iowa. Amos owned exactly three square miles of fertile Iowa land. Amos used ten acres for a home site and space to park his considerable collection of farm machinery. Year after year, Amos raised corn on the remaining one-thousand-nine-hundred-ten acres.

His unshakable religious convictions, and the watchful eyes of his wife Rebecca, would never allow him to raise Cain. In good-natured jest, though always behind his back, friends and neighbors called him colonel kernel, the first word referring to his strictly regimented lifestyle and the second an obvious reference to his corn-filled existence.

A Protestant work ethic was deeply ingrained in the Brown elders. Both were sure that God looked favorably only on those who stayed the narrow righteous path. They toiled hard, dawn to dusk, never complaining. And they reaped ample material rewards for their labors.

They believed strongly that parents should pass such virtues on to their children. Excessive partying, which they defined as more than two social events per month for the children, and a life of even minor dissipation were for the lost and weak.

Indirectly, Amos Brown was simply a hog farmer. With corn in the field, there was pork on the plant. With corn in a hog's tummy, there was pork growing on the hoof. And, of course, the sole reason for this chain of events was to get corn in the form of pork on the tables of American consumers. Amos's bright yellow corn became the other white meat of America.

Amos chose to deal exclusively with the plant-raising link in this food chain. He had no desire to get involved with hog raising, because hog excrement is one of the foulest smelling substances known to mankind. Amos was happy to leave that smelly link of the local money chase to the folks who lived downwind of him. He always tried to live by the biblical Golden Rule, but this came with limits when hog manure was involved.

At a very young age, Josh had also learned this truth about raising hogs. His less fortunate classmates, those whose parents fed Amos's corn to their pigs, carried a fowl porcine smell with them everywhere, notwithstanding repeated scrubbings with strong soap and pumice bars. The stench of pig shit seemed to penetrate deeply into the pores of their skin, as well as saturating the fluffy fabric of clothing. Their social lives suffered.

The Brown family was Methodist, which imposed an additional stiff code of ethics on an already puritanical way of life. Regular attendance at Sunday's church service was obligatory, even during the almost sacred season of corn harvest. The family was generous when the collection plate appeared. They supported all church-sponsored activities.

Josh's parents had even named him so his initials would spell out one of their most admired Old Testament characters. Mr. and Mrs. Brown hoped and expected that Josh would stand up to life's trials as successfully as their Holy-Land hero Job had, so many generations earlier.

And of course, consumption of alcoholic beverage was absolutely forbidden in the Brown household. All Methodists know that the devil himself resides in liquor bottles, and that the road to heaven does not pass through Milwaukee or any of those other Wisconsin towns and their many breweries. Neither Amos nor Rebecca had ever consumed one drop of alcohol, at least knowingly. Methodists even refused to use wine at communion, although the church's liturgy included this volatile word. Unfermented grape juice was the substitute of choice. As an additional example of their firm stand against alcohol, Rebecca Brown was the perennial president of her community's chapter of the Women's Christian Temperance Union, who's acronym meant "we'll see to you!" by those who enjoyed an alcoholic beverage now and then. Carry Nation was Rebecca's heroine and role model, all wrapped up into one sober body.

Josh was the oldest of three children. As the only son, his father's long-term plan was to pass the land and farm machinery along to him, so he could carry on in the grand corn-raising tradition. As Josh entered that magical age when he could safely operate tractors and other farming equipment, and also understand the implications of his father's plan, he was pleased. The novelty of controlling huge machines was exhilarating, and a life of financial security was his for the taking.

For years, Josh followed the road of life prescribed for him by his parents and their religion, thinking he was as happy as a child could be. This primrose path extended into his junior year at high school. He then took a detour. Or perhaps it took him. Neither he nor anyone else living in Chickasaw County would have guessed that this straight-laced young man was about to start down a road that would eventually lead to being a lazy, though rather harmless, pot-head camped out in the rainforest of Hawai'i.

The turning point occurred at a party in celebration of winning the state's AAA Conference football title. Josh was a sure-handed pass receiver on the local team. One of his circus catches had clinched victory. He was the focus of much jubilation at the party, one of those few parties he was permitted to attend. No elders were present.

But compared to his classmates, he wasn't having much fun. That suddenly changed when the team's slightly inebriated quarterback threw Josh a perfectly spiraling can of Grain Belt Beer from across the party hall, and then convinced him to drink some…for a change.

The first swallow tasted slightly bitter but extremely refreshing. Yummy! His classmates were watching, mostly in disbelief. Josh grinned and took another swallow. He tried, but failed, to suppress a foamy beery burp. Classmates laughed at his embarrassment over this unusual, for him, body noise. Josh caught the general mood, smiled and took another swallow. Bobby, the quarterback, slapped Josh on the back, triggering another burp. The team's cutest cheerleader, Betsy, walked up to face him and smiled invitingly.

"Wow, Josh, you were great in the championship game. Everybody says that we couldn't have won without you. Even Bobby says no one else could have caught that game-winning pass."

Josh wasn't sure what to say. Most everyone in town agreed that Bobby was best at everything athletic. Bobby certainly felt that way. The room was dark enough to hide Josh's blush as Betsy continued babbling her praise.

For years Josh had watched from the sidelines as his friends, male and female alike, seemed to enjoy parties more and more with each drink of the Methodist-forbidden brew. Now that he had finally dared to join this crowd, he was beginning to understand what the enjoyment was all about. Beer made him a little bit lightheaded and pleasantly relaxed in a way that he had never before experienced. He could actually have fun, laugh, tell jokes, and feel comfortable in the presence of girls. He and Betsy talked awhile, held hands, and danced right up through the final slow one. Josh didn't even mind that Betsy's dad was one of those who raised pigs.

"Can I see you home, Betsy?"

"Sure!"

They talked about the game and school and beer and other teenage stuff. At the door, Betsy stood on tiptoes and gave Josh a wet kiss on the lips, his very first one. He was relaxed enough to start to give one back, as she turned to open the door. He missed his mark a bit, but was feeling fine anyway. Josh's face was plastered with what his classmates called a S.E.G., all the way home.

He was a convert to a new way of life, though a pretty sober one. While some of his classmates drank to the point of dizziness, he was always a safe designated driver. Beer became his social drink of choice, but in moderation. With strategically timed consumption of those little black beads called Sen Sen, the most effective beer- and tobacco-breath camouflage known to teenagers in his part of the country, trusting parents never suspected that a new son was being hatched.

Beyond the beer, they would have been shocked to know that he now practiced something called French kissing, with Betsy and his other dates.

The next lifestyle revelation, as Josh emerged butterfly-like from his cornfield chrysalis, was the discovery that a common weed growing in most ditches along roads that surrounded his father's cornfields could also give him the kind of pleasant buzz that came from a beer or two.

For years, he had heard rumors about this magical weed, but had never believed them. He was a farmer. He knew a weed when he saw one, and all weeds were undesirable by definition! With just one successful experiment, though, he understood a new meaning for the word. All he had to do was roll this plant's leaves into a cigarette paper and smoke away at what his more worldly classmates called a reefer.

What an enjoyable complement to an ice-cold beer…and a few kisses from Betsy or Donna.

Now, the mind-and-body-numbing hours spent in the hard metal seat of Amos's farm tractors, cultivating row after row after row of corn plants, could be made bearable. All Josh had to do was stop at the edge of the field, pick a few leaves from the magical plant, and roll a good one.

He destroyed a few corn plants, instead of adjacent thistles, when smoked leaves led to challenged tractor steering. But his father never seemed to notice. Abundant corn rolled in at harvest time. New money accumulated in the Browns' bank account as pork appeared on the American table.

As his senior year wound down and high school graduation approached, Josh would have been a fallen soul in the eyes of his parents and the Methodist Church…had they but known. But appropriately timed consumption of Sen Sen hid sin sin. His new habits were a secret, shared only with his closed-mouth classmates. He was a very happy camper at parties…and a seemingly serious nose-to-the-grindstone son at home.

Josh felt pretty sure that he was on a collision course with his parents. He didn't know how or when his double life would be resolved into one. But that perfect pendulum of Mr. Hermes was on its way to the left extreme, with Josh tenaciously hanging on.

CHAPTER 9

GEOLOGISTS VERSUS RESTLESS VOLCANO

While a restlessly sleeping Josh was struggling through conflicting personal emotions, caffeine-alert Andy was struggling with professional confusion. His nose was once again being rubbed in the fact that book learning and experience with real things of the material world are often separated by a chasm of contrast.

Like most geologists before him, and probably those yet to follow in his footsteps at HVO, he had already misjudged the behavior of Kīlauea enough times to increasingly imagine that an irrational supernatural power, such as Pele (rather than the so-called laws of physics), might partly control what the volcano did. Yet surely all that training at Stanford made him an expert who could observe, chart, and ultimately understand the inner workings of a volcano, without having to factor the power of Pele into the equation. After all, he had majored in geology, not religion!

Well-trained scientist or not, he was now thoroughly puzzled by Kīlauea. During the past several weeks, the HVO seismometers had sporadically transmitted the wavy signals of this tremor back to the charts recorded at the observatory. His schooling, including a multitude of profound lectures by internationally famous professors, had described volcanic tremor in a sterile academic way. But nothing had been taught about tremor and the possibility of a pending eruption. For sure, something shaky was afoot underfoot. Everyone agreed that magma was on the move somewhere down there, but was it ready to erupt?

The HVO staff was faced with a daunting scientific challenge. Pele, Kīlauea, or Mother Nature had thrown down the gauntlet. Andy and colleagues would pursue this challenge. The excitement of an occasional scientific discovery along the way was their main motivator. Maybe the next breakthrough would be about tremor.

There was also a political motivation to understand the volcano. Scientists hated this, because politics tended to get in the way of science. But history had repeatedly demonstrated that politics should not and could not be ignored if HVO was to thrive rather than fall victim to the misdirected swing of a budget axe.

Most of the undesirable political side of life at HVO emanated from Washington D.C. Power struggles began there within the U.S. Geological Survey itself…just which of that agency's programs should get a healthy piece of the USGS budget pie this year?…and permeated on through the Department of the Interior and the Legislative and Executive branches of the federal tree.

Just a few months earlier, congressional Republicans back in D.C. had tried, yet again, to permanently shut down HVO, and the entire USGS for that matter. Behind the Washington scenes, word was that a prominent southern congressman reasoned that "It shouldn't cost anything to run a volcano," not understanding that any "running" involved, at places like Kīlauea, Mount St. Helens, and that long string of Aleutian volcanoes in Alaska, was the other way around. Only in Hollywood's fertile imagination do people control the energy and fury of a volcano.

Mr. Congressman also obviously didn't understand that knowing what these powerful outlets of earth's internal heat might do next is of critical importance to the national and even international economy. People, factories, cities, and aircraft harmed or destroyed by volcanoes are not ignorable trivia.

Another of the many rumors circulating across the informal communication channels of D.C. quoted a fundamentalist congressman from a northern industrial state as wanting to destroy any agency that believed in a world billions of years old. After all, this lawmaker knew in his heart that the correct age of the earth came from a literal translation of the Bible. Bishop Ussher had the age thing right all along, with Earth's creation at 4004 B.C. No logical arguments based on scientific observations could create a chink in this congressman's monolithic faith. What better way to deal with a contradictory idea than to simply eliminate it?!

A rather special balancing act was imposed on HVO by being within a national park. The fact that HVO had been established before that park existed would seem to have grandfathered in rights for HVO to do what is necessary to carry out volcano-hazards studies. However, conscientious and well-meaning park superintendents viewed the volcano as something to preserve, while equally pure motives at HVO saw the critter as something that needed to be dissected in various literal and figurative ways. Occasional clashes were inevitable.

On the international scene, wily oil-producers in the Middle East created times of temporary havoc, even at HVO, with unpredictable petroleum embargoes. The embargoes inevitably triggered a string of energy-conservation edicts from Washington.

During the biggie of the early 1970s, all federal office lights were to be turned off at the end of the workday…no exceptions. The HVO staff had tried diligently to contribute its part to this laudable effort. However, when the juice to the network of seismic instruments was accidentally turned off (not once, not twice, but thrice), the resulting loss of earthquake records was deemed far more damaging than consumption of a few more kilowatt-hours of energy…especially since those records would have permitted the staff to predict an eruption of Mauna Loa that had wiped out part of Hilo. Big Island politicians had been very unhappy about this snafu, though they admitted that D.C. politicians, and not HVO scientists, had been the source of the problem.

In spite of such mini disasters, all of the political crises seemed to disappear as easily as they appeared. Once arm waving, finger pointing, and seemingly pointless national debates had run their course and produced the politically desired sound bytes, reason prevailed. Through all the stink, the USGS, including its age-old HVO, continued to advise the country on how to deal with such matters as natural hazards and the natural resource stuff of building and sustaining the American economy.

In spite of the most recent set of political bumps, Andy and the rest of the HVO crew kept their jobs. But they felt an increasingly heavy mantle of responsibility to warn the public about how to avoid becoming another of Kīlauea's toasted victims.

For both the science and the politics, Andy agonized over the meaning of Kīlauea's fits of tremor. This wasn't just the background noise of congressmen. It was time for serious consultation with his observatory colleagues.

Looking up from the instruments, he saw a coworker step out of his office.

"Hey Rob. We just recorded several more minutes of tremor. Do you have a few minutes to talk about this? I'd like to know what you make of it this time."

Rob shuffled down the hall at his typically slow and deliberate pace, head slouched a bit as though weighted down by his shoulder-length jet-black hair. Like Andy, Rob was in his twenties and carried high-powered education credentials.

❧   ❧   ❧

Rob had completed a bachelor of science degree in geology at Berkeley in four years, in spite of attractive distractions in the form of readily available mind-bending substances of various chemical compositions and an abundance of friendly female classmates.

Berkeley was still Berkeley, but Rob's focus was on completing an education that would carry him out of the kind of dead-end life that had consumed his parents. They had come from Mexico with legally obtained green cards in hand. Three children soon appeared, born into U.S. citizenship.

To finance the family, the parents had been stoop-labor workers in the huge agribusiness fields of the San Joaquin Valley. Both died in their early forties, with the hunched backs and arthritic hands that come from seemingly endless hours of tending to the crops of absentee-owners. But their deaths were not in vain, for even labor-shortened lives had allowed the parents enough time to instill high ambitions into their son Roberto Armando Garcia and his two older sisters. The parents had also accumulated enough savings to get the kids started at reputable universities.

The sisters went on to become successful professionals, one an interior designer in Sacramento and the other a small-animal veterinarian in Davis. Rob set his sights on a career in earth science. The lure of low in-state tuition led him to begin his higher education at Berkeley. If the earth had taken his parents prematurely, perhaps it would give him something back. But payback probably required some knowledge of the payer.

A scholarship-supported Ph.D. from Columbia University's Lamont-Doherty Institute followed his B.S. degree from Berkeley. There, Rob learned more than most anyone might want to know about a volcanic rock called basalt.

He learned that basalt is the stuff of the earth. If you partly melt and squeeze the earth's interior, out squirts basalt lava in hot volcanic eruptions.

He learned that over geologic time—a mind-boggling concept described as "deep time" by writer John McPhee in his attempts to help the masses comprehend billions of years in contrast to a human lifespan—massive outpourings of basalt lava had covered extensive areas of several continents. Equally mind-boggling, some of these lava floods had changed the earth's climate long enough to disrupt plant and animal life worldwide. No, it wasn't just Noah's flood at work, thank you Mr. Congressman.

Rob most especially came to know basalt as the linoleum on all ocean floors, which account for nearly three fourths of the planet's rocky surface. Like any lived-in home, much of this rocky flooring is dirtied with a veneer of gritty detritus washed in by rivers and by the accumulated corpses of once-living sea creatures…the spilled cookie crumbs, spaghetti sauce, and mustard of the sea. But underneath the messy veneer is a thick carpet of basalt, all erupted from a great system of planet-girdling fissures that map out a pattern imitating the seams of a baseball.

While a student at Columbia, Rob also learned that he was not cut out for a long-term diet of oceanographic cruises, the platform from which he learned so much about basalt. He had sailed the Atlantic, Pacific, and Indian Oceans and sampled their bottoms in his quest to understand basalt. But when at sea, no medication could convince his stomach to pass swallowed food on down the digestive tract, rather than back up his esophagus. He alone had added a significant amount of messy food scraps to the carpet of seafloor basalt.

In order to put his extensive knowledge of basalt to good use, he needed a land-based job. He scored that position at HVO, knowing that the Hawaiian islands are nothing but basalt, give or take a few fringing coral reefs and patches of white sand derived from them by a constant pounding from near-perfect surfing waves.

"Ummmh" was Rob's thoughtful-sounding though painfully useless answer to Andy's question. He, too, was puzzled by these bursts of volcanic tremor. He mulled possible explanations silently in his mind, rather that blurting out half-baked ideas that might later prove to be silly. His upbringing in poverty had taught him to be cautious. Silence ensued for several minutes, as both geologists seemed steeped in scientific thoughts. Andy, being Andy, let his eyes focus briefly out the window at a procession of young female tourists.

Finally, Rob was ready to talk.

"I'm not sure what Kīlauea's trying to tell us, but the same brief message has been sent so many times that we can't discount it as meaningless noise. If we'd seen a burst of tremor just once or twice during the past several weeks, we might relax about the possibility of an impending eruption. But we have now recorded what, thirty or thirty-five bursts in ten weeks, more or less evenly spaced in time? This isn't coincidental or trivial."

Rob was again briefly lost in thought and then continued in his carefully crafted cadence.

"Look, volcanic tremor is most likely caused by the underground flow of molten rock, the stuff that feeds eruptions. We all know that…or at least think we know that. So, we need to find a way to chart the pathways that molten stuff is following and try to get a handle on how much is involved. We need to somehow map Kīlauea's system of lava plumbing to determine what is flowing where down underground.

"Judging by how often past eruptions have occurred, the next one seems way overdue. This alone worries me about what might be brewing in the bowels of this volcano. She may have some pipes ready to burst."

The concept of plumbing within a volcano can seem bizarre to the uninitiated, but the analogy is useful and not far from reality. Molten rock moves through pipe-like conduits and opens cracks underground, creating tremors and a few small earthquakes as it shoulders aside hard and brittle rocks in the process. The subsurface frozen dregs of this moving rock syrup appear later in the eroded innards of old volcanoes, graphically illustrating the system of plumbing involved, like a road map in the rocks.

Andy slowly nodded his head in agreement. He, too, was increasingly concerned that the world's most active volcano had gone without eruption for an uncharacteristically long time. When he mentally combined this lengthy period of quiet with the tremor indications that molten stuff called magma was moving about inside Kīlauea, he was almost forced to conclude that HVO had a potentially explosive situation developing.

This was quite an about-face from the initial reaction that both he and Rob had had to the earliest bursts of tremor, which had occurred weeks ago.

At first, both believed that the tremors might be artifacts of the earthquake-recording equipment or of human activities, rather than visceral stirrings of the volcano. Both knew that the traffic of heavy trucks can cause a nearby seismometer to shake and tremble in a way that creates a record of tremor. One of the HVO instruments was close to the site of construction for a huge hotel at the local golf course, just outside the national park. However, the truck possibility was eliminated when it became apparent that seismometers far from the construction site were simultaneously recording the same message of tremor.

Andy and Rob then considered the possibility of shaking caused by strong winds. Typical Hawaiian trade winds, occasionally punctuated by a strong hurricane, regularly push flags into a flapping, extended position, without the need for a starchy stiffener of the sort used on the stars and stripes that astronauts planted on the windless moon back in 1969. These same trade winds can stir a seismometer into tremor-like shaking, during strong gusts. So, they checked the weather records. Most of the tremor recorded at HVO during the past several weeks had occurred on salubrious days of gentle breezes. This eliminated wind from the list of possible sources of tremor.

A continuing process of elimination drove both to the conclusion that the volcano was stirring back to life. Kīlauea was going through spasms of her own, not human- or weather-caused, tremor. And that tremor probably meant subterranean molten rock on the move.

The million-dollar question now was whether this molten stuff would ever see the light of day, or would instead stay beneath the earth's surface and cool to solid rock there, out of people's homes and lives. Actually, a valid answer to the outstanding question represented much more than a million dollars in value, especially if the HVO staff were to make a mistake in prediction that stirred those murky congressional waters.

They stood staring at the seismographs. Rob appeared thoughtful and pensive. Andy uncertain and a bit nervous. Outside, tourists were still enjoying the crater-within-caldera panorama. A passing child pointed through the window in admiration and delight. His shouts carried through the glass.

"Mom, Dad. Look at the volcano experts! That's what I want to be when I grow up. Can I? Can I?"

Andy and Rob were feeling like anything but experts at the moment. They needed help. Two minds on a single track arrived at the same conclusion, in unison.

"We'd better huddle with Ben, sooner rather than later."

Andy continued: "He may recognize a message embedded in the tremor that we're overlooking. He's out of town until Friday. Let's watch for more tremor until then."

CHAPTER 10

HAY-SEED TEEN DISCOVERS HEAVEN AND VALERIE

In his fitful sleep, Josh was reliving irony. His current laid-back, pakalōlō-filled lifestyle was the unintended result of an elders-hatched plan meant to bond him ever more strongly to a corn-raising life in Iowa. Seriously sober intentions had gone awry.

By Chickasaw County custom, pleased elders and other community stalwarts treated each graduating class to a "vacation" trip, as a reward for successfully completing their high school education. For Josh's class, a select subgroup of the elders, led by Amos Brown, crafted an itinerary designed to consolidate the solid framework of education already accomplished at home.

Amos and elders included a little fun in the itinerary…but not excessive fun. Just how much was clearly spelled out in a guidebook they wrote. Each student was expected to study this in preparation for the trip and to carry it for reference along the way. A typed report titled "What I Learned in Hawai'i" was required of each student not more than ten days after trip's end.

And so it was that twenty graduates of the class of 1980 flew west from Iowa corn-and-pig country for ten days of education (and some fun) in Hawai'i. Their chaperones, football coach Butch Kaster and his wife Fanny, were far more interested in conjugal pleasures than watching after the students.

Fun on Oʻahu came first in the form of snorkeling at Hounoma Bay, followed by swimming and body surfing at the white sand beach of Waikīkī. For a history lesson (chapter one, page six of their guidebook) at Pearl Harbor, Josh and classmates visited what's left of the unfortunate battleship Arizona, still harboring human remains and leaking diesel fuel where Japanese bombs had sunk it in 1941.

Maui fun began with a day of deep-sea fishing. Josh and classmates caught far more rays of solar, than piscine, variety. Tropical sun baked the white winter skin of the Iowans to a fiery red, a process that had started at Waikīkī.

Maui day two got underway with a pre-dawn drive to the crater rim of Haleakala Volcano. A yawning sunburned group watched the sun grow right up out of the ocean.

Once back down the long slope of Haleakala, they drove southward along the coast through masses of chaotic jungly vegetation to the quaint village of Hana. Plant variety posed a stark contrast to the corn, corn, and more corn of back home. There was a lesson in botany, (chapter two, page three), something about the advantages of controlling plant variety to maximize the useful production of crop.

A bit beyond Hana, they passed the fun-filled place called the Seven Sacred Pools (where one of Hawaiʻi's few perennial rivers cascades step-wise over thick masses of lava, polished to a brilliant black sheen by millennia of splashing water) on the way to the site of more education. This somber lesson came at the cemetery where Charles Lindberg had chosen to be buried.

As Josh read that Lindberg had been a famous pioneering aviator, who let his admiration of the Germany's WWII Luftwaffe accomplishments drag him into messy politics and bigotry (chapter two, pages four and five titled "Stay Focused on What's Right"), he was thinking mostly about the incredible contrast in landscapes between this resting place and that of Lindberg's upper Midwest origins.

Josh could certainly understand abandoning a Little Falls, Minnesota (or anywhere Iowa) winter in favor of a daily embrace by the warm tropical arms of Hawaiʻi. Even now, he felt those comfortably encompassing limbs wrapping ever tighter around his body, muting his will and diluting his desire to follow in Amos's footsteps.

The Big Island was the trip finale. If Josh had any lingering doubts about falling in love with Hawaiʻi, this island erased them. The name was so appropriate. The Big Island has twice the land area of all the other Hawaiian Islands combined. Big included up, too. The neighboring peaks of Mauna Kea and

Mauna Loa rise to more than 13000 feet in elevation, 12000 feet higher than any part of Iowa.

The class saw these majestic volcanoes as their Aloha flight from Maui made its approach into the Hilo airport. The lumpy rounded top of Mauna Kea was dotted with the domes of astronomical observatories. Though late spring, a trace of snow still capped Mauna Kea. The Loa version of Mauna was a smoother broad shield-like pile of raw black lava indented by what looked like the product of a giant cookie cutter.

According to the guidebook and an in-flight magazine, geologists call this depression Mokuaweoweo Caldera. They say the top of the mountain collapsed when lots of molten rock was erupted from a huge pot of the stuff stored just below the surface. With the cellar support suddenly gone, the roof caved in.

Another story claimed that during winter, one could snow ski on Mauna Kea and water ski at a fine Pacific beach, on the same day. This combination of back-to-back activities was quite impossible to experience in Iowa.

A non-stop succession of Iowa-compared-to-Hawaii contrasts battered Josh as they travelled north from Hilo, along the lush windward Hāmākua coast, up and over a pass between Kohala and Mauna Kea Volcanoes, to Waimea and beyond, into the leeward side that's about as dry as west Texas. They went from coconuts to cactus in thirty miles and thirty minutes!

Josh was once again thinking that the flat, ancient, and tired land of Iowa was pretty boring by comparison. On the Big Island, entire volcanic hills and plains were created in less time than it took for a field of corn to ripen back home.

Their last day was spent at Kīlauea, the centerpiece of Hawai'i Volcanoes National Park. They followed Crater Rim Drive, around Kīlauea's two-mile-wide cookie-cutter caldera. This was not only a large collapsed hole in the ground; it was also a stinkpot. Though different in scent, the strength and stench of the volcanic fumes reminded Josh of hog manure. Both he and his quarterback buddy were choking on the fumes.

"Hey, Bobby. Do you recognize the smell? It's a little like back home, isn't it."

"Yup, you got it, Josh. Does this mean that Kīlauea's a pig? Notice how no one is living directly downwind of this source of stench."

Along the caldera rim, they visited displays that explained what scientists know about the inner workings of Kīlauea. A nearly equal amount of display space and information were devoted to Pele and her relationship to Kīlauea.

Josh started wondering if the scientists really did understand the volcano. As if in partial answer to his silent wondering, one display cabinet contained the partly burned boot and pant leg of a geologist who had fallen into a moving lava flow several years earlier. A sign explained that the seared geologist had been pulled to safety and was now living a fully active life right there in Hawai'i. Josh winced in shared pain at the very thought of immersing any part of his body into a liquid the temperature of molten rock.

"Hey, Bobby. Maybe we could have used this guy on our team…hot footing it off tackle when we needed a few yards."

"Naw. Anyone clumsy enough to fall into lava would never have made the first team cut."

"Yeah, you're right. What a dumb accident for someone who's supposed to understand the volcano. The last thing in the world I'd do is get caught up in this lava stuff!"

Next came a tour of Kīlauea's east rift zone, that long tapering ridge pointing toward California at a place called Cape Kumukahi. Their guidebook said that the cape had grown another quarter mile closer to California during an eruption in 1960, barely twenty years earlier.

Josh marveled again at how alive the Big Island is, growing acres of *new* land each year. At the same time, erosion was removing hundreds of thousands of tons of *old* Iowa, washing sand, silt, and clay downstream to the Gulf of Mexico.

Creative "For Sale" signs posted on patches of new lava told Josh and his classmates how realtors took advantage of their growing island.

"Don't buy old tired land. Buy this brand new never-before-used earth. Get it today, before time takes its toll."

Naive Todd, the class dreamer whose career goal was to escape his family's tradition of raising pigs…by becoming a real estate agent…wondered aloud: "Do you guys think these signs are serious, tongue-in-cheek, or the work of slime balls? Serious or slime, I could never use that pitch about land at home, could I?"

Now back on the wet side of the island, the class was driving through dense rainforest. A century earlier, lava had oozed through the area, leaving a stand of pipe-like sticks, called tree molds, where majestic 'ōhi'a trees had once thrived. How bizarre! Flowing lava had molded against tree trunks and froze there as a skin of hardened rock. The encased trunks burned away because of the intense heat.

When Dorothy Pender, from a corn-raising family, climbed into one of the hollow molds to pose for a round of photos, Josh was reminded of a story about a farm girl from Kansas visiting a Wonder Land. Compared to the Big Island, though, what place could possibly be a Wonder Land. Sweet-smelling Dottie Pender made just about any place even better!

It was time to move on. Coach Kaster suddenly came to life. "Hey, class. Our next stop is where Mother Nature's version of *your* mother's pressure cooker has been harnessed to generate electricity. If this sounds like magic, well, maybe it is, just a little bit."

Scientists and engineers had drilled wells into a pocket of high-pressure steam, where magma heated groundwater to way above boiling temperature. The engineers piped this gift of nature into a turbine that generated electricity for the island. Coach Kaster, who also taught environmental studies, finally had something of special interest to him.

"Okay, class. Remember that back in Iowa and most of the rest of the mainland, steam for making electricity is created by burning dirty old coal or diesel fuel. The electrons here, though, are flowing through Big Island power lines from a nice clean natural source of steam. These volcanoes can be friendly and beneficial as well as violent."

As if to reemphasize that thought, the class next swam at nearby Pualaa Park, where the pleasantly warm temperature of a large tidal pool was the tepid result of magma heating water.

"Gifts from Mother Nature," said Kaster as he splashed about. "Gifts from Pele."

By this time, Josh was giving serious thought to dropping out of the corn-raising money chase of Chickasaw County and living in the natural abundance of the tropical paradise called Hawai'i. Long before he had come on this trip to Hawai'i…nudged along by Grain Belt, reefers, and his more worldly classmates…he had had second and even third thoughts about a life like that of his father. Josh was an increasingly confused young man, poised to rebel and cast away the life his parents had planned for him. But he was still uncertain about the wisdom of doing so.

Then came Valerie, who unexpectedly helped Josh make his life-changing decision. She appeared on the wooden walkway outside a shop in a funky little town called Pāhoa, the very last stop before the Hilo airport and a flight home.

The elders of Chickasaw County had selected Pāhoa for the class's last stop, as an example of the non-tourist side of Hawai'i. A working-class village, located in rainforest near the east rift of Kīlauea, Pāhoa was the antithesis of clean-and-wealthy Waikīkī, Lahina, and Kona. The elders, and most especially Amos Brown, were sure that this last look would help the students appreciate their good life in Iowa, and long to hurry home, even more for the contrast. How very wrong those elders were…in Josh's case. Amos's plan was about to backfire.

Town was a single gently curving street, about three quarters of a mile long, lined with small and very old looking one- and two-story shops. Most shared walls of inexpensive wood construction. Painting of exterior walls was clearly a low-priority exercise. Random stretches of concrete, wood, and natural dirt formed a ramshackle network of shop-front walkways, presumably reflecting the net result of decisions by individual shop owners, rather than something dictated by a town ordinance.

Unlike the merchants in slick and squeaky-clean tourist towns, Pāhoa shop owners displayed chaotic and dusty piles of the necessities of day-to-day living…toilet paper, soap, rain coats, brooms, cane knives, shovels, rubber boots. A gas station, small grocery store, and a couple of cafes rounded out the commercial section. At the south end of the town's main street sat the largest building, by far…a faded-yellow old wooden structure on stilts, the town's public school.

The people of Pāhoa looked as unpretentious as the material things of their town. Dress was earth tone and working class to the extreme. Most of the population reflected the multiracial look so characteristic of Hawai'i's melting pot, with Japanese, Filipino, Portuguese, Chinese, European, and native Hawaiian genes stirred together in various proportions. Black hair and bronze skin were everywhere. So were tens of nondescript brownish shorthaired dogs that looked to be the product of interbreeding run amok.

Another local look harked back to the 1960s hippie days of Berkeley and San Francisco. Long hair, beards, and unshaved female legs were not enough to hide the true light skin colors of mainland haoles. Apparently, part of Haight Ashbury and the like had moved to Pāhoa, a tropical refuge for those unable to exit the laid-back anti-materialist hippie life and get on with the me generation and mega-consumption of the 1970s and beyond.

Having recently discovered the joys and scent of reefers, Josh easily recognized the smell of burning marijuana emanating from several of the store fronts as he ambled along, looking for gifts that he might buy for his sisters. Was this place his nirvana or was he dreaming? As he pinched himself to test for consciousness, Valerie drifted out of one of these stores as quietly and gracefully as a wisp of reefer fume might have escaped Josh's nostrils, had he been smoking.

She was lovely and smiling…perhaps the smile of stoned friendliness? She was five foot three at most, and probably weighed no more than ninety-five pounds. A patterned but formless tent-like dress covered what Josh imagined to be a firm and beautifully shaped body underneath. She wore no shoes. Her straight blond hair hung down to her hips. Lack of makeup seemed to accentuate twinkling eyes set in a smiling oval face, with perfectly proportioned ears, nose, and lips.

She walked right up to Josh and started a conversation as though they had been the best of friends for years. She made him feel instantly at ease, something that had never come easy for him with girls, although the recent discovery of beer and reefers had helped in that department.

"Hi. I'm Valerie."

"Hi Valerie. I'm Josh."

"You look new in town. I'm fairly new to Pāhoa, myself. It's a nicer place than it looks like at first glance. Want to hear about what I've discovered over a cool drink?"

"Sure. And you're right. This *is* my first time in Pāhoa."

She took him by the hand and led him into a small cafe. They ordered mint-flavored iced drinks, as though they had planned this meeting long ago. They sat and locked gazes in mutual attraction, fascination, and wondering.

"So, first tell me about yourself, Josh."

"Well, uh, I'm from Iowa. My whole high school class is here. You probably saw some of them walking around town, with either pasty white or red sunburned skin exposed. We're on a trip to celebrate our graduation."

Valerie nodded and kept her attention focused on Josh.

"I'm a farmer. Here. Look at these abused hands."

Valerie took Josh's hands and rubbed her thumbs over callus-hardened palms. Josh could feel her stroking just enough to fantasize about where such rubbing might lead. He put his hands back around his drink glass.

"My father raises corn, lots of corn. He, aaah, plans to pass his farm along to me when he retires. That'll probably happen in just a few more years. Then I'll have a ready-made financially secure life dropped in my lap." Josh waited for a reaction.

"Well, that should take a load off your mind. I mean, lots of guys your age are struggling to figure out what career they want, and how to get it going." Valerie could see some creases of doubt form across Josh's face.

"Sure. You're right about that. But I'm not so sure I *want* that farm, even though it's big and a big money maker. I hope this won't insult you, but my feelings about the farm are all wrapped up in a personal problem I've got with religion. It's a problem I'm having a tough time dealing with."

Valerie noticed Josh's facial creases deepening.

"You see, my parents are practicing Christians. Actually, they're Methodist…I mean, *extremely* Methodist…ridiculously, fundamentalist Methodist."

Josh took Valerie's silence and unchanged expression to mean that it was okay to talk about religion this way. "I've got nothing against believing in a god and behaving like a decent Christian, you know, observing the Golden Rule and all. But in my family that means almost none of the fun times that my classmates always seem to have. Well, that all changed about a year ago. I discovered the relaxing pleasures of beer and reefers…and that this stuff doesn't send you straight to hell. Of course my father and mother don't know about my discoveries."

Valerie interrupted briefly with "Actually, here that leafy stuff is called pakalōlō. Welcome to the pakalōlō capitol of the Big Island."

Josh grinned. "I thought I smelled something familiar in the air." He pronounced p a k a l ō l ō slowly, almost musically. "Ummh. That word sounds as pleasant as the pleasure it gives.

"Anyway, since I found another way of living, I've been leading a double life. Father and mother still think I'm following the straight and narrow Methodist path. And that's what they'll expect and demand when I get the farm. My being an adult won't change their thinking. But I'm not sure a free farm would be worth the long-term personal pain. The farm wouldn't be free anyway, would it? Lots of moral strings would be attached."

Josh hesitated briefly as though gathering some deep inner thoughts. "And now, having seen so many neat things about life in Hawai'i, I just feel like dropping out and living off the land. I've seen three of the islands during the past nine days, and I think I could do that here on any of the three. I like the Big Island best, though."

Josh was feeling pretty emotional. A tight voice reflected these feelings when he continued. "The fact is, I'm confused as hell. We're supposed to head for the Hilo airport and the flight home in about thirty minutes. And I'm not at all sure I want to go home."

Josh read sympathy into Valerie's attentive expression. Her story was about to push Josh to the most momentous decision of his life, to date.

"Josh, Josh. I've been through the same kind of gut-wrenching inner turmoil that's eating away at you right now. I rebelled at my parents' way of life. And I've made my break from that. Meet a four-week Pāhoa hippie, from the very wealthy banking district of New York City."

At this point, they began to hold hands across the table.

"Believe it or not, just weeks ago I was still living the life of a high-society debutante in the financial capital of the world. My father's a highly successful banker there. The social side of our family life was important for bringing in new customers. I was expected to be part of this recruiting game, as soon as I was old enough to mix with adults, father's potential and established clients."

As Josh listened, he tried to imagine this plainly dressed female in the kind of elegant gown demanded for a coming-out party. She was plenty attractive in a sack dress.

"I played my family social role through the first two years of college. But I was never interested in the high-society money chase. Mother and father knew that I hated that life."

Josh's attention was riveted to Valerie. He had never before met a New York City society female. Here he was holding hands with a real debutante.

"Most of the men I met were preppies of the Andover, Choate, Deerfield, and Exeter variety."

Josh had no idea what these schools were. But he nodded as though he did.

"These guys went on to Harvard, Yale, Princeton, or maybe Dartmouth, whichever place was in a particular family's tradition. They were all so alike and so malleable. Each was willing to be molded into the person his parents had planned for even before their child's birth. Josh, I don't think any of these guys had even experienced life outside their precious and sheltered eastern seaboard society. I'm sure they had never walked through a cornfield."

Josh wasn't sure how to take this comment. He'd been in too damned many cornfields. But he wasn't a preppie and had never been to New York, or any other sophisticated city. Well, maybe he had. Someone once told him that Des Moines was French.

"I wanted some variety in my life. I became desperate to break out of this molded and moldy social scene."

Josh was trying to compare life as a strict Methodist with that in the social scene described by Valerie. Though totally different styles, both stifled independent behavior and thought…those things called thinking and acting outside the box. He was starting to think that he and Valerie had a whole lot in common.

"I was, and still am, lucky with the family situation. My parents sympathize with my plight…maybe in large part because I'm an only child. Mother isn't able to have more. So, mother and dad have agreed that I can pursue whatever lifestyle I want for a few years. There will be no questions asked, with the understanding that I'll return to their New York place for a two-week visit, twice a year. Other than those visits, I'm on my own. They send no money, no letters. We avoid those kinds of contact."

Valerie went on to explain that, meanwhile, the New York financial social scene of her parents believed that she was attending an exclusive finishing school for advantaged young ladies, somewhere in Western Europe. This lie was easily passed off as truth by the semi-annual visits back to New York.

Valerie had "discovered" Pāhoa a few years earlier on a family vacation, much as Josh was discovering the place at that moment. She had returned and took up residence just one month earlier, because the town provided her with the quiet and hassle-free environment that she wanted, as she tried to sort out what she really wanted to do with her life. It was obvious to her that Josh was in much the same predicament that she had experienced pre Pāhoa. It was also obvious that there was little time for him to think through what his future should be. His class would be boarding their van in less than thirty minutes for the short drive to the Hilo airport. What should she do?

Valerie's mind was a whirlwind of thoughts. This guy was no clay-ball preppy, as her earlier male companions had been. He was her diamond in the rough. He had a lot of corny and naive edges that were attractive and almost entertaining at the same time. She could polish those rough edges, although maybe they should be left as is. In short, she saw much in Josh that had been so sorely missing in her New York escorts. She wanted to share her current lifestyle with this soul mate, and see where that relationship would take them.

Valerie and Josh continued to look into each others' eyes with a depth of understanding and mutual pleading that needed no verbal expression. Josh could hear the voices of classmates calling his name. Time was short. He resisted hardly at all, when Valerie smiled her iceberg-melting smile, took him by the hand, and led him out the back door into a rainforest that was to become their shared home from that day on.

The Chickasaw County coach, his wife, and the other students searched the main street of Pāhoa for Josh, frantically and in vain, as their departure time loomed desperately close to being missed. They could wait no longer. Their van crept down the line of Pāhoa stores and out of town to the north toward

Hilo. They boarded their Hilo-Mainland flight rather than forfeit the cost of the homeward leg of their journey.

Once back home, it quickly came to light, through elders' intense questioning of Josh's worldly and earlier tight-lipped classmates, that for the past two years, Josh had been a regular, though moderate, consumer of beer and reefers.

Amos and Rebecca were shocked, aghast, angry. How could they have missed seeing such sinful behavior? In the spirit of their beloved Old Testament eye-for-an-eye philosophy, they could not forgive Josh. Instead, they set about refocusing their energies on grooming Josh's sisters and their husbands-to-be into inheritors of the family corn-farming business. In the selfishness of their public embarrassment, they chose to forget Josh, as though he had never existed. He had failed to live up to his initials. He could, and in their opinion, should roast in hell. Little did they know that their son's fate would in fact be a hot one, at least here on earth.

Back on the Big Island, Josh and Valerie set up housekeeping in the rainforest of Kīlauea. They were friends, sometimes lovers, but mostly soul mates, each searching for their preferred way of life. They demanded little of each other beyond companionship and a sympathetic listener. They quickly cleared their "homestead" along a broadly tapering ridge of land within convenient walking distance of Pāhoa. They learned that, with minimal scavenging, they could live off the natural bounty of this land. Pakalōlō from their small garden served simultaneously as a life-enhancing consumable and a widely accepted medium of exchange.

Valerie was pleased with her new living arrangements, although she still intended to carry out her part of the agreement with her parents. She also expected to return to some form of their life, beyond her window of living as she chose.

In his newfound independence and freedom, Josh was serene. He was content with his spartan lifestyle and new friend. The occasional feral pig rooting through their Hawaiian homestead triggered waking-hour thoughts of his former family life. But even these unwanted intrusions mostly served to remind him that he was now corn-free. He could deal with the feral pigs. They were few enough and so much on the move, that not even the stench of their manure was an aggravation.

※ ※ ※

Huge tropical raindrops simultaneously woke Josh and Valerie from their hammock slumbers, partly because of the brisk splash of drops on their skin and partly from the tympanic drumming of drops on the roof of their shelter. As was often their custom on warm summer days like today, not that winter days were much less warm, they stayed naked in their hammocks and slowly rotated long enough to complete a pretty thorough and effective all-over shower. Sometimes they even used soap for this ritual, but mostly the pelting of another inch or two of tropical rain was sufficient cleansing for their lifestyle.

If the rain continued more than several minutes, they would retreat to the shelter. Otherwise, the reappearance of the warm tropical sun would so quickly dry them that they need not leave the comfort of their sling-like beds. Today's was one of the short-lived showers.

Josh remembered once reading that native Hawaiians had dealt with the frequent tropical rains this same way, before European missionaries arrived and browbeat the locals into covering their bodies with a Christianly proper amount of clothing. Josh often thought that God would not have been happy with his disciples, knowing that the lengthy process of drying out rain-soaked clothing, in contrast to wet skin, chilled many Hawaiians into bouts of illnesses, often resulting in death. It seemed that Christianity often hurt people in the name of love and understanding.

But Josh was now free to pursue the tropical Hawaiian style of life. He was released from the strictures of John Wesley, as interpreted and practiced by Amos and Rebecca. His lifestyle pendulum was on its leftward swing, and he was determined to keep it moving in that direction.

With that pleasant thought, he sighed and slipped back toward a clean-bodied pakalōlō-induced slumber. Her steady breathing told him that Valerie was already there. Tomorrow, they would put on a few clothes, walk into Pāhoa, chat with friends, and trade pakalōlō for meat, beans, and beer.

CHAPTER 11

BEN, THE EARTHQUAKE MAN

Ben was the earthquake specialist on the HVO staff. He was arguably the world's brightest and most experienced volcano seismologist. Like his widely advertised Wall Street counterpart, when Ben spoke, wise people listened...if they wanted to know what the seismic shaking of a volcano meant.

Born of Filipino parents who had immigrated separately to Hawai'i as teenagers without much money or education, Benito Antonio Ruayan's childhood was one of manual labor. Mostly Ben helped keep food on the family table by raising vegetables and by caring for other people's landscape plantings for the money to buy what could not be grown in the back yard.

When time and parents permitted, Ben enjoyed free recreation offered by the Big Island...fun at a beach and an occasional hike to a remote part of the island's rainforest-covered slopes. His father sometimes took him to illegal though ever-present cockfights, wanting to maintain as much of the homeland culture as possible. His father thought that his son would enjoy this Filipino tradition, but blood sport never appealed to Ben. He was interested in plants, not animals...and in nurturing living things, not maiming them.

During childhood, Ben was no stranger to the eruptions and earthquakes of Kīlauea. He grew up near the village of Mountain View (just a few miles from Kīlauea's caldera), where it was impossible to ignore the volcano's tantrums, even if he had wanted to. As a pre-school child and later as a teenager, he watched repeatedly from the sidelines as towering fountains of lava were thrust high into the Hawaiian sky and then splashed down to cover acre upon acre of lush rainforest with a new frosting of basalt.

By age twenty-five, Ben had witnessed more than a dozen eruptions. His favorite happened in 1955, just a few miles south of his home. The east rift of Kīlauea had split open as though suddenly cleaved by some huge diabolical sugar-cane knife, and then blood-red lava spewed out, covering miles of roads and acres of papaya fields. His second favorite, in 1959, was the two-thousand-foot-tall lava fountain at Kīlauea Iki near the top of the volcano, mostly because this was an all-time record height. Somewhat disappointing, though, was the fact that all of the erupted lava just collected in a deep crater, rather than spreading out across the landscape to produce the kind of inferno that seems to thrill young boys. Large and destructive or small and benign, all the pyrotechnics of nature that Ben had witnessed were visually fascinating. Plus, new volcanic ash made excellent soil for tropical plants and successful vegetable gardening.

Ben's love of plants and the superb gardening possible in a mild tropical climate eventually seduced him into the tranquil adult life of raising flowers for export to the mainland. After he had acquired his own acre of rainforest at 2000 feet in elevation, and a wife, in that order, he specialized in raising a shiny-leafed plastic-looking flower called anthurium. The climate allowed year-round growing. Anthuriums shipped well, and the unabashedly phallic shape of this flower's reproductive system protruding from the cleft of a bright-red, heart-shaped leaf seemed to create a consumer demand beyond that generated by a more conventional flowery house decoration. Business was brisk. Anthuriums were especially popular on Valentine's Day. Life was good for Ben, his wife and the three boys who came along during the first three years of marriage. Another part of Ben's body seemed as fertile as his green thumb.

But as Ben's hands cared for the flowers, his mind wandered and wondered about how an active volcano like Kīlauea worked. He visited the Hilo library and read all materials he could find on Kīlauea and other volcanoes. He observed Kīlauea's eruptions from as close as law-enforcement officials would allow. He haunted the halls of the observatory on days when they were open to public visits. He pestered the observatory staff with myriad questions about volcanoes.

He began to keep systematic records of Kīlauea's behavior…the when and where of eruptions, the size of earthquakes that rocked the island as part of the eruption story, and any other tidbits of information that he thought might be important to understanding the volcano. He became frustrated by the knowledge that he needed sophisticated instruments and more access to the mountain to go beyond a superficial level of understanding.

Given his passion for Kīlauea, it was inevitable that Ben's avocation became his vocation. He had an academic and inquiring mind trapped in the body of a gardener. As a middle-aged adult, he crossed the Pacific Ocean and North America, where he matriculated at Princeton University to learn how to apply seismology to an active volcano. He excelled at this pursuit, while his family stayed at home and maintained the flourishing flower farm. Soon he was the HVO seismologist. The pesky visitor with a myriad of questions evolved into the expert with ready answers.

Ben's office was small and windowless, the better to view seismogram charts on a TV monitor in their electronic form, an efficient alternative to dealing with those bulky plain-paper tracings. He spent hours studying the charts, converting the information imbedded in their squiggly lines into precise locations of earthquakes within the earth...a place that scientists call the hypocenter...and up above on the surface, the so-called epicenter. He also calculated the intensity of each quake...a measure of the amount of energy released during an earth spasm.

Within a year at HVO, he could recite, from memory, the where when and intensity of all significant quakes, going back to the 1950s when a network of electronic instruments was first installed. He was *the* walking encyclopedia of Kīlauea's shakes.

Recently, Ben had become especially interested in tremor. Its tracing was so unlike that of a conventional earthquake that no one before him had fully understood how to deal with it. As is often the case when confronted with the unfamiliar, most people before him had ignored the tremor puzzle. All that was really known at this point was that tremor probably signaled the underground movement of magma. This wasn't enough information for defining the probable time and place of the next eruption. Ben was determined to delve deeper.

During the past several months, he had made the study of tremor his personal passion. While others on the HVO staff were kicking rocks out in the field or pretending to study the seismic signals at the tourist-watching window, Ben holed up in his dark office, staring at records of past tremors. He methodically measured the height of each wavy tremor tracing from crest to trough, something his textbooks called amplitude. He determined the time it took for one complete waveform to be recorded, the tremor frequency. And he determined the duration of each spasm of tremor, from its onset to finish, to a fraction of a second.

A pattern was emerging. It was time to share his thoughts. That Friday when Andy and Rob showed up was indeed an opportune time.

❦   ❦   ❦

The three of them crowded into Ben's office and positioned themselves in front of a twenty-seven-inch monitor that could display any or all of the observatory's seismic records at the stroke of a computer key. Ben took charge as the other two listened. He began by looking up toward a large map of the Big Island, taped to the office wall, behind the monitor. Ben led the conversation in his typical pseudo-formal style.

"Gentlemen, I've been looking over old and recent tremor records for some time, and I think I see a pattern of behavior that can help us understand Kīlauea. I haven't shared these ideas with anyone else yet, because some of my interpretations are kinda shaky…no pun intended. You two are the first to hear my thoughts; you are my guinea pigs. I want to get your reaction before I go to our boss, The Don."

Pointing to the map with a yardstick, he continued. "First, remind yourselves that we have seismometers all over the island, fifty of them to be exact. Most are here on Kīlauea, and all of them record electronically. Six also record on those paper drums by the window. As we all know, that window dressing is as much for the entertainment of tourists as for our own use, which seems to include a bit of window-aided mental undressing of selected tourists…by some of us."

Ben pointedly glanced at Andy with this last remark. His wry, blunt, and understated sense of humor was beginning to seep into the conversation. He turned and reached toward the top of the Big Island map with his stick.

"The seismometer farthest from Kīlauea is on Kohala, the most northerly of the five volcanoes that make up our Big Island. That's about sixty-five miles from us as the nēnē flies."

Ben liked to use the native Hawaiian goose as the Big Island straight-line-distance bird of choice. A nēnē has a lot more character than any crow that he had ever seen. Besides, he knew that the word is French slang for the human female breast, a fact that usually pumped up Andy's pulse a beat or two.

It was working today. At this point, loverboy Andy was grinning, as his imagination created an Escheresque squadron of flying firm breasts, nipples at attention, headed straight for Kīlauea from Kohala. "Not a bad idea for a tee-shirt design" he was thinking.

Ben continued describing the network of seismometers, always looking at the map. "Now, coming south from Kohala toward Kīlauea, the instruments are spaced closer and closer together, from Mauna Kea, to Hualālai, to Mauna Loa. In fact, our seismometer coverage on this island is about as thick as gull shit would be on the Hilo pier, if only we had seagulls. With just one more instrument, I swear the island would sink."

Andy and Rob winked at each other and chuckled silently as they recalled Ben's pet peeve about already having so damned many instruments deployed that he never seemed to have time to study all the records. A few Republican congressmen would agree with Ben, seeing an opportunity to save a few dollars to the embarrassment their Democratic counterparts. But no other scientist, Republican or Democrat, would agree. Of course, those scientists didn't have Ben's day-to-day task of analyzing all of the incoming data.

Finished with the map lesson, Ben looked squarely at Andy and Rob. "Okay, so here's what I've done. First, I looked at the amplitude of tremor...you guys know about that, right?...the vertical distance between the top of a wavy tracing to its bottom. Our seismometers are all calibrated the same. So this distance should increase with intensity of the shaking and also with how close a particular seismometer is to the source of shaking. Like any other violent physical action, other things being equal, the farther away the less the action is felt. Hey, here in Hawai'i, no one felt the direct impact of that first A-bomb dropped on Japan, did they? But everyone in Hiroshima sure as hell did."

Ben talked about the Pacific theater of WWII a lot. His parents had fled the Philippines as teenagers, mostly to escape the craziness that was developing in their country as Japan cranked up its war efforts. They never let Ben and his siblings forget how fortunate they were to be in Hawai'i, during war or peace.

"Well, I've got news for you experts. The difference is small, almost too small to measure. But for every series of episodes of tremor that led to eruption ever since HVO's seismometers have been functioning, the amplitude increased as the time of eruption approached. Unfortunately, tremor rising from beneath Kīlauea is too weak a signal to be recorded as far away as Kohala, or even Mauna Kea, but still we have enough information to see this pattern."

Ben suddenly jerked around and used the yardstick to point to a piece of graph paper taped to the wall, near the Big Island map. The vertical axis was labeled "Amplitude, in millimeters." The horizontal axis was simply "Time, in days," with values of zero at the lower left corner of the graph. Ben had hand drawn a line that nicely passed through a hot-dog-shaped blizzard of data points from day one to the end of the graph, and that line rose ever so slightly from left to right. The amplitude definitely increased with time.

"This example is for several episodes of tremor that preceded the 1959 eruption at Kīlauea Iki, just a couple of miles east of where we now sit. Do you two remember reading about that one? At 2000-feet tall, it produced the highest lava fountain ever recorded at Kīlauea. Tourists sat, mai tai in hand, on the lānai of the Volcano House Hotel, just across the caldera from where we are now, and watched that towering orange-colored aerosol spray. Jumping Jupiter that was a fantastic experience, although I was a bit too young to be drinking a mai tai then. As a teenage kid, I watched it with my dad. I imagine that you boys were barely a gleam in your daddy's eyes back then."

Still pointing to the graph: "As you can see, the amplitude of tremor peaked as eruption began, in this case during the evening of Saturday, November 14, 1959. The damn volcano couldn't wait another thirty-six hours, for official work time, could it?"

Ben, Andy, Rob and all other HVO employees were well aware of the fact that Kīlauea seemed to have a perverse habit of starting eruptions on weekends, holidays, or at night. Over the years, many a family celebration or a good night's sleep had been interrupted, if not ruined by an eruption-alert phone call from the person on duty at HVO.

"I've found the same behavior of amplitude peaking for other eruptions that I've graphed. Once eruption begins, the general pattern is for tremor to vibrate along at a more or less constant level and completely die out when eruption stops. Neat, huh??!! If I do say so myself, this info is as tasty as five-day poi."

Ben was referring to the fact that the Hawaiian food staple, poi, ferments in its package as it sits on store shelves. The consumer who wants a small but pleasant buzz from his poi buys the stuff that is several days old. According to local legend, five-day poi wins in the overall taste-and-kick contest. Ten-day poi has more kick but has gone a bit bitter. Most mainlanders would argue that some fermentation is needed to make poi of any age palatable.

To Andy, this starchy substance…extracted by pounding the roots of taro plants…was reminiscent of the consistency and color of plain old library paste…that white stuff that came in half-gallon jars to every elementary school on the mainland. But unlike poi, at least library paste always tasted good, fresh out of its container or even months later.

Andy and Rob smiled at each other knowingly and silently urged Ben to get on with the tremor story.

"I also looked at the time it takes for a wavy tracing to repeat itself. This is what my pointy-headed professors at Princeton called frequency."

Andy and Rob could see by the look on Ben's face that he was about to go off on one of his famous tirades. He had been an excellent student at Princeton, but he never fit comfortably into the rather stiff and formal academic environment and its use of excessive jargon for simple ideas. As a result of those Princeton years, he still had some haunting personal demons embedded in his psyche. He kept them at bay by railing against academia from time to time.

"God, some of them were prissy, stuffed-shirt, self-important assholes at times…with predictable frequency in fact."

This feeble attempt at humor didn't tickle Andy and Rob at all. They were starting to get excited about the scientific breakthrough that Ben seemed headed toward. They could do without his time-consuming asides at this point.

"Well, it seems that Kīlauea is a monotone, as predictable as one of my Princeton professors, good old one-and-only Herr Hertz. Kīlauea's tremor is stuck on a repeat time of about one second, whatever the amplitude may be."

Next came a wry grin across Ben's face, which usually preceded his expounding a colorful, if not downright fanciful idea. "Could there be some primordial message imbedded in the fact that the world's fundamental unit of time is also the one note played by molten rock as it flows through its underground plumbing? This behavior is a bit like the single tone that comes with a certain flow of air through the pipes of a bugle. The one-second repeat time isn't very helpful to us in trying to predict when that molten stuff might erupt, but at least it tells us when Pele's syrup is on the move. Can't you just picture Pele's hot lips down there blowing molten rock through a musically resonating pipe?!"

His expression reverted to a more serious character. "As you esteemed colleagues know, the record of an off-the-shelf earthquake, like the ones that regularly rock California, contains repeat times almost all over the map, all much briefer than that of our one-second tremor signal. If we could jack all of these up to the pitches of vibrations audible to the human ear, a California quake would play us a symphony while Hawaiian tremor would sound more like my family's monotonal whining. Hey, please don't tell them I said that, huh. I have enough problems at home now that I work at HVO while wife and kids are left with the anthurium growing."

Andy and Rob nodded their assent to this minor conspiracy. They knew that Ben's mid-life decision to pursue a career in volcanology had not been universally applauded on his home front. Ben had essentially dropped an entire burgeoning business into the hands of those who earlier had only been helpers, so he could pursue his personal dream.

"Okay, now here comes what I think is the clincher." Ben's dark brown eyes, set into a rather broad flat face, grew to be even larger orbs than usual, as he started to explain why he thought an eruption was coming soon to Kīlauea. "I have pretty hard evidence that our network of seismometers tells us when our volcano's one-note magma is getting close to the surface. This part of my story is a bit of a stretch, but bear with me.

"The original network of seismometers, back in the 1950s, was just on Kīlauea. With time, instruments were placed further and further from Kīlauea, and today, as I mentioned earlier, the network reaches all the way to the north end of our island. This gives us some interesting and incredible leverage. You remember your physics lesson about levers, don't you? The longer the lever, the more you can lift. And with levers of greatly differing lengths, you can pretty easily calculate differences in the loads they can lift.

"Okay, so Kīlauea's magma starts its life deep in the earth, about sixty-five miles beneath the island's surface. At least, that's where it first starts to trigger earthquakes on its upward journey. When this liquid stuff first starts breaking and pushing those brittle rocks aside and surging through the openings, the tremor that it generates gets to all the seismometers at about the same time, simply because the length of the journey from magma to seismometer is about the same everywhere. The length of that journey is our imaginary lever.

"But, and this is the real kicker guys, when that magma gets to within about ten miles or less of the earth's surface, we have levers of vastly different lengths. The tremor now gets to instruments right above it here at Kīlauea sooner than to those farther away, say on the flank of Mauna Loa. It's simple geometry."

Ben took one step back from the TV monitor and made the grand gesture of a deep bow. "Gentlemen, I believe that I can measure that difference in time!"

Andy and Rob stood in stunned silence. They knew that the concept Ben just explained was valid and quite simple. And they remembered that many people before Ben had tried to measure the difference in time between the first arrival of a spasm of tremor at instrument A versus instrument B versus instrument C and so forth, but had always given up in frustration. They wondered what new stroke of genius Ben might have up his sleeve.

In their own, and greatly contrasting ways, they were reminded that sometimes the greatest of breakthroughs comes from the simplest of thinking and observation. Andy's mind still tended to gravitate toward the mundane, even irrelevant, while Rob's was sharply analytical and to the point.

Andy: *Hey, the discovery of ethyl alcohol and its pleasant effect on the state of human consciousness was an accident of natural fermentation of a sugary fluid and the resultant giddiness of those who drank the fermented liquid. This was a simple yet profound discovery.*

Rob: *Ben is applying the elementary equation "velocity multiplied by time = distance." The velocity at which the tremor moves through the earth is probably constant. However, distance to instrument A versus instrument B and therefore the travel time both change as magma reaches shallow levels beneath the volcano's crater. But could Ben really measure a difference between the arrival of tremor at Kīlauea versus more distant stations?*

Ben read the mix of disbelief and awe on the faces of his colleagues. With a twinkle of his big spherical brown eyes he continued, obviously in great delight. "Timing, gentlemen, excellent eyesight, and a dollop of imagination. My entire conclusion rests on precise timing and my ability to identify the exact moment when tremor squiggle begins, where other eyes have failed. We've come a long way from sundials, burning candles, hourglasses, windup springs and the pink bunny that keeps on going. Once our HVO system of seismometers was a wounded beast, dependent on a whole gaggle of unsynchronized timekeepers. Each instrument was a slave to its own separate clock. But about twenty years ago, we got the entire network on a single and highly precise clock. That is a key ingredient.

"My 20/10 vision helps the cause, too. And, finally, my willingness to see an emerging squiggle where others see a flat line. I can't say that this part is an exact science, but it seems to work for me.

"Voila, as the French would say!!" Then looking directly at Andy: "There's more to life than an attractive couple of nēnē, even in France."

Ben stood in front of the monitor and punched a few computer keys. A series of parallel lines, the tracings of seismometers, appeared across the screen. The left half of each trace was flat and horizontal. The right half of most was squiggly, obvious recordings of tremor that looked like a bunch of worms marching from right to left, or was it left to right, in tight military formation. A few of the lines were flat all the way across the screen, because those instruments were so far from Kīlauea that none of the tremor shaking could travel that far.

"Watch this." Ben now created a razor-thin vertical line across the screen with the swish of a mouse, followed by a left click. He could move the line, back and forth, in increments of any chosen size, by tapping the horizontal arrows on his computer's keypad.

"I'll start with the vertical line on the left side of the screen, in the area where *all* the tracings are flat. Obviously, this represents a time when the ground wasn't shaking at all."

The screen looked as though a scissor had cut across all fifty lines, at precisely right angles.

"Now, I'll bring the line slowly to the right, until it touches the first squiggle. I could move all tracings simultaneously to the left and get the same result."

Andy and Rob watched, as Ben tapped the right horizontal arrow on the keyboard until that first squiggle was touched.

"Well, what do you see?"

They moved from side to side, to get different angles on the screen. They took magnifiers and examined the crossing lines up close. They stepped back a couple of strides, scratching their heads. Then in unison: "Hey, Ben, what is this…one of your bad jokes? There's no difference at all across the entire set of tracings. The vertical line exactly touches the beginnings of all the squiggles."

Ben grinned, a grin of extreme pleasure.

"Excellent, gentlemen. Both go to the head of the class. Your conclusion is exactly the same as mine. But I didn't want to bias you by suggesting what you should or should not see in this set of data. You're looking at the tremor that was recorded in September, about 10 weeks ago. This was the first spasm we got of the stuff that has been coming in sporadically ever since.

"Okay, now look at this data set." Ben cleared the screen with a double click of the mouse and then brought up another set of lines. Superficially, they looked just like the first set. With a knowing grin, Ben continued: "Let's bring the vertical line over to touch the onset of squiggles. You do it this time, Andy."

Andy moved the vertical line in such tiny increments that the human eye could not see the movement triggered by a single tap of the arrow key. Eventually, though, the beginning of a squiggle was touched. Andy stopped, while he and Rob again did their side-to-side and magnified viewing. The vertical line touched about a third of the squiggles, a third were not touched, and the rest were the flat ones too far away to record any tremor. For the squiggles not touched, some were further from the vertical line than others.

Andy and Rob spoke in unison. "Hey, Ben, enough of this teasing. What's going on here?"

"This, gentlemen, is the spasm of tremor that came in just yesterday. The lines that are being touched are those from instruments closest to Kīlauea's caldera. The other lines, those not touched, are the tracings of stations further away, on Mauna Loa or way off on the flanks of Kīlauea. And the further away from the caldera, the wider the gap between the vertical line and the tracing. Those longer levers seem to be doing their thing. As I said earlier, timing and the ability to recognize the very first onset of a squiggle are everything. Either we've got some pretty damned exciting stuff here, or the world's best atomic clock and my eyes are out of order. We're talking about differences of less than a second."

Ben was in high performance mode. He was the master of ceremonies at the premiere of a unique show, and he was thoroughly enjoying his role.

"I could show you data sets from times between the two we've seen. Not surprisingly, they give intermediate results. Let's not go into the details right now, though. My conclusion, gentlemen, is that we are seeing strong evidence for the rise of magma right up into the volcano during the past ten weeks. I think I can even calculate the approximate present depth of this rising batch of magma, but let's also save this for later."

In keeping with his personality and relatively shallow thinking, Andy was immediately sold on Ben's story. This was expressed by a quick and enthusiastic "Way to go Bruddah Ben!" accompanied by the back-and-forth Hawaiian waggle of his right hand, little finger and thumb extended. He had jumped to conclusions without a lot of thought most of his life. Sometimes this put him in trouble, even in jail a couple of Stanford nights. But Dad and his dough had always been there to bail him out. Post Stanford, he was trying hard to think more for himself, especially in his science endeavors. He was making progress, but he still had a ways to go.

Rob, with caution bred from a childhood of poverty and disappointment, was not so quick to accept Ben's story. Rob would be the devil's advocate for awhile. He stood in silent thought for a couple of minutes and then turned directly to Ben.

"Your story about the tremor seems logical and pretty convincing, but how does it stack up with other kinds of information? What about the regular old earthquakes that Kīlauea generates? You can make plots of those in space and time, too. Do they also indicate that a new batch of magma is moving up into the volcano?"

Ben had anticipated this question. The first word of his answer overlapped the last word of Rob's question...*volca yes no.*

"Yes, I've got reams of plots that show when and where regular old earthquakes have shaken up Kīlauea. This is all very interesting stuff, and it helps map out where the main magma pipes and underground storage tanks are located. But, and this is important, this style of volcano shuddering is happening more or less all the time, throughout the entire body of Kīlauea. So, even though it helps us map out the system of plumbing, it doesn't tell exactly when and where a given batch of Pele's syrup is on the rise. Only the tremor does that."

Rob seemed satisfied with this explanation. But there was more on his mind.

"Okay, then, what about the volcanic gases that leak out of magma as it rises toward the surface? Some of our colleagues say that they can tell a new batch of magma from an old one by the proportions of carbon dioxide and sulfurous fumes that leak out at those gas vents we call fumaroles."

Ben had a barely controlled hair trigger on this topic: "Gases, molasses!! The people who study this ethereal stuff are full of their own product...nothing but hot air. I happen to think that their gassy science is basically groundless and full of crap. Hell, much of what they study even smells like an overripe bean-fed fart. The stuff they long to capture is mixed into the atmosphere and on its way to California before they can get their hands on it."

Ben stared directly at Rob, and moved up to within a couple of nose lengths of his face.

"You know those fancy glass bottles they use to collect gas? I think they just run off to the field and fill them with whatever is convenient. Have you ever even seen one of their samples? Those damned bottles look completely empty, coming and going, to me. Those folks have the biggest con game of volcano science going."

Out of mutual respect and Rob's hatred of spittle spray in his face, both backed off a couple of steps.

"A rock, you can get your hands around. And you can show it to your colleagues later. If they don't believe it's real, just bop them on the head with it. Earthquake damage is another tangible thing. A broken building, broken ground, photos and the recollections of those in the area of damage are very real. But ask a gas scientist to show you something real, and all you get is an empty bottle or a graph that anyone could create out of whole cloth."

Rob and Andy had heard this kind of venting from Ben many times before, when it came to the gas people. Even the gas people themselves admitted that they had a tough line of research to tackle, most especially because the tacklee was indeed invisible and highly mobile. But magma does emit a variety of gases, and this product, though difficult to capture, has a useful story to tell if only the sampling problems could be effectively solved. Rob kept hoping that someday Ben would lighten up a bit in his criticism.

Ben took charge again.

"What I propose is that we meet with The Don and let him in on the tremor news. If I'm right about the meaning of these recent spasms of tremor, we've got an explosive situation developing, right underfoot. I think we need to resurvey the entire volcano to see if she really is bloating up like a balloon about to burst. We need to remeasure the ground elevations here in the caldera area, to see if new magma is pushing up the way it usually does before eruption. It will be a ton of work, but I think it's a must."

Ben, Andy, and Rob all nodded in silent agreement. Ben continued as master of ceremonies.

"In spite of my excitement and concern about what our volcano friend may be doing, I think we have adequate time to get ready for whatever's coming. It's Friday today. I need to spend the weekend helping my family with the flower business. You guys probably have some social plans. Let me go talk with The Don right now and set up a staff conference for Monday morning. Unless you hear to the contrary, we'll meet at nine o'clock."

The three of them drifted out of Ben's office in different directions. Ben headed for The Don's office. Rob needed the quiet of his own office to think carefully through what he had heard during the past hour. Andy headed back to the seismograph window, hoping to ogle a few more sexy female tourists and to daydream about his plans for a weekend of non-stop partying on the Kona Coast.

CHAPTER 12

RICH BOY'S EPIPHANY II

Sunday morning. Nine o'clock.

Andy was regaining consciousness slowly, incrementally…and painfully. His taste buds sensed a mix of bile and something akin to unswallowed lye soap. The inside of his mouth felt like it had just finished a strongly astringent gargle…maybe with some of that liquid used to unclog bathtub drains. If so, the stuff had only partly cleared away the hair-in-mouth feel that came with this severity of hangover.

His head felt as though the sack around his brain was being inflated with a high-pressure tire pump…or was the pressure on the outside pushing in? Either way, the pain was real and at a constant level, except for a sharp additional spike that came with each beat of his heart. He was wondering, yet again, how much abuse of this sort his brain could tolerate before permanent damage set in. Neurobiologists claimed that consumption of too much alcohol can kill brain cells, and these buggers-the cells not the biologists-were not known to regenerate.

The first rays of morning sunshine that entered his eyes…when he finally pried the lids open-literally-with his fingertips…registered with the rods and cones as though sharp metal pins had pushed through the retina, instead of a few waves of that normally painless electromagnetic radiation called visible light.

He was on his back, staring up at a white stucco ceiling that looked down at him with the rough-and-sparkling texture of garish kitty-litter. Ugh! Some of those flakes of stucco even looked kitty-poop stained. Flashes of light reflected from the clean bits of pseudo litter, further aggravating the eye pain.

God, he felt awful.

He rolled onto his right side and peeked at the floor. Good. The carpet was clean. He hadn't upchucked sometime between getting into bed and waking up. At least that was something to be proud of, or maybe just thankful for.

The bed was comfortable, but whose bed was it? He rolled onto his left side and moved his right hand under the sheet, onto a motionless lump of humanity next to him. His hand started low and moved upward. Ah, the curving hip and warm full breast of a female. Thank the mating muses, he hadn't made a gender blunder in last night's stupor.

But who *was* he in bed with...Tracie, Chantal, Sandy, someone else? He honestly couldn't remember, and he surely couldn't tell by feel alone. Ray Charles could boast about identifying specific lovely ladies with his sensitive braille-trained fingertips. But that talent came from a lifetime of daily practice that Andy still lacked. He was working on it, though.

Andy selected his females by looks. He had rigid standards. Dull though it may have seemed to other guys, all of his dates looked the same, and even felt the same if a relationship got that far...short, slender, firm full breasted, and with long hair. Other female sizes and shapes were definitely worth watching, but actual dating and what went with that was restricted to his select subgroup of datable ladies.

Hair color mattered not, but length certainly did. He wanted something to hold for stabilization, during gymnastic changes of love-making position.

The height thing? Well, he had never felt comfortable looking up to a woman—except when he and she were both horizontal—part of a need for dominance learned from his businessman father, he supposed. And he was definitely not enamored with robust Rubenesque body types.

Whoever his bed partner was, she was definitely zonked. Through his pain, he smiled to himself and thought briefly of waking her to start anew the kind of frolic that was last night's love making. That had been supreme...lots of rough-and-tumble foreplay followed by entry into their joint journey along the slippery slopes of love. If Andy concentrated hard enough, he could briefly retaste the pleasant saltiness of female sweat and stale sex on the tip of his tongue, even now through the salivary bitterness of too much booze.

He sighed and smiled as he also recalled the almost uncontrollable vibrational shuddering climax of Sandy, or whoever was under the sheet, and wondered if there could be any link to the earth tremors that Pele had recently released at Kīlauea. Could his lovers help him understand that enigmatic goddess and her volcano home that was his job to study? What a homework assignment this could be!

Whatever, the pain coming from almost every possible source above his neck…even smiling hurt a little…convinced him that the level of pleasure a morning frolic might add would pale in comparison to the associated increase in his continuing hurt. Besides, his bed partner might be in as much hangover Hades as he was.

He rolled back to the right, pivoted sideways on his butt, set his feet on the floor, and sat upright. A brief spasm of vertigo passed, and then he was standing. He looked around, walked to the bedroom door while reflexively scratching his scrotum, and recognized the floor plan and furniture as that of Tracie's place. Okay, that would explain the lack of sand between last night's sheets. It seemed that Sandy, the beach nymph, always brought her namesake to bed in any number of interesting body traps. Even a moderately quiet session of love making with her released enough grit to turn soft sheets into coarse sandpaper. Wild sex created a virtual sand box.

He continued to wander the apartment until he found his clothes. Once he got onto the right line, this task was easy. His sandals were just inside the entry door. There was nothing unusual about this, given the widely practiced Hawaiian custom of leaving foot attire at the door, either just inside or out. The habit was so firmly ingrained into the island population, that even sometimes drunks, like himself, remembered the practice.

About two paces into the apartment, he found his aloha shirt, resplendent with colorful palm trees and parrots, in a crumpled pile on the floor. A line between shoes and shirt projected straight to the bedroom door, fifteen feet away.

Next in line were his tan khaki trousers, the fly only partly unzipped…presumably in the frenzy of passion to get on with love making…but at least unzipped far enough to not threaten to put him in the soprano section of a boy's choir.

And finally, there were his favorite bright-red bikini briefs with the Valentine's Day heart-pattern motif, right at the bedroom door.

Except for sandals, two pair of which were piled up together at the door, Tracie's clothing was distributed along the same beeline, spaced between his stuff. Andy's shirt, then Tracie's tanktop. His trousers, then her miniskirt. His red briefs, then her purple panties. The clashing colors of those last two items gave his gut a brief upchuck twinge.

He *thought* his stomach back to calm and then smirked, realizing that Tracie must have been even more anxious to get naked between the sheets than he had been. They always undressed each other, and his shirt had come off first. At least one of them had remembered to shut the apartment door. Otherwise, folks in neighboring units would have been regaled with even louder noises of love making than they must have heard anyway.

Starting with the article of clothing nearest the bedroom door, he got dressed. He left a shaky hand-written note saying "Thanks for a great night!" taped to the inside of the entrance door, slipped on his sandals, and stepped outside onto the second-level deck. The fresh morning air felt good.

Using the handrail for support, he descended to the apartment parking lot, where he discovered that the battery of his Toyota truck was dead, dead, dead. He must have left the headlights on last night. He couldn't even get a feeble squawk from the horn.

Like most places on the Big Island, the land here sloped to sea. He pushed enough to get his rig coasting downhill, jumped in, shifted into second gear, popped the clutch, and relaxed as the engine snorted to life. He cruised on down to the waterfront and joined Ali'i Drive.

Downtown Kailua was deserted, except for a stream of loyal parishioners headed for morning services at Moku'aikua Church. He recognized a couple of attractive middle-aged ladies who had been in the audience at the King Kamehameha Hotel's floorshow, where he picked up Tracie last night. Unlike him, they must have stayed sober. Or perhaps they were looking to atone for last night's overindulgences, if not true sins, hung over or not.

Andy turned right onto a narrow street that angled up to a city parking lot, just a block uphill from a giant banyan tree whose canopy extended completely across Ali'i. He parked, backing into a downhill-sloping space, and walked to the waterfront shops. Two cups of strong Kona coffee at Buzz's place helped soothe his throbbing head. After last night's gross mistreatment of the digestive system, it was still too soon to try solid food.

He walked back to the Toyota, went through the clutch-popping routine again, and maneuvered through Kailua's streets to Highway 11, part of the perimeter route around the Big Island. He was southbound, headed toward his small rental house on stilts in Volcano Village, just Hilo side of Hawai'i Volcanoes National Park.

Because of the abundant twists and turns in the road, especially in the Kona district, the hundred-mile drive back home normally took at least two hours. His challenged reflexes this morning kept him at a three-hour pace, which was fortunate at this time of year. It was the season for hundreds if not thousands or maybe even millions of overripe mangos to splat onto the pavement from huge trees overhanging the highway. As attested to by many rusted hulks of autos, lying dead in ditches along hairpin turns, friction between tire and road was almost zero when squishy mangos came between rubber and asphalt. Of course, some of those metal corpses were more the victim of mai tai than mango.

Much as Andy tried to simply relive the mostly carnal animal pleasures of last night, he found his mind returning to a theme that had been increasingly haunting him of late. He seemed cursed by self-introspection. For better or worse, his mind kept returning to the same topic, like a flawed LP record stuck in one monotonous groove: Enjoyable as his weekend party life in Kona had been ever since he moved to Hawai'i, an inner voice claimed that this lifestyle was not fulfilling a nagging and growing psychic need.

It had all started just two weeks ago, when Chantal asked about his long-term personal plans during the afterglow of lovemaking, and then went into a crying jag when he answered, "Oh, I've got nothing specific in mind."

Her reaction had made him wonder, for the first time, if his lovers actually expected and hoped for something other than fun from him. Maybe he was being a selfish brat, just screwing his way through life, taking but not giving? These were heavy thoughts for a Stanford party boy.

With each new episode of inner turmoil, Andy was reminded of how he had come to feel about his first two student years at Stanford. That life of drunken debauchery had been salvaged by the example of David Johnston at Mount St. Helens. The resulting life-changing experience had been mostly professional, while his current dilemma was more personal. But really, the two parts of his life were so intertwined in his mind that he was repeatedly falling back into the kind of funk of dissatisfaction that had so engrossed him at Stanford.

His mind snapped back to more mundane things, as the highway entered a sparsely vegetated football-field-wide swath of black lava that extended as far as he could see, up the flank of Mauna Loa and down toward the ocean. There would be about a half dozen of these along this stretch of highway. They were Pele's roads, paved with rough-surfaced lava that spilled from high on Mauna Loa and extended like arthritic fingers pointing the way of their paths into the sea. Most had been created during a spectacular eruption in 1950. One was of 1919 vintage and more difficult to recognize, because of its age. Some vegetation had already grown back. The entire mountainside along this stretch of the highway was a thick sheet of overlapping finger-like lava flows. Most, though, were old enough to be covered with a uniform-looking matt of trees, shrubs, and grass.

As suddenly as the black lava had appeared, the road was back onto heavily vegetated ground. Simultaneously, Andy's mind switched from things volcanic to those personal.

Both his mind and body were getting tired of the weekend late-night frenzies of booze and babes, two of the three Bs that had been the mainstay activity during his first two years at Stanford. And, somewhat surprising to himself when he really thought about it, he was also tired of and feeling a little bit disgusted (and guilty?) by waking up in a different bed the morning after almost every weekend night of partying. Could it be that his youthful period of sowing wild oats was giving way to an age of wanting the security of a steady harvest of affection from a single known partner? This idea frightened him a bit. But then, he *was* approaching those late twenties, an age when so many people "married and settled down."

Whether marriage was in his near future or not, maybe both his mind and body were no longer capable of sustaining the irresponsible lifestyle that had so characterized his high school and early college years. This possibility reminded him of a recent galling experience that had left him wondering if he was even still able to unequivocally identify a beautifully dressed woman when she walked right up to him. Cracker-barrel wisdom claimed that the loss of memory was the first sign of old age. Could his first age-related loss be gender recognition?

Andy's recent wake-up call happened at HVO and created incredible embarrassment for him. His colleagues wouldn't let him forget the snafu. Andy the Romeo, Andy the Don Juan…Andy the fool!

The incident had started innocently enough, at that large window behind the seismic recorders. He was there alone, pretending to study the instruments, while in fact he was mostly looking for lovely female tourists who might just stare through the widow and lean over a bit to get a clearer view of those tools of science. The entire staff knew very well, from scores of experiences, that such leaning could produce great nēnē watching, in the French translation of that word. All agreed that tourist watching was a swell way to pass some quiet time.

On that fateful day, he was rendered temporarily speechless when four tall…about six feet tall in fact…stunningly gorgeous young ladies strode right up to the window and did an extra deep stoop, given their height, to view the seismic display. Smooth tanned skin was exposed on necks, faces, arms, and legs protruding from tasteful short-cut summer dresses. Intermediate-length hair, on two blondes, one brunette and one red head, was elegantly coiffed. They chattered away in English—a California accent?—while using their small soft-looking animated hands for emphasis and punctuation.

They were the most attractive eyeful that Andy had seen in days, if not weeks or months. After only brief surreptitious ogling, Andy felt the need to peek straight down, sensing the growth of an embarrassing bulge, as an extra surge of blood flooded his groin. Best to temporarily retreat.

Gathering his composure, Andy summoned the entire HVO staff. All quickly assembled. They acted convincingly interested in what the seismograms were showing. In fact, of course, everyone was sneaking peeks at swelling mounds of paired nēnē, partly exposed down the gapping necklines of the fulsome foursome.

Once these tourists walked away, toward the Halemaʻumaʻu overlook, an animated HVO staff exchanged their evaluations of the remarkable display of female anatomy just seen. Discussion continued sporadically throughout the day. And everyone, even the females (cross gender sexism was not a problem at HVO) on the staff, said, "Thanks, Andy, for calling us to the window! What a show!!" before leaving the office that afternoon.

The next morning, however, Andy's pride, and a bit of his manhood, were diminished when Ben presented him with the Entertainment Section of the *Hilo Nūpepa*. The feature article highlighted four talented female impersonators from San Francisco who currently were the lead show at Hilo's Naniloa Hotel. One glance at a picture of the group instantly deflated Andy's ego. His discovery of yesterday had not been what it had appeared to be.

Casanova Andy was crushed. He was the instant butt of jokes and jibes questioning his manhood. He continued to haunt the window for female viewing, in spite of his blunder. Hey, the rest of the staff had been bamboozled, too. But he was far more cautious about calling colleagues to share attractive viewing with him.

❦ ❦ ❦

The road entered another sparsely vegetated swath of black lava. Andy recognized this one as coming from an eruption in 1926. A fast-moving flow had even wiped out the coastal fishing village of Hoʻōpūloa. Crusty old Thomas Augustus Jaggar II, HVO's founder, had been so devastated at his helplessness to stop this destruction that he had redoubled efforts to find ways to divert lava flows from their natural paths.

Andy mused that, unfortunately for things in Pele's way, the situation today wasn't much changed from that of Jaggar's day. It seemed that if people felt they must build on Pele's terrain, they should be prepared to move when she decided to repave the land with her brand of asphalt. Such moving was inconvenient, but then people in Hawaiʻi were fortunate because Pele usually gave them enough time to save themselves and most of their easily movable earthly possessions, unlike the situation near more explosive volcanoes like Mount St. Helens and Mount Pelée. If only they could speak, David Johnston and the citizens of St. Pierre could attest to this truth.

Once again, the road slipped back into a heavily vegetated countryside whose green cover thinned incrementally over the next ten miles or so, as Andy's lane arced slowly around to the east. Then, bang, Highway 11 passed right onto a sterile black lava landscape that looked like yesterday's offering from Pele. Andy shifted down a gear, to help the Toyota climb up and over the broad crest of a long tapering ridge headed to the sea, a zone of cracking and rifting all the way down the side of Mauna Loa, where lava oozed out every decade or so. Houses of an obviously new and growing subdivision were scattered here and there across this sterile landscape.

"Why," he wondered again, as he did each time he drove through this area, "do people build where they know a threat from more lava flows is so real? And then why do they expect the government to bale them out financially when their houses and land are buried by new lava?" Incredibly enough, even a couple of HVO's scientists from earlier years owned land and homes here, on a part of the Big Island most threatened by lava flows. "It's just something about human nature" he rationalized silently.

Human nature was also telling him that his bladder would burst if not soon relieved of its liquid contents. Once across the rift zone's suburbia nonsense, he stopped at a small café in Nāʻālehu for pee and tea. He also gobbled down a bowl of steamed rice. This gooey stuff usually calmed a squeamish stomach for him. He guessed that once consumed, it formed an impenetrable plug that would only allow other stomach contents to go further down the digestive tract, rather than hurry back up. It worked for him again. He was feeling a lot better.

He was back in the Toyota now and on old number 11, descending several hundred feet to sea level and Honuʻapo Bay. Then came the long steady and nearly straight climb across the west flank of Kīlauea, up and over the top of the volcano, through a thin slice of the national park, and on into Volcano Village where his little rental house sat perched on ten-foot-tall stilts. The garage was the open space under the house.

It was mid afternoon. Andy decided that a soak in the tub would be a nice lead into flaking out in bed for what he hoped would be sufficient sleep to make him a worthwhile contributor to the HVO staff meeting that Ben had set up for tomorrow morning. Additional personal reflection during the soak led him to vow that he would get his love life aimed at developing a stable relationship with one special woman, yet to be identified, as soon as the apparent volcanic crisis at HVO was behind him.

If Ben was right about a new batch of magma pushing up into Kīlauea, there would be a ton of work for the entire staff in coming days and perhaps weeks. Eruption, if it came, would make life in the near term even more hectic. But whenever calm returned to his day-to-day life, Andy made a pact with his conscience that he would replace the frantic weekend life of booze and babes in Kona with a search, maybe starting nearby in the much more sedate Hilo, for Ms. Right.

The 1980 eruption of Mount St. Helens had earlier gotten his student life turned from dissipation to production. Perhaps an eruption of Kīlauea would help straighten out his love life.

"It's unlikely," he thought, nearly hidden beneath the foam of cherry-scented bubble-bath, "but weirder things have happened to me." Andy then fell asleep. He woke up two hours later sporting the classic shriveled-prune look of too much time in water.

CHAPTER 13

HAK, THE HAWAIIAN HOOD

As he sat in his plush office chair, puffing on a huge (smuggled) Cuban cigar, Gregory Hakonē looked anything but prunish. He was a robust Hawaiian whose bronze wrinkle-free skin appeared to be stretched to its elastic limit. He was kamaʻāina…born and raised on the island of Oʻahu.

He was also the closest thing to a neighbor that Josh and Valerie had. Hakonē and two partners in crime were raising pakalōlō in bulk quantities on their piece of rainforest along Kīlauea's east rift zone, just up-rift from the garden of Josh and Valerie. The Hakonē enterprise existed for one reason, and one reason only…to make a lot of money for the three partners. They smoked a little of their agricultural product, but they sold most to a growing stable of clients, located in Hawaiʻi and on the U.S. mainland.

Through the genes inherited from his parents, Gregory was a potpourri of Filipino, Japanese, Portuguese, Hawaiian and mainland haole blood. The haole part came by way of a U.S. sailor who had managed to get into his great-grandmother's bed for one night.

The parents had inherited the old family place, where Hakonēs had resided for three generations. This unpainted one-story house with a metal roof and dirt floor sat on the windward side of Oʻahu. Gregory and his siblings grew up there.

The windward side of Oʻahu took the brunt of trade-wind storms, and there were plenty. Lots of rain, second-rate swimming beaches, and big waves were the norm. Surfing was often excellent, if you were talented enough to handle thirty-foot curls. Over the years, many a novice surfer got wrapped up in one of these curls and disappeared into the deep Pacific.

By contrast, the leeward side of Oʻahu was typically baked in sultry sun and caressed by gentle sea breezes. Friendly waves, whose open-sea force was tamed by a fringe of coral reef not far offshore, lapped at miles of beautiful white-sand beach. Tourists, big money, Waikīkī, and Honolulu were the core of this scene.

The poor and the working class were relegated to the windward side, where ramshackle housing was at least affordable. Like the weather, life on the windward side was stormy, while that on the leeward was downright benign.

During Gregory's childhood years, and still today for that matter, his mother, Lillie, was a maid at the Royal Hawaiian Hotel at Waikīkī. For the entire third floor, she kept clean sheets on the beds, clean towels near the showers, hair wads out of shower drains, and cockroaches at bay. Her husband, Joe, tended lawns and flower gardens for the wealthy residents of Honolulu. Six days a week, Lillie and Joe commuted together to their jobs, up and over Nuʻuanu Pali, in the rusty hulk of what once had been a shiny blue Ford pickup. The rig looked, sounded, and behaved used-up by the time they could afford it. Including the commute time, twelve-hour workdays were the rule. Commute time was increasing as the Ford's six-cylinder engine lost compression and power. A stop at a filling station was turning into "fill her up with oil and check the gas" instead of the more usual order of the day. They could never seem to accumulate enough money to upgrade.

Still, they somehow managed to find time for more than sleeping while home. Seven children were the result, before Lillie and Joe decided to quit…or just plain got too tired to continue. With so many mouths to feed, the family budget was stretched really thin. But no one went hungry, and few clothes were needed at sea level in the tropics.

Gregory was the first child to come along. In a traditional Hawaiian family he would have helped fill in as parent to his siblings. But there was something perverse about Gregory from day one. He cried incessantly as a baby. Later, when he was old enough to help around the house, he refused to pitch in with the household chores, including the care of his siblings. As a teenager, he sat expressionless and watched as his two-year-old sister was badly mauled by a pack of roving poi dogs, rather than help her at some risk to himself. He seemed angry that he even had siblings. He wanted, and took by force, the few "luxury" material things that the Hakonē parents could afford for their flock. And he seemed to like the sight of blood, so long as it wasn't his.

Gregory was not a role model. Eventually, even his name came to sound evil. When he was a pre-teenage child, his family and neighbors called him Greg. By the age of puberty, with his male anger and aggression increasingly emerging, he decided that Greg was too soft, gentle, and sissy-ish. He renamed himself Hak. This fit him well, he thought.

At age sixteen, Hak joined a rough motorcycle gang that patrolled and controlled the streets of a large part of the windward side of Oʻahu. In imitation of the Al Capone era of Chicago, windward merchants could buy gang-provided protection from imaginary criminals. If not, well…

Hak's gang-member trademark was to chop off the little finger at the last joint of the dominant hand of an upstart rival or uncooperative merchant, as a permanent visual reminder of who was in charge in this territory. Ambidextrous enemies lost the ends of both little digits. Hakonē was Hak, and don't you forget it! An early bout with TB had also left him with an ugly-sounding hacking cough that came and went.

By the time he was twenty-five, Hak was two-hundred-thirty pounds of mean flesh. Though not soft, he had the rounded and robust Polynesian appearance that usually came with generous daily portions of poi. He was tiring of the windward scene on Oʻahu. The place was getting too crowed for his tastes. More gangs were forming, some with pretty tough members. He needed more space. He wanted less competition in pursuit of his rough lifestyle.

So, Hak and several of his gang friends shipped their Harleys to Hilo, and began a new life on the sparsely populated Big Island. He and his fellow tough guys cruised the island's few highways with their bellowing and barking bikes. They drank beer, caroused, and made general nuisances of themselves at public beach parks. They bloodied the occasional hippie, a life form whose value they could not comprehend from what they perceived to be their lofty and highly evolved Darwinian perch. A growing number of young men with unnaturally short little fingers began to appear on the Big Island. In short, Hak and friends were the stereotypical badass motorcycle gang. A few years earlier they would have been members of the Primo Warriors, named for a popular island-brewed beer. But the Primo brewery was now defunct. Hak and his buddies were the Big Island Warriors.

Having grown up in stinking muddy poverty—he funded himself with his strong-arm activities—Hak eventually decided that he would reverse this situation by becoming a wealthy pillar of the Hilo community. He knew about the link between supply and demand, and he also knew about a huge unfilled demand for pakalōlō. He would establish an illegal business behind a solid facade of tax-paying legitimacy.

His time on the Big Island quickly taught him about "free" fertile land on Kīlauea's east rift zone, a place where he could safely grow his illegal cash crop. He selected two partners from the motorcycle gang. The three of them retired their Harleys and hacked their way into an isolated part of the rainforest. With sugarcane knives flailing, they opened space for a garden, carefully preserving trees and large bushes as a canopy of camouflage. Their business venture was soon underway.

Hak's plantation, as he liked to call it, was less than a straight-line mile from Josh and Valerie's place, but the two may as well have been separated by light years in terms of accessibility. That rainforest was nearly impenetrable, without a large sharp cutting weapon for clearing a path. Still, the two growers knew about each other.

They kept their distance. Josh and Valerie were pursuing a private lifestyle, while Hak and his partners were seeking big money. Both operations were highly illegal. Without speaking, they agreed to ignore each other in everything but their mutual need to avoid the law. Their unwritten memorandum of understanding called for joint efforts to thwart the law, whenever necessary. Neither group wanted to lose their chosen pursuit. At the same time, the river of trust between them ran as deep as Josh's love of hogs.

As soon as profits from the sale of their illegal product permitted, Hak and partners replaced their hogs with new Toyota Land Cruisers. Each of them also bought a comfortable, though not overly showy, house in Hilo. They rented office space on Kamehameha Boulevard, near Hilo's waterfront, and hung out their business shingle…HAK'S HUI. They mingled socially as clean-shaven conservatively dressed businessmen. Their lifestyle transformation appeared complete.

They bought ten acres of land near Kapoho in the Puna District, where they undertook the legitimate business of raising papaya for export to the mainland. Theirs was simply one of many papaya orchards in this part of Puna. And they did, indeed, raise this savory fruit and successfully ship many crates of the product of their labors to grateful consumers in California. Though not one to dwell on deep intellectual thoughts, Hak recognized a spot of irony in the fact that a miniature, scaled-down version of a papaya leaf looked a lot like the leaf of his other cash crop.

No one, and most especially the law, bothered the employees of Hak's Hui and their seemingly legitimate business enterprise. Citizens and police alike were simply delighted that three former Big Island Warriors were now businessmen whose desire to fit into the local scene was apparently genuine.

To capitalize further on their acceptance into the Big Island business community, Hak joined Hilo's south-side chapter of the Rotary International Club. Hak's somewhat cynical view of this organization led him to conclude that everyone blindly accepts the notion that a Rotarian is a rock solid citizen. Though he didn't realize it at the time of his initiation, his membership in Rotary International would be critical to the continuing success and growth of his illegitimate business.

Until then, genuinely good Rotarians would travel to other parts of the Big Island and occasionally to one of the other Hawaiian islands to tend to their commerce, while a business trip for the three employees of Hak's Hui usually meant disappearing into the rainforest of Kīlauea's east rift zone, to tend to their flourishing field of pakalōlō.

Hak, his two partners, and their hippie-ish neighbors were cultivating Kīlauea for profit and fun. The staff at HVO cultivated the mountain to harvest clues about how the volcano worked…clues to when and where it might erupt next. In wildly contrasting ways, the east rift zone was very important to both endeavors.

Hak sucked in one last drag on his cigar, blew a few smoke rings toward the office ceiling, and snuffed out the butt in a large carved-basalt ashtray. He was alone, talking to the world.

"Smoking pakalōlō makes me relax, and sometimes feel happily giddy. Smoking Cuban cigars makes me feel important, like I'm a significant cog in Hilo's business machinery. What's the harm here? Why are so many pleasant, fun, and sometimes useful things in life illegal?"

Just then, his partners walked in. It was time to plan for the next pakalōlō and papaya harvests.

CHAPTER 14

AN INCREASINGLY RESTLESS VOLCANO

At The Don's request, all twelve members of the HVO staff assembled in their makeshift conference room at 9:30 Monday morning. Space was limited at HVO. This was the only room big enough to accommodate the entire staff at once.

The floor covering was scuffed-and-cracked eight-inch linoleum squares of probable WWII vintage. The original pattern had apparently been slightly marbled in shades of gray, but the surface was now so worn and deteriorated that the best description was simply earth tone. Brown splotches here and there attested to the inevitable coffee spills that come with a bunch of daydreaming, if not occasionally spastic scientists. Around its edges, the floor was decorated with delicate-looking walnut- to tennis-ball-size creeping fuzzies, those finely interwoven and elusive orbs of dust, hair, and grit detested by fastidious mothers and neatness-freak personalities of all ages.

The conference room housed a poorly equipped but better-then-nothing library, whose shelves were warped boards salvaged from a park storage shed torn down years earlier, a large and obviously homemade mobile bulletin board mounted on an unstable rectangular arrangement of inadequate-looking six-inch-diameter wheels, a four-by-ten-foot table made from hand-me-down sheets of splinter-rich plywood, and the six seismographs at the large window where tourists were invited to look in and see the instruments of science at work. Chairs, like so much of the HVO property, were from government surplus warehouses on Oʻahu. No two were of the same design or color.

Sturdy, artistically stone-covered outer walls belied the grubby interior of the building. The casual passing tourist might easily carry away a false impression of the quality of HVO workspace. Other than the staff, there was nothing attractive about the inside. An interior decorator would have fled screaming…or scheming about how to get a cushy government contract to redecorate the place.

The attire of the HVO staff mimicked the quality of that interior workspace. Though consisting of professionals holding doctorate, masters and bachelor degrees, supported by a highly trained and competent technical cadre, the workforce at HVO could be mistaken for factory manual laborers in another setting. Dressing up meant coming to work in recently laundered cotton jeans and work shirt. Dressing down was an oxymoron within the group, on Friday or any other day of the week.

One reason for the dreary sartorial habit was comfort, pure and simple. Formal attire of the starched-uniform variety probably would have created calluses on derrieres that had no padded chairs to use. Those Army-surplus hand-me-down seats were either flat cold metal or hard wood. Besides, much time was spent in the field, breathing volcanic fumes, walking through blowing ash and grit, and occasionally kneeling or sitting on the hard and sharp surfaces of lava flows. Subjecting decent clothes to such conditions made no economic sense.

In fun-loving spirit, the HVO staff also practiced their dress code of choice as a means of reminding park rangers that not all employees of the Department of the Interior are equal. Ongoing competition of many sorts between the two groups was almost as old as the national park presence at Kīlauea. Old Thomas August Jaggar II and his cronies had worn neckties on a regular basis, probably as a holdover of university habits. But that kind of formality disappeared with Jaggar, when he retired in 1940. All along, though, rangers were required to wear green and beige departmental uniforms with identifying nametags. Today's rangers, heads squeezed into incredibly uncomfortable Smokey the Bear hats, viewed the HVO crowd in their patched jeans and torn chambray shirts as an embarrassment to the department. At some level, perhaps they were right. Embarrassment or not, those HVO folks certainly were comfortable. Even The Don, whose salary exceeded that of the park superintendent, dressed in HVO casual, and in so doing spoke reams about not judging a person by his clothes.

The Don's actual title was Scientist in Charge, SiC in acronym form and not-feeling-well, literally, in sound. Because Scientist in Charge was clumsy and time consuming to say, and because no one wanted to hint that the man in this position was anything less than healthy, title "The Don" had been adopted as a little in-house joke. Although The Don was not a violence-prone Corleone type of person, he was the boss. He was the guy at the tippy-top of the local USGS organizational pyramid. Besides, so many SiCs had carried the birth-certificate name of Don over the seven decades of HVO's history that it seemed doubly appropriate to use an implied reference to a mafia-like organization as in-house humor. Such silliness helped develop camaraderie, a feeling of being on a harmonious team when the staff had to complete long, arduous, and often boring volcano-wide surveys.

A few imaginative young thinkers hoped that they would soon need to address the boss as Doña. But the USGS was still a good-old-boys club, as it had been from its very origins. Change in this bureaucracy moved about as fast as most geologic processes, volcanic eruptions excepted.

Jack A. Richards was the current Don. Decades earlier, he had learned enough about volcanoes to get a Ph.D. from the University of Oregon. In 1979, he had replaced the SiC, Don Jackson. Jackson had bid goodbye to the USGS when he decided to try a stint in academia at Northern Arizona University in Flagstaff for his remaining few professional years. Richards himself was only a few years from retiring. The *old* in good-old-boys seemed a prerequisite for becoming The Don.

Richards now sat at the head of the table…or was it the foot…the end closest to his office. It didn't much matter how one labeled his position, because on-the-job formalities within the HVO staff only extended to being considerate enough to contain bodily flatulence until outside, where the putrid human gas bursts were lost in the general volcano-fume stink. It seemed senseless to be more formal when the staff occupied such cramped shabby quarters and worked so closely inside and in the field.

As always for these gatherings, Andy sat to Jack's left. This positioned him on the side of the table with a clear view of the seismograph window and its tourist traffic. He was sufficiently rested from his Kona weekend of debauchery to feel at ninety-nine percent mental capacity. He still remembered his Sunday vow about focusing future love-life energies on finding a single Ms Right. But that was no valid reason to let attractive women walk past the window without an appreciative glance. "Look but don't touch" would be his new motto. He guessed this dictum should also apply to his relationship with the fine lady that always sat next to him at these meetings, where their hands and other body parts could, and often would meet under the table.

That was Liz, one of the three multi-talented and youthful technicians. She had been born and raised on the Big Island. She stood five foot two on tiptoes, and had eyes of blue and waist-length straight blonde hair. She was also single and fun loving...characteristics that forged a mutual attraction between her and Andy from the day he had arrived on the HVO staff. They had known each other more than once in bed, as well as on the job. Though she couldn't have known it at the moment, the heat of their friendship would cool considerably in the coming days and weeks...if Andy was true to his recent vow.

Next came Frank, a sexagenarian mechanic and general handyman, who somehow kept the HVO fleet of old and tired vehicles running; Howard, a middle-aged machinist, who could transform a sketchy design into a functioning whatsit from the HVO stock of scrap metal, and who also changed the paper charts on the seismographs each morning; and Bruce, another of the technicians, whose job it was to help whatever non-technician needed help.

Allan Springs sat at the foot of the table, on the assumption that The Don was at the head. Allan was a tall and lean, serious kind of guy who seemed to live in a world of mathematics and physics, at the expense of interpersonal relationships. Like The Don and Rob, Allan carried a Ph.D. His came from the Colorado School of Mines in Golden. For his thesis project, he had developed an electrical technique to prospect for deposits of gold. He didn't find the mother lode in his quest for a Ph.D. Now, here he was prospecting for molten rock, a far cry from King Midas's precious metal. The tools of his trade were general enough to be applied to essentially anything buried from sight, within the earth. The beauty of explaining the information he gathered with his various Rube-Goldberg looking instruments was that he had a nearly infinite number of solutions to all his problems.

Allan's brand of earth science, known as geophysics, was simultaneously gratifying and frustrating...usually gratifying to Allan and frustrating to the rest of the staff. With so many possible solutions to the problems he explored, no one could prove Allan wrong, unless they dug deeply enough into the earth to expose the source of the geophysical signal that he measured at the surface. Since such digging wasn't practical, Allan was always secure in knowing that he had the right answer...hell, he had a whole basket of right answers for all geophysical questions. In spite of the obvious potential for frustration, the rest of the HVO staff agreed that Allan's contributions were important in trying to understand a volcano.

Jeb and Jane, technician and secretary, respectively, sat to Allan's left. Jane doubled as a land surveyor when needed and tripled as the only person who did enough housekeeping to save the observatory from drowning in its own refuse. She conscientiously emptied wastebaskets when they overflowed and swept the floor when the odor of spilled food tinged the office air. But somehow her broom never quite reached to the perimeter population of fuzz balls.

Rob, the basalt guy, sat next to Jane; then came Kabana, the administrative officer, and finally, Ben, the earthquake expert.

After a couple of minutes devoted to "hi and how was your weekend," The Don took charge and got the meeting underway.

"I know how you informally share what you're up to with each other, so you already know that for the past few weeks we've been recording some seismic signals that might indicate a new batch of magma pushing up into Kīlauea. Ben has some new ideas on what the recent bursts of tremor might be telling us about this possibility. I'll ask him to give us his story in a few minutes. First, I want to hear from Andy, Rob, and Allan. Do you guys see any signs, other than the tremor, of the volcano being unusually restless?"

As the rock-deformation geologist, Andy spoke for himself and Rob.

"Well, the results of our routine weekly measurements up here around the caldera have been just that...routine. We know that the caldera area has been swelling a little bit. It's about two inches wider than it was three months ago. We also know that a broad gentle bulge has been growing, somewhere on or near the floor of the caldera. But the ground has pushed up only a few inches at most. That's hardly unusual for Kīlauea, even an at-rest Kīlauea."

This kind of stretching and doming might have seemed extreme and troublesome to someone with a house built on the moving earth. But in fact what Andy described was nothing more than the typical flexing of Kīlauea between eruptions. The entire HVO staff understood that the volcano might well be yawning in boredom, rather than ratcheting up to eruption. Either way, there certainly were no threatened buildings on the caldera floor.

"Okay, guys. Thanks.

"Now, Allan, what do you have to tell us?"

A few barely stifled yawns and some glazed-over eyes appeared even before Allan started to talk.

"I've been deploying some of my electrical anomaly gear to see if the body of Kīlauea has electrons flowing in unusual patterns or if the rocks of the volcano are changing their electrical properties. As I've told you all before, that

EAG is very portable and versatile. That's why I don't need to call on a lot of help from you techs."

A barely audible (to all but Allan) sigh passed the lips of Liz, Jeb, and Bruce. At one time or another each of them had been called on to help Allan in the field. And not one of them found excitement or pleasure in stringing out lines of wire, pounding metal rods in the ground, and then watching a few silly dials twitch or not twitch.

"I can measure tiny differences, down to milli-amps and milli-volts. And if the electrical conductivity of rock changes the wee wee-est fraction of an ohm-meter, I'll record it."

The Don wanted to keep the meeting moving.

"So, Allan, do your milli-amps, milli-volts, and ohm-meters tell you anything about the state of Kīlauea?"

"Yes, I have picked up a few anomalies here and there."

"And they mean?"

Well, it's impossible to tell, exactly. Our unusually heavy rainfalls during the past three months could have changed the electrical conductivity of the rocks simply by soaking them with more water. Distant tropical thunderstorms send electrical surges through the entire earth, so I always need to consider worldwide weather, too. Closer to home, the high-voltage transmission lines of Hilo Electric, the ones that pass through our park, have had lots of unusual voltage surges lately, and that can affect my surveys. There *is* the possibility that electrical anomalies are caused by new magma entering the volcano. Oh, and some of my recording equipment has been acting up recently. I need to huddle with you, Howard, about this."

Howard nodded toward Allan. "Sure, anytime."

As usual, the rest of the crew saw that this was a typical case of his volcano geophysics. Allan might eventually understand the source of the electrical aberrations, but only *after* Kīlauea erupted the answer.

A few moments of complete silence around the table, heads nodding knowingly, was code for "this may be interesting science but what help is it in forecasting an eruption?" Rob, the thoughtful and careful scientist, raised his hand to get everyone's attention.

"Let me try to summarize, to make sure we're all on the same page, so to speak. Allan, you've measured some electrical anomalies. They might be the result of heavy rainfall, voltage surges in nearby transmission lines, faulty recording equipment, a powerful thunderstorm in Africa, or possibly, just possibly new magma pushing up into Kīlauea. Or some combination of all the above. Well, *now* we're getting somewhere."

A few snickers broke the silence. But always immersed, if not lost, in his own world of geophysics, Allan was impervious to such criticism. Still, The Don tried to smooth over a slightly awkward situation.

"Thanks, Allan. Crew, you should all keep Allan's results in mind as you think about the other volcano measurements we make. There might be some important correlations with the electrical stuff. Okay, Ben: Tell us what you see in the tremor."

As Allan sat, slowly, mumbling to himself and scribbling a few notes on a scrap of paper, Ben stood up and took charge. Without the help of his computer monitor and the sets of squiggly lines that represented bursts of volcanic tremor, Ben summarized what he had told Rob, Andy, and The Don the previous week.

Next, he walked to the other side of the table and spun the mobile bulletin board around so the blackboard side faced the group. He then got about as serious as he ever did and launched into an explanation of why he believed that a new batch of magma was approaching the surface, probably getting ready to erupt fairly soon…pretty heavy news to report. The ever-present grin on his face told everyone that he was the same old fun-loving guy they had always known.

With a hint of a bow toward Liz and Jane: "Ladies and gentlemen, it's easiest to explain what I think is behind all this tremor, with the drawing of a drop-dead simple triangle."

With that introduction he turned toward the blackboard and drew a single horizontal line extending about three inches from his left to right. He labeled the left end "Mauna Loa" and the right end "HVO." He then drew a vertical line from the HVO end, extending nearly three feet, down to the bottom of the blackboard and forming the second side of a triangle. He completed the triangle with a third line, whose length was only marginally greater than its vertical, nearly parallel neighbor. Next, he wrote the label "earth's surface" along the horizontal line and "source of tremor" at the bottom of the vertical line. He stepped back to admire his handiwork, and then spun around to spit out his story.

"This heap of broken and shattered rocks we call a volcanic island does a pretty miserable job of transmitting earthquake energy. Sure, powerful earthquakes shake all the way through the pile and record on our seismometers, from Kīlauea to Kohala. But something as feeble as tremor is easily absorbed in the loose rock before it can travel far."

A widening grin told his audience that he was about to make a joke, or what he thought passed as a joke. "The bottom line is (PAUSE) that there is no line…at least no line recorded as tremor on many of our seismograms."

Ben continued very slowly, deliberately, and with exaggerated emphasis. He put his hands on Andy's shoulders, which were just in front of him. "B U T, and this is a big but…about as big a butt as Andy was the day he mistook female impersonators as stunningly beautiful women right over there at that window…tremor that comes directly up from the roots of Kīlauea usually records on instruments out about as far as six miles from HVO, and this gives me enough leverage to see new magma rising."

Andy, Rob and The Don knew exactly what Ben was talking about, because of his earlier explanation to them. Allan probably also understood Ben's point, at least his facial expression gave one that impression. In fact, his mind was probably busy creating multiple explanations for what Ben had said, in the true spirit of geophysics. The rest of the staff just seemed puzzled.

Ben turned back to the blackboard and continued. This time he labeled the horizontal line as six miles and the vertical line as sixty miles.

"Here's the deal, colleagues. When the source of tremor is roughly sixty miles beneath HVO, or even deeper, the earth vibration travels to an instrument six miles away from HVO in the same time as it travels to us right here. Actually, it should take a little longer to arrive at the distant instrument, because that travel path is a little longer. But the clock for our seismometers can't measure whatever that small difference might be.

"What I've noticed during the past ten weeks, though, is that eventually I could measure a difference in travel time. And that difference has been getting bigger and bigger with each new burst of tremor."

Ben then redrew the triangle to represent a vertical side only four miles long. He talked with his back to the group, which is what he tended to do when experiencing a lot of uncertainty.

"When the source of tremor is only about four miles deep, like I've drawn here, the difference in travel times should be about one second. And that's what I've been seeing for the most recent bursts of tremor."

Ben turned slowly around, looked directly at The Don and continued. "I know there's a lot of slop in my method, lots of uncertainty, but the trend is there even if the exact difference in time is in doubt. I'm pretty sure that a new batch of magma is rising up beneath Kīlauea, and that it may be as shallow as three or four miles. I suppose that hot stuff could be even shallower, and that's why I think we need to quickly resurvey the entire volcano for elevation changes. We know the volcano inflates like a balloon when new magma comes in, and measuring a rise in elevation is the best way to track this happening. That bulge that Andy told us about may be a small pimple on a much bigger pustule."

He broke what was by now a pretty serious mood with his patented grin of intended mischief. "Our Latin American volcano colleagues call tremor *tornillo*, their Spanish word meaning screw. I guess the tremor signal on a seismogram looks kinda like the threads on a screw, when viewed with enough imagination. Well, I'm afraid that we're going to be royally tornilloed, if we don't figure out what Kīlauea is doing, and real soon."

Ben sat amid grins and a little titter from his friends. The Don took over.

"Troops, I agree with Ben…about new shallow magma, but not necessarily about getting tornilloed. So, kiss off your social life…and your family life if you have one…because we are going to blitz this mountain with an elevation survey. We've all been through this before, so we know just how much work it means. It's important to finish the job as quickly as possible.

"Rob and Andy, each of you will lead a four-person team. Pick who you want, and remember that we don't discriminate by gender around here."

Briefly forgetting his new vow of relative chastity, with involuntary reflex Andy reached over to squeeze Liz's knee under the table, and to let his hand slide several inches up her leg. But his hand stopped just short of contact. He turned and smiled at Liz, who, having expected the under-the-table feel of Andy's fingers, looked back, a bit puzzled.

"One team will start in Hilo, at the tide gage on Hilo Pier, and work its way up the mountain along Highway 11. The other team will start at the Volcano Store, on Highway 11 just outside the park, and then cover all of the ground here around the top of the mountain. If weather, your health, and our instruments cooperate, we'll have our answer, at least *an* answer about whether the volcano is getting bloated with new magma, within a week or so. Have fun, troops, and remember our motto."

From past experience, everyone knew that this signaled the end of the gathering. They also knew that it was time for the HVO team chant. All twelve stood, raised right hands high with clenched fists, and repeated loudly in unison.

NE PLUS HAUSTAE AUT OBRUTAE URBES! (No more burned or buried cities). The sound easily carried through the window behind the seismographs.

Tourists looking in that window must have thought these people were daft, a holdover from Nazi Germany, or a mysterious island cult. But the HVO staff, from The Don on down, knew that this was simply one means of maintaining group morale.

Old Thomas Augustus Jaggar II probably would have smiled from his grave, to know that the motto he had adopted for HVO back in 1912 was a source of camaraderie as well as a lofty objective still pursued, decades later. More morale boosts of this sort would probably be needed during the long days and drudgery of leveling that would begin tomorrow.

From her lair deep within the roots of Halemaʻumaʻu, Pele *did* smile. She knew that the message of Jaggar's motto was hers to make or break. She began anticipating fun interactions with the HVO staff during the coming days. She knew full well that She could tease or please (even maybe a little of each) as they scrambled to take the pulse of her volcano home.

As the HVO crew dispersed, The Don asked Andy to come to his office.

CHAPTER 15

POLICE VERSUS PAKALŌLŌ

It was also Monday morning at the Hilo office of the Big Island Police Department. While the HVO staff was discussing the possibility of an impending eruption of Kīlauea, Lieutenant Herbano sat at his desk, fuming mad, about to erupt himself.

His weekend had been an unmitigated disaster...well almost unmitigated. He had planned a two-day fishing trip on his forty-foot boat, the Hooker, with buddies Joe and Cory. There was to be nothing but beer, cholesterol-laced food, country-western music, fishing, guy talk, and untold uncensored burps and farts...nirvana for good ol' boys alone. If a razor was found on board, it would be thrown into the Pacific.

But Herbano's wife, Maria, torpedoed these plans at the last minute when she insisted that he instead attend Saturday and Sunday soccer games of the teams that his two young sons were members of. Never mind that the boys, much as he loved them, would play little if any, given their lack of natural athletic ability.

So, as usual when Maria insisted, he had stood along the sidelines, part of the time in pouring rain, trying to act interested as he watched what seemed like all Hilo kids, except his own, flail away at a little white ball that rarely found its way into the netting of a goal.

Why? Well, Maria had a powerful lever that controlled much of what he did, and she knew when and how much she could apply this tool to her advantage. Herbano smiled and felt a warm glow grow between his legs, remembering that at least those weekend nights at home had been more fun than hanging out with a bunch of stinking fish and two unwashed buddies would have been. The boat would keep. There would always be fish to catch. And boatless buddies anxious to have a free ride were a dime a dozen.

But here it was, only Monday, and already the workweek seemed a shambles. His crack and covert Pakalōlō Obliteration Team, which was supposed to have carried out a search-and-destroy mission in the Puna District over the weekend, had failed miserably…again. This group had a growing history of failure, a dismal record already longer than the tail on a whippet. Maybe the team's POT acronym was still clever, but that's about as far as cleverness and results went with this group.

It was now Herbano's unsavory task to explain to Captain Chan why yet another mission to control the illegal growing of pakalōlō in their jurisdiction had yielded no results. Chan would be pissed, because he would then have to explain this new failure to Tanaya, the chief of police, who would carry the bad news higher up the governmental pyramid and political food chain of the Big Island and so forth, until the report would land on the desk of Hawai'i's governor.

Heads would role, figuratively, although the same chain of repercussions had happened so often that the protestations of all those directly involved were mostly window dressing for the public and for federal politicians. Failure was so common that the public came to expect it.

In spite of such low expectations, the feds, heads usually in sand (or in rectal-cranial posture, as patrolman Chan liked to joke), always projected a positive spin. They backed their public pronouncements with lavish continuing amounts of funds for the control of controlled substances, under the ridiculous dictum that if money was spent, then some positive results must have accrued. Given the lengthening history of failure, though, the whole charade was pretty laughable to any thinking person.

It wasn't for lack of trying on the part of the Big Island police that pakalōlō plantations, especially those in the Puna District, seemed to flourish undeterred. Herbano's agents had mounted repeated ground attacks there during the past couple of decades, but this elite POT team had never been able to locate pakalōlō plantations in the nearly impenetrable cover of Puna's rainforest. Without exact knowledge of where access trailheads were located, POT team members did nothing but thrash about in tangles of fern and bushes when searching for passable routes to desired, yet unknown, destinations.

An added hazard came from unexpected encounters with vegetation-covered fissures, the open rocky scars left behind by earlier eruptions along this part of Kīlauea's east rift zone. No POT operative had permanently disappeared down one of these gaping cracks, but a leg or two had been broken over the years, when that first step into a fern thicket proved to be a deep one. Through no fault of their own, some of Herbano's troops were injured yet living, thanks to vegetation, examples of the folly of attempting to cross a chasm in more than one bound.

A couple of times and at great expense, specially trained scenting dogs had been brought in from the mainland. The simple-minded idea was that even if trailheads weren't visible, they must be smellable. This style of search was complicated by the fact that rabies-free Hawai'i detains incoming dogs through a one-hundred-twenty-day quarantine before they are released to chase crooks, cats, or anything else. The scenting dogs were doomed to fail anyway, because telltale human odors are quickly and very effectively washed away by frequent rains, sending howling hounds running in meaningless circles.

The only noticeable benefit to the police force from all of these attempts at raids was a cadre of officers in excellent physical condition (once broken limbs were healed) from their frequent struggles against vegetation. Pulling at a tangle of ferns was the green equivalent of stationary steel at the departmental gym.

Herbano had once ordered aerial attacks, but the broad canopies of large trees pretty effectively hid illegal garden plots from such prowling. Growers realized from the beginning that pakalōlō plants distributed randomly simply look like a part of the natural green vegetation beneath large trees. They planted their crop accordingly. More than once, though, a police surveillance plane had accidentally passed over a pakalōlō garden, only to be ignored if the growers felt they had not been observed beneath their green camouflage, or otherwise used for target practice. The first few bullet holes in wings and fuselage convinced Chief of Police Tanaya that losing an expensive aircraft, to say nothing of pilot and observer, wasn't worth the potential benefit of wiping out an illegal garden. Besides, troops on foot would have to destroy the gardens, and those access trails were still hidden from the sight and scent of police detection.

Further confounding the police efforts to enforce their marijuana law was the fact that most Puna residents were unconcerned by the pakalōlō growing in their district. At best, from the police perspective, the locals were passive and neutral. At worst, they actively worked against the police by refusing to cooperate in any useful way.

More than once, residents threatened lawsuits against the police over misuse of federal funds devoted to marijuana eradication. This threatened litigiousness resulted in the loss of hundreds of thousands of dollars that might otherwise have supported the POT team, or been squandered on this group, depending on your point of view. The Big Island government returned real substantial money to Washington D.C., rather than risk going to court against the very citizens who were, in theory, being protected from the local pakalōlō growers.

In short, the police were fighting a steeply uphill battle against the camouflage of lush green vegetation, seemingly bottomless open volcanic fissures, and Puna residents.

As though these three adversaries weren't challenge enough for Herbano and his POT squad, there was an additional roadblock that came with law enforcement officers of the national park. Though no visible boundary was apparent on the ground (how could there ever be such a line in the tangle of tropical vegetation?), everyone understood that much, and perhaps most of the pakalōlō growing was within the park. Given this situation and the inevitable jealousy between competing law-enforcement agencies, Big Island and park service cops worked mostly at cross purposes. They frequently advised each other to stay within their own jurisdictions, even though they had little idea where the dividing line was in the field. They certainly did not freely share evidence and information.

Pakalōlō growers were aware of this intra-cop feud of feds versus locals. How could they not be, when the feuding was so public? Growers were in the enviable position of watching police expend mountains of energy fighting each other, rather than directing a cooperative blitzkrieg at the naughty weed.

Herbano was stuck in the middle of this messy bureaucratic maze. He was all too aware of the improbability that his POT squad would ever succeed. Yet, his job demanded that he behave like success was just around the corner. So, he sighed and girded himself for another verbal dressing down as he walked toward Captain Chan's office. Herbano knew that by the end of their conversation, they would both pretend that the past weekend's failure was the product of just a bit of bad luck, and begin plans for the next attempted raid.

When would this nonsense end? His young sons had a better chance of scoring a wining soccer goal than his elite POT commandos had of scoring a pakalōlō hit.

CHAPTER 16

AN INVENTORY PROBLEM

As Herbano walked dejectedly toward Chan's office, weekend and Monday morning mostly ruined, Hak sat smiling smugly and sipping Kona coffee in his second-story corporate office just a few blocks away. He loved the location and comfort of his office. It was so centrally located in the rather small but growing downtown business district that banking and other errands were a short walk at most…providing so little exercise that his girth was on the rise.

Though the office was an unimaginative rectangular shape, at seven hundred square feet the hui's needs were well served. A wet bar and small refrigerator occupied one corner of the back wall. At the other corner of that wall, a small but modern restroom provided comfortable relief when the digested residue of wet bar libations needed release. Shelves and file cabinets filled in between the corner functions.

Hak's desk and a well-padded high-back chair on rollers, the only substantial pieces of furniture, sat squarely in the center of the room, the clearly stated focus of power. An overhead fan provided all of the air conditioning needed for comfort, even on the hottest of Hilo days. Two metal chairs and a small table between them were positioned in front of Hak's desk, so he looked down on them. Only his partners used these chairs; no one else came calling. The hui needed no outside visitors to succeed. And there was no question about who was in charge of Hak's Hui.

The end walls of the office were tastefully decorated with large framed color photographs of the hui's papaya orchard, and eruptions of Hawaiian volcanoes. The land at the orchard had been resurfaced with basalt lava and ash during an eruption in 1960, on the very spot where a small town once stood. A photo, immediately below the one of the new and fertile papaya field, showed this place during that eruption. A village that had been called Kapoho was being overrun by lava. Hak had insisted that the two framed photos be exactly the same size and shape. He felt clever knowing that whatever might be left of that little town was not far below his cropland; in fact, it was not much farther down than the distance between the photos. These decorated the office's south wall.

The north office wall was a collage of action shots showing various eruptions of Mauna Loa. One scene showed lava burying a few Hilo houses back in the late 1970s. Another, Hak's favorite, showed a bomb, of human rather than volcanic origins, blasting a hole in the levee of that lava river. Several of his Rotary brothers still talked about this eruption. Hak had been amputating little fingers from enemies on Oʻahu at the time.

All of the office art was the handiwork of talented Big Island professional photographers. Unlike those early days of his bike-riding youth, Hak could now easily afford to hire such talented people.

A large ocean-side window framed an eastward view, looking over Hilo Bay. As recently as 1946, this scene would have been impeded by a tangle of ramshackle waterfront businesses. Then, a huge tidal wave (or rather, tsunami, in his rapidly growing vocabulary of the sophisticated Rotarian) came visiting from Alaska and washed the slate clean, literally, out to sea. Incredibly, local politicians were wise enough to avoid a repeat performance of this kind of house cleaning by banning reconstruction of the waterfront businesses. Their wisdom paid off just fourteen years later, when an equally huge tsunami came visiting from the coast of South America. This one simply washed across a huge grassy-strip park, which afforded people like Hak an unobstructed bay view from his office, two streets inland of the water.

That water was smooth as a mirror this morning, reflecting sunshine toward downtown. Hand up to shade his eyes, Hak could see a few tourists already exploring Coconut Island, connected to shore by a two-hundred-foot gently arched concrete walkway. Local fishermen probably had been there since sunrise, and were never enamored with tourist noises, distractions, and predictably inane questions about "gettin' any."

Hak's partners had just visited him to give their weekly crop reports about the two Ps…papaya and pakalōlō. They were now headed back to the east rift zone plantations for the usual caretaking and a bit of harvesting. They had brought news that was simultaneously elating and a bit problematic, though problematic in a very positive way.

The complication, the kind of challenge any conscientious CEO should savor, was that Hak's Hui was producing pakalōlō crops so bumper that temporary storage, in preparation for trans-shipment to customers, was strained beyond capacity. There was plenty of demand, and growing, for their product, but the flow from garden to consumer was not continuous. It happened in spurts and slugs, between which safe storage was needed for accumulating inventory.

Over periods of a couple of months or longer, production and sales balanced out almost perfectly, in terms of weight of product produced and sold. But within a given week, with increasing frequency Hak was sometimes burdened with several kilos of high-quality weed on hand, waiting for the next opportunity for shipment to the mainland.

His business had grown from the humble beginnings of nickel bags sold daily on the Big Island, to demand for several kilos per month from contacts he had developed on the mainland. His product was now so well regarded that consumers asked for it by name. Knowing that product recognition is important to such a burgeoning business, he had spent many a night thinking about an appropriately catchy name, usually while smoking a joint to the melodious voice of Bob Marley. What better environment for inspiration.

He'd been too stoned to remember when inspiration struck. But now, within the islands, Kīlauea Kiya was as well known as Maui Wowie, O'ahu Wahoo, and Kaua'i High. Users seemed to like products with rhyming names. On the west coast of the mainland, where Hak's business tentacles were growing outward from a head centered in Las Vegas, Kīlauea Kiya was keenly competitive with most North American brands.

Business was great. His earlier life of poverty was a thing of the distant past. Damned if he would send any of his growing mound of money back home to the parents and siblings, though. His greatest gift to them, and he guessed that they just might agree, was leaving that miserable shack called home on windward O'ahu. That made one less mouth for the parents to feed.

Meanwhile, buyers in Las Vegas seemed to have an insatiable appetite for his product. He had developed what seemed to be a foolproof and safe means of transporting the stuff to them, but someone else controlled the frequency of his business trips. To minimize the risk of detection, he traveled only on a monthly gambler-special charter flight, non-stop from Hilo to Las Vegas, and greased a few palms with cash along the way.

The usual luggage checks for these chartered mainland-bound flights, including an inspection for possibly tainted agricultural products, were observed in the breach. After all, most passengers were highly respected Big Island businessmen, with a few adventuresome politicians mixed in for variety and flavor. None of these people would be expected to take plant stuff with them to Vegas, just clothes and the minimum three-thousand-dollar bankroll of gambling money required for free round-trip passage on the plane.

And so it was that Hak could stuff a suitcase or two with hermetically sealed packages of pakalōlō and have no fear that the agricultural inspectors at the Hilo terminal would even suspect any wrongdoing. They, usually two Japanese gardeners who preferred this job to pulling weeds from someone else's landscape, simply nodded and accepted generous tips from Hak as he carried his bags untouched through their station and checked them with the smiling Gambler's Special ticket agent.

"Yup," Hak mused to himself as he continued to appreciate the view of Hilo Bay, "business is great. But I've *got* to figure out a better system for inventory storage. It's always been too risky to stash the stuff here in Hilo...just plain too great a chance that it would be accidentally discovered, possibly during one of those random searches so loved by police."

Experience had already shown that leaving packages on the ground at the plantation invited the nearly instant growth of mold on the product, if those damned feral pigs could be kept away long enough for any mold to grow. Hak needed to come up with an effective storage solution soon.

He finished his cup of coffee, rose slowly from his comfortable plush chair, and headed for the office door. By the time he walked to the downtown offices of the First Hawaiian Bank, they would be open. He would check a few recent entries into his rapidly growing savings account. Then he would stroll on down to Makana's Place for a gossip session with friends until the noon luncheon meeting of his Rotary club.

CHAPTER 17

A SWINGING ADVENTURE IN A WEBBED-ROPE SCROTUM

Andy and Rob huddled to draw up the two surveying teams, as soon as the Monday morning staff meeting concluded. They had been through this exercise once before during the past year. They opted to repeat what had worked well then.

Andy would lead a team consisting of Liz, Jeb, and Kabana. Rob's team would include Bruce, Jane and Allan. Andy had never developed the patience needed to work with Allan, on any project. Rob's early life, however, had instilled in him great patience for any well-intentioned person. Allan certainly wasn't ill-intentioned; he just lived in an almost hermetically sealed cocoon of geophysics and its tools.

Frank would be a substitute for Andy's team, in case a regular got sick, literally, or sick-and-tired of the surveying routine to last out the entire job. Howard was Rob's sub. Ben would be spared the tedium of surveying, mostly so he could keep a continuous watch for more bursts of tremor. The Don's job was to keep HVO functioning while the in-office staff was badly depleted.

Once selected, each team gathered the equipment they would need for the next several days...a surveyor's leveling telescope on its tripod, two stadia rods, a "dependable" vehicle from the HVO motor pool, and enough blank data books to record what would be literally hundreds of measurements.

Andy's team got the 1950s vintage green Ford station wagon. This group would start in Hilo and survey up the mountain along heavily traveled Highway 11. They needed the most dependable HVO vehicle and the Ford was it, in spite of its age and more than 200000 miles logged, before the odometer self-destructed. Besides, it was bound to rain on them from time to time, and the Ford had a Frank-designed-and-built, foot-operated control for the windshield wipers. This kept the driver's hands free to steer and to write down the numbers that would be shouted out by the telescope operator, while running the wipers as needed with his foot.

Rob's team got the next-best vehicle, a notoriously undependable 1960s International Scout. This team would be working mostly cross country on foot, once they completed the few miles of road work between their starting point, the Volcano Store just outside the national park, and the summit area of Kīlauea. They would be fine if the old army-surplus Scout would last for only another ten miles. Then Frank could work his mechanic's magic to coax yet another day or two of work out of what was basically a piece of junk.

Everyone in the vehicle-procurement process…from The Don on up through the USGS headquarters, to the General Services Administration, in Washington D.C.…knew damned well that Japanese-made rigs would have been far more cost effective for HVO's needs. In the private sector, Toyotas were everywhere on the islands. They were readily available, more dependable than American-made counterparts, and less costly to buy and maintain.

However, under its Buy American policy, the feds would allow foreign automakers the chance to compete for government contracts only if they agreed to add twenty-five percent to their bid price. Laissez faire and the free market cornerstones of the U.S. economy obviously did not extend overseas.

So, HVO was effectively stuck with American machines, and only hand-me-down surplus military vehicles at that. It was a credit to Frank that the HVO motor pool was mobile at all. His up-from-the-ashes pride and joy, a WWII military jeep, vacuum-operated windshield wipers and all, would be the backup rig for the surveying crews.

With a little searching in dank closets and dusty office corners, every piece of necessary equipment was in place to get started early the next day. Andy's team agreed to meet at the Hilo Pier, seven o'clock. Rob's group would meet at the Volcano Store, also at seven o'clock.

Others headed back to their offices, to try to enjoy what would be the last bit of low-stress relaxation until the survey was complete. Andy joined The Don to see what he wanted.

"Andy, before you guys start the leveling survey, I want you to make one more flight over that gaping crack at the head of the Puʻu Kapupapu Pali. That crack still worries me. If it's changed at all since your last visit, it may give us a clue about what Kīlauea's up to.

"I've already made arrangements for Wilbur to meet you at the usual place at about noon. You two soul mates can once again surreptitiously play your war games, without our uptight headquarters folks knowing about all the safety rules you'll be breaking. They'd shit painfully sharp-edged bricks if only they knew what you guys do under the banner of official government business."

The crack The Don mentioned had formed in 1975, when a powerful earthquake shook the entire island. Shaking had been so fierce that a huge piece of Kīlauea along the south coast dropped twenty-five feet as it slid about the same distance seaward. The ocean slosh this landslide created had washed landward, drowning a few campers. Once the disturbed water came to rest, the shoreline ended up a lot further inland than it had been.

Since then, the new Kapukapu crack had served as a kind of bellwether of volcano behavior. When Kīlauea was restless, the crack opened a little wider. And when the volcano was tranquil, so was the crack. This was a handy indicator for HVO, but Kapukapu was so remote that the only practical way to visit was by helicopter.

Enter Wilbur, helicopter pilot extraordinaire, survivor of many near-death experiences as a military chopper pilot during the Vietnam war, free-spirited bachelor. He and Andy shared a lot of bravado and macho traits. They were a natural team. They had worked out a system whereby Andy, the Stanford-educated expert on rock deformation, could take vertical photos of the crack and then later detect any additional opening by photo-comparison analysis, back in his office. It would have been easier, faster, and more straightforward to simply land and measure the width of the opening. But a park biologist had declared the Kapukapu area too environmentally sensitive for landings. Low-level hovering was deemed okay, though.

They met at the usual staging area, just outside the park. Andy was waiting there, polishing off a cheese-and-pickle sandwich, noticing first the sound and then the sight of the chopper. Wilbur landed quickly, the tips of the main rotor blades whirring within a few feet of Andy's car. He shut down the engine, released his seat belt, and jumped out. They did a high-five hand slap.

"Aloha, partner! How ya been?

"How's the nooky norgling at Kona?"

With his recent vow of relative chastity in mind, Andy chose not to pursue the nooky question. Besides, if he and Wilbur got off on sex-tangent talk, they might never get their job done.

"Hey, I've been fine. You, too, I hope. But the damn volcano seems to be gettin' a little restless, so the boss wants me to check that Kapukapu crack again." Though he knew what Wilbur was about to say, for the umpteenth time, Andy still had to chuckle to himself.

"Well, old buddy, if there's a crack that must be considered kapu, I'm sure glad that it's a cold gash in solid rock, instead of what you and I prefer."

"*Acuerdo, amigo mio*. But, hey, let's get rigged up. I want to get home early and put in a good night's sleep. I'm facing some long and tedious days of work for the rest of the week."

Wilbur got the message. He opened the chopper's small luggage compartment and extracted a rope-webbing cargo sling. He and Andy spread it under the chopper's cabin and began tying it to the skids.

During a normal cargo-carrying operation, the sling would be attached to a single metal clamp beneath the cabin. When in use, it would hang (according to Wilbur) "like the scrotum on a horny Brahma bull." But for today's purpose, they tied the sling up as tight as possible to the leading and trailing edges of the skids. They wanted to form a flat trampoline-like surface beneath the cabin. That would be Andy's perch. Once aloft, it would sag a foot or two from his weight. But it would work fine as a platform from which he could photograph the crack, looking straight down, as Wilbur hovered one hundred feet above the ground.

They finished tying net to skids. Andy crawled under the cabin, face down, camera in hand. There was less than a coconut-diameter clearance between his back and the bottom of the cabin. Both he and Wilbur were well aware that if Wilbur were ever to land over a slight hump, Andy would be squished between the ground and chopper cabin, like an overripe guava under a car tire. Andy trusted Wilbur's judgment. He was ready to fly.

The helicopter was an old Hiller. It looked like some kid had assembled it from a set of metal tinker toys. Inadequate-looking skinny interconnected tubing extended here and there. The slick and painted fuselage of fancier choppers was absent. You could see right through the Hiller from almost any angle. Access for maintenance must have been a piece of cake.

The cabin could sit three across, very cozily, within a small plastic bubble. Even someone in the middle spot could feel unduly susceptible to falling from this tiny fishbowl. Acrophobics need not apply.

The engine, fully exposed, was a gas-burning six-cylinder reciprocating beast of Lycoming make. At idle, noise precluded any normal conversation. At flying rpm, eardrums were mistreated.

After the relatively slick modern machines he had piloted in 'Nam, Wilbur loved the primitiveness of the Hiller. It made him feel like a pioneer, an Orville or Wilbur Wright…an Igor Ivan Sikorsky. And he knew that Andy liked working with him and the Hiller…birds of a feather, you know, both preferring a dangerous challenge to being coddled.

In flight, they communicated through Andy's hand signals that Wilbur could watch in slightly convex mirrors, one attached to the leading edge of each skid.

They were on their way and were soon over the crack. The air was smooth today; the job should be easy. Wilbur positioned the Hiller directly over the photo spot and went into hover mode. After so many return trips, he recognized *the* crack as easily as Andy did. Wilbur watched Andy in the mirrors, as another roll of twenty-four frames was exposed. Then, Andy's left thumb came up, with camera cradled in the right hand, which signaled mission complete.

Wilbur slowly twisted the throttle for addition power, gained a bit of altitude and headed back to the staging place. About halfway back, something suddenly tugged the machine to the right. Had he encountered a little turbulence? Maybe, but it was such a quiet and smooth air day.

A couple of seconds later, Wilbur felt a tug to the left and realized that he had already instinctively compensated for an unbalanced load. He knew his machine well enough to know that something was amiss. He looked for a hand signal from Andy to see if he, too, was aware of something out of whack.

My god! What *was* out of whack was Andy and his photography nest. The cargo sling had somehow come loose from the left skid and was swinging back and forth like a pendulum, attached to the right skid. Andy was hanging on for dear life, with one hand. The camera was bouncing off Andy's belly as it swung, in its own pendulum arc, from the strap around Andy's neck.

Wilbur felt his unstable load whip back and forth through one more cycle. He caught a glimpse of Andy, who now had both hands firmly clutching the rope webbing. If anyone could hold on for the duration of the flight, it would be strong, athletic Andy.

Though he knew that Andy couldn't hear him, Wilbur shouted "Hang on buddy. We'll get through this okay. Just hang on damned tight! Pretend the net is Sandy."

The back-and-forth tugging on the machine was decreasing as Andy and his net started to hang straight down. Wilbur was getting a little adrenaline surge. He was smiling. He started singing "Up in the air, junior bird man…" This was kinda shades of 'Nam all over again, but without the hazard of enemy fire.

Hand signals weren't going to happen in this situation. Wilbur simply continued toward the staging site, as smoothly as possible. Three minutes later he was slowly descending over that open spot next to Andy's car. Wilbur glanced at the right mirror and sensed an okay, as Andy looked him in the eye while nodding his head up and down.

Down, down, down. Finally, the tip of the cargo sling hit earth. Another ten feet, and Andy's feet hit earth. When Wilbur saw Andy safely off to the side, waving, he set down the Hiller as gently as a mother lays her new baby in its crib. He cut the engine, and stepped out. Andy had pulled his shirt up and was examining his belly.

"Hot damn, Andy. You should get a circus job with a trapeze act. That was some stunt you just pulled."

Andy was grinning, between spasms of pain that occurred each time he touched another stomach bruise.

"Yah, but next time I'm not taking the camera. Look at this pattern of hurt from the banging of Nikon on flesh."

Andy's open right hand rubbed his stomach in a slow circular rotation. At the bottom of one cycle his hand paused.

"I'm damned glad that neck strap wasn't a foot longer!"

Wilbur looked at a dappling of black-and-blue on Andy's abs, with apparent disinterest. He involuntarily crossed his legs in reaction to the strap comment.

"Not to worry, buddy. Those bruises will disappear in a couple of days. In the meantime, they can be badges of honor during your frolics with the fairer sex."

Neither of them was about to admit that fear had been a factor during Andy's cargo-sling swing.

"I wonder how that sling came loose, anyway?"

They looked, but found no obvious answer to that question.

"You know, *amigo*, that was actually fun, once I realized I had a strong enough grip on the rope to avoid free fall. Let's keep this little mishap a secret. If The Don finds out what happened, even *he* would probably ground us for good. And I just may want to dance the cargo swing again, only on purpose so I can avoid that initial moment of not knowing what might happen.

"Deal?"

"Deal!"

Andy powered up his car and headed home. A long soak in his claw-foot bathtub would help soothe bruised stomach muscles.

Wilbur stuffed the cargo sling into the luggage compartment, got the Lycoming barking at top volume, and headed back for the Hilo airport. What a great day it had been. He'd have to find Laura tonight and share the excitement. She loved to listen to his tales of helicopter exploits. Her rapt attention often led to two tightly wrapped bodies and exploits of the flesh. And *her* restlessness indicator was anything but cold stone.

CHAPTER 18

A BONUS FOR ROTARIAN HAK

With Andy off on a helicopter mission and the rest of the staff following up on his instructions, The Don was in his office getting some notes and photographs together for a talk he had earlier agreed to give to a group of Rotarians in Hilo. He was to be their lunchtime entertainment today. The topic was Hawaiian volcanoes. He wouldn't talk about the developing restlessness of Kīlauea…there was no need to unnecessarily worry the locals until he had harder evidence that the volcano was stirring…but he would try to educate them about some of the geology of Kīlauea and the rest of this dynamic island that they call home.

As Scientist in Charge, The Don had received and accepted many invitations to give talks to gatherings of various organizations…Rotary, Lions, Kiwanis, AARP, Hilo Chamber of Commerce, Hawai'i Visitors Bureau, school groups, even the local chapter of AA. It was easy to impress listeners, at least those who would stay awake, with slightly embellished tales of eruption and earthquake damage of times past, and with spectacular photographs of lava flows and towering fountains.

With a little luck, some of his audience today would listen with enough interest to ask a question or two. From past experience with similar groups, though, he anticipated many heads nodding in near slumber during the talk, especially since they would be in a hot room following a huge meal, heavy on hard-to-digest starch. Even worse, the window shades would be drawn and lights turned off for his slide show. Listen or not, these Rotarians always had kind words of thanks at the door, as they headed back to tend to their real business of the day...finding ways to enhance their particular style of commerce.

The Don didn't much enjoy encounters like this, but reaching out to the community was an important part of his job. At the least, he got a free lunch for his efforts. At the most, he got lunch plus a newly educated convert or two who would be better informed and perhaps even enthusiastic about Hawai'i's volcanoes.

With luck, with a lot of luck that is, some of such enthusiasm might even slop over into politics and eventually benefit HVO in a very tangible way. More than once, newly engendered buoyant enthusiasm had risen through the old-boy's network to the level of Hawai'i's U.S. congressional delegation, resulting in a bit more money for HVO's budget. Yes, giving lectures like today's was all part of a money dance, and The Don was expected to carry out a pas de deux with many a partner.

Ironically, today his main accomplishment would be to inspire a crook to even greater criminal heights. Of course, The Don had no way of knowing that this was soon to happen. After all, he would be speaking to Rotarians, pillars of the community.

Whether he succeeded or failed to energize locals about their volcanoes, he would be retired in two more years. Then he could build a dream house on his piece of Mauna Loa's southwest rift zone...his hunk of land with a mind-blowing view of South Point, the most southerly part of the United States, with the crystal blue Pacific Ocean as a backdrop beyond.

Though he hadn't yet had the courage to tell the HVO staff that he was one of those crazy volcano guys who wanted to live in danger of wipeout by eruption, he wouldn't be able to hide this fact once retired. It was becoming increasingly hard for him to listen silently as Andy ranted and raved about the stupidity of intelligent, educated people putting themselves so squarely in harm's way, each time he returned from one of his Kona weekends, a route that took him very near the place where The Don would build. But this retirement spot was one of The Don's dreams, and had been for several years. Besides, once retired he could ignore the stinging words of criticism from professional colleagues without any fear of career setback.

Thoughts, notes, and 35 mm slides organized, The Don drove down to Hilo. As usual, he used his personal vehicle, a habit he had developed early in his tenure at HVO, after missing or arriving embarrassingly late for several meetings because his company car had again failed him.

His destination was K. K. Tei, a popular Japanese restaurant near the waterfront. But as earlier experience had taught him, the fine food would be served to customers out front, while the Rotary group in a rear meeting room once again gnawed on rubbery chicken, overcooked vegetables, and all the poi you could eat. He never understood why a group of rather wealthy citizens would tolerate such trashy victuals, but he had never yet been with a gathering of Rotarians who ate well.

Today's attendance was impressive. Five men were seated at each of six round tables. Pre-meeting jabber was fully underway. The president of the group, a haberdasher named Mr. Takashi, was at the table closest to the American and Hawaiian flags, the figurative head position. With a wave of his hand, Takashi invited Richards to sit at that table. The Don chose a place that offered a view of the rest of the tables. Then, as Takashi stood, the room became silent.

"Ferrow Lotalians," he said with a distinctive Japanese lilt of mangled Rs and Ls, "pleath lise to the Predge of Arregance to the USA's frag."

Takashi was a recent immigrant from Japan. His mastery of the Hawaiian version of English pronunciation was in the very early stages of development.

Whatever the accent, Richards had heard this use of the phrase "USA's flag", rather than "our Nation's flag", at other Rotary meetings on the Big Island, and wondered if it wasn't deliberate. Hawai'i had become a state only about twenty years earlier, and many of the island's inhabitants were first-generation immigrants who maintained close family and patriotic ties "back home".

Wherever their true first-order allegiance might have been, all stood, placed hand over heart, and followed Takashi's lead in reasonably correct recitation of The Pledge. Then, by slowly lowering his outstretched palms-down hands, Takashi signaled others to be seated, while he remained standing.

He next ran through a brief business agenda, basically a recap of all the good works their chapter had completed so far this year and a summary of those yet to come. From his description of what the chapter had accomplished to date, an outsider might conclude that this small Hilo Rotary group rivaled the United Nations and International Red Cross in missions of peace and charity.

Self-congratulatory back-patting arms nearly twisted off, it was time for the ritual joke telling. The Don had never heard a joke truly worthy of laughter at one of these meetings, but he had learned early on that the best way for a non-member to weather out a Rotary meeting was to follow their behavioral leads. So, he smiled when they smiled. He stood when they stood. He sang when they sang. He ate when they ate. And now he was laughing as they laughed over some pathetic tale of a haole wahine in distress. The Don was almost always the only haole at these gatherings, and he couldn't help but notice that Caucasians were the butts of most Big Island Rotary jokes. After all, Caucasian was definitely a minority racial group here.

Next came the ritual of fines. For the most trivial of trumped-up offenses, Takashi fined members from one to ten dollars, cash payable to the treasurer on the spot. The Don never quite understood this part of the business meeting, but he supposed that such fines somehow kept the chapter solvent enough to schedule the next luncheon.

"Blotha Tamaño," droned Takashi as he stared at a middle-aged bald guy at an adjacent table. "I didn't hea or see you raughing at joke. You've been with gloup long enough to undastand that this is unacceptable behavia. So, this will be ten dolla to our tleasalla, light now."

The Don recognized Tamaño as a rotund Hilo mortician. It was well and widely known that this master at his profession could, and probably would go without laughing, or even smiling, in the company of Don Rickels, to say nothing of amateur joke teller Takashi.

Takashi looked to a gentleman at one of the back tables and continued. "Ahh, blotha Temprano. You appalently think you sneak in undetected, late, by sitting in back of loom. Not so, my good ferrow. Five dolla to the tleasalla, light now, pleath."

Richards recognized Temprano as a high school science teacher with a reputation of punishing his students for being even a minute or two late to class. Perhaps Takashi had a child in Temprano's class and was feeding this man some of his own medicine? Whatever, that fine was paid, and so forth, apparently until Takashi felt he had raised enough money this time around. The good news was that guests like The Don were not subject to fines.

"Although many of us not lecognize the religious significance of Chlistmas, we all cleally undastand its business value. So, pleath, stand alound you table, hold hands, and farrow me in singing, in celeblation of this horiday time."

With Christmas less than a month away, The Don had been expecting, and a little bit fearing, a sing-along. This would be his least favorite part of today's Rotary ritual. Though not a hard-line ultra-male macho type, he preferred to choose the men whose hands he would hold. So far, this had included his father, when The Don was little Richie, and his now-adult sons when they were pre-adolescents. But this kind of selectivity was neither encouraged nor allowed around a table of Rotarians.

The Don would, and *could* never forget his first Hilo Rotarian Christmas experience. It had been about a year ago, with the downtown chapter. A hand-holding neighbor had gently stroked The Don's palm with the tip of a well manicured index finger, and then watched him with a curious smile when they got to the line about donning gay apparel. This had been one hell of an unwanted surprise and was enough of a shock to temporarily raise his voice an octave. Thank God, the sweaty and non-callused hands of his neighbors today had no special message to massage.

However, as their impromptu a cappella choir slipped into Silent Night, a Rotarian facing The Don from a nearby table received a surprise message. The Don couldn't help but notice a wry smile grow across the lips of that man, whose nametag said "Rotarian Hak." Hak was reacting to the fact that the hand of the neighbor to his left was probably a victim of his earlier Big Island Warriors lifestyle. Hak didn't recognize the guy. But this man was missing his little finger beyond the last joint.

Takashi led the group in one more carol…Rudolph the Red Nosed Reindeer, which was not a bad description of gin-loving Rotarian Rudy Hoshita…after which the group sat.

Finally, came the food. Large portions of poi in plastic tubs disappeared quickly. Ditto for globular mounds of steamed rice in carved Koa-wood bowls. Platters of mushy unidentifiable overcooked green and yellow vegetables were also consumed, probably, The Don thought, because they were easily confused with poi from their paste-like consistency. Most of the rubbery chicken, however, bounced right back to the kitchen, headed to its final resting place. Hilo's landfill would continue to be the source of great volumes of gas produced from fermenting food.

"Probably better for gas production there than in the stomachs of my audience" mused The Don.

Warmed sake was offered as an after-dinner drink. Members were finally adequately stoked with food and drink for the general-interest talk. Takashi stood.

"Gentlemen, I give you honable Docta Jack Lichads. You know him as man in chalge of Hawaiian Volcano Obsavatolly. He now tell us about geology of Hawai'i."

As Takashi sat, and began to pour himself another glass of sake, all others oriented their chairs toward a broad white wall, where The Don would project his slides.

Richards breathed in deeply, bit his tongue just a bit, and got underway.

"I thank you for the honor to address such a remarkable community group as your Rotary Chapter. It isn't every day that I have such an opportunity."

The unspoken final phrase of "Thank God" quickly flashed across his mind.

"And thank you for the good fellowship in recognition of the Christmas season, and for the filling meal we all just consumed. It isn't every day that I eat like this."

Though Richards was purposely including ambiguous phrases in his opening remarks, Takashi and his flock were soaking up his words as pure high praise. With his audience smiling and nodding in self-gratulatory pleasure, once again, the unspoken final phrase of "Thank God!" registered in The Don's mind.

"In heartfelt sincerity and truthfulness, I can say that of all of my past experiences on the lecture circuit, being with a Rotary chapter very much like yours was by far the most memorable."

While Takashi and his flock continued to bask in the notion of being excellent hosts, The Don was silently reliving that damned index finger stroking his palm. That certainly was *memorable*!

Now came the meat, and it wasn't rubbery chicken. First he painted the big picture with a broad brush…the story about how the crust of the earth is really just a thin skin, broken into a dozen or so pieces that float around on earth's hot interior like segments of skittering scum on a near-boiling pot of water.

"We humans naturally prefer to believe that we live on terra firma. But while terra it is, firma it is not."

The Don's audience, living on an island with active volcanoes and fairly frequent feel-able earthquakes, could identify with this notion in a way that folks living in middle America could not.

Next came the story of the Hawaiian Islands, how all three-hundred-seventy miles of the eight links in this island chain are progressively younger from northwest to southeast, right on down to the Big Island with its active volcanoes. The Don reminded his listeners that links at the old end, the dead volcanoes of Niʻihau and Kauaʻi, formed about five million years ago.

"If you're familiar with just a bit of Hawaiian folk lore, you know that the early Polynesian settlers of the islands recognized the age progression long before our so-called modern high-tech science did. Remember that Pele has always lived in an active volcano, and to do so she has had to move from Niʻihau on down the island chain to Kīlauea, here in our back yard. Those early settlers certainly knew how to read the landscape."

With a combination of words and a couple of slides projected on the big white wall, The Don illustrated how the floor of the Pacific Ocean is sliding over a very hot stationary place below, where molten rock is created and then rises buoyantly, like a cork in water, to form the line of volcanoes. One of his pictures showed a cutaway view of earth, with the devil aiming an oxyacetylene torch up toward the Pacific. He could tell that most of his audience was awake and following his story, from the several heads nodding in amused agreement, rather than in near sleep.

The Don looked down at his watch. He had already used up ten of his allotted fifteen minutes. It was time to focus in on Kīlauea. Since his audience was familiar with the legend of Pele, he was sure these Rotarians would want his opinion about whether to believe today's scientists or to heed the teachings of Pele when in conflict with science. This was always a tough nut to crack, because it pitted unquestioning faith in the truth of something against the establishment of truth through the experimental results and observations of science. It was the classic nonsense of comparing apples and oranges, without admitting that apples are not oranges.

The Don skirted this issue with a steadily changing background of spectacular eruption photos projected on the wall.

"At least fifty eruptions have occurred on Kīlauea since written records were first kept in the early 1800s. Colorful descriptions of some of the earlier eruptions are embedded in the oral traditions behind Pele. All eruptions were either at the top of the mountain, in what we geologists call the summit caldera, or within long narrow zones of cracks and fissures, called rift zones."

A slide illustrated that one rift zone radiates southwest from the caldera to the Pacific, while the other starts off in a southeast direction, and then turns straight east, slicing right across the Puna District and into the sea.

The Don noticed that Rotarian Hak, the guy with the wry smile during Christmas carols, become extra attentive when the label "Puna District" appeared on the wall.

"The two rift zones are connected by a third band of broken and cracked ground called the Koa'e fault system."

With more slides as visual props, he showed how the Koa'e extends six miles westward from the elbow, the bend in the east rift zone, until it merges with the upper part of the southwest rift zone.

Some in the audience now appeared to be nodding off, victims of too much food, too much heat, and not enough interest in something other than ways to promote commerce. Fairly accustomed to addressing rather disinterested crowds, The Don simply continued with his story.

"Something a bit strange and unusual, though, is that unlike the southwest and east rift zones, the Koa'e has rarely ever been the site of eruption. The neat thing about this fact, at least to us geologists, is that fissures and cracks there are literally open for inspection. They haven't been flooded with lava flows. Many of the cracks are so wide open that people can climb down in, descending more than one hundred feet into some."

While most others were now nearly asleep…Rudy Hoshita was audibly snoring…Rotarian Hak was sitting on the edge of his chair. He was straining to hear The Don's every word.

"Geologists have discovered lava tubes exposed down in the walls of some of the open fissures."

Hak was happily stunned to next hear that some of these tubes were hundreds of feet long and tall enough for human exploration. A sudden coughing fit from Hoshita caused Hak to miss the final bit of description. As Hoshita convulsed, The Don was saying that through time, Koa'e fissures open incrementally further, when an eruption from a newly formed nearby crack in the east rift zone pries the volcano apart a little more. Then he added that occasionally fissures also partly close, especially when magma rising up beneath the caldera pushes toward the Koa'e.

"We call this kind of behavior accordion tectonics. The cracked and fissured ground in the Koa'e behaves kinda like the changing motions of the pleats in that musical instrument so popular with gypsies. It's just that over time the fissures always open more than they close. Our rock accordion keeps getting wider."

Though Hak missed the bit about accordion tectonics, what he did soak up about the Koa'e was music to his ears. Those lava tubes might provide excellent temporary storage for his occasional inventory gluts. He would visit the Koa'e himself as soon as possible.

Meanwhile, The Don concluded to an appropriately polite round of applause, which began softly and grew louder as sleeping Rotarians awoke. Lights came on. Takashi approached The Don.

"As memento of you visit with us today, we, membas of Hilo's South Side Chapta of Lotaly Intanational, plesent you with official liting instlument."

To a second round of polite applause, Takashi handed The Don a bronze with silver trim, retractable ballpoint pen, emblazoned with the Rotary International name and industrial-gear logo.

"Thank you so much. I will value this gift as I have others I've received from groups like yours." The Don would add the gift to an already substantial dust-covered collection of similar cheap pens whose ink eventually would dry up from extended disuse.

Members dispersed back to their business ventures. Hak stayed long enough to ask The Don for directions to the Koa'e.

CHAPTER 19

LET THE SURVEY BEGIN

Tuesday was an exceptionally busy and important day for HVO and Hak's Hui. Both organizations had critical work to get underway, and both would be focusing their energies on Kīlauea Volcano. The HVO surveying crews wanted to know if the surface of Kīlauea had gotten any higher since the last time elevations had been determined, several months earlier. And Hak, the CEO of the hui that carried his name, wanted to know if Kīlauea could provide a safe warehouse to store an agricultural product that enhances a feeling of being higher…if not actually being so relative to sea level.

Andy and his crew were at the Hilo Pier by seven o'clock. Each member wore a brilliant orange vest over work clothes. They wanted to be easily visible. The streets in this industrial part of Hilo were plenty busy, and once out of town they would be surveying along the shoulder of heavily traveled Highway 11. During past years of surveying, no HVO employee had been hit by a passing vehicle, but some of those wizened elderly Japanese farmers steering their ancient pickup trucks to Hilo's vegetable markets seemed directionally challenged to the point that vests were the minimum advisable precaution. HVO's old Ford station wagon wore a police-style flashing orange light, attached magnetically to the roof and powered through the dashboard cigarette lighter.

A couple of freighters were offloading cargo, but otherwise the pier was empty. The long steel fingers of derricks were swinging from ship deck to shore, placing slings of cargo directly on eighteen-wheeler flatbed trucks, and positioning the contents of other slings nearby on the pier. Three forklifts were buzzing about, seemingly moving pallets of freight back and forth without accomplishing much, in the spirit of teamster make-work. All of this activity was far enough from the tide gage to allow Andy and crew the access they needed to their starting point. Weather was overcast and wind free, excellent conditions for surveying.

Decades of tidal records indicated that sea level was rising at Hilo. It seemed that the weight of the island itself, increasing with the addition of lava during each eruption, pushed slowly yet inexorably downward, depressing the seafloor, much as a heavy rock sinks slowly into a bucket of cold tar. Sinking at a speed of only a very small fraction of an inch per year, though, the pier was safe from inundation for centuries, if not millennia to come. Sea level was unchanging for the purpose of the HVO study.

Andy would start as the "gun man," the person who operates the surveyor's level. Liz and Jeb would be "rod men," or more accurately rod woman and rod man, the people who carry ten-foot-long metal poles...one surface of which is precisely graduated in feet, inches, and fractions of an inch...from survey point to survey point. Kabana, HVO's administrative officer, was good with numbers. He would drive the Ford and record the numbers that Andy called out with each reading. By the end of their days-long survey, everyone would have a chance to change tasks at least once. Job switching was part of an attempt to stave off the mind-numbing boredom that comes with multiple days of repetitive motion.

Their survey was a game of technical leapfrog. Jeb set his metal pole vertically on a firm footing, called a turning point, facing Liz. Andy set up the tripod with surveyor's level between the two. Sighting horizontally through the telescope, he read the number (feet, inches, fraction of an inch) on Jeb's rod and called it out to Kabana, the recorder, sitting in the Ford next to Andy. Then, as Jeb moved to his next position, down the road to a point beyond Liz, Andy swiveled the telescope to sight on her rod and called that number to Kabana. Kabana subtracted one number from the other, and, voila, there was the difference in elevation between points one and two.

Then Andy, shadowed by Kabana in the Ford, walked to a spot between Liz and the repositioned Jeb. Andy did the *read, call out numbers, spin, read, call out numbers* process again. This style of leapfrogging would be repeated seemingly ad nauseam, as the crew worked its way up the mountain. Intellectual stimulation was at a minimum. Later, they would compare the new results with earlier ones to see if any changes had occurred from time one to time two.

When working along a road, Kabana could drive to successive gun positions, sometimes transporting the gun man and his instrument on the flopped-down rear door of the station wagon. Liz and Jeb, though, were expected to walk, and sometimes run, between positions, getting lots of exercise in the process. By the end of the survey, they would have carried those damned ten-pound rods thirty miles. And at an average of about seventy-five feet between rod man and gun man, the old setup-turn-and-move, setup-turn-and-move routine would be repeated nearly five hundred and fifty times.

It was a boring low-tech business, and a classic example of how dull so much of the nuts-and-bolts of science can be. But it was the only reliable way to find out if the volcano was inflated with a new batch of molten rock.

Andy and crew completed eight miles of leveling that first day, all the way to Kea'au Village, without tempers lost or mistakes made. That was a great success. Rob's crew started at the Volcano Store, entered Hawai'i Volcanoes National Park, and completed leveling around Crater Rim Drive. Both crews were tired but satisfied with their progress by the end of the day.

CHAPTER 20

THE LAVA TUBE WAREHOUSE

While Andy and his crew were completing their first setup on the Hilo Pier, Hak was in his hui office getting stuff together for a visit to the Koa'e fault zone that Dr. Jack Richards had so graciously described for him and other Rotarians yesterday. If Richards's story of those gaping cracks and lava tubes was accurate, Hak would find the safe-haven warehouse he so sorely needed. He had to reconnoiter the area to be sure. He wanted to get an early start to minimize the possibility of encountering other tourists as he snooped around the Koa'e. His two hui partners were at the Puna plantation, harvesting yet more product that would need proper storage if it was to be in prime sale condition at the time of his next Gambler's Special flight to Las Vegas.

Hak put a lunch of cone sushi and poi, a two-quart canteen of water, two hundred feet of climbing rope, a pair of leather gloves, a flashlight, and a hard hat into a backpack. He kicked off flip-flops, pushed his large flat Hawaiian feet into a pair of sturdy leather boots, and laced them up tightly. He wore tan khaki pants, a light cotton shirt, sunglasses, and a S.F. Giants baseball cap. Any ranger encountered should logically conclude that Hak was off on a day hike.

Hak stepped outside, locked the office door, walked down to ground level, and crossed Kamehameha Street to a parking lot. He threw the backpack onto the front passenger seat, got behind the wheel of his Land Cruiser, and turned the ignition key. As usual, the reliable six-cylinder engine rumbled to life. A minute later, he passed the turnoff to Hilo's airport and was headed toward the national park on Highway 11.

At the edge of town, he slowed and eased partway into the car-free oncoming lane to avoid interfering with what appeared to be a surveying crew for the Big Island Department of Transportation. He changed his mind, though, when he noticed that one of the surveyors was female, a very attractive young female. Gender discrimination in hiring was still rampant in the BIDOT part of Big Island government. He decided the crew might be students from the local vocational school, learning a marketable skill.

Thirty-five minutes later as he turned left off Highway 11 and entered the park, he encountered another surveying crew. This one also included an attractive young female. A bit puzzled, but fairly uninterested because he couldn't imagine that these crews had anything to do with his business, Hak continued on. A couple hundred yards further, he hung another left. He was on his way to the Koa'e promised land of Dr. Richards.

The road was in dense, tangled rainforest. Hak noticed the fresh cuttings of recent ditch mowing, without which vegetation probably would reclaim the paved-over land in just a few months, if not weeks. He could smell the newly cut stuff, too. The rainforest parts of the island always smelled like fermenting vegetation, an odor that newcomers from dry climates often found objectionable. Hak had grown up with the smell, though, and found it nose-ticklingly pleasant…whenever he actually thought about it. This landscape was a lot like that of his pakalōlō plantation, but at 4000 feet in elevation rather than 2000.

The road was narrow and winding. The Land Cruiser whizzed around a curve, and almost collided with a mower, mounted on a small John Deere tractor driven by a bored-looking guy in park service garb. Hak careened around the green machine. The driver didn't acknowledge the near collision. His ears were sealed behind the oval coverings of headphones, while his torso from the waist up bobbed and weaved, presumably to the rhythm of weed-cutting music.

Around a few more curves, the road widened into a parking lot. A large sign announced "Thurston Lava Tube." Two diesel-smoke-belching tourist buses were hogging most of the space. Japanese tourists were offloading, like a stream of humanity extruded from a metal container. Once afoot, they milled about, photographing almost anything that didn't move. Hak slowed to avoid hitting a particularly careless photographer who had strayed into the center of the through-going traffic lanes. He silently mused that if Japan ever again chose to attack Hawai'i, the Emperor would have one hundred percent detailed photo coverage of the war zone, in advance.

A short-haired middle-aged blond couple, with stark winter-white skin protruding from multi-colored shorts and aloha shirts, looked nervously worried about being smothered by the flood of wriggling humanity as they inched through the oriental throng, toward a path leading to the lava tube.

Cruising past the lava tube sign, oversized in national park style and nearly covered with mildew from rainforest humidity, Hak smiled in anticipation of discovering his own, unnamed and unknown (by others) tube in the Koa'e. This would be a place for safe storage of his crop, a place where there would be no tourists, a place that not even the voracious consumers of Fuji film would be able to photograph.

Another half mile of roadway twists and turns and the rainforest seemed suddenly to consist mostly of tree ferns. Some were as tall as thirty feet. The bottom half of each was a scaly (at least prehistoric if not dinosaur-age in appearance) cylindrical vertical brown trunk that mimicked a farm-field wood fence post in diameter and uniformity of appearance. Each trunk was topped with a sunburst of tall green leafy fern stalks, many with rows of finger-like protrusions that seemed to be caught in the act of opening upward, toward the life-giving sun. Where stalk attached to trunk, the union was masked by a mass of tan soft shaggy growth, reminiscent of uncombed hair on one of those recent hippie immigrants from the mainland…the type Hak had once enjoyed roughing up and defingering.

Seeing so many of these unusual trees unexpectedly triggered the memory of a singsong phrase his mother had used on him and his pre-teenage siblings while trying to teach them some words of the Hawaiian language. She had worried so that the language might go extinct, if parents didn't teach their children at least a few words.

To the repetitious cadence of a Hawaiian chant, she would repeat "Pulu grows on hāpu'u. Pulu grows on hāpu'u. Pulu grows on hāpu'u." And then she would prompt the children to sing her song, both singly and together. Without understanding why, the kids had enjoyed this game…even angry Hak, who was still Greg at the time.

Well, here he now was, surrounded by hāpu'u, those characteristically Hawaiian tree ferns. And there was plenty of that fuzzy soft pulu growing on them, too…material once used to stuff pillows and couches before artificial fibers became pillow stuffing of choice, probably saving these strange-looking trees from extinction.

Mother had told the kids all about these trees. Hak was thinking that learning the words would have been easier and maybe even meaningful and more fun if his mother could have conducted her lessons surrounded by the real plants. But life for the Hakonē family, at the edge of poverty on windward Oʻahu, simply did not include leisurely visits to virgin forests of tree ferns.

Hak cleared his mind of family thoughts, looked in the rearview mirror to be sure he had a customarily scowly expression on his face, and drove on. One more mile of cruising in his Cruiser and Hak hung a left turn, southeastward onto the Chain of Craters road. He was now following the upper part of the east rift zone. If he remembered correctly, Dr. Richards had said that the far eastward extension of this rift zone, a mile-wide swath of cracked and busted-up ground, passed right through the Puna district. If so, both his papaya and pakalōlō plantations were probably in the path of rifting, too.

Two more miles, and Hak turned right onto the Hilina Pali road, heading southwestward. Richards's directions so far were perfect, and these roads were all very well marked with large national park signs…so large that Hak figured the rangers must judge most visitors to be visually impaired. In spite of their earth-tone color, the signs did not blend inconspicuously in to the natural landscape.

Hak slowed a bit. The Hilina Pali road was only one-lane wide and had more curves than an old Coke bottle, or the gyrating hips of a hula dancer. Within a few hundred yards farther down the road, he slowed even more. The surface had become incredibly rough…so rough that he stopped and got out to be sure that the roughness was in the road and not in some broken spring or flattened tire of his Toyota.

Aha! The truck was fine, and the landscape was just as Dr. Richards had said it would be. The bumps were the product of a multitude of formerly open earth cracks, cutting right across the road. It was kindergarten-easy to visualize how opposing jagged edges could be mentally fit back together like pieces of a jigsaw puzzle. Road repairs filling in the cracks had created less than a smooth finished surface, perhaps in recognition that a swarm of new breaks would appear in a month or two anyway.

Whatever the reasoning behind a sloppy repair job, for Hak rough was good. It told him that he was within the Koaʻe fault zone.

He drove on another mile or so, and pulled off at one of the few spots wide enough to let other traffic pass by, if any should appear. He grabbed the backpack from the passenger seat, got out, locked his rig, swung the pack into place, and gazed off in a westerly direction. This should take him to the land of volcanic warehouses.

The weather was sunny and practically wind-free. His decision to not bring a raincoat had been the right one. Even if he didn't find what he was looking for, the hike should be enjoyable. He wondered why the place wasn't teaming with tourists, those not afraid to leave the security of a bus temporarily behind. Just then, the low rumbling of internal combustion engines intruded on the silence of his surroundings.

Hak waited and watched as two white Ford vans pulled in and parked some forty feet behind his Toyota. He pretended to get busy with something in the luggage space of his rig, as twenty incredibly noisy and obviously happy adult haoles spilled from double side doors opened by the van drivers. The gender split was about half and half. A persistent cacophony of laughter and unintelligible simultaneous conversations filled the air.

Like Hak, everyone in this group was dressed appropriately for a hike. Backpacks were plentiful. Some of the men were using peculiarly shaped hammers of the geologic profession as juggling pins, quite unsuccessfully. One person was distributing white cloth bags for carrying rock samples.

Hak pretended to ignore the group, while sneaking furtive glances in their direction. These chatterboxes, probably all from the mainland judged by their uniformly pale skin and mildly southwestern accents, seemed oblivious to his presence. Finally, one of the group shouted for attention, and surprisingly, the chaotic mass morphed into a class of ordered and attentive students.

"Geology teachers," thought Hak.

Everyone focused on the leader…an average-looking guy, a bit grayer and perhaps older than the rest. In profile, Hak noticed a nascent paunch where flat muscular abs might have recently occupied that body space in a somewhat younger and robust geologist. He wore faded blue jeans, a pale blue chambray shirt, and an even paler blue trucker's hat whose band was ringed with several concentric white stripes, the salty residues of evaporated sweat. Only these salt stripes and his tan hiking boots were a color other than blue.

"Okay, guys and gals, all you'll want here is few of the sample bags. No hammers needed. This is the spot I told you about earlier where you can collect Pele's version of pumice to take back to the classroom for your students. So, here's today's test. Who remembers what this strange frothy Hawaiian rock is called?"

A tall and lean mustached teacher, who was crouched on one knee in a shooting posture that seemed to demonstrate a memorable elk or deer kill to an attentive colleague, turned his face to the leader long enough to shout "Pele's pumice!" This obviously wrong answer met with howls of laughter and scatological catcalls detailing the respondent's ignorance.

"Come on, come on. Didn't any of you listen to the lectures I gave in preparation for this field trip? Maybe we should have just stayed home in Flag. Remember, you've got to take some new information back to the classroom, or you'll never get your school system's permission to go on another of these boondoggles."

Hak was soaking up all this playfulness, correctly concluding that these folks were no threat to his plans. They were totally self-absorbed, fun loving, and harmless to him. They still seemed unaware of his presence.

"Reticulite."

A strange sounding word that Hak had never before heard came softly from the lips of a willowy dishwater blonde female lost in the sea of mostly taller people.

"We're here to collect reticulite."

"Hey Dolores, a gold star for you. Okay, test is over. You may now collect reticulite to take back to your science classrooms. You'll find walnut-sized pieces of this fragile stuff hidden under the protection of small bushes and in clumps of grass. There's just one more bit of important information, though, that I must provide as your leader. Attention, please."

At this point, Hak noticed, the leader very purposefully turned his back to the group, which had begun to disperse like a bunch of well-trained cats, eyes to the ground in search of reticulite. The teachers spread out in an expanding shotgun pattern to the east, away from the leader. They paid as much attention to him as a typical airline passenger does to a flight attendant droning out the pre-flight dos and don'ts. Mr. Leader spoke at a volume audible only to himself.

"Remember that we are in a national park, and that it is illegal to collect rock samples without a special permit…which our group does not have. I'll just wait here by the vans while you do what you must do. You have twenty minutes to learn the lessons of this place. I'll give a blast of the horn when it's time to reassemble and leave."

By the time this little speech was finished, Hak noticed that not one of the teachers was in sight. They were still within shouting range, though. Hak heard a bout of high-pitched cackling laughter from the piercing voice of the one called Julie…or was it Eileen?

Feeling completely unthreatened by this happy-go-lucky gaggle of teachers from the mainland (hell, they'd probably be off the island and headed back home before he had serious need of his hoped-for volcanic warehouse), Hak headed out in a westward direction, as Mister Blue settled into one of the vans and began reading a book.

This part of the Koa'e was sparsely vegetated; the only trees were 'ōhi'a. Hak wasn't a botanist, but everyone who lived on the Big Island recognized 'ōhi'a trees by their red and occasionally yellow bottlebrush-like flowers. Understory consisted of a few small bushes; he wasn't sure what they were. They looked a bit like the 'ōhelo berry bushes that grew in abundance up around the summit of Kīlauea. These berries in the Koa'e, though, were small, hard, and bitter...he discovered as he bit into one and quickly spit it out...compared with the real 'ōhelo variety. Whatever kind of berry it was, their bushes and the 'ōhi'a trees were so few that the landscape was open for easy walking and good visibility.

He could see that only a little farther west, a quarter of a mile or so, there was virtually no vegetation. Richards had said the Koa'e was in Kīlauea's rain shadow, and he sure was right about that. No matter how much wandering around Hak might do out here, it should be easy to relocate the Toyota.

Human company was even scarcer than vegetation. Other than the two vans loaded with harmless science-teachers high-grading rocks from a national park, he had seen no vehicles on the Hilina Pali road, and he was alone in the Koa'e. This wasn't too surprising since the road ended abruptly at the lip of a 1000-foot cliff just a few miles beyond where he had parked. And now as he walked over an undulating surface of smooth pāhoehoe lava flows, partly covered with cinders, he saw no footprints, human or otherwise. Here in the rain shadow, footprints would remain for weeks and months on end, before the odd storm would wash them away. Apparently, Hak would have this place to himself whenever he chose to visit. This situation was perfect for his needs.

A horn honked in the distance, back to the east. Hak knew now that he truly was alone, or was about to be alone, in this part of the park. He continued a slow amble mostly westward, toward the broad outline of Mauna Loa Volcano, looming far in the background. He was taking in the rather stark yet intriguing landscape and thinking about what a pleasant stroll this would be for even the most nonathletic of people, when he nearly plunged forty feet to his death...or at least to an unwanted hard landing at the base of a cliff.

Without warning, the smooth lava surface underfoot dropped away, as though someone or something had torn the landscape in two and failed to reassemble the pieces on the same level. He inched closer to the edge of the precipice, looked down and saw, at the base of this vertical cliff, the kind of open gash that Richards had described just yesterday. This looked like a giant version of the kind of repaired cracks he had seen cutting across the Hilina Pali road.

Since there was no one around to hear, Hak released a shout of joy.

"Yes! I've found a candidate for hidden warehousing!"

Walking along the top of the cliff, a landform his mother had taught him to call a pali, he found a place where the face had collapsed into a jumble of blocks. He used these as stepping stones to the lower level. Once down, he followed the open gash until he found a place where he could enter safely.

The opening ranged from about one to three feet wide, depending on just how much broken lava had tumbled in from the inward-facing crack walls. But by working his way back and forth along the crack, he should be able to descend at least twenty or thirty feet, as far down as he could see from the surface. There were enough irregular steps along the sidewalls of the opening that he would not need a rope. He donned hardhat, took a drink from his canteen, tucked his flashlight into a hip pocket, laid the pack in the shelter of a huge overhanging boulder, and started his descent.

The first change he noticed was a temperature drop just a few feet into the crack. He felt cool compared to being exposed to the sun at the surface. He started a conversation with himself.

"Ummh. This underground temperature should be ideal for storing my crop."

Down another thirty feet or so, crouching under a huge boulder that spanned the entire width of the crack, sunlight was getting thin. He didn't yet need the flashlight, but that would come soon. He watched both walls of the crack closely as he descended, hoping to find one of the lava tubes that Richards had mentioned.

"Damn. I'm seeing nothing but old gray lava flows, stacked up in a boring layer cake."

He continued his descent, precarious step by precarious step. He right foot slipped on what felt like loose marbles. He aimed the beam of his flashlight at his foot and saw brilliant red cinders in a layer about two feet thick, sandwiched between lava flows. This stuff looked totally out of place, both for its color and for being loose pieces easily dislodged by hand, or foot, rather than being stone-solid lava.

Hak played the light beam along this layer. Some foreign object was sticking out of the cinders at the far reach of his light. He scuttled along a lava ledge until he came face to face with a tree branch as thick as his arm.

"Must have been buried by fallout from a giant lava fountain."

He snapped off the end of the branch. His fingers came away black. Heat from the cinder blanket had cooked the branch until it was pure charcoal.

"I *could* take this stuff home and use it to BBQ my next steak. But I'm on a different mission today. I hate to think what would happen to a person who got buried by a rain of hot cinders."

Hak descended another thirty feet, a total of about seventy now, he figured. Using the flashlight was a must. He still hadn't found a lava tube, and he could go no deeper. The crack at this level was completely filled by rocks tumbled from higher levels. He drifted horizontally, eastward if his sense of direction was correct, along a level where two lava flows were in contact.

"Man, it's dark down here…and cool and ghostly quiet."

Though he would never admit so to another human being, Hak was a bit frightened and enervated, simultaneously, realizing that he was within the bowels of the world's most active volcano.

"No eruption today, please, Pele."

Hak shivered with the persistent coolness. He made a mental note to bring a warm jacket next time. He imagined that someone trapped here could shout for help until out of energy, to no avail, unless someone happened to be directly above listening at the surface. Without a rescue, it would be a chilly and slow death. The notion that the trapped person could be himself kept Hak moving laterally along the crack, guided by the beam of his flashlight. The lens was warm enough to bring additional feeling back to cold hands.

Then suddenly, there it was…the almost perfectly circular opening of a lava tube, part of Pele's subway system, extending straight back into the wall on his right. Hak's pulse increased with the excitement of discovery. His shivering stopped. As he entered the tube, he instantly forgot about the possibility of getting trapped underground.

"Let's see. It's about seven feet top to bottom, easy to stand up in. I wonder how far it goes back?"

He aimed the flashlight along the tube. He saw that broken blocks of lava filled the tube to its ceiling, no more than twenty feet in from the crack.

"Damn! The ceiling must have collapsed. I want more storage space. I'll keep looking and find a bigger tube."

Hak was getting cold. He began the climb up and was warming himself in tropical sunshine only five minutes later. He leaned back against a large rock, facing the sun for maximum warmth, and dug the lunch out of his pack. He interspersed bites of cone sushi with globs of poi, scooped from a plastic tub with a great substitute for a spoon, a paddle formed by the index and middle fingers of his right hand. He thought about what to do next. He talked it out with himself as he ate.

"Richards said that the Koa'e has lots of gaping cracks with lava tubes. So, I can either go back down this crack and explore it some more, or I can look for a different crack to explore."

By the time all of the starch-of-the-taro-root and rice were in his tummy, washed down with water, Hak had decided to search for another crack. Since his lunch-spot crack ran east-west, he figured that his best bet to find a different one was to head north, or south. No one, not even his worst enemies and detractors, ever accused Hak of being stupid…mean, overly aggressive and selfish, yes, but not stupid.

With the snow-capped top of Mauna Kea, far to the north, as his guidepost, he started walking again over the gently undulating surface of pāhoehoe. A twin-engine tourist plane buzzed overhead in part of its broad circle around the caldera, that big hole in the ground at the top of Kīlauea. Hak reflexively looked for cover, temporarily forgetting that he was not at his pakalōlō plantation and this was not a police flight. Remembering that he was in fact a legitimate tourist today, he relaxed and laughed at himself for the unnecessary, albeit brief, increase in pulse rate.

And then there he was again…at the brink of a pali. Looking down, he saw what he sought, a gaping gash inviting him to explore. He made his way down another makeshift staircase of tumbled rocks against the face of the pali. He stood at the edge of the open cleft. This one extended east and west as far as he could see, seemingly unchanged. He found an easily recognizable place to leave the pack. This time he took his gloves to avoid chilled fingers.

Descent was easier than in the first crack. Irregular protrusions of rock from both walls formed steps almost perfectly spaced for his stride. Quickly, he was at least seventy feet below ground level, flashlight in hand, and going even deeper. The crack narrowed as he went deeper. He had to squeeze his robust body between walls several times. But continue on he could and did.

At what he guessed was about one hundred feet depth, the crack was filled with debris tumbled down from above. So, like before, he headed east along this uneven floor. And also like before, he soon encountered a lava tube extending back into the wall on his right. Unlike before, the beam of his flashlight illuminated an eight-foot-tall conduit open as far back as he could see. He began to explore.

"Alright! This tube is open back more than fifty feet. That's way more than enough storage space."

With gloves off, Hak ran his fingers along the wall of the tube. He smiled in the dark and told himself how lucky he was.

"Here in the rain shadow of good old accommodating Kīlauea, the tube is not only cool, but also dry. I've got controlled environment, air-conditioned space at no cost to the hui. Man, this will be perfect for the health and preservation of the inventory. Wait 'til the partners hear."

Back on the surface, Hak looked around and made detailed mental notes of landmarks…a uniquely shaped six-foot boulder next to his crack entrance, a pair of stunted-looking ʻōhiʻa trees about fifty feet to the east, and that ramp of tumbled rocks on the face of the pali an equal distance to the west. He was pretty sure he would be able to find this place again.

Once back at the top of the pali, he looked to the southeast and was gratified to see a bright reflection of sunshine from one of the windows of his Toyota, maybe a half mile away. He could only inwardly grin at the ease with which this was playing out. He headed back to the Toyota.

"God, I really owe Jack Richards great thanks. But I don't think he would be pleased to know why!"

There were no signs of the teacher group at his parking place, other than a bunch of human footprints in cinders, an accidentally dropped white sample bag, and the short arcing sets of tire tracks left where vans had been jockeyed back and forth to turn around on the narrow road.

Not wanting to bring attention to this spot, Hak picked up the sample bag. He used it as a broom to sweep away the tire tracks before stuffing it into his pack. Sporting a Cheshire cat grin across his usually scowling visage, Hak fleetingly thought that maybe life really was as good as his mother and other optimists said it was cracked up to be. He cruised on down to Hilo feeling as high as his product could take anyone.

CHAPTER 21

LET THE SURVEY CONTINUE

Seven o'clock Wednesday morning.

Andy and the rest of his crew were sipping Kona coffee, rubbing sleep from their eyes, yawning, and talking about stiff muscles from yesterday's work. Tired or not, though, here they were at Kea'au Village, ready to start where they had left off barely thirteen hours earlier. When everyone seemed coffeed up, Andy spoke.

"Okay, crew. I want you all to start with the same job you had yesterday."

Liz and Jeb put on their longest sad facial expressions, looked at Andy, and moaned in unison.

"I want us to start this way…at least until we all get warmed up, into a comfortable rhythm, and are cruising along like the well-oiled machine that we are."

This bit of ego stroking changed sad expressions to happy faces. While Liz and Jeb were retrieving the rods from the rack on the station wagon, Kabana was examining the leveling records from the most recent previous survey. A quick glance told him that the elevations determined yesterday showed no change from the earlier ones; this was good news. Changes, if indeed there would be any, should appear higher up on Kīlauea. That's where new magma would rise up into the volcano. That's the position of the metaphorical underground balloon that inflated when the new hot stuff arrived. Rob and his crew would likely be the ones to measure ballooning. You couldn't be sure, though, until the survey was complete.

Number two day got underway okay for Andy and crew. By late morning, though, tempers seemed frayed, patience worn thin. Repetition and miles of walking were taking a toll.

Liz growled and scowled at Andy when he brushed into her chest as she moved past him from one turning point to another. Usually, she invited such contact and greeted it with a warm smile, complemented by an "accidental" stroke of her hand against Andy's thigh. There was no hand job today, though. Only a "Watch where you're going, klutz."

What frowning Liz didn't realize was that Andy's contact with her was unintentional. He'd been daydreaming about his new approach to a relationship with the opposite gender. At the moment of bump, his mind and body had been disconnected.

Jeb was limping and complaining of a raw blister on the heel of his left foot. Apparently, some pain really was involved. On one advance to the next turning point, he swung his rod into traffic, almost grazing the side of a passing car, as he stumbled on his sore foot. Andy had never before seen Jeb so clumsy.

They couldn't afford to damage a rod. Those simple looking tools were expensive. They were a special type of steel called Invar, an alloy that doesn't expand or shrink in response to changes in temperature. The crew could be sure that a foot measured in direct hot sun was exactly the same length as a foot measured in the coolest of Kīlauean mist. HVO had only four of these rods. If one were damaged, only one crew would be able to work. The surveying job would be stretched out many more days than anyone wanted to consider.

Kabana was complaining of eyestrain. Even with light eye work back at his office desk, the staying power of his clear vision was marginal. Kabana had worn glasses from age two, and the amount of correction needed for clear vision had progressed right along with his age to the point that his present lenses were so thick that their weight left permanent impressions on the bridge of his nose. Over the years, he had developed calluses there. Today, he was removing his glasses, rubbing the bridge of his nose, and replacing his glasses so frequently that hands needed for writing and driving were otherwise occupied to the point of slowing their rate of survey progress.

At lunchtime, Andy decided to shuffle the deck.

"Jeb, that's a nasty looking blister. I want you to take over for Kabana for the afternoon. With the Ford's automatic transmission, you won't even have to move your left foot.

"Liz, you take the gun. That'll give you something different to do. You'll still be walking; but I know damn well that you're in excellent physical shape."

Liz and Andy exchanged knowing grins.

"Kabana, you and I will team up on the rods. That should give your eyes a rest. Let's go!"

Switching jobs accomplished what Andy hoped it would. Attitudes turned upbeat. The team became downright cheerful. A little shouting and singing replaced the morning silence of gloom and pain. At one point Liz chided Andy for sloppy work. She was sighting toward Andy, trying to read numbers on a wavering rod.

"Hey, lover boy. Haven't I taught you by now how to keep your rod straight?"

That brought a chuckle from everyone, even Andy, who had been daydreaming again about his new approach to a love life.

They completed only three-and-a-half miles of leveling on day two, finishing just a bit uphill from the village of Kurtistown. Part of the slowdown, compared to day one, was due to the boredom-and-pain syndrome. But most was because they were now working their way uphill, rather than along the nearly flat ground of yesterday. With an increase in slope, the distance between gun and rod men had to be shortened. Otherwise the gunman would be looking through a horizontal telescope at pavement in the uphill direction and sky in the downhill direction, with no numbers to read.

❦   ❦   ❦

Rob and crew worked on foot all day. They completed a random-looking circuitous route back and forth across the floor of the caldera. Though their path may have looked like that of a dizzy dodo to the uninitiated, they were filling in gaps needed to paint a complete picture of Kīlauea's behavior, once all the data were gathered.

❦   ❦   ❦

That Wednesday morning, Hak and his two partners were considering data of their own. The next Gambler's Special flight to Las Vegas was scheduled for the first week of January, nearly four weeks away. Several bricks of their harvested pakalōlō were piled up at the plantation, and several more would exist before Hak could get safely to his mainland buyers. Threats of damage from mold, rot, and curious feral pigs demanded that they move the bricks soon, real soon, or see thousands of dollars of their product disappear.

The plan they hatched was this: The partners would return to the plantation early the next morning, with backpacks. At exactly nine o'clock, they would emerge from the rainforest at an isolated spot where they could transfer the content of their loaded packs into Hak's waiting Land Cruiser. They would then hike back in, because more crop was ready for harvest, while Hak drove up to the national park to make his first deposit in the lava tube vault. Hak thought of the tube as a vault with foot-thick-steel walls and door. The tube was *so* remote. Hak felt confident that the law would never find this place.

CHAPTER 22

PAKALŌLŌ IN STORAGE

Thursday's activities were playing out on schedule, exactly according to plan. On his way out of Hilo, heading toward the Puna District and the pakalōlō transfer spot, Hak stopped at a KTA store to buy a nylon-bristle house broom with a hollow plastic handle. His partners would be at the plantation by now, filling their packs with those valuable bricks, the building blocks of the hui's wealth.

Low clouds and a thin mist shielded Hak and his partners from any possible aerial observation, as they transferred the bricks from backpacks to the luggage space of the Land Cruiser. Hak threw a dirty old blanket over the bricks. Even a snoop would see only what might be a lumpy pile of stuff left there since last weekend's picnic.

On the drive from dirt rainforest track back to pavement, Hak encountered a young couple walking toward Pāhoa. He recognized them as his hippie neighbors in pakalōlō production. Hak and neighbors studiously ignored each other, as they passed with only inches of separation.

Hak was now cruising through the village of Mountain View on Highway 11, more than halfway to the park from the Puna plantation. There was that survey crew again, the one he had seen at the outskirts of Hilo on Tuesday. This time the lovely young lady was looking through the telescope, instead of holding one of those long metal rods. As he drove by, Hak admired the contours of her derriere, as she bent over the instrument.

Though he now had no regular lady, he had often enjoyed the pleasures of the flesh during his biking days. Like most everything else back then, he simply took a piece when he wanted it. He still appreciated the sight of a nice female ass, the seat-cushion of love, naked or clothed.

Today, Rob and his crew were leveling along the Chain of Craters road, on their way to the Hilina Pali road, which would take them angling across the Koa'e toward the southwest. Once across, they would turn and level their way back on foot, heading due north, toward HVO. The entire loop would take two full days. With luck, or at least without unanticipated mishaps, they could finish the part along the roads today and do the cross-country part tomorrow. At the moment they were about a mile from the turnoff onto the Hilina Pali road.

So far, Rob had been able to avoid serious deleterious effects of boredom and burnout within his crew by simply rotating tasks. Today, Allan was the gunman, Rob and Jane were rod men, and Bruce was driver/recorder. The old International Scout had not failed them yet, and today's route was all gently downhill. Rob hoped that this excuse for a truck might just last through another bout of work without the need for Frank's healing touch. Downhill was a plus for the weak engine, and *gently* downhill was a plus for the brakes, which were about as dependable as the engine.

As they leveled past a crater named Lua Manu (which translates to English as Bird Crater or Bird Toilet, depending on one's druthers), the first tourist car of the day appeared. It was a tan Toyota Land Cruiser, as common as cockroaches on the Big Island and as dependable as the rising sun. Seeing this rig reminded the crew that their Scout would be lucky to get through the day without some mechanical failure.

The driver of the Toyota, a middle-aged, Hawaiian-looking guy with less than a smile across his face, slowed and watched them in apparent recognition as he skirted past rod man one, gun man, and rod man two.

Hak recognized these folks as the same crew he had encountered yesterday, near the entrance to the park. He had no idea what they were doing, other than maybe surveying in preparation for some roadwork. He did wonder about all of this surveying between Hilo and here, though. If a large road construction project was in the offing, he would have heard about it through his Rotary group. There would be cushy government contracts for Rotary brothers to seek.

At the moment, as he turned onto the Hilina Pali road and headed to his parking spot, the staging ground for Operation Pakalōlō Transfer, he just hoped, and assumed, that this crew would continue down the Chain of Craters road. The fewer people he saw on his mission, the better. Those rowdy teachers of Tuesday had been enough unwanted company.

He could take only half of the bricks in one load. The rest stayed under the blanket. In addition to gloves, water, and a flashlight, this time Hak also put a lightweight nylon jacket in his pack. He then unscrewed the handle from the broom he had bought at KTA; the sweeping part went into the pack. He carried the light-brown handle, pretty convincingly disguised as a walking stick.

Land Cruiser locked, he set out in a direction that more or less split the difference between the tops of Mauna Loa and Mauna Kea. With its cap of snow, Kea was living up to its Hawaiian name. At over 13000 feet in elevation, Loa was wearing a similar mantle this time of year.

As he walked along, Hak made mental notes of landmarks underfoot. He would need these on days too cloudy for the big mountains to be visible. Within twenty minutes, he was at the entrance to his subterranean warehouse vault. Finding the spot had been easy. Today he would take everything down into the crack with him. About halfway down, he removed the backpack and hand carried it. The crack was too narrow at this depth and deeper to accommodate the combined girth of his poi-fed body and attached pack. He had to carry the pack alternately to the side and in front of him, as he descended to the tumbled-rock-strewn floor of the crack. He then sidled horizontally eastward, toward the tube opening.

Flashlight in hand, Hak examined the tube in more detail than he had yesterday. The floor was fairly flat and smooth, the same kind of surface as the ground of the Koa'e. He ran his fingers over the smooth rock. Mother had taught him that Hawaiians call this type of lava pāhoehoe. It looked to Hak as though a very shallow stream of lava, a last gasp of flow through the tube, had frozen in place. This floor covering was the rocky equivalent of a dark shag carpet.

The sidewalls were even smoother to his touch. They looked glassy in the flashlight beam. Both the feel and look reminded Hak of the glaze on his favorite ceramic coffee mug back at the office. The ceiling of the tube was similarly glazed. It was also decorated with hundreds of inch-long skinny protrusions. Hak imagined them as tiny fingers reaching down toward him. What did they want? He stretched up to meet them, but could not quite touch the ceiling.

Hak saw bench-like surfaces perched along the sides of the tube. Each was about two feet wide and a foot above the tube's floor. It was almost as if a carpenter had constructed shelves for his use. He stood on one and rubbed a couple of the downward pointing lava fingers. If anything, they were smoother than the sides of his coffee mug.

He stepped back to the floor and opened his pack. He spread his windbreaker as a cushion on the bench where he had been standing. He laid the bricks of pakalōlō there, carefully, to avoid puncturing their hermetic plastic seals on the sometimes-spiny surface of his inventory shelves.

Smiling the grin of complete satisfaction…Hak figured he couldn't ruin his tough-guy reputation if he smiled here in the dark…he turned to climb out and return to the Toyota for the second round of Operation Pakalōlō Transfer. He didn't need his jacket for warmth today. His body was generating plenty of heat from the excitement of his accomplishments.

Trip two went as quickly and smoothly as trip one. Hak now had about a hundred pounds of pakalōlō stored in a safe and environmentally friendly place that no cop would dream existed. His part of Pele's subway system now contained, what?…about $100,000 of inventory value once transferred to the mainland and sold to users in Las Vegas. There would be no more losses due to mold or pigs. From now on, he would be able to convert essentially one-hundred percent of his harvested crop to hard cash, thanks again to Dr. Richards.

"Man-o-man, I love those civil servants! At the next meeting of my Rotary chapter, I'm going to propose a strong resolution to work toward increased federal funding for HVO."

For this return trip, Hak reassembled the broom and swept away telltale footprints as he walked back to the Toyota. He did not see the surveying crew again. He guessed that they had indeed continued on down the Chain of Craters road.

However, as he turned left onto that road, he met the oncoming government-green car of a park ranger. This vehicle had a set of colored lights attached to the roof. It was a cop car. The driver, a male haole with a marine-style crew cut, was alone. His stared at, if not right through, Hak as their cars passed slowly. Hak's imagination surged with wild thoughts and then calmed. He had no incriminating evidence in the Toyota.

Maybe this ranger gave all tourists an evil-eye stare. Maybe he was one of those who resented park visitors, because visitors complicated an otherwise simple job. Whatever the reason behind the cop's behavior, he just cruised on by.

An hour later, Hak was relaxed comfortably in his office chair, enjoying the view of Hilo Bay. He gloated about how smart he was, and mumbled a few thoughts about his hui's business.

"Time to make arrangements for another shipment of papaya to California consumers. It seems to be the designer fruit of choice in La La Land right now.

I think the hui could make a profit selling only papaya, if we chose to go straight. But then those fickle Californians probably would switch to kiwi, or some other product. Pakalōlō will never go out of style."

CHAPTER 23

THE CONVICT CHARADE

Friday morning. Seven o'clock.

Andy and crew were gathered on Highway 11 near the village of Glenwood, yesterday's stopping point. This was to be the fourth straight day of leveling. Everyone was tired and bored. But they were beyond the point of no return, at least in terms of total miles to be surveyed. This was no time to relax and let down.

As his crew's leader, Andy planned a little trick that might boost morale. This scheme would involve the public. His planned ruse was corny, but it had worked in the past and should work again today.

Andy would run the gun. Kabana and Jeb, whose blister was covered with enough moleskin padding to dull pain, would be the rod men. Liz would enjoy the relative comfort of driving the Ford and writing down numbers as Andy shouted them out.

The starting point was at an intersection. A secondary road ran north from Highway 11. A large sign pointing in that direction spelled out Kulani Prison Camp. This was home to some of the Big Island's less desirable inhabitants. Kulani inmates were low-risk, petty theft kinds of crooks. Still, nearby locals were not pleased to have such neighbors, even under lock and key. These misfits of society were considered lazy ne'er-do-wells, slopping at the public trough rather than earning a living by their own legal labors.

Andy would exploit these feelings to raise the morale of his surveying crew. He walked to the back of the Ford and dug out a shopping bag stuffed with three light-blue cotton shirts. The back of each had a seven-digit number stenciled in two-inch-tall black print, above which was the damningly bold label BIG ISLAND PRISONER. As his crew gathered around, he removed his own brown work shirt, and donned a blue one that made him inmate number 9678863. Should anyone think to dial this as a phone number, they would reach HVO.

"Kabana, I now bestow upon you the questionable honor of being Kulani inmate 9678820."

Kabana cackled so hard his glasses damn near fell off. He changed into the blue shirt.

"Jeb, you're crook 9678809. And, of course, you, Liz, are the officer in control of this scumbag group. We're counting on you to look and act your role."

Andy attached large magnetic signs to the grill and side doors of the Ford. The common message advised readers that this was a work crew of prison inmates.

Liz had an in-dash control that triggered a police siren installed by Frank. The siren was legitimately useful during eruptions, when HVO staff needed to identify themselves to the public as officials who wanted clear and immediate passage through traffic snarls that inevitably developed near eruption sites. Today the siren would be that of a policeman, or rather a police lady. The shirts were the brainchild of one of the earlier Dons, who had led HVO with an incredibly sensible and successful sense of humor during his years as Scientist in Charge.

Costumes and signage in place, the fourth day of leveling got underway. Time and again, passing motorists slowed to shout out their thoughts about making lazy crooks work for a change. The driver of an eighteen-wheeler tank truck, loaded with potable water for the park, slowed enough as he passed the crew to give them a piece of his broad mind.

"Nice ta see ya assholes workin 'stead of loafin! If you ever get out of jail, get a legit job."

Another passing motorist, a teenager with a vacant expression plastered across a flat face, thought he was clever as he grinned and shouted at Kabana.

"Hey, bruddah four eyes, why don't ya put dat pole where da sun don't shine!"

These and similar statements of the kind one might expect from intellects that would be in favor of capital punishment for even minor offenses were in fact morale boosters for the crew. The public, at least the folks speaking out, were accepting the phony identities without question. And they were letting loose barely latent hatred and narrowmindedness, feelings that apparently didn't take much prompting to activate. It made one wonder who the bad guys were...real Kulani inmates or bigoted "law abiding" citizens.

Inmates Andy, Jeb, and Kabana would sometimes react to the verbal abuse by looking sheepishly guilty of lord knows what crime. Or they would silently raise the middle digit of each hand, and occasionally snarl back, *sotto voce*, at the intolerant idiots. Fortunately for all, no motorist stopped for a punch-out. Andy wasn't sure he could explain his way out of their game, should an angry driver stop to pick a fight.

Liz, the civilian-clad supervisor of the work crew, would occasionally emerge from the Ford and loudly castigate her inmate charges as being slow and lazy...siren blaring in the background. At times she had a roadside admiration society composed of housewives and merchants whose homes and stores line the highway through Glenwood. More than once, she proclaimed a punishment that resulted in the rod men, Kabana and Jeb, going into their running mode, between turning points. Cheers and jeers from the sidelines were plentiful.

By the end of the day, the crew was exhausted yet exuberant from the charade. Boredom and physical pain had been forgotten in the passion of play-acting. They had advanced another five miles. Weather and the equipment god permitting, they could finish their part of the elevation survey by early afternoon tomorrow.

Yes, tomorrow would be a weekend day. And no, there would be no overtime pay. But camaraderie went a long way. Besides, they all understood the importance of completing their survey in as brief a time as possible. Pele never took time off, and she might just do something over the weekend that would force them back to a start at the Hilo pier, if they rested over the weekend.

Nobody wanted to start all over, now that the job was almost done.

Friday was the day for Rob's crew to level south to north, right across the Koa'e fault zone. It would be a day of nothing but walking over an undulating pāhoehoe surface broken here and there by fault-zone palis. But they had only four miles of such walking before linking back to the Crater Rim road, where they had leveled on Tuesday.

Yesterday, while leveling down the Hilina Pali road, they had encountered a parked car, the tan Land Cruiser that had passed them near Bird Toilet Crater earlier in the day. They saw no indication of where the driver had gone. Natural curiosity led to a peek into the vehicle. The rig was empty, save for a grungy looking blanket spread over something lumpy in the back luggage space. It was still there on their return to HVO at the end of the workday.

Today, as Howard drove Rob and crew down the Hilina Pali road to their starting point, the Land Cruiser of yesterday was gone. Apparently, the driver had simply taken a day hike from his parking spot, returned after they had finished their work yesterday, and was safely back home, wherever that might be. There was no need to notify rangers of a possible lost tourist, wandering in the wilderness called Koa'e.

This was fortunate for both rangers and tourist. The ranger staff consisted of one female naturalist and five brawny male law enforcement specialists, aka cops. It was widely known across the Big Island that these ranger cops hated to leave their offices, except to get into their patrol cars. And they hated to leave their cars even more, except to write a ticket for the unfortunate park visitor who parked outside marked spaces or exceeded the speed limit by a measly five mph.

The lone naturalist was so overworked that she rarely got beyond the main visitor's center in fielding questions from tourists. According to national statistics, though, the ranger staff at Hawai'i Volcanoes National Park was balanced about the same as in other national parks across the country. It seemed that someone in the staffing department believed that national parks are long on crime and short on natural wonders.

CHAPTER 24

BUREAUCRATIC B.S.

While the survey crews were putting in long and arduous hours in the field, The Don, Ben, Frank, and Howard tended to business at the office. As usual, Howard changed the paper charts on the seismographs by the tourist window each morning. He then delivered the tracings to Ben, who was diligently watching for additional indications of Pele's unrest. The rest of Howard's time was spent in his workshop, machining a new instrument of geophysics for Allan, from metal stock recently declared excess from a WWII U.S. Army cache on Oʻahu. As with vehicles, HVO got military metal hand-me-downs, too.

In his small dark office, Ben noted that several minutes of tremor were recorded around 11 PM Wednesday and again on Friday morning. The source of tremor still seemed to be pretty shallow, up within the below-sea-level part of the volcano. Ben couldn't tell if the source was getting shallower with time or not. He would just have to keep close tabs on whatever was happening. Past experience had shown that the shake-rattle-and-roll of Kīlauea's uneasiness tended to accelerate in power and frequency just hours to a day or two before actual eruption. So far, the trends looked constant to Ben, suggesting relative stability and no need to panic the public with an eruption forecast.

Frank spent most of his time tinkering with the old WWII vintage military jeep. Vehicles as sturdy and mechanically simple as this weren't made anymore. Frank wanted to keep such a prized antique running forever, if possible. Besides, HVO was unlikely to get a replacement.

The Don held the hands of worrywart bureaucrats at USGS headquarters. There was the usual stuff about budget. The Don was certain that the salary equivalent of time spent on HVO budget worries by people at headquarters exceeded HVO annual spending. From the HVO perspective, it was kind of hopeless to get too involved with budget. All the big decisions were made in what seemed like a vacuum at headquarters anyway.

At the moment, the federal government was two months into a new fiscal year, and Congress was still haggling over an appropriate level of funding for the entire Department of the Interior. The department was functioning in the mode of "Continuing Resolution", whose acronym was affectionately back-translated to Constipation Regime by most employees. As in past years, because this same budget stalemate occurred almost annually, CR triggered orders from USGS headquarters that The Don could spend only at the average monthly rate HVO had spent the previous year. Never mind that real events, especially those related to an active volcano, might dictate otherwise.

Furthermore, using the past as an indicator of the future, by the time congressional fiscal constipation was overcome and the HVO budget was set, half the fiscal year would have elapsed. Then, given the required advance time for making significant purchases, something beyond envelopes and paperclips, this situation would lead to the catch-22 of not being able to responsibly spend what was finally made available. To add insult to injury, The Don and his staff would be ordered to spend money rapidly during the final month of the fiscal year even if they didn't want to, in order that no money be returned to Congress at the end of that year. It was impossible, you see, to carry money from one year to the next, and congress would interpret this year's unspent funds as funds not needed, ever.

So, The Don and those budget people in Reston were yet again speculating on what HVO might get eventually, even though they were already two months into the new budget year. Having been through such an exercise so many times before during his tenure as Scientist in Charge, to The Don this was a form of mental masturbation that never resulted in a satisfying climax. But folks at headquarters seemed to need to be stroked, anyway. He was doing so via the phone right now.

"Yes, yes. Okay. We'll keep our rate of spending to that monthly figure you just gave me. You'll see the results on our monthly reports back to you."

The Don had made similar promises in earlier budget crunches like this. What he knew, but folks in Reston didn't, is that Kabana had ways to cook the books when need be. Kabana could make large and rapid spurts of spending dictated by whims of Kīlauea look like even outlay at the rate dictated by

Reston. All it took was a few creative invoices from Big Island vendors…who were also close personal friends.

While saying yes, The Don was thinking no.

"What a stupid way to run an organization! Especially one whose job is to quickly and effectively react to the hazardous whims of nature. I'd like to trap a bunch of congressmen between the enfolding arms of a lava flow, and explain that rescue will happen when the HVO budget is approved. Lava flows move much faster than Congress acts."

The real hot potato of the moment, though, had less to do with money and Congress, than with Reston's view that The Don had a smart-aleck on his staff who needed some stern disciplining. The problem was over a recent memo sent to all USGS employees by the headquarters safety officer. The message embedded in this memo, if a reader could get beyond the bureaucratic mumbo jumbo, was that employees should be especially careful to avoid injuries in their office environments. Specific guidelines were offered. For example, "Don't string electrical extension cords where you might trip over them." And "Don't lean back in a chair that might tip over."

The memo was a classic example of reiterating common sense…the obvious. Even to one of average gray matter, the main accomplishments of such memos seemed to be the ever-escalating destruction of paper-producing forests and a feeble justification for the safety officer's job. To one with above-average gray matter, a steady stream of this verbal diarrheic sputum was a festering aggravation. Most thinking employees dealt with their memo rage by recycling the paper, following a quick read of a feckless message. Recently, though, an HVO employee had reacted to one of these memos in a manner insulting to the safety officer. Headquarters was out to defend one of its own.

Rob was the culprit. His early life had instilled in him a lack of patience for nonsense, when the world and its peoples had plenty of real problems to deal with. Like most employees, he usually bit his tongue and recycled the nonsense on paper when it arrived. However, on the particular day that the memo in question sullied his mailbox, he was in no mood to humor the system. He stayed at work late that night and composed his own memo, one dripping wet with not-so-subtle sarcasm. He sent copies to managers at each organizational level of the USGS bureaucracy, right on up to the top of the power pyramid.

DEPARTMENT OF THE INTERIOR
U.S. GEOLOGICAL SURVEY
NOVEMBER 27, 1982

MEMORANDUM

To: Ernest A. Bodie
Safety Officer, USGS Headquarters
From: Roberto Armando Garcia
Research Geologist, Hawaiian Volcano Observatory
Subject: Safety in the Office

Though we've never met, I feel that I know you well. Ever since joining the USGS, I have been a regular recipient of your frequent advice about safety issues in the workplace. Your missives, over time, have helped me create a pretty clear image of their creator, and his Ernest passion for the job. You are a busy Bodie.

You are obviously tireless and unrelenting in your efforts to identify any and all situations that might lead to injury of employees while in the line of official duty. You relay that information, via hard copy, promptly and profusely to all of us office occupiers. I think it only fair, even perhaps overly modest, to say that, on balance, your record of productivity, documented again and again in the detailed messages of your memos, is weighty, indeed.

It is an understatement to sum up your career to date as quite substantial...and truly remarkable. My colleagues and I here at HVO *frequently* remark about your work. Judged from your record to date, I'm sure that you will issue many more inciteful messages, as new workplace hazards come to your attention. I fervently hope that your supervisor is fully aware of your activities and *properly* recognizes them for how they impact the day-to-day mission of all USGS employees. I trust that I'm not overstepping the bounds of propriety by sending him a copy of this memo, in hopes that it will spur him to a heightened consciousness of your output.

I do *so* want to be sure that he and other high-level managers in the organization know how *deeply* I feel about your contributions. In fact, your most recent memo, the one dated November 22, 1982, and titled "New Safety Issues for the Office" is what prompts me to write.

Who else, but someone as observant as you, would have recognized an electrical extension cord, slithering clumsily right across an office floor, as a hazard. I'm sure that I *never* would have tumbled to this conclusion on my own. Your superior prescience has provided just one more example of how badly we all need help in not injuring ourselves on the job.

To make a longer story short, over the years I have painstakingly collected your memos in the top drawer of my five-tiered, army-surplus metal filing cabinet. While inserting the November 22 piece of paper (that drawer really is quite full, you know!), the added weight tipped the entire cabinet right over onto me. (I guess the old straw and camel's back came into play.) I'm pretty athletic, but I was barely able to retreat fast enough to avoid the accumulated impact of your messages. Several bones in my right foot were nearly crushed by the cabinet and its contents.

I may be pushing logic to its limits with this next observation (though I *know* I can count on you to help me see the situation clearly), but I think there is a new office-safety issue to be learned from my experience. I wanted you to be the first to analyze what almost befell my poor foot, so you can alert all employees with one more of your cogent memos…if you think my near accident merits such action.

Thank you in advance for your careful attention to this issue.

Copies:
Director, USGS
Chief Geologist
Office Chief
Branch Chief
Jack Richards, SiC of HVO

In keeping with a pervasive lack of a sense of humor at headquarters, the safety officer had not been amused. His formal complaint, yet another memo from his office, had gone all the way up to the USGS director, who passed it back down a different branch of the bureaucratic tree to The Don's immediate supervisor. The phone conversation ended with The Don promising to take immediate and appropriate action on this issue.

He hung up, grinning in the satisfaction of knowing that "appropriate action" would be to somehow get a one-time cash award into Rob's hands, for creative problem solving. He recorded a brief message for Kabana.

"Kabana, my friend, I have another fun challenge for you to tackle. With your encyclopedic knowledge of USGS regulations, this one should be a piece of cake, as well as enjoyable. It seems that our boy Rob has pissed off the USGS safety officer and his backers in Reston. They want me to punish Rob. But I want you to find a way to reward the guy. Hell, we all hate those stupid memos about safety in the office. So, get your creative juices flowing. I want something on my desk to sign ASAP."

The Don had accomplished this sort of anti-establishment task before. Meanwhile, he would talk with Rob and try to convince him to avoid butting heads with headquarters again, at least not in the near future, even if the folks back there often seemed to work at odds with the goals of HVO.

CHAPTER 25

BEN FINDS A BULGE

Saturday was a day of mopping up for both leveling crews. Each had about a half day of work left. It was also a day of considerable mopping off. A light but steady drizzle coated the lenses of the leveling telescopes, blurring the numbers seen on the rods. As gunmen for this last push, Rob and Andy used up what seemed like a ton of absorbent tissue, repeatedly drying the lens on their instrument long enough to complete a reading.

Half-length raincoats were the protective clothing of choice. By the end of the workday, a body was soaking wet from the waist up, anyway, mostly with sweat generated because of the raincoat seal. A body from the waist down was soaked with rain runoff from the coat tails and from splashing through puddles. Working conditions were unpleasant, but by noon all leveling was completed.

Andy's team started at an elevation of about three thousand feet, where they had left off yesterday at the conclusion of the prisoner charade. In a unanimous show of chivalry, Andy, Kabana, and Jeb insisted that Liz be the driver of the Ford. She put Frank's creation, the foot-controlled windshield wiper, to extended use. When the last reading was completed, at the Volcano Store, Andy bought the crew a celebratory round of beer, flaunting the rule of no alcoholic beverages in a government car.

Liz wisely kept her bottle of brew capped until they arrived back at HVO. Even though the HVO and the National Park Service were sister agencies in the Interior Department, it was well known that sibling rivalry, rather than love, was what motivated the park law enforcement specialists, most especially that military-style head cop, Jefferson Davis Pickett. The last thing the crew needed at the end of their successful stint of leveling was another traffic ticket to hand to The Don, who would then have to grovel before the park superintendent to have the ticket forgiven.

That Saturday, Rob's crew was once again on foot. They measured elevations along two miles of trail across the southwest rift zone, just a mile or so outside Kīlauea Caldera. This crew slogged back into HVO wet, tired, and alcohol free.

Together, the two teams now had enough information to create a map that would show how elevations had changed on Kīlauea since the previous leveling binge, six months earlier. Creating this map would wait until Monday. Yesterday evening, The Don and Ben had assured them that Kīlauea was not in a crisis mode, at least as judged by a relatively low level of earthquakes and tremor. The Don urged the staff to rest up during what remained of the weekend. They would gather on Monday to evaluate the results of their labors.

Both leveling crews took this advice to heart and dispersed toward home. Andy chose to head to his little house on stilts and enjoy a long soak in the claw-foot bathtub, bottle of chilled white wine within reach. He was too exhausted to even think of an athletic bout of lovemaking with one of his Kona ladies. Besides, he remembered his recent vow to settle down. He was trying hard to do so; he hoped Kīlauea would follow suit.

Ben was so fascinated and frankly kind of worried by the many bursts of tremor during the past couple of months that he worked up a map of elevation changes on Sunday, while the rest of the staff enjoyed a well-deserved rest. Late that afternoon, he finished calculating the changes and plotting them up as contour lines on a map. He was astounded at both the magnitude and pattern of what he saw. He had never before seen such a large elevation increase, and in such an unusual place, during his entire fifteen years on the HVO staff...or even in the old *Volcano Letter* records that went back to the early part of the 1900s, for that matter.

Thinking he may have screwed up the math somewhere, subtracting hundreds of old readings from the new ones, he left the map on his office desk and headed home to salvage his family life. The wife and the boys were getting increasingly tired of running the anthurium business without his help.

CHAPTER 26

A COMPUTER FINDS BEN'S BULGE

Eight o'clock, Monday morning. Nineteen days 'til Christmas.

Ben grabbed the map he had created yesterday and went to see The Don. He had to wait at the office door. The Don was on the phone, finishing the inevitable start-of-the-week round of phone calls from headquarters. Micromanagement was alive and active. It seemed that The Don could hardly go to the crapper without someone in Reston wanting to know if everything came out okay in the end…and did he flush the toilet? Given the normal content of these conversations, flushing was appropriate.

Phone finally back in its cradle, Ben quickly entered The Don's office and rolled out his hand-drafted map.

"Look at this. I worked it up yesterday, without benefit of a computer. Maybe I screwed up my math, subtracting old and new elevations. If not, we've got something bizarre going on."

Ben's tone and volume of voice reflected how surprised and shocked he was with his results. Following a cursory glance, The Don mumbled his agreement about using the word bizarre.

"Jesus, Ben. What've you been smoking? I sure *hope* you screwed up somehow. This isn't the Kīlauea that we all know. It looks like some aboriginal kid from Australia's outback was asked to draw his favorite toy."

The contours on Ben's map traced out the form of a giant boomerang. The Don and Ben stared in silence, scratching their heads.

A COMPUTER FINDS BEN'S BULGE   171

"Let's sit on this until Andy and Rob finish entering all the new data into a computer spreadsheet. Then the computer can create a map. Don't say anything to them. We don't want to bias them in any way."

The computer part of the process was underway as Ben and The Don talked. Once finished, the machine would do the math that Ben had done manually. It would also print out a map of contoured elevation changes. Under normal circumstances, this computer product should be ready by about noon. The staff would then huddle to evaluate results.

Andy and Rob were still tired from last week's long work days. They were well aware that residual fatigue was tugging at their level of energy. Data entry was advancing more slowly than normal. To minimize, and maybe even avoid exhaustion-caused errors, they printed out copies of the in-progress spreadsheets about once an hour, so Jeb and Bruce could compare these entries against the numbers hand-written in field notebooks. The job was only about two thirds complete by noon.

The brown-bag lunch around the conference room table was unusually quiet and quick. The usual verbal sparring between Andy and Liz, replete with soft-core double entendres, never took place. Andy even ignored the parade of tourists, some of them attractive females, past the window. He and the rest of the HVO staff wanted to see the final results of their Herculean efforts, ASAP. A couple more hours of mind-and-body numbing keyboard tapping were needed to complete this advance in the science of volcanology. Data-entry drudgery was about as non-glamorous as the office part of their research got.

At three o'clock, both survey crews gathered around the printer. A map of contoured elevation changes came chug chug chugging out of the machine's bottom end. Jeb spread the map out on the conference room table. What they saw looked more like the product of a lower-tract anatomical outlet, than a printout of science from one of Hewlett Packard's best. Andy and then Rob reacted as they stared at the map.

"This map is a piece of crap! The maximum amount of elevation increase, the high spot here, is way way too much, at least compared to past experience. I might've expected a foot or so since we last leveled. I mean, we know from tremor that *some* magma has been pumped into that thing we call the balloon. But enough to push the ground up four feet? No way! I think we need to recheck the computer data entry against numbers in the field notebooks more carefully. Someone must have been myopic or dyslexic at the keyboard."

"I agree, Andy…a piece of *mierda!* And what in the name of Pele's house is the high spot doing way down there between the Koa'e and the south edge of the caldera? In the past, the high spot has always been *inside* the caldera…not necessarily at the same place, but always somewhere within the big hole in the ground. I mean, that's basically why the hole is where it is. The big magma balloon is right underneath it."

Andy and Rob kept staring, pointing, and shaking their heads.

"And hey, Rob. As if the amount and place of bulging aren't bizarre enough, look at the overall shape. We've got a giant boomerang instead of the usual bull's eye. One boomer finger's pointing down the east rift zone and the other one's pointing across the floor of the caldera, just about at us."

The assembled group stared silently at the map in shared confusion. Everyone knew that, historically, bulges tended to be as circular and prominent as an unwanted pimple at the tip of one's nose on prom night.

Rob called The Don and Ben. They came quickly. Ben laid his handcrafted version of the map next to the computer-generated one. They were uncannily similar. Still, everyone agreed that both maps were so very different from any other map of uplift at Kīlauea, going back decades in time, that the entire process of data entry and computer processing should be repeated.

"We're going to start from scratch on creating a map of uplift…tomorrow, after you two guys have had another night's sleep."

Visions of the great unknown were dancing though all heads as the staff dispersed for home. Being leaders of the surveying crews, much mental madness was haunting Rob and Andy. Had they screwed up in the field somehow, and essentially wasted all of last week's time and effort? Not likely, because all closed loops in their survey network balanced out to zero change, just as they should. No, their field measurements were good…very good, as usual.

If the fieldwork was fine, then maybe there was a screw-up in the manipulation of data back in the office. Andy, in his overly hasty, somewhat shallow, fickle, and flighty way, was confused about what might be happening. He silently decided that Pele must be responsible for his confusion. It was the old "blame someone else" when all else fails. Rob was his usual cautious and analytical self. He was thinking of possible explanations based on hard science. Deep down, though, where logic confronts the problem, each felt fairly certain that the map reflected the real situation, not some weird human mistakes. After all, that similar hand-done version by Ben was independent of any data entry mistakes they might have made.

An hour of high-meditation yoga on his living room floor allowed Rob to sleep soundly for eight hours. An hour of consuming beer and junk food brought on sleep for Andy. His head and stomach might pay a price tomorrow, but the magic of Kona coffee and steamed rice would help him through another boring stint of data entry.

❧   ❧   ❧

Eight o'clock, Tuesday morning.

Now reasonably well rested, Andy and Rob were back at the data entry routine. They finished shortly before noon. Everyone agreed that lunch could wait while the printer produced another of its lower-tract outputs.

Chug, chug, chug, chug…line by line the printer worked at its job, feeding its three-foot-wide roll of paper through in tiny incremental steps. They watched in tense anticipation as the edge of the map began to emerge from the machine. The north part of the area appeared first. There was that stretch of Highway 11, arcing around the edge of the caldera and heading off westward in the direction of the Kona coast. This part of the map showed no uplift.

Chug, chug, chug, chug…next, the edge of the caldera came into view. But still no contour lines of uplift appeared. A few more chugs and the exposed part of the map was near the center of the caldera. Contours of uplift were now being traced. First the one-inch contour, then the two-inch contour, the three-inch contour and so forth, in a nested pattern that mapped out the shape of an index finger pointing north-northwest, toward Puʻu Ulaʻula high on Mauna Loa.

Chug, chug, chug, chug…the index finger, defined by the one-inch contour line, had grown to the equivalent of about a half mile in width on the ground as the exposed part of the map extended south of the caldera and across adjacent Keanakakoi Crater. The contours also showed that the thickness of the ridgeline of the finger of uplift had increased, up to a foot now.

Chug, chug, chug, chug…the finger grew a little more in width and a lot more in uplift height as the edge of the exposed part of the map marched southward. Now two feet of uplift, next three feet of uplift, and finally four feet. Then, as contours less than four feet began to swing eastward…whirl, and the four-foot contour closed on itself to form a nearly perfect circle. This marked the spot of maximum uplift.

Chug, chug, chug, chug…another index finger was being created. This one pointed eastward, down the center of the east rift zone. A boomerang shape was being fleshed out. By this time, the HVO staff could see that the computer-generated and Ben's hand-generated maps of yesterday had not been mistakes.

Silent confusion reigned, just as it had yesterday with the appearance of the first edition of the map. Everyone moved to the conference room. Jeb tacked the map onto the mobile bulletin board. People walked around and examined this strange beast from every conceivable angle. It still didn't make sense...at least not within the range of experience of these people.

Support staff tended to stay silent in the background, waiting for profound pronouncements from their Ph.D.- and B.S.-toting colleagues. But no believable explanation, hell just plain no explanation at all was forthcoming. Instant brilliance was elusive. It was time for The Don to assert his stature as being in charge.

"Okay. We've got a new creature to try to understand. Sitting here silently picking noses won't accomplish anything. Go about your normal business, but keep thinking about what the map might mean."

The staff heeded The Don's advice. No one, not even Andy, spent time tourist watching at the big window. The conference room was devoid of people the rest of the day. But that strange map hung there, like a bizarre and unique Chinese puzzle, challenging anyone in the group to translate its contour riddle into an understandable tale.

Tuesday ended in silent confusion.

CHAPTER 27

IT'S HAPPENED BEFORE

Wednesday began the same way. But while the rest of the HVO staff, including The Don, stayed in their offices, partly as a way to think undisturbed about the puzzling map and partly as a way to hide their lack of useful ideas, Rob was in the conference room dragging dusty volumes from library shelves, reading and taking notes.

At exactly eleven o'clock, he discovered a publication titled U.S. Geological Survey Professional Paper 856, "Structure and Origin of the Koa'e Fault System, Kīlauea Volcano, Hawai'i." For the next hour, he carefully read this anonymous-looking booklet cover to cover, in spite of the fact that this was literally and figuratively gray literature.

The covers, originally cheap gray paper, were now a light faded gray. They were also coated with seven years' accumulation of gray dust. The color reminded Rob of battleship gray, and set him wondering if paper, like most everything else at HVO, was simply hand-me-down from the Defense Department.

In recognition of the (lack of) spirit projected by such a dull and dusty color, Rob, like the rest of his geology colleagues, knew that almost no one reads USGS Professional Papers. They are difficult to obtain, too often about obscure topics of limited interest, and always written in the most boringly bland prose imaginable…the ultimate distillate of government word-usage rules and editing, no matter how talented a writer the author may have been. To top it off, the publication in his hands was so thin, only twelve pages of text, that it had almost gone the way of many of its skinny companions…freefall off the back of a library shelf into an eternal graveyard between shelf and adjacent wall.

Yet this insignificant-looking little runt seemed to have the explanation, or at least a possible explanation for the origin of that unusual pattern of uplift still staring out from the map on the bulletin board, challenging all passersby.

With a growing sense of excitement, Rob called everyone to an early brown-bag lunch at the conference table, so he could share his new information. As the rest of the staff ate, Rob stood next to that enigmatic map and told his story, holding PP 856 high with his right hand.

"Hey crew! I've just discovered that about ten years ago one of our HVO predecessors completed a detailed study of the Koa'e area. This guy was mostly interested in looking for patterns in the hundreds and hundreds of cracks, faults, and fissures out there. Most of his published story is straightforward and not surprising. He mapped swarms of east-west trending open cracks and palis. But, listen to this: he also describes a two-mile-wide semi-circular pattern of arcing, concentric cracks whose center, or focus, is exactly at the bull's eye of our map of uplift."

Through the slurping, gnawing, swallowing, and burping sounds of lunches being consumed, Rob suggested that since this spot apparently was a center of volcano inflation in the past, as shown by the concentric pattern of cracks, it's reasonable that the same place could once again be a center of inflation. The "why here now, and not in the caldera?" question was another issue.

"We've got to believe that our map is correct. And we've got to learn all we can about this new bulge and how it fits into the PP 856 ideas."

No one spoke, but The Don smiled broadly and gave an enthusiastic two thumbs up. His body language accurately reflected everyone's feelings. But it seemed that not even a possible scientific breakthrough could compete with the eating of poi. The only sounds of approval were those of slippery poi being consumed by smiling faces plastered across with agreement, motioned by up-and-down nodding heads.

Rob finished his summary of PP 856 by noting that the bull's eye on their new leveling map and the focus of those old concentric cracks was a patch of high ground called Āhua Kamokukolau. Most of the staff knew enough of the Hawaiian language to realize that āhua means a mound or a swell.

"Could it be that ancient Hawaiians witnessed the growth of this mound?" asked Rob with an uncharacteristic twinkle in his eye. He was obviously excited by his discovery in the gray literature. And he was thinking that like so much of his life, especially his early life, color was not necessary for substantial and significant accomplishment. In fact, by this point in his life he was almost certain that color, in both its literal and figurative senses, was commonly camouflage for lack of substance.

Active minds around the table began to silently plan ways to test Rob's suggestion. Allan knew what he would do. The uplift bulge was where he had weeks ago measured some weird electrical signals coming from the ground.

Rob would also be going to the Āhua Kamokukolau area. His crew had leveled right across there, but he hadn't been thinking in terms of a bull's eye bulge at the time.

Andy was anxious to see that place, too. With so much uplift, there was a good chance that new cracks had formed, the stuff of Andy's Stanford training.

Ben would stay at HVO and continue to monitor for tremor and other earth shakes. Bruce, Jane, and Jeb were asked to print out and distribute a couple dozen copies of the new map, for use in the field and office.

The Don would basically hover, exuding moral support and projecting silent-but-helpful vibes of leadership, attributes that seemed to come naturally with his age and experience.

CHAPTER 28

THE BULGE HISSES STEAM

Thursday morning was cool and misty. Rob and Andy were on foot, crisscrossing the bull's eye area of their uplift map. They paused briefly at the brass benchmark cemented into the small hill called Āhua Kamokukolau and stared down, deep in thought. This had been one of Rob's leveling points just six days earlier. An elevation of 3494 feet had been etched deeply into the benchmark, back in 1960. Well, they now knew that this number was wrong. The place had been raised four feet within the past six months.

They walked away from the benchmark, heading south toward the core of the Koa'e. A myriad of short hairline cracks broke the pāhoehoe lava underfoot...nothing unusual there. But it was difficult to know if these were new products of the recent uplift, or old breaks that had formed much earlier. Then, bingo, a few steps further, they hit the jackpot.

About fifty yards south of Āhua, they entered a several-foot-wide belt busted up with many obviously new cracks, all running roughly east-west. Each crack was open no more than a quarter of an inch. Most exposed unmistakable rootlets of living grass stretched G-string tight across, from one side to the other. A few of the roots had been extended beyond their breaking point. Like the opposing walls of the cracks themselves, these fine organic strands could be mentally put back together like pieces of a jigsaw puzzle. So, this area of upward bulging had also been pulled out laterally beyond the breaking point of both rock and root.

"Jesus, look at all these new cracks, Rob! I knew there had to be some; no rocks get punched up four feet without breaking. To think it could be otherwise would be a real stretch."

Knowing that rocks do, in fact, stretch a bit before they break, Rob smiled briefly at Andy's attempted humor. They continued to walk southward, eyes glued to the ground.

Then came the clincher. One of the new cracks was emitting steamy vapors, weakly yet warm to the hand. This tepid outlet of nature's heat, called a fumarole, was obviously new. It carried the sulfurous smell of aged egg. It had not yet been active long enough to rot adjacent lava or coat it with telltale crystals of yellow sulfur, little messengers from magma.

"I guess I and my crew didn't see this steam because our route was a bit too far off to the west to notice such a feeble wisp of a white cloud. Ditto for the new cracks."

Rob's mind was racing around now, trying to put these discoveries into an eruption-scenario context. He suddenly remembered reading about another patch of ground, no more than a mile to the northeast, where a once verdant landscape of rainforest had been reduced to cracked, hissing, and sterile ground in 1938. Back then, HVO geologists had concluded that a batch of magma had pushed up under the area, causing shallow groundwater to boil and cook plant roots to death. In fact, the resulting sterile patch of ground, nearly a quarter-mile wide, was still steaming a bit and visible from the Crain of Craters road, almost forty-five years later. Few passing motorists noticed this handiwork of Pele. Rangers had never erected an explanatory sign.

"Hey, Andy, do you remember that patch of steaming ground that formed near the Chain of Craters road in 1938?"

A slight nod of the head signaled yes.

"Well, I'm betting that our Āhua bulge, cracks, and steam are working up toward another one of those."

As his mind worked logically through the remembered information, Rob realized that this entire part of Kīlauea was a literal and figurative hotbed of shallow magma-filled pockets, positioned here and there barely underground. The current Āhua hump was just another in a long history of magma-inflated earth. Maybe the biggest balloon-like pocket was beneath the caldera, and was most frequently active. But apparently lots of kiddy balloons were outside that caldera, getting pumped up now and then with batches of molten rock.

Rob and Andy headed back to HVO feeling confident about the accuracy of their map of elevation changes. They were also extremely worried about the meaning of that new fumarole. If there was enough new heat to be boiling away shallow ground water, could the magma be far behind? And was it still on the move, or had it got stuck somehow, destined to cool underground rather than erupt? These were questions that the HVO staff needed to consider carefully…and very soon.

CHAPTER 29

HAK MEETS OFFICER J. D. PICKETT

Early that same week, while the HVO staff was stewing about the significance of their leveling survey, Hak was in his Hilo office stewing over what to do, or not do, about his new pakalōlō warehouse.

On the one hand, his first deposit there had been in storage since last Thursday. He thought it would be sound business practice to visit the warehouse and check on the condition of the product. Perhaps there were unsuspected hazards to the integrity of his inventory. In his imagination he could see rats or mongooses, savaging the bricks. Unlikely, he thought, with the Koa'e being so dry and so far from any agricultural fields. But the uncertainty was nagging and tugging at his nerves.

On the other hand, he didn't want to create unwanted curiosity within the staff of park rangers by visiting the Koa'e too often. That part of the park got very few visitors. A sudden increase in visitation, especially by one person, might trigger questions in the minds of typically suspicious policemen, which, Hak believed, is what most of the rangers in this park were. He shuddered briefly, remembering how that Marine-looking ranger cop had stared right through him a few days earlier.

So...what to do?

By Tuesday afternoon, he decided to visit the warehouse the next day. If the bricks he had deposited there last week were unmolested, dry and in pristine shape, he would return in the future only to add to, or remove from, the warehouse inventory.

Early Wednesday morning, Hak loaded his backpack into the Land Cruiser. This time, he took only flashlight, gloves, and jacket. He knew he wouldn't need climbing rope. Being seen with a hard hat would provide an observant person with a strong clue to his ultimate destination. No need for that.

Forty minutes later, he was about to turn onto the Hilina Pali road when he saw the unmistakable flash of red-and-blue lights in his rearview mirror. He pulled off into a wide spot just beyond the intersection and waited. Thank goodness, he had nothing illegal or incriminating in the Toyota.

The ranger pulled in behind and got out of his government green machine, lights still flashing. In the rearview mirror Hak could see that it was the same mean-looking guy of last week. He braced for an unwanted interview.

As the man approached, Hak could see hardness in his eyes, an indication of a personality type that Hak had encountered repeatedly during his gang years. Hak would deal carefully with this officer. He wore a service revolver and nightstick on his right hip, and what looked to be an aerosol can of mace on the left. He would be no good-natured Andy Griffith.

Hak rolled down the window. Mr. Ranger stepped up and stared through, legs in the slightly spread position of a person ready for action. Hak read the bold raised print on the officer's metal badge...J. D. Pickett.

"How ya doin', sir? Welcome t'our national park."

Hak recognized a southern (Mississippi? Alabama?) mainland accent, a sound he had learned from movies.

"I'm fine, officer. What's the problem?"

"Well, a family of California tourists say their pet dawg got away from their rental van 'roud here a cupla hours back. I'm just wundrin' if ya might a seen it. I seen ya signal ta go right, down the Hilina Pali road. Very few folks go that way, ya know. I thought I otta stop ya so I could ask ya ta keep your eyes peeled for a stray hound."

Hak was continuing to develop a personality profile of J. D. Pickett, and it wasn't complimentary. First of all, given anti-rabies quarantine laws that discourage importing a dog into Hawai'i, Hak knew that it was unlikely any tourist would bring a pet on vacation here.

Whether the dog story was true or just fabrication, ranger Pickett exuded the aura of a bully, someone who would not hesitate to use his position to take advantage of and maybe even take something of value from an unsuspecting, if not intimidated park visitor. He stared down at Hak with a mixture of smirk, smile, and snarl decorating his face. A four-inch scar diagonally across his left cheek helped emphasize the snarl part his expression. Hak found himself wanting to add little-finger disfigurement to the man.

"No, I haven't seen a dog out here, but I'll be sure to contact park headquarters if I do. I was heading down the Hilina Pali road for a little sightseeing and maybe a short hike if the weather cooperates. I like to get out of my Hilo office for a bit of outdoor exercise now and then. Your park is a great place for that."

Both were quiet for what felt like a long time, at least to Hak. Ranger Pickett seemed to be waiting for something from Hak, and Hak thought he knew what was coming down. Hak had a strong feeling that this guy had taken many a bribe during his park service career. After all, Hak had played that kind of role himself, but without the official-looking uniform, during his youth on O'ahu. That experience now helped him hear the unspoken invitation and threat coming from Mr. Civil Servant there above him.

"Well, I surely do thank ya for those kind words 'bout our little piece of 'merican heaven here. By the way, if ya want ta see a truly amazin' sight that ain't on the regalur park beat, just hike on in there a couple hundert yards." Ranger Pickett was pointing north, across the Chain of Craters road, toward fairly dense rainforest.

"There's a really deep hole back there in the woods. People call it Devil's Throat. It's wider than the longest eighteen-wheeler, and deeper than a ten-year pit dug under an Alabama outhouse. It's like the bottom fell out from a piece of our earth. I do believe the devil hisself lives and does business there."

Hak took this bit of unsolicited information and Pickett's grin as hints of where to pass something of value to the ranger with no fear of detection, for either of them. Another round of awkward silence ensued. Finally, Hak spoke.

"Thanks, officer, I'll remember that place on a day when I'm better prepared to accept your invitation to explore, and have extra time without other plans in the way."

"Well, okay. Enjoy the day here tourist…"

"Hak."

"T o u r i s t Hak" drawled out Pickett, while extending his hand through the Land Cruiser's window for a farewell shake.

Hak was no weakling, but Pickett's grip was nearly bone crushing and seemed loaded with meanings well beyond goodbye. As Ranger Pickett walked away, Hak was sure that this cop wanted and expected something of value, should they meet again. Hak was almost positive that the deep pit called Devil's Throat was way more than a special volcanic curiosity. Back in Hak's badass gang days, it would have been known as a drop point. This deep throat probably was a place where the devil in the form of J. D. Pickett did business with intimidated tourists.

Pickett walked back to his patrol car, reached in the window, and turned off the flashing lights. He removed the nightstick from his belt, threw it into his car, and slid into the driver's seat. He was careful to not cramp his revolver or mace can under his butt. He then stuck his left arm out the window and signaled Hak to leave first. Hak hung a U-turn and went left, down the Hilina Pali road. He would complete his mission as originally planned. Having told Ranger Pickett that he was in the park to visit this area, it would look suspicious not to.

As he headed down the rough road, Hak watched for, but didn't see, the ranger's car in the rearview mirror. Pickett was either still sitting at the encounter spot, or had continued east down the Chain of Craters road. Perhaps he was looking for another tourist to visit with.

An hour later, Hak had taken his hike and was back in the Land Cruiser. His new warehouse had been easy to relocate. The bricks stored there were in fine condition. He would no longer worry about the integrity of his lava-tube warehouse. He would visit only to deposit or withdraw, minimizing the chances for another encounter with Ranger Pickett.

That same hour later, J. D. Pickett was still thinking about his chat with tourist Hak. He rechecked his notebook to be sure he had jotted down the license number of Hak's Land Cruiser. Pickett was pretty sure that this guy had been hiding something during their conversation, sort of holding back, but he couldn't sort out just what that something might be. If for no other reason, skin color made Mr. Hak a suspicious character in Pickett's way of thinking. Well, he would watch closely for tourist Hak and pull him over for another talk if the chance should present itself.

He didn't need justification to do so, at least not in his mind. He was a policeman with the school of thought and practice that citizens are guilty until proven innocent. He had once heard about a long-time-dead French guy named Napoleon who had this same approach to justice. JD had seen a painting of this Frenchy, though, and he was way too much of a physical wimp to represent the kind of good cop values that JD actively embraced.

HAK MEETS OFFICER J. D. PICKETT

❧   ❧   ❧

Jefferson Davis Pickett was the only child of poor white farming parents in rural Alabama. He had inherited their lack of intelligence and something between distrust and hatred of colored people. He also inherited his daddy's burly build. Helping to work the farm had added hard rippling muscle to a naturally sturdy body.

In high school, JD was the toughest lineman on the football team. His vicious style of tackling, a modified form of body slam he learned by watching professional wrestlers on TV, had resulted in more than a few broken bones and concussions, for opponents.

JD was also the state heavyweight wrestling champion during his four high school years. Basketball and baseball, though, required eye-and-limb coordination and grace that were not part of JD's physical attributes. He could throw the twelve-pound shot-put ball damn near all the way across Tallapoosa County, though.

Through the grace of a misguided public school policy called social advancement, JD graduated right on schedule at age eighteen. About then, the Vietnam War came along and the Marines were asking for a few good men. JD wasn't necessarily good, even by a Marine definition. But he surely was a man. He toughed out the most grueling training they could throw at him in Camp LeJeune. His only mishap was suffering a deep barbed-wire gouge across his left cheek, during a training exercise that required his thick body to squirm supine under a low obstruction.

He was fully trained and ready to ship out to 'Nam when an unexpected physical flaw interfered. JD came down with such a case of bursitis that he was unfit for combat. He was given good-conduct walking papers from the Marine Corps and was faced with the heavy question of what to do with his life.

The one thing he knew about life was that he was tough and that he liked to use that toughness on others to get whatever he wanted. He liked to intimidate. He liked to control. He liked to be above others, both physically and symbolically, though he surely didn't think much in the abstract.

During a weekend of leave from LeJeune, he had visited Washington, D.C. There he saw lots of policemen in fancy uniforms, up on horses, patrolling and controlling crowds of visitors like himself. Now *this* was a job he could enjoy.

Once mustered out of the Marines, JD returned to D.C. to apply for the job. His good-conduct record with the Marines gave him lots of bonus points with the U.S. Civil Service Commission. It also helped that he had lots of experience with horses…mules, actually, but he said horses on the application form. Within a couple of months, J. D. Pickett was a mounted ranger with the U.S. National Park Service. He was in uniform and in a position to legally work the crowds of the D.C. mall. The job didn't pay much, but he was so happy that his bursitis hardly ever flared up.

These were the early 60s, times of many anti-war and civil-rights demonstrations on the mall. All sorts of interesting folks gathered to champion their causes. Crowd control and law enforcement were necessarily a substantial part of Park Service service. JD quickly discovered that his position of authority and power could bring a variety of fringe benefits.

For overlooking this-and-that breaking of the law, while simultaneously dropping only the slightest hints of how to please him, JD supplemented his salary with such goodies as food, alcoholic beverages, mighty good marijuana and, occasionally, even sex. Eventually, though, it became hard to hide his unofficial activities from his mounted-patrol colleagues.

It was time to move on, which was easy. His employer encouraged periodic transfers. A promotion usually greased the skids of transfer.

Next came Rocky Mountain National Park, in Colorado. JD had to trade his horse for a green Chevy Impala said to have about two hundred horses under its hood. But whether on horse or in a car, most of the general public seemed to have unduly high respect for him as an officer of the law, especially since he looked and sounded like he could easily bust your arms and legs on a whim. JD discovered several ways to attain a Rocky Mountain high, while living in comfort that his daddy and mama would never believe, were they still alive.

The next two rungs on his career ladder were Glacier and Yosemite National Parks. Like the previous two, these assignments kept him living in middle-class luxury, in spite of a somewhat paltry salary. Tens years into his job, and he had only advanced from level 3 to level 5, on the U.S. Civil Service pay scale that topped out at level 15. At this rate, it would be another ten years before he got halfway to the top. This was unacceptable to J. D. Pickett.

He continued to rationalize his ripping off of tourists by believing that those damned feds were so stingy that he had to keep supplementing his salary to maintain a decent lifestyle. His time at Glacier Park was okay for gathering extra pay, but the extracurricular action there was slow.

By contrast, Yosemite was wild, wooly, and wealthy. Hippies from the San Francisco Bay Area were taking over practically the entire valley. While valley air was once polluted by hundreds of wood-burning campfires, it was now more often thickly tainted with the combustion products of top-grade marijuana. Hippie visitors readily agreed not to trash the park if Ranger Pickett didn't trash them. JD found his supplemental remuneration of free victuals, free pot, and free love most enjoyable.

He moved westward, ever westward, staying one step ahead of having his illegal activities discovered. Twenty years into his park service career of law enforcement found JD at Hawai'i Volcanoes National Park. By now, even mentally limited JD had a plan for the rest of his life. Adding in his marine time, he had to work only six years in Hawai'i to qualify for full voluntary retirement from his federal employment. He vowed that during those six years, he would be especially watchful for opportunities to supplement his regular salary. What the heck, maybe lady luck would shine on him and provide a huge score in the autumn of his career.

Then, he would go back to Alabama, move into the old family house that he'd inherited from daddy and mama when they died, and watch hired hands do all of the farm work. Meanwhile, he'd be guzzling RC Cola, beer, and bourbon as he rocked in the comfort of daddy's favorite chair on the front porch.

This was Jefferson Davis Pickett's plan and state of mind when he disembarked from the United Airlines flight into Hilo, where he was met by Fritz Kamph, the park superintendent. This was still JD's plan and state of mind four years later, as he and tourist Hak started dancing around each other to see which one would blink first.

CHAPTER 30

A TWENTY-FIVE WATT BULB

Friday morning. December 10.

The Don, Rob, Andy, Ben, and Allan huddled in the conference room to discuss discoveries of yesterday in the Āhua area. At The Don's request, Andy started.

"The new cracks range from hairline to open as much as an inch. And there are lots of them. I think we all know that new cracks aren't necessarily cause for alarm, though. Good old Kīlauea has been busted up this way many a time...without erupting."

They all knew that the volcano acted like a heap of loose blocks, sort of a giant version of a kid's sand pile, poised to slip and slide with little if any help from magma (or little Billy) pushing at it.

There was something else, too, that Andy was straining to remember...something from one of his classes at Stanford. It had to do with the configuration of the area of greatest uplift...that bull's eye zone at the nub of the boomerang. The width of the edge where four feet of uplift dropped off rapidly to only several inches might be important.

"Uh, I don't remember exactly, but...I think the fact that the patch of greatest uplift around Āhua drops off pretty fast out along the arms of our boomerang tells us that new magma is really shallow under there. There's some rule of thumb...something like the width of the steep drop-off being a reasonably good indication of the depth to the magma pushing from below. I need to double check this in one of my old textbooks. The idea sure fits with Ben's thinking that tremor is shallow."

Just as Andy was finishing his point, a burst of tremor began to record on the bank of seismograms by the tourist window.

"Oh boy! Ride 'em cowboy," shouted The Don. Before getting interested in volcanoes, he had been a ranch hand in Montana.

The four stared at the instruments, transfixed, until tremor died away. Next, analytical Rob got into the discussion, with his take on what might be happening.

"Andy's right. New cracks alone aren't necessarily cause for alarm. But the fumarole that Andy and I found is unmistakable evidence of new heat. That new heat, combined with the four feet of uplift, means magma right below…really shallow if Andy and Ben are right. And tremor means magma *on the move*, not just hangin' out stagnant down there. I think we're sittin' on a dangerous situation."

Rob looked at The Don "…maybe as dangerous as a frisky Montana bronco."

Allan uncharacteristically jumped into the conversation at this point, without being asked. "Remember what I said at our meeting two weeks ago, about measuring some unusual electrical currents?"

Three heads nodded yes.

"Well you didn't pay much attention to me then, but I think you will now."

In fact, the entire staff had gone through its head-nodding routine as a way to hurry Allan along, so he wouldn't get off on another of his obtuse geophysical primers. Now was the time for Allan to expound. He positioned himself beside the map of uplift, still tacked up on the bulletin board. He began what the others hoped would not degenerate into another academic-style lecture.

"As you know, I tend to work alone, or with Jane, Jeb, or Bruce when I need an extra pair of hands. And I tend to experiment with all sorts of instruments to see if Kīlauea gives off geophysical signals of what she's up to."

Heads were already starting to nod, not in understanding and appreciation, but in a let's-get-on-with-it sense of urgency. Allan understood the sign language.

"To make a long story short, one of my experiments has been to pound a couple of metal posts into the ground at various spacings and connect them with a piece of copper wire. Then a meter tells me whether or not the ground between the electrode posts is carrying an electrical potential."

Andy, Rob, and The Don had studied *some* geophysics on the way to a Ph.D. in geology. They had a notion where Allan was headed. They raised their hands to chest level and started spinning them in opposite circular motions universally understood to mean "Get on with it!"

Allan took the hint.

"Well, four months ago my readings indicated no unusual electrical potentials anywhere on Kīlauea. Then two months ago, about the same time that the bursts of tremor started to come in, small potentials started to show up. They've kept increasing with each remeasurement, and just two weeks ago, shortly before we started our leveling binge, I measured enough potential to light up a twenty-five-watt bulb."

By this time, even head-in-the-clouds Allan could see that he had an audience he could play like a well-tuned piano. He kept them in suspense briefly by extracting a large red handkerchief from a hip pocket. He slowly and loudly blew his nose, even though there was no bodily fluid reason to do so. He continued this ruse by carefully refolding the handkerchief before reinserting it into his hip pocket.

"Well, my fine geologist colleagues, this electrical-potential anomaly is centered right over Āhua. From there it radiates out down into the east rift zone and up into the caldera. It's something we geophysicists call a streaming potential, because it originates when a fluid streams, or flows, through a porous and permeable medium."

Impatience was once again showing on the faces of his listeners. This was getting way too academic.

"In layman terms, my measurements indicate that normally cool groundwater has been heated. Once heated, the water started to rise buoyantly and to circulate through the cracked and broken rocks of the volcano. That circulating water is called a hydrothermal-convection system. It's basically a giant underground version of a roiling pot of about-to-boil water on the kitchen stove. The fumarole that Rob and Andy found is steam leaking from this underground hot water."

His audience found the story very convincing…further hard evidence that a new batch of magma was pushing up into Kīlauea. The Don knew that it was time for him to take charge. He thanked Allan and called the rest of the staff to the conference room.

"Okay troops. We've got plenty of evidence of an increasingly restless volcano underfoot. We've got bursts of tremor, getting shallower with time. We've got as much as four feet of uplift during the past six months. This also seems to be saying that magma isn't far below. We've got new ground cracks near Āhua, one of them bleeding off steam from a body of underground hot water. And we've got Allan's electrical whatchamacallit.

"Liz, Jeb, Bruce, Jane. Talk to Andy, Rob, and Allan later about the details of their recent discoveries. Meanwhile, here's our battle plan, before we go public with any announcements of impending eruption.

"Andy, Rob, and anyone they want as helpers will revisit the area of new cracks and the fumarole near Āhua, at least once a day. I want to see a map of those cracks updated daily. And I want to see a daily plot of the temperature of the new fumarole right beside that map. If anything seems unusual, I want to be notified immediately, day or night, weekday or weekend.

"Ben, I want you watching for additional bursts of tremor, as closely as Andy usually watches the tourist window. Again, anything unusual gets to me right away.

"Everybody be especially alert to volcano behavior that seems restless and changing. Talk to each other. Don't sit on an idea, thinking it may hatch into something significant later. And remember, there is an alarm wired into my house. That will be triggered when so many earthquakes and tremor bursts happen that our seismometers can't keep up with the shaking. That's what Kīlauea has always done right before past eruptions, and we should expect that that's what she'll do before the next one. If you get a late-night phone call from me, you'll know why without thinking."

With a final "What do you say?" from The Don in a louder-than-normal voice, the entire staff stood with raised right hands clenched into fists.

The sounds of *NE PLUS HAUSTAE AUT OBRUTAE URBES* once again rang through the conference room, from twelve voices in unison.

Tourists at the window were surely confused.

The ghost of Thomas Augustus Jaggar II surely grinned.

Pele continued to slumber, although somewhat restlessly.

CHAPTER 31

TWO WEEKS 'TIL CHRISTMAS

That weekend and most of the following week were eerily quiet at HVO. Kīlauea was in a holding pattern. No new cracks were discovered near Āhua. The temperature of the fumarole hovered around 110 degrees Fahrenheit, warm to the hand. Two more short bursts of tremor were recorded, one Monday morning and the other on Thursday afternoon. Ben could find no evidence in their squiggly lines that the magma triggering this shaking was any shallower than it had been during the previous couple of weeks. Regular earthquakes were being registered at a normal background rate for the volcano. Allan's streaming potential never got beyond the twenty-five-watt bulb strength, a pretty dim light. This dimness developed into a new in-house joke about the level of intellectual brightness at USGS headquarters.

"What's the level of that streaming potential today, Allan?"

"Well, it's still resting at one Reston."

Beyond such background humor, everyone at HVO was on edge, expecting a sudden daytime convulsion from Kīlauea or, more likely, a late-night phone call from The Don. A long string of previous timing perversity suggested that eruption would begin anytime other than during working or waking hours. Relaxation at the workplace was a lost luxury, temporarily they all hoped.

Relaxation at home was elusive. Christmas was less than two weeks away. Gift buying, tree decorating, and partying with friends were planned family activities. Past experience had taught understanding spouses and friends that an HVO employee might be called to duty at any time, damaging one's social life. What spouses and friends didn't know, at the insistence of The Don, was that yet another year-end holiday season might very well be disrupted by the antics of Pele.

As anyone who knew how to read her signs could see, Pele was getting increasingly restless. She was still abed deep in the roots of Halemaʻumaʻu, but a spate of dreams was interfering with sound sleep. One in particular was recurring. It carried a message to remind Christians that theirs was not the only religion on earth…and that they were latecomers to the Hawaiian scene.

What better way to make this dream come true than to emerge violently from her Halemaʻumaʻu home, disrupting the lives of people celebrating Christ's birthday? If She did so, She would not, *could* not, be ignored.

Centuries earlier, when her sister Hiiaka stole her lover, Lohian, Pele had staged eruptions as punishment, the molten rock equivalent of taking an unforgiving cat-o'-nine-tails to the wrongdoers. Not a scheming sister, not an unfaithful lover, and not even a praying Christian could ignore being the target of one of Pele's lava flows.

CHAPTER 32

THE FATAL BUG

If the staff at HVO was tense, Hak was harried. The holiday season itself presented no high-stress personal problems. His family ties had been permanently severed long ago, when he took his Harley and moved to the Big Island. As a reclusive bachelor, he had no other-gender socializing duties to think about. Plus, he and his two hui partners made it a practice to share business but not pleasure pursuits. He had absolutely no social obligations that came with Christmas, New Year, or any other holiday.

Hak was concerned about his main cash crop. His partners had harvested and packaged enough pakalōlō during the past ten days that he should make another inventory deposit in the Koa'e warehouse vault, soon. That was fine and mechanically easy to accomplish, but Hak was still haunted by his evaluation of the character of Ranger J. D. Pickett and the not-so-subtle hints thrown out by that guy when they talked last week. Hak didn't want to encounter Pickett again, but might very well do so if he reentered the park, the domain of Pickett's law-enforcement jurisdiction.

After considering his options, Hak decided that he should take the chance of being stopped by Pickett again (and maybe searched?), rather than let the mold and feral pigs of Puna ruin thousands, or even tens of thousands of dollars worth of inventory. Hak was pretty certain that Pickett could be bribed if necessary. He was familiar with this type of person and could offer a very attractive bribe, in either cash or crop.

Early Wednesday morning, Hak met his partners at the transfer point along that obscure dirt road in Puna. The second round of Operation Pakalōlō

Transfer was underway. Two more backpacks full of the valuable bricks were loaded into the luggage space of the Land Cruiser. Hak headed for the park.

He entered without incident. A smiling curly-haired brunette at the entry booth waved him through as he held up his Golden Eagle pass. Another fifteen minutes of uneventful driving, and Hak was parked at what was becoming his personal trailhead. He put fifty pounds of pakalōlō bricks in his backpack.

The first trip to the underground warehouse went without a glitch, as did the second. He swept away his footprints on the second trip out. Hak now had about $200,000 of inventory in safe storage. He smiled to himself knowing that in less than three weeks, he would be withdrawing most of this product for the next Gambler's Special flight to Las Vegas.

What Hak didn't know, as he left the park and headed back to Hilo, was that the friendly rangerette at the entry booth had recognized the Toyota's license number as a "hot one." She had immediately radioed chief law enforcement specialist J. D. Pickett. Pickett surreptitiously followed Hak to his trailhead parking spot.

There, while Hak was on his first trip to the lava tube, Pickett slid under the Land Cruiser and attached a powerful miniature radio-beacon transmitter to the frame, effectively hidden from the view of even an overly observant grease monkey. With his receiver, Pickett was now able to locate and track Hak's Toyota up to ten miles away. He had this Hak guy under his thumb.

CHAPTER 33

MESSAGES FROM MAGMA

Given the events of the day, Friday the 17th could have been mistaken for the 13th. Maybe the tone was set early on, when all HVO employees had to walk under a ladder to enter the building. Frank was on the top rung, hanging a Christmas wreath over the door to help celebrate the spirit of the season. And maybe Pele, who does not celebrate Christmas or other Christian holidays, was somehow responsible for what happened. Life was about to get messy at HVO.

All was quiet and routine throughout the morning and during the noontime brown-bag lunch around the conference-room table. As the demands of work tasks permitted, the staff exchanged homemade Christmas gifts. Ben gave everyone a dozen anthuriums. Other gifts included such consumables as Santa-shaped cookies, pohā jam, ʻōhelo-berry wine, banana bread, and traditional rock-hard and steel-dense fruitcake. Though strictly illegal in a government building, at least this was the ruling from ultra-conservative headquarters, the staff members would feast on alcoholic fruit punch and tropical pūpūs at the end of the workday. In deference to the distant bureaucrats, this celebration would take place in Howard's workshop where even a hint that the beverage might be alcoholic would be out of public view.

But the party never got started.

At exactly 2:37 PM, a burst of tremor began to shake the seismometers of the HVO network. At first, this was not considered unusual or cause for special concern; there had been plenty of bursts of tremor during the past three months. But twenty minutes later, when tremor continued unabated, Ben was wondering what to make of this longer than usual shake. None of the previous bursts had lasted more than ten minutes.

Everyone knew that continuous tremor went with eruption. The entire staff scanned the horizon, from east to south to west, from the tourist window. No fountains of fiery molten rock were visible.

After forty-seven minutes, tremor ceased and the crew relaxed a bit. Ben did one of his calculations for depth; he discovered nothing to heighten his concern. But he was getting worried that his technique might not be able to recognize small, yet important differences in how shallow the rising magma might be.

While Ben was pondering the long new burst of tremor, Andy and Bruce were scouting the area around Āhua. They were on the daily run to measure the amount of opening across the cracks discovered there just eight days earlier, and to search for any new breaks in the pāhoehoe lava surface. The area had been unchanged since Thursday the 9th. What they found on Friday the 17th, though, was as startling as the extra-long burst of tremor. Since just yesterday, several new cracks, with those telltale stretched-to-snapping grass rootlets, had formed.

Andy lifted a metal measuring tape from his backpack. He rolled out a couple of feet and handed the end of the tape to Bruce.

"Walk this end of the tape over there, to the masonry nail on the other side of the belt of new cracks."

Andy positioned himself over another nail they had earlier pounded into pāhoehoe lava at the north edge of cracking while Bruce pulled out enough tape to reach the nail at the south edge, about thirty feet away. Andy pulled the tape taught and read the distance. He mumbled softly, "hmmm" and "holy shit."

"The distance is seven inches more than yesterday. The ground is being pulled apart. And you know what, Bruce? I can't hold my finger over the fumarole anymore because of the heat. The steam hissing sounds louder, too."

While Andy pondered these changes, Bruce scrounged around until he found a dead branch fallen from a nearby ʻōhiʻa tree. He attached a thermometer to the branch and positioned the thermometer at the base of the steam plume for about a minute, long enough for the instrument to attain the temperature of the steam. He extracted the thermometer, read the temperature, and shouted, "Wow!" in both pain and surprise.

"Jesus, I shouldn't have touched this thing. I've already got puffy blisters on my thumb and index finger. The reading is a hundred eighty degrees. That's seventy degrees hotter than yesterday."

Andy wrote the temperature in his notebook, along with the new distance between nails. He and Bruce snooped around some more. Both noticed that small crystals of yellow sulfur now lined the lip of the fumarole crack. A little steam had also begun to hiss from a nearby new crack.

"Bruce, buddy. We've got multiple messages from magma. That stuff can't be far beneath our boots. Let's get back to HVO."

Andy retrieved a two-way radio from his backpack and reported their findings to HVO. He had no idea that an unusually long burst of tremor had stopped just a few minutes earlier. Andy's concern grew by an order of magnitude when told about the tremor. Relaxation at HVO was interrupted when told about the new cracks and hotter fumarole.

Andy and Bruce put tape and thermometer away, and left. Back at HVO, the entire staff gathered in the conference room. In spite of gut-wrenching inner turmoil, The Don projected considerable outer calm. He asked Rob, Andy, and Ben to work over the weekend. They would continue intense monitoring of seismicity and ground-truth observations in the Āhua area.

"I want the rest of you to go home. Try to relax and carry on with your personal holiday plans. Don't get too far from a phone, though."

The Don explained that within an hour he would start a series of phone calls needed to notify local officials and USGS headquarters that Kīlauea was on Code Orange Alert. This was the official way of publicly announcing that if the volcano continued her current level of unrest, eruption was possible within the next two weeks.

Deep in the bowels of her Halemaʻumaʻu home, Pele was laughing at the frantic scientists attempting to anticipate her next moves, as She continued to slowly awaken. Apparently, stretching and thrashing about in her fluid-filled bed had not only lifted and shook Kīlauea, but it had also created new cracks in her coverings, allowing steam to leak out at the surface. From considerable past experience, She knew that the scientists would scurry and scamper about, doing the best they could to gather enough information to anticipate the volcano's next moves. But they would always be at least one step behind, missing a key piece in their attempts to solve the puzzle. She would see to that.

CHAPTER 34

CODE ORANGE ALERT

The Don returned to his office, opened the upper right drawer of his desk, and retrieved a list of names with phone numbers to be called about official public statements of volcano unrest. The first call went to headquarters. Given five time zones between Virginia and Hawaiʻi, USGS employees would be home, Christmas shopping, or partying.

Nonetheless, when The Don's superiors returned to their offices the following Monday, they would expect to have received notification of his announcing Code Orange Alert before anyone else. As all properly trained bureaucrats know, knowledge is power, and the Reston crew wanted to be the first to notify the Hawaiian congressional delegation of possible volcanic action in their home state. This made the headquarters staff look smart, responsive, and devoted to congressmen…good for them personally and good for the future of the USGS. The Don left a series of voice-mail messages. He covered his butt from any possible accusation of tardy notification by immediately sending a backup fax to each name on the headquarters list.

The next call went to Fritz Kamph, the park superintendent. Jack Richards explained that if eruption occurred, it was expected to be away from heavily visited areas of the park. Fritz thanked Richards and said that he would inform his staff immediately. He would also post the Code Orange Alert at the visitors' center, for the public to read and digest. Even if eruption did not occur during their visit, Kamph knew that tourists would later speak fondly and excitedly about his park, spreading the word and hopefully increasing future visitation numbers. The way the park system worked, more visitations should translate into a larger budget. Eruption was a cash cow to Kamph, and he would milk this beast for every squirt of money he could get.

Finally, The Don made a call to notify all levels of government on the Big Island. Pronouncements of this sort were always funneled through Frank "Fuzzy" Chee, the Big Island's minister of civil defense, at his long-standing request and insistence.

Chee listened to Jack Richards, thanked him for the information about Kīlauea, and returned the handset of his phone back into its lavender cradle. The fingers of his left hand combed his goatee, as he evaluated the situation. Chee understood that an eruption, if one occurred, would most likely stay entirely within the national park, outside his jurisdiction. Still, he would personally spread the message of Code Orange Alert throughout the Big Island, thereby gaining considerable public exposure and appearing to be one of the island's most-knowledgeable civil servants. As a personal bonus, if the properties or lives of Big Island citizens were somehow damaged or destroyed by eruption, he could not be held responsible. In fact, he would be able to take credit for minimizing such losses, as the original source of warning the public about impending disaster.

A grinning Chee immediately arranged for a taped TV interview in his office. He appeared that night on the six o'clock and again on the ten o'clock Big Island TV news reports. He sounded professorial and intelligent, goatee waggling in sync with his lower jaw. Fortunately for Chee's public image, no foreign objects dropped from his moving chin whiskers during TV taping. Uninitiated viewers might have concluded that he was a world-renowned volcano expert, rather than simply a civil servant conduit for information.

Once the initial TV news was broadcast, all Big Island radio stations started to carry Chee's story. The next day's edition of the *Hilo Nūpepa* ran an extensive interview with Chee as their lead story. The entire front page was printed over an orange-colored background, to emphasize that Code Orange Alert was in effect at Kīlauea. The *Honolulu Advertiser* ran excerpts from the Hilo extravaganza. Even just the possibility of an eruption was an opportunity for enhanced personal aggrandizement for civil servant Chee. He certainly made the most of it.

By contrast, eruption, including events leading up to and subsequent to, was treated as a source of scientific data and discovery for The Don and his staff. They sought knowledge, not fame. They hoped to contribute to HVO's motto, no more burned or buried cities, in the process.

Hak watched the TV version of announcing Code Orange Alert at Kīlauea and read more of the details in Saturday's newspaper. He recognized Chee as a fellow Rotarian. Hak understood that either or both of his plantations in the Puna District could be destroyed by an eruption along the east rift zone. Dr. Jack Richards's talk to his Rotary group had explained that. But there was nothing he could do to control the volcano. Besides, his pakalōlō inventory was safely stashed in the Koa'e, a place that Richards had singled out as virtually eruption free. The sales proceeds from inventory could carry him long enough to develop a new plantation, if eruption made that necessary.

Josh and Valerie heard nothing about the Code Orange Alert. They had been to Pāhoa to barter for food and drinks on Thursday. By that evening, they were back at their isolated pakalōlō garden…smoking, and talking about what they wanted to do with the rest of their lives. Josh kept insisting that he would be perfectly happy to spend the rest of his life right there, with the occasional walk into Pāhoa for food, drink and conversation.

Valerie believed he was sincere. In fact, she was becoming concerned that Josh was simply losing an appreciation of the joy of living, in whatever lifestyle he might choose. Valerie, too, was happy living there in the rainforest of Puna…for the time being. But ever since her most recent visit back home, she had been thinking more about reestablishing a life somewhere in an environment that her parents considered to be civilization. She and the parents still shared a strong bond of mutual love and respect. Furthermore, each visit home reminded her that she still enjoyed many material things. She realized that she wanted more than her present subsistence level of living. Just so an increasingly materialistic lifestyle didn't include those crazy New York City banking and financial-market scenes, overrun with predictably dull preppies cum Ivy League finishing school.

Chaotic California would be preferable.

If She could only be seen, Pele was smirking in the knowledge that her mood swings were creating such a variety of strokes for different folks. With a growing probability of eruption, Kamph lusted after more money for his park. Chee longed to be recognized as a savior, to be adored by the public. And USGS leaders in Reston once again endowed themselves with the intelligence and knowledge of the actual workers in the field.

A common theme across this diverse gallery of people was enhancing one's personal image. It had long disturbed Pele that the scientists would work long hard hours only to have their discoveries usurped and manipulated by others in various bureaucratic food chains. She was doubly upset when even the scientists succumbed to hubris. On the other hand, their occasional games of one-upmanship with each other guaranteed that they would never fully recognize the big picture...never truly understand how volcanoes work. Pele knew that the human inability to focus outward, rather than on personal gain, would assure her place as a goddess forever.

She was also thinking more about the possibility of moving to a new volcano home. She had enjoyed Kīlauea over the millennia, but parts of the place were getting uncomfortably crowded...especially the rapidly developing housing areas in the Puna District. She was starting to wonder if She should do an extensive remodel, which would include major reduction in the burgeoning housing density of humans, or just move away from their mess.

She decided to sleep on the thought, for the time being. As She closed her eyes, She rolled over in bed, sending one more shudder of tremor through her volcano home.

CHAPTER 35

STEADY AS SHE GOES

Eight o'clock. Monday morning, December 20.

Allan, Bruce, Frank, Liz, Howard, Jane, Jeb, and Kabana arrived at work perky, rested, and smilingly happy. There had been no late-night phone calls from The Don over the weekend. Instead, each of these cheerful creatures had completed preparations for Christmas, which was now only five days away.

In stark contrast, The Don, Rob, Andy, and Ben were dog-bone tired. They looked like they had been chewed up and spit out by some prehistoric carnivore. Blood-shot eyes, unshaven faces, thoroughly wrinkled clothes, and more than a hint of BO mimicked the characteristics of skid-row down-and-outers in Hilo's Mamo Theater district, rather than attributes of highly educated and well-paid research scientists.

They had set up housekeeping at HVO. Two army-surplus cots and sleeping bags were the bedroom furniture. The Don's wife, Martha, brought meals in the morning and evening. Ben's wife, Stishia, provided a noon meal. Bachelors Andy and Rob were happy to eat anyone else's cooking.

All four stayed awake during daylight hours. Ben and The Don watched the incoming seismic recordings closely, while Andy and Rob visited the Āhua area two or three times each day. At night, two of the crew stayed awake to watch for any unusual surges of tremor or earthquakes while the other two dozed…in three-hour shifts. And what was the reward for massive loss of sleep? Nothing…at least nothing in terms of increased volcano unrest. But that was reward enough, depending on one's point of view.

The Don had been through so many eruptions during his career that he suffered from burnout. He would be pleased to go into retirement without another volcanic crisis added to his résumé, thank you. He was unenthused about this need to frantically scurry about in response to Kīlauea's whims, in yet another exercise of trying to save people and their possessions from volcanic violence. He was quite ready to change places with Joe Citizen, by putting himself, Martha, and a new retirement house at risk on that piece of island paradise along Mauna Loa's southwest rift zone.

Ben's feelings were mixed. Like The Don, Ben had already experienced several eruptions. His adrenaline still surged in pleasure and excitement, though, each time Kīlauea came alive. Yet he knew that he owed his family more of his time. And he knew that he should address this issue before family bonds suffered irreparable damage. Maybe it was time for him to return full time to the anthurium patch, and leave volcano studies to a younger seismologist…maybe…right after this next eruption.

As youngsters and relative newcomers to the study of restless volcanoes, Andy and Rob were openly hoping for a major, even record-setting eruption real soon. Their résumés included lots of empty spaces that could use filling.

Allan? Well, Allan couldn't be bothered to think about much other than a new piece of equipment that Howard was building for him. That doodad would help him show these geologist doubters the value of geophysics in understanding volcanoes!

Monday and Tuesday passed quietly. A few brief bursts of tremor were recorded, but nothing unusual enough to cause increased concern. The new cracks and fumarole near Āhua were unchanged. Code Orange Alert was still in effect.

But by Wednesday morning, public awareness of a possible eruption was back at ground zero, right where it had been before Code Orange had been announced. The Don was providing daily updates to all official parties on his to-call list, but in typical media fashion, no follow-up stories were appearing. Fuzzy Chee stayed quiet for fear of being tainted with the reputation of crying wolf one too many times. The lack of continuing information prompted John Q. Public to reasonably conclude that Kīlauea was no longer threatening to erupt.

Even the experts at HVO were concerned about the crying-wolf syndrome. They faced an almost insurmountable challenge. Big Island government officials and the public wanted information, answers, and predictions in black and white, rather than shades of gray. However, eruption prediction is a game of chance, an attempt to define the probability of what is to come and when. The odds of being right with a specific prediction were about the same as consistently winning at craps. The house always comes out ahead.

Trying to make the public aware and appreciative of these realities was a bit like pissing into the wind. You always ended up with something undesirable on your face, to say nothing about the shoes, pant legs, and shirt. The HVO crew would play the hand they were dealt. They could do no more, and would do no less.

Hak was one of that multitude of citizens unconcerned by the fact that Code Orange Alert was still in effect. Yes, his present concern was about Kīlauea, but only with regard to making one last deposit of pakalōlō into the Koa'e warehouse before his next trip to one of the world's highest risk places, Las Vegas.

Hak reasoned that Christmas Eve would hold the least likelihood of an encounter with J. D. Pickett. He figured that even that cretin would relax a bit for the holidays. Most federal employees were dismissed a few hours early from their jobs that day. Hak would make his last deposit of the year during the late afternoon of December 24.

Then, he would relax in his Hilo home until that early January departure to Vegas. When he got home from the selling trip, he planned to buy himself a special "Christmas" gift, a Cessna 210 and enough lessons to become a licensed pilot. He had plans of expanding and accelerating the distribution and sale of Kīlauea Kiya, up and down the Hawaiian island chain, with his own wings.

CHAPTER 36

CODE RED ON CHRISTMAS EVE

As public awareness of Code Orange Alert plummeted to near zero, Kīlauea became increasingly restless. When Rob and Andy visited the Āhua area on Wednesday morning, they discovered two more inches of opening across the zone of cracks and five more degrees of temperature at the fumarole. Enough brightly colored sulfur now encrusted the fuming crack to give the impression of huge yellow lips, exhaling white smoke.

That same morning, three long bursts of tremor shook all of the seismometers on Kīlauea. Ben still couldn't determine whether the source of tremor was rising closer to the surface. But he already knew the source was well up in the mountain itself. And the increasing number of minutes of tremor each day translated into more minutes of molten rock flowing around down there. Magma was increasingly on the move.

The pattern of increases in crack opening, fumarole temperature, and duration of tremor continued for the next thirty-six hours. The pace of unrest was accelerating, and this was a pretty universally agreed upon sign, within the volcano brotherhood, that a volcano was at the verge of eruption.

At 1:43 on Friday afternoon, following a sixty-nine minute burst of tremor, The Don declared Code Red Alert. This announced that eruption was possible within twenty-four hours. The usual phone calls were made. Santa was already making his rounds in Reston.

The Code Red warning was almost universally ignored in Hawai'i. After all, it was only a statement of a "possibility" of something happening within the next twenty-four hours. Santa Claus was scheduled to arrive on the Big Island in just a few hours, following his trans-Pacific flight from California. Top priority for almost everyone was to observe the holiday.

On his way out the door, heading home, Kamph posted Code Red announcements on bulletin boards. But even before his thumb pushed in that first tack, the entire park staff was gone, on official early dismissal. All visitor facilities were already locked.

Fuzzy Chee was not about to be the one to interfere with his constituents' enjoyment of Christmas. He could lose a lot of popularity by being the harbinger of badly timed inaccurate news. Because he did not act on Jack Richards's phone call about Code Red, no one outside the national park knew of the heightened threat of eruption.

While the rest of the world went about enjoying Christmas Eve, once again The Don would have to give up spending that holiday at home. Someone had to be at the office, just in case Code Red transformed into red-hot lava, from those two incendiary-sounding words. Being The Don meant being that someone.

At four o'clock that December 24th afternoon, he wished the rest of the HVO staff a Mele Kalikimaka and sent them home.

CHAPTER 37

THE LAVA TUBE SCUFFLE

At four o'clock, Hak was entering the park with his load of pakalōlō bricks beneath the dirty blanket in the back of his Land Cruiser. There was no ranger at the entrance booth. He cruised on through and headed toward the Koa'e.

At four o'clock, Jefferson Davis Pickett was in his government-owned house, no more than two hundred yards from the entrance booth. He was watching Hawai'i Five-O on TV, while feasting on pork rinds and a moon pie. This tasty southern food was being washed down with alternating swallows of ice-cold RC Cola and beer. Since he never had been able to decide which beverage he liked better, he preferred to drink them back-to-back. His culinary tastes were as finely honed as his education.

As usual, his radio-signal receiver was on and within reach, right there on the coffee table beside his chair. He hadn't seen Mr. Hak for nine days, since attaching the signal transmitter to his car. JD was kind of antsy for another encounter; that would help make his Christmas a day to remember.

At first, he thought the ear-piercing whining signal was part of the cops-and-robbers TV program. But soon it was obvious that his receiver was picking up the program he loved most. His prey Hak was somewhere nearby, on the move.

JD left the TV blaring, bolted outside, and jumped into his ranger car. All the important tools of his trade were already there…revolver, shotgun, mace, handcuffs, nightstick, and flashlight. The direction indicator and range finder of his radio-signal receiver showed Hak to be about a half-mile away and moving southward. JD grinned, knowing that tourist Hak was headed for his favorite park place, the Koaʻe. JD followed, sure that he was only a couple of minutes behind his quarry.

At the now-familiar spot along the Hilina Pali road, he approached Hak's parked Land Cruiser slowly, hand on holster. JD made no attempt to hide his presence; he was ready for action. But Hak wasn't there. The hood of the Toyota was still warm…hardly a surprise, but it made JD feel smart to copy this investigative technique of his favorite TV character, Detective Steve McGarrett of Hawaiʻi Five-O.

The Toyota was locked. JD peeked in and saw nothing but a dirty and rumpled blanket draped over something lumpy in the luggage space. As he scanned the ground near the Land Cruiser, he saw no signs of what Hak might be up to…except for a set of roughly size 11 boot prints leading off in a westerly direction. It was time to put one of his truly accomplished talents to work…tracking. Back in Tallapoosa County, his daddy had taught him well in the art of tracking possum, deer, and black bear. Daddy also taught him to track coon, "In two meanins of the word, if ya git ma drift" daddy had liked to say, with a twisted smile across his nearly toothless face.

First, JD moved his ranger patrol car smack dab in front of Hak's Toyota, another trick that McGarrett used to slow a crook's getaway. Then, he began tracking what his warped mind thought of as the Hawaiian equivalent of an Alabama two-footed coon. The job was easy; Hak was heavy footed and seemed unworried about concealing his route.

Twenty minutes later, JD was standing at the edge of a huge open crack, straining to see motion or hear the sounds of a human down there. Soon there was no need to strain. Someone was deep down in the crack happily singing a ditty whose words sounded like complete nonsense…something about pulu and hāpuʻu. Given the season, JD figured it was a Hawaiian Christmas carol never heard in Alabama, or D.C., or in any of his other earlier duty stations. With a full array of police weapons on his belt, he quietly began his descent into the crack.

Down below in the lava tube, Hak had no idea that JD was in pursuit. In fact, he was in an unusually festive mood. He had entered the park without seeing a soul, and presumably without being seen by a soul. He was now positioning the newly delivered bricks, the first of two loads, with the rest of the warehouse inventory, on the lava bench. Everything was going according to plan.

This would be a special Christmas for him, in its own way. While the children of happy families enjoyed visions of sugarplums dancing in theirs heads,

Hak was envisioning his Cessna 210. In an uncharacteristic fit of nostalgia, he even remembered some happy holiday times as a young child growing up at home. His parents had tried hard to make a little seem like a lot. Yes, most material things had been lacking, but there was always the family laughter, even from angry Greg at times. These memories brought an unseen smile to his face and a Don Ho-ish rendition of "Pulu Grows on Hāpu'u" to his lips.

Life was good at the moment. He stood silently and thought about that for a while. In spite of his evil ways, he seemed blessed. Then he turned to climb out and head back to the Land Cruiser for the second load. His flashlight illuminated something unexpected...first the boots, and then the muscular torso of what he immediately recognized as Ranger J. D. Pickett. Pickett's face was wearing a sinister-looking grin.

Pickett aimed his flashlight back and forth from Hak to neatly stacked packages on a low lava bench along the lava-tube wall. A brief conversation began. "Well, well ma friend. What have we here? Are ya gonna tell me that you're Santa hisself, and that this is where ya store the Christmas goodies before delivery?"

Because his entire park service career had included contact with marijuana in its various forms of packaging, JD immediately recognized those bricks for what they were. From the tone of voice and facial expression, Hak knew that Pickett knew. And intellectually slow though he was, Pickett knew that Hak knew that Pickett knew. Both were playing with full decks so far as the content of the brick packages were concerned.

Hak's mind was spinning with confusion and possibilities. How should he handle this guy? He decided it was time to play the bribe card. What else could he do?

"Well, how nice to have you drop in for a Christmas visit, Ranger Pickett. I certainly could be your Santa Claus and a very generous one at that. Yes, you're right. These packages are gifts. One or more could be yours."

Hak aimed his flashlight beam at JD's face and tried in vain to read meaning into a opaquely blank expression.

"But if these gifts seem clumsy or aren't exactly what's on your list for Santa this year, perhaps a stack of Ben Franklin photos on fine green paper would be appropriate. I keep those in Hilo."

The two of them held their ground, facing each other no more than six feet apart, flashlight beams trying to illuminate and anticipate any quick or tricky moves by the other guy.

Again, because of his on-the-job experiences, JD knew exactly what was being offered. He was thinking as fast as his small volume of gray matter allowed. He imagined two possibilities.

Number one: He could work out a level of bribe agreeable to both of them, and let Mr. Tourist Hak go free. JD was sure he had the upper hand in this kind of deal making. Or, number two: He could arrest Hak, turn in just enough of those bricks to put the guy in jail for many years, and secretly keep the rest for himself.

JD had no inkling that what he had stumbled onto was part of something really big, that this was only a single arm in a large, complex, and very profitable set of drug tentacles. Instead, JD assumed that this was simply a one-time situation, a take-it-or-leave-it-now setup. After a few moments of silently figuring this and a few other angles, JD settled on option number two.

With number one, Hak might turn the tables and find a way to blackmail him. He might even come after him with violence. JD didn't doubt that he could best Hak in a one-on-one hand-to-hand fight. But a hired assassin with the cover of darkness held a different potential balance of power.

With option two, though, Hak would be in jail, out of circulation at least until JD had retired and moved back to that secure family farm in Alabama. Hak might claim foul play, that there had been much more pakalōlō and that Ranger Pickett had taken it. But chances were that a policeman's word would trump an illegal drug producer's.

So, number two it was. JD stepped forward, closing the distance between them.

"I'm 'fraid I got t'rest ya, bubba. Y'all come quietly now."

Hak struck out with his flashlight, his only weapon. A blow caught JD on the left cheek. The puny plastic instrument seemed to bounce off the two thick parallel ribs of scar tissue there. With his much more substantial U.S. Government-issued law enforcement flashlight, JD pounded metal down on Hak's head. Hak went to his knees. JD had him cuffed before he could begin to recover. It was a blood-free scuffle.

While this short-lived brawl was underway, an observant person sensitive to motion would have noticed that the ground had begun to inexplicably shake. The motion was much more than the jostling and banging of bodies.

But by the time these two undesirables realized what the volcano was doing to Hak's hideaway, it was too late…permanently too late. Pele's jailhouse door had slammed shut.

CHAPTER 38

ERUPTION!!

Beginning at exactly 5:27 that Christmas Eve, lasting through and long after the struggle between Hak and J. D. Pickett down in the lava tube, the odds of eruption in the near future ratcheted right up to a certainty. Unlike the strong hints of impending eruption one week earlier, this time the eruption indicator was unmistakable.

The Don was standing at the tourist window, looking out at Kīlauea Caldera and that smaller inset hole called Halemaʻumaʻu Crater, when suddenly all of the instruments in front of him went into wide gyrations of recording tremor. The pens on the seismographs were slapping back and forth so violently that they clicked loudly against the metal edges of their holders. This seismic signal continued, showing no signs of letting up.

The Don watched the pens flapping wildly and unabated for several minutes, before admitting to himself that he knew exactly what was happening. He had been through this very drill several times before during his career with volcanoes. Magma was either hurrying on its way to eruption, or was already there, coating the surface of Kīlauea with yet another layer of Pele's asphalt.

This late in the afternoon, daylight was rapidly dimming. Tourists were on their way or already back to comfy hotels. The Don was looking out the tourist window in the direction of Āhua and beyond, as magma's orange glow, reflected from the bottom of low clouds, illuminated the sky. All of the preceding measuring, calculating, speculating, and warning pronouncements were now history.

Eruption was underway.

The Don went to his office, retrieved the list of phone numbers from the upper right desk drawer, and once again began making calls. There was no fancy candy-coated color-coded message this time.

"At exactly 5:27 PM Hawaiian time, on December 24, eruption began on the upper part of the east rift zone of Kīlauea Volcano. All activity is within a relatively remote part of the national park. Eruption is continuing at the time of this phone call."

When messages had been left and family festivities disrupted, he went back to the window to watch the glow coming from out there about five miles distant. In spite of his several past eruption experiences and the accumulation of a certain patina of indifference that comes with familiarity, The Don was still in awe of Kīlauea spewing molten rock. There was something primordial about what was happening. Land was being born, slipping out from nature's gash right there in his presence. He almost felt like a midwife. Birthing symbolism seemed endless.

The process also represented an incredible display of power, way too much power for any human attempts to control it…and there had been many over the years. Berms had been built, and bombs had been dropped…most recently on the Hilo-facing slopes of Mauna Loa a few years ago. A few years before that experiment, tons of icy cold north Atlantic water had been sprayed on a lava flow in Iceland, in hopes of stopping its advance by quickly cooling it to solid rock. But mostly, lava flows moved on as they saw fit, paying little heed to human interference.

The resulting sense of helplessness went beyond the human ability to rationally comprehend. The Don thought that such a feeling must be why ancient Hawaiians discovered or invented Pele, and why so many contemporary Hawaiians and miscellaneous converts still believe in the goddess.

The Don continued to stare toward the eruption in silent wonder, realizing that just being here, watching such an incredible display of pyrotechnics and raw power probably was the most unique and special Christmas gift one could ask for. He called Martha, waiting at home, to share these thoughts. They wished each other a Merry Christmas, reaffirmed their shared love, and said goodnight. Neither expected to see the other that night…maybe not for days to come, depending on how the eruption evolved.

Being The Don meant being on the job when the volcano erupted. He would wait for the arrival of HVO staff members he had called. There was nothing more for him to do until they came, anyway.

CHAPTER 39

A SQUEEZE BOX PLAYS A DEADLY TUNE

While Hak and JD were struggling in the lava tube, flashlights banging down on heads, magma that had been pushing up beneath the Āhua area for the past months and weeks finally gained enough buoyancy to make a final breakthrough toward the surface. On the way up, this surge of molten rock pushed the ground directly above it even higher. It also shouldered adjacent rocks off to the side.

The compression part of the accordion style of Koa'e crack behavior (which The Don had described for the Rotarians but Hak had not heard because of a gin-lover's coughing fit) was being put into play. While a new fissure opened to spew out molten rock, pre-existing nearby open cracks of the Koa'e were squeezed partly closed.

This had happened before during the life of the volcano and would happen again. But partial crack closing had now trapped humans underground. As The Don watched the orange glow of eruption from the HVO building, those trapped men were as unaware of their fate as The Don was of their predicament.

When Hak was cuffed, giving both men a chance to stand still, if only briefly, each felt the ground shaking underfoot. Simultaneously, they heard rocks falling within the open spaces of the crack that was their passageway to the surface. A couple of bowling ball sized chunks of basalt ricocheted back and forth between the crack walls, down to the level of the lava tube, and then rolled out on the floor.

Hak and JD backed away, moving a little farther into the tube. Both were confused and frightened, but neither expressed their feelings. To do so would be to admit fear, and these were two tough guys…just ask them. They waited for what seemed twenty, and was maybe as long as two minutes. There was still a tickling vibration singing up their legs from the ground tremor, but no more rocks were tumbling down the crack. What they didn't yet realize was that Kīlauea's version of a rock accordion had just played a dirty trick on them. Their access and escape route was now much narrower than it had been minutes earlier.

JD broke the silence.

"O.K., tourist Hak, I'm takin ya in. You're unda arrest as a drug runna. Don't be givin' me trouble if ya don't want a couple more lumps on the noggin'. Let's get otta here."

Hak obeyed. With his hands cuffed, it was futile to struggle. He was sure he would lose in hand-to-hand combat with Pickett, anyway. His life as a successful businessman had softened what used to be muscles on a motorcycle dude. He still had substantial weight, but his flesh was soft. His belt size had increased from thirty-four to thirty-eight inches with the softening. By contrast, he had seen the rippling of muscle under Pickett's shirt during their first encounter. If Hak were to take this guy, he would need an element of surprise and the help of a lethal weapon.

Hak led the way to the exit. Pickett followed close behind, aiming the beam of his flashlight at their feet. Pickett pushed Hak into the crack. Climbing with cuffed hands was clumsy enough, even with the cuffs in front. But soon another obstacle presented itself. Hak couldn't find the passageway he had been using all along. He mumbled this to Pickett and asked for more light. JD obliged. More light was not the answer. Hak could not find an opening large enough for his body. Access had always been tight, but other than rubbing shirt and pants on sidewalls of the crack a few times, access had been easy.

"I can't get out of here. Maybe if you took the cuffs off…"

"No way. You're not the trustable kind. Git back down here."

Hak backed down the fifteen or so feet he had ascended and stood in the entrance to the tube. Though he couldn't see it, he heard a grin on Pickett's face as he said, "Now don't ya run away, while I'm findin' the exit."

Pickett got no farther than Hak had. At first he was sure he just needed to move laterally one way or the other to find the way he had used to get down.

Trouble was, he basically couldn't go up or sideways. He scrambled here and there as much as he could for ten or fifteen minutes, before he gave up, puffing and frustrated.

Down in the darkness of the tube, Hak first heard the scuffing sounds of Pickett's body rubbing the walls of the crack as he searched for free passage. Then he heard the sounds of puffing added to scuffing, and finally the longest and most obscene string of expletives imaginable, made to sound even worse than normal by a heavy southern accent.

Silence was followed by more puffing and scuffing and finally the reappearance of the flashlight in Pickett's hand.

"Prisoner Hak, it seems that both of us are prisoners. The volcano musta done somethin' to close up our passage and send boulders tumblin' down. We got a big problem here to work on togather."

CHAPTER 40

IT'S LAVA AT FIRST SIGHT

A hundred feet above Pele's prisoners and four miles to the east, a fifty-foot-tall wall of bright orange lava gushed in a jet-like roar from a quarter-mile-long fissure in the east rift zone. A classic Hawaiian curtain of fire was unfolding.

Splashing back to earth, the molten rock gathered into a river that flowed northward through the rainforest. Lava burned and buried trees, bushes, grass, ferns, and flowers as it advanced. Squealing mongooses and feral pigs ran to safe ground. Squawking birds in the path of destruction quickly changed trees. A few muffled mortar-like booms pierced the air, as moisture-rich vegetation exploded in steam blasts.

The fiery fluid oozed downhill where it encountered the Chain of Craters road. Asphalt burst into flames, polluting the air with billowing black sooty smoke. Lava continued to follow the downslope contour of the land until it spilled into nearby Pauahi Crater. A hot churning lake of bizarre Christmas pudding quickly formed in this six-hundred-foot-deep pit.

Not one human was present to witness this fantastic natural performance of sound and light, heat and fury.

By 6:15, while everyone else in Hawai'i was enjoying Christmas Eve with family or friends, Andy and Rob were at HVO with The Don. Ten minutes later, Ben, who lived halfway to Hilo, arrived. The immediate plan was that Andy and Rob would drive down the Chain of Craters road for a close-up view of the eruption site. The Don and Ben would stay at HVO to watch the seismic records coming in. Office and field crews would maintain radio contact.

Rob and Andy took the Ford and headed toward the eruption site. From HVO, they could see the bright orange light from the curtain of fire reflected off the bottoms of low clouds hanging over Kīlauea. They arced around the south edge of the caldera on Crater Rim Drive. Two college-aged tourists at the Keanakakoi Crater pullout, camera mounted on tripod, were carefully photographing a large sign that warned "NĒNĒ CROSSING. DRIVE SLOWLY." They were ignoring the nearby rare birds feasting on 'ōhelo berries. As nearly dark as it was, those folks must have been desperate to photograph the sign. They were also missing the usual fun of Christmas Eve with friends.

Andy looked at Rob and grinned. "I'll give you a hundred to one odds that those two are French!"

"No bet, buddy. I'm too smart for that."

They turned right onto the Chain of Craters road. The first landmark of the rift zone was Bird Toilet, next the still warm and treeless patch of ground that had formed in 1938, then the intersection with Hilina Pali Road (Devil's Throat hidden in rainforest to the left), and suddenly, WHOOSH. The Chain of Craters road was no more. A lava flow was oozing across, right to left, in front of them, on its path to a deepening lake of molten rock in Pauahi Crater. The curtain of fire was visible about a quarter mile off to their right.

They turned the Ford around, and got out, leaving the key in the ignition. They were set for a quick departure, if necessary. Backpacks in place, they jogged the short distance to the orange river. Neither had seen flowing lava before.

Most of the flow was crusted over with a thin black film of just-formed basalt rock. Cracks in this crusty cover exposed viscid still-molten stuff moving underneath. The flow was sluggish, advancing at the pace of a comfortable walk, easy and safe to approach on foot.

The thin crust provided enough insulation for Rob and Andy to safely walk right up to the edge of the lava river without fear of burning skin. Special heat-reflecting attire was unnecessary so long as their skin was covered with something as simple as cotton. They watched briefly in silent fascination. Then.

"Woowee!! Basalt, my favorite rock. I sailed the high seas to learn about this stuff, barfing my guts out most of the way. I never got to see it being formed, in eruption, though, 'til right now.

"It doesn't get much better than this, does it Andy?! This is the kind of stuff that coats most of the earth's rocky surface, and here we are watching it happen. Give me five!"

The slap of flesh on flesh and the childish giggling sounds of two delighted adults rose above the hissing and clinking of flowing lava. Andy and Rob were experiencing the kids-in-a-candy-store thrill that hits all volcano scientists when they first see molten rock on the move.

"¡Ay Dios, y todos los Santos!" as my Hispanic Stanford friends would say.

"This is like a religious experience, almost as good as hot sex. It's one thing to read about erupting magma, to look at pictures, to listen to fancy word descriptions from the mouths of professors. But seeing, hearing, smelling, and feeling an eruption first hand makes all that classroom stuff seem grossly inadequate, almost phony. My motto is geology-in-action is the best way to learn'…as long as that geology isn't the study of meteorite impacts."

They stood transfixed for several more minutes, in silent awe and admiration. Eventually, the first-time novelty started to wear thin. They remembered that there was more to studying an eruption than just watching. The Don would expect them to return to HVO with samples and measurements…rocks and numbers.

Rob walked back to the Ford and extracted a long metal pole-like tool, with an attached instrument about the size of a shoebox. He walked up to the edge of the flowing lava and inserted the metal probe of the pyrometer. Watching a dial on the instrument, he began to call out temperatures as Andy recorded the numbers in his notebook.

"Two thousand seventy. Two thousand ninety five."

Twenty seconds into the experiment and the metal probe was still rising to the temperature of the lava.

"Two thousand one hundred and fifty. Two thousand one hundred and seventy. Two thousand one hundred and seventy five. Two thousand one hundred and seventy five. Okay, that seems to be the equilibrium temperature."

As Rob walked the pyrometer back to the Ford, Andy stepped cautiously up to the flow and pierced the black crust with the sharp end of his geology hammer. Fourteen years earlier, an HVO geologist had slipped into lava up to his knee while trying to sample this way. Andy didn't want to repeat that accident. The pick's point made a thud on thin crust as it penetrated several inches into the orange stuff underneath. Andy swiftly withdrew the hammer, whose head came out draped with taffy-like molten rock that cooled to glistening glassy solid black basalt within a minute or so.

"Hey, a rock sample doesn't get much fresher or more pristine than this, does it, Rob?!"

It took another several minutes of cooling before the newly minted basalt bullion could be handled enough to insert it into a labeled cloth bag, ready for study back in the lab.

They estimated the width and depth of the lava river. They timed how long a piece of crust took to flow fifty feet downstream. Later, they would calculate the volume of lava flowing past that spot each minute.

Finally, they documented the scene with photographs. Mission accomplished, they radioed a report to The Don, powered up the Ford, and headed back to HVO.

The time was now eight o'clock. The eruption was two-and-a-half hours old, and seemed to be in a holding pattern. A steady diet of tremor, punctuated by a few small earthquakes, was being fed to all seismometers near the eruption site. This was the normal result of magma surging upward in a curtain of fire. The Don and Ben agreed that nothing special need be done so long as this behavior persisted. The eruption was in a remote part of the park. No homes were threatened…or people as far as they knew. The public, immersed in Christmas activities, apparently was unaware that eruption was underway.

The Don phoned Fritz Kamph at home to relay the observations of Andy and Rob. Kamph would have to get a ranger or two on site, soon, in anticipation of hordes of tourists once the word was out that an eruption could be safely viewed up close.

When Rob and Andy got back to HVO, The Don urged them and Ben to return home, and enjoy at least part of their Christmas festivities. He insisted that they stay near a phone. He would take up residence again at HVO. Martha would join him, and together they could keep tabs on the eruption. The team of Mr. and Mrs. Richards had done this before.

CHAPTER 41

RANGER RITA HOLDS FORTH

Christmas and the following day were peaceful at HVO. Martha had moved in with The Don. She visited their house, just three miles away, to prepare meals, which she brought back to HVO. With the help of an ancient refrigerator, filled mostly with HVO's supply of photographic film, and a hot plate that was a piece of equipment in the chemistry lab, she and The Don ate well. Though bureaucrats at headquarters would have been mortified, had they but known, the two shared a bottle of properly chilled Dom Perignon on Christmas Eve and a bottle of homemade 'ōhelo berry wine, a gift from Ben and his family, with Christmas Day dinner…right there in a USGS building.

Once again, surplus army cots and sleeping bags were the bedroom furnishings. Unlike the earlier episode of live-in volcano watch, though, the gentle and unhurried lovemaking of a retirement-age couple exercised those cots each night in the privacy of Howard's machine shop. Vise, band saw, drill press, and lathe watched in mute amusement.

"What do you suppose those bean-counting bureaucrats back at headquarters would think about this use of government facilities?" The Don wondered aloud in smiling afterglow.

"I'm sure they'd be jealous, though they would never admit it" replied Martha as she headed down the hall to wash up.

On Christmas morning, Fuzzy Chee managed to pry himself away from the breakfast table long enough to contact all Big Island media. He avoided an interview this time, because he had in fact screwed up by not communicating the earlier Code Red warning.

By noon of Christmas Day, word of Kīlauea's eruption was widespread across Hawai'i. The orange reflection from the bottoms of clouds had been visible all the way to Hilo on Christmas Eve. Akamai locals who stepped outside that night knew exactly what this colorful sky meant. They also chose to save eruption watching until the next day. They knew that Santa visits but once a year. Pele's visits are less regular but more frequent.

By noon that next day, the viewing public began to descend on the eruption site in droves. Kamph's staff had its hands full.

Since chief law enforcement officer J. D. Pickett was nowhere to be found, his second in command, Archie Boggs, supervised traffic flow and parking. Visitors were made to park at the turnoff for the Hilina Pali road, and walk a mile or so to where the lava river oozed across the Chain of Craters road. In eagerness to see their first eruption, visitors' parking was somewhat haphazard and chaotic.

Archie and his minions found this behavior to be sufficient justification for writing tickets. Almost all visitors were so delighted to witness a real-live eruption that they accepted their fines without complaint. Still, the spirit and purpose of the national park system were not enhanced by strict enforcement of picky spur-of-the-moment traffic regulations.

At the eruption site itself, a carnival atmosphere tended to smother any bad P.R. generated by Archie and his meter men. Wood barriers were set up across the road to keep visitors a safe distance from the edge of the lava river. Scores of locals and out-of-state tourists alike were ooohing and aaahing, pointing, shouting, laughing, and clicking photos.

The park's lone naturalist, Rita Jensen, was barraged with non-stop questions. Two unpaid geology-student volunteers, undergraduates from the Hilo campus of the University of Hawai'i, were helping her as best they could. There were myriad queries from interested thinkers.

"How hot is the lava?"

"Two thousand degrees…about as hot as Bessemer pig iron."

"Can I touch it?"

"No, you cannot. Why would you want to, anyway, as hot as it is? You still have all your fingers. I recommend you keep them."

"Where does it come from?"

"A place about forty miles straight down beneath us. Geologists call it the mantle."

"Where's it going?"

"Well, it's flowing into the rainforest over there, and it spills into a deep hole in the ground called a pit crater, about three hundred yards out of sight. If and when that crater fills, we'll have to move to a safer viewing spot."

"How long will the eruption last?"

"To be honest, none of us, including the geologists who study this volcano, has the foggiest idea. It could stop any minute now. Or it could go on like this for years. Though they've tried many times over the years, humans don't and can't control volcanic eruptions."

"Can I take a piece of the new hot rock?"

"Not while I'm here. Park rules."

Mark Helpburn stared almost passionately at the edge of the lava river, where coagulated liquid solidified to rock and added to an already substantial rubbly levee along the main channel. He introduced himself to Rita as a San Francisco attorney who specializes in real-estate law.

"This is a fascinating performance that nature is putting on. Do you know who actually owns the new land forming here?"

Rita shrugged. She was not about to get mired in a discussion of that legal morass. Plenty of litigious folks were already pursuing the problem, and had been for years.

Visitors interested in most anything other than torts threw Rita the inevitable questions about whether scientists know how volcanoes work…the when-and-where they would erupt? Or did the goddess Pele control Kīlauea? Interesting mind games and philosophical discussion of the limitations of science sometimes followed. She and her helpers got a heavy dose of oral tradition versus the scientific method.

Rita had a great time with these interactions. This was the very stuff she had trained for on her route to a park service job. The wonders of nature were the foundation of so many of the national parks. She just wished, again, that she had another professionally trained scientist to work with her at times like this. The students were helpful, but they were learning as much as teaching. As always, Rita rationalized her situation by remembering that the nation's premiere geologic park, the Grand Canyon, had not even one geologist on its staff. People came from all around the globe to see earth's rocky history exposed in the walls of that humongous trench. Yet a real live person educated to explain the landscape was not on the park staff. There were plenty of Archie Boggs types, though.

Rita and her helpers had to police the visitor area when overly enthusiastic and inquisitive folks went beyond the barriers. Their concern was for personal safety, not law enforcement. Tickets were not issued. Sensing an overwhelming enthusiasm for a closer encounter with active lava, Rita occasionally dropped hints about how and when someone might safely get right up to the edge of the lava river.

As day one of the eruption moved into days two and three, Rita and her volunteers were exhausted by the end of their twelve-hour sessions on duty. Once they left their post, visitors were on their honor to obey the KEEP BACK message tacked onto the barriers. Archie and his crew weren't about to staff the eruption site after normal work hours. What went on after dark was a whole different scene from daylight visitor behavior.

Having watched HVO geologists sample the edge of the lava river, several after-hours tourists came with hammers and other metal tools to dip into the hot orange taffy. Squeals of delight were only occasionally interrupted by squawks of hurt when overly eager hands touched still-hot souvenir treasures dangling from the ends of hoes, rakes, and picks.

Experienced locals came equipped with shovels and upward flaring metal pails. When quickly filled with scooped-in lava, the pails served as molds that produced truncated cones of basalt, used widely as landscape accent rocks on the Big Island. Other people pushed coins partway into the soft liquid lava, and collected the solidified product for use as a paperweight or shelf-decorating knickknack.

These and other styles of lava sculpting were limited only by the creativity of the sculptors. A few minor burns and the occasional cut from glassy lava were injuries tolerated without complaint. These were well worth the fun and excitement of interacting with "live" lava. The park reaped a pile of positive PR, simply by staying out of the way.

Rita knew what went on at night. And she knew that she was supposed to discourage, well, actually, her marching orders were to *prohibit* sample collecting. But she also knew that the collectors did not visibly mar the landscape. A scoop from the lava river healed itself almost instantaneously as more lava filled the temporary void. Besides, the amount of continuously erupted lava was so much greater than the trivial amount carried away by people that no one would or could notice the loss.

Rita also knew that many of the filched samples would be returned. Park information brochures made clear that Pele would bring down all sorts of ill on any person who carted away pieces of her volcano home. And so it was that many a collector returned his basalt treasure to the park, accompanied by a letter filled with remorse and contrition, when some unexpected misfortune struck shortly after his Hawaiian vacation.

Through all of this, Rita and her student volunteers had a great time interacting with a delighted visiting public. Meanwhile, Archie Boggs and his dour staff directed traffic and wrote parking tickets. The whereabouts of Pickett remained unknown.

CHAPTER 42

A CARBONATED FAREWELL FLING

By Monday, with the character of the eruption unchanged, a steady stream of tourist-carrying airplanes circled the upper east rift zone when clear weather permitted. The eruption site remained officially open for tourists on the ground, during daylight hours. Unofficial nighttime fun continued.

Martha moved back into their house early that morning. The makeshift bedroom cots were folded and stored along with the sleeping bags. The Don was alone when the HVO staff started to trickle in for work.

He immediately called an all-staff meeting around the conference room table, to bring everyone up to date with what had changed at the eruption site over the weekend (basically nothing other than the deepening of the lava lake in Pauahi) and what the plan was for the coming days.

"Rob, Andy, and anyone else who wants to visit the eruption site: I want you to head down there and make another temperature measurement of the flow. Collect more of that supremely fresh rock, too…some of today's basalt…and get some photos of what's happening."

As usual, Andy was seated next to Liz as The Don continued his instructions. There hadn't been any of the old under-the-table body contact between them since Andy's decision to stop philandering. There wasn't even the usual above-the-table shoulder and eye contact of earlier times. They simply listened attentively to The Don.

"Eruption's been underway long enough for us to think about starting a series of measurements to track the filling of Pauahi. So, I want some of you to see if you can walk safely in to the lip of the crater and get that little project going. Since all of the lava is ponding there, a record of how fast the lava-lake surface is rising can tell us what volume of magma is spilling out onto the earth each day. It might be interesting to compare that number with the number Andy calculated from the size and speed of the lava river where it crosses the road. Any other ideas?"

Thoughtful silence.

"So far, the eruption's been incredibly stable. But Pauahi is filling fast enough to overflow in a few days if nothing else changes. We need to be able to give the park folks a heads up in advance. Ben and I will stay here and monitor the seismic action."

Andy was mentally formulating a modification to The Don's work plan…one that could address both HVO's and his own personal needs. Ever since his vow to leave the variety pack party life behind and find that one special woman, he had meant to have a heart-to-heart talk of explanation with Liz. Their relationship definitely had changed from hot to cool with the new vow. Even party boy Andy felt that he owed Liz more than nothing for an explanation. They had shared much during the past couple of years. At the very least they were close friends. You didn't just dump a close friend without explaining why. A trip to the eruption site could provide an ideal opportunity to carry off what might be an emotionally difficult conversation…on neutral ground, out of sight and sound of anyone else.

"Hey, Liz. How about coming with me to recon the vent area, while Rob and his helpers try to bushwhack into Pauahi? We could use up-to-date info on where the lava is spilling out on the ground as well as where it's ponding."

Liz gazed into Andy's eyes, trying to read any additional information that might lie behind this invitation. They had hardly spoken for days. She got no interpretable vibes, but was thinking, "why not."

"Okay, Andy. Let me get into my field boots and grab a backpack with a few supplies. I'll meet you out at the Ford."

Meanwhile, Rob was assembling and outfitting his own crew. He, Bruce, and Jeb would see if they could open a trail downstream from the tourist spot to Pauahi. They would have pretty tough bushwhacking through the rainforest. And they would have to be careful to avoid getting surrounded by a curling errant finger of lava. But three strong backs and six eagle eyes should be able to do the job.

It was about ten o'clock when Rob turned the Ford onto the Chain of Craters road. A tourist car partly obstructed their lane near a large sign announcing "DON'T FEED THE NĒNĒ." The tourists were photographing the sign. As the Ford slowed to pass this scene, Andy stuck his head out the passenger-side window and shouted "*Bonjour, mes amis.*" Tourist heads immediately snapped in Andy's direction, betraying an understanding of their native language. Everyone in the HVO Ford erupted into laughter.

They drove through the crowded parking area that had been designated for eruption watchers. One of Archie Boggs's staff took a long enough break from writing citations to help clear a safe path through waves of pedestrians. At the eruption site, they positioned the Ford, headed out, near Rita Jensen and her current gaggle of deliriously happy visitors. Much to the additional delight of these folks, the HVO geologists collected a sample of flowing taffy-like lava and measured the temperature of the lava river with that proboscis-like metal pyrometer probe. Rita gave a blow-by-blow description of what was happening. Many roles of Kodak, Fuji, and Agfa film were consumed.

The HVO crew huddled back at the car.

"Okay, Andy. We'll head for Pauahi, while you and Liz see if you can get close to the erupting vent. Who knows how long it'll take either of us. Let's try to meet back here at about noon. We have the two-way radios for communication if anything unexpected crops up."

"Sounds like a plan to me. Take care. See ya soon."

Rob, Bruce, and Jeb, cane knives at the ready, disappeared into the rainforest greenery in the direction of Pauahi. Andy and Liz slipped out of sight toward the curtain of fire at the vent.

Andy led the way. The two remained silent as they wended their way among clumps of fern and grass beneath the branches of 'ōhi'a trees. They were able to advance slowly without needing knives to slash vegetation.

Fifteen minutes later, Andy stopped. He turned and waited for Liz to catch up. He looked her straight in the eye as she approached.

"Liz, there's something I've been meaning to tell you recently. But I couldn't find the right place or time."

From the tone of his voice and seriousness of facial expression, Liz knew that heavy news was coming down…anything from "I'm dying of cancer" to "I think you're a twit." They were separated by two feet of charged atmosphere.

"Ya know, I've…I've really enjoyed the fun times we've had, ever since I first met you…when I came to Hawai'i to join the HVO staff."

Liz cracked a muted smile of agreement. Andy read this as disbelief.

"I mean it. You're a lovely lady who believes in living *carpe diem* to the hilt. Until a couple of weeks ago, I was a full-fledged *carpe diem* person, too. But I've had a change of heart. Believe it or not, I want to find a special woman, settle down, and be true to her. I'm not kidding. Please don't laugh."

Liz could tell that Andy was completely serious. A few moments of awkward silence ensued, gazes locked on each other.

"And uh…well, the thing is that you're not *her*, much as I've enjoyed our times together and consider you to be a great friend."

You could have heard a leaf drop for the silence. It was, in fact, uncharacteristically quiet, save for a low jet-like hiss coming from the curtain of fire, a couple hundred yards farther into the rainforest. There was absolutely no wind, meaning no swishing of 'ōhi'a branches or fern fronds. Andy and Liz remained mute, each trying to read meaning into the other's facial expression.

Finally, the high-pitched twittering of an 'apapane broke the spell.

"Andy, Andy. We're more in tune with each other than you think. Like you, I've been wanting to move on with my life recently, too. But I couldn't quite bring myself to tell you. Well, now it's all out in the open for both of us, and there's no need for morose moodiness or rivers of tears."

"Really? Just like that?"

Andy's ego was thinking that he should be a little harder to leave.

"Really."

The 'apapane was now singing an aria of glee. They sighed, hugged, and backed off an arm's distance, holding hands. It was all very chaste and platonic…a mood that was pretty short-lived. Liz formed a cutely mischievous smile, the kind of smile that Andy had seen many times during their fun-and-games days. He sensed what was coming.

"But before we go our separate ways, friend, I propose a farewell frolic in the grass…one for the road, so to speak. What do you say?"

Andy spent a nanosecond deciding to break off this relationship with one last session of lovemaking. They embraced again, this time in non-platonic passion. They stepped back and grinned in anticipation. Andy led Liz by the hand, in search of the perfect setting for their final fling. He soon found a shallow swale, about the size of a gigantic circular bed in a Las Vegas hotel. The overhanging canopy of a large 'ōhi'a tree partly shaded this au naturel playpen. They could hear hissing and clinking from the nearby lava river, perfect background mood music for geologists. Yet they were in no danger of being inundated by this fiery neighbor.

Liz slipped off her backpack. Before dropping it to the ground, she extracted a small rectangular package whose wrapping crinkled in familiar sound as she tossed it to Andy.

"Here, lover. Be sure to put this in the right place at the right time. We don't want to create a keiki as a result of our fun."

Andy smiled and shook his head back and forth thinking "Who but Liz would carry a supply of condoms in her backpack."

Clunky field boots off and backpacks aside, they began the ritual of undressing each other. Since Liz had asked for this last tryst, she began. She slowly unbuttoned and stripped off Andy's blue cotton work shirt. There was no undershirt and no male jewelry, only a very masculine hair-matted chest. Liz ran her fingers through the hair, waiting for Andy's first move. She was starting to purr.

"Ummm. I *do* like this."

Andy also started at the top. He lifted Liz's tee-shirt over her head, exposing a customary lack of bra. Lack of tan lines bore testament to hours of nude sunbathing. Andy slowly and gently twirled Liz's nipples between thumb and index finger. They instantly hardened. He briefly licked and nuzzled her breasts. He was hardening, too.

"Ummm. I *really* like this."

Next, off came Andy's jeans, Liz's expedition slacks, Andy's briefs, and Liz's panties. They were naked in the forest, ready to share the fruit of love to the core, one last time.

Andy spread their clothes out in a patchwork blanket, positioned within the shade cast by the 'ōhi'a tree. They lay down facing each other and began rehoeing familiar ground. At the right moment, Andy had the presence of mind to unwrap and position that special protection before consummating the lovemaking.

At the instant of supreme pleasure, Andy found himself thinking that orgasm seemed more ecstatic than ever before. He also found himself remembering a book he had once read, a book that explained how partially choking off of one's air supply is said to enhance the pleasures of the sex act.

Finished and exhausted, they rolled onto their backs and looked up into a profusion of lovely red 'ōhi'a lehua blossoms. They lay silent.

Dizzy with the afterglow of sex, at least that's what he thought his dizziness was, Andy wanted more conversation.

"Liz, I *do* want us to stay friends, even though the lovers part is over."

When she didn't respond, he repeated the thought.

"Hey Liz. Are you listening? I want us to stay friends, even though we won't be bedding down together."

Liz still didn't respond. Andy gently nudged her. No reaction. He then not so gently pushed on her. Her body was as limp as a soggy rag. Her breathing was becoming raggedly uneven.

Andy suddenly realized the cause of his dizziness and her limpness.

"Liz, wake up! Liz. We've got to get out of here!"

He thought he was shouting, but his voice was barley audible.

She wasn't responding. Andy was getting a little delirious and finding it increasingly difficult to breathe. He struggled to his feet. He tried to lift Liz, but didn't have enough strength. In desperation, he grabbed her by the heels and unceremoniously dragged her naked limp body no more than twenty feet, up and out of their cradle of love.

As his head rose above the lip of the swale, breathing came more easily and smoothly. Liz was still apparently comatose.

"Liz, wake up, damn it!"

He slapped her face a few times, getting no response. He started mouth-to-mouth resuscitation. A half dozen or so hard blows into her mouth, nose pinched to force the air inside, and Liz started to cough and wheeze. Her chest rose and fell with each gasping breath. She sat up, blinked a few times, and looked at Andy with a "what's going on?" expression.

"¡¡*Caramba!!* Liz. We damn near died down there in our love nest! We got a little careless.

"Remember how carbon dioxide is always bubbling out of active lava. Well, some of that gas must have fizzed off of the lava river and flowed into our sunken forest bedroom...enough of it to push out most of the lighter oxygen."

Liz's head was nodding in apparent agreement.

"We would've been safe, except that there isn't enough wind today to stir the carbon dioxide back into the rest of the atmosphere. We could easily have bought the farm. Wouldn't the discovery of our naked bodies have generated a gaggle of entertaining stories."

They looked at each other, trying to reason through what had just happened. Liz was trying to get her mind around what Andy had just said. Both were still a bit disoriented from not enough oxygen.

"We were just a minute or two from being victims of an invisible volcano hazard that most people don't even know about...carbon dioxide suffocation."

They sat motionless until breathing became the easy involuntary action it should be. Ever the optimistic upbeat and fun-loving one, even in the shadow of near death, Liz looked at Andy and grinned.

"You know, partner, making love with you always did take my breath away. But this is a bit extreme, don't you think! I mean, just because it was the very last time…"

A few hugs, kisses, and giggles later, Andy took a deep breath and held it as he retrieved their clothes and packs from the bowl of death soup. They dressed. It was nearly noon. Andy fished the radio from his pack, flipped the switch to ON, and thumbed the transmit key.

"Rob, this is Andy. Rob, this is Andy. Over."

"Hey, this is Rob. Where are you? We got into Pauahi okay, and are back at the car."

"Well, Liz and I had more than enough excitement, even though we couldn't get right up to the vent. We're on our way back. Should be there in about twenty minutes."

Andy and Liz faced each other, holding hands. They promised to be lifelong friends, swore that the saga of their final lovemaking would be their secret, and headed Fordward.

As they walked, Andy reflected on the fact that twice he had almost died during the past two weeks. Maybe he wouldn't live long enough to find that special someone and settle down. If so, maybe he should enjoy his remaining time in former *carpe diem* fashion.

Maybe he should consider a career change.

CHAPTER 43

WHERE'S OLD JD?

By Monday noon (at least that was the day and time according to Hak's gold-trimmed Rolex; JD's watch had been smashed against a rock when he was struggling to find the exit route), Hak and JD were in a dark funk, more than a little dispirited. Hak's flashlight no longer worked. JD's facial scars had been sturdier than cheap plastic. JD was nursing the batteries of his flashlight by sitting in darkness most of the time.

By peering up the access crack, they could see faint daylight. But where light and fresh air passed freely, robust bodies could not.

Following their initial brief scuffle, JD kept Hak cuffed, not being sure that an exit route to the surface didn't exist somewhere other than up that main crack. After they gave up on exiting through the crack, together they had walked into the lava tube as far as possible, only to discover passage sealed off by the rocky rubble of a collapsed roof, less than a hundred feet downstream. So, they went back to the tube entrance and thought in darkness and silence about possible ways to escape their bizarre prison.

The cuffs came off. Hak wasn't going anywhere; they were in this mess together. It seemed that either both escaped, somehow, or both died of slow starvation there in their underground jail cell. An unspoken bond was being forged from shared need.

By Rolex Monday night, they still had not hatched any brilliant escape plans. Stomachs were rumbling in hunger. But more critical, large bodies were becoming increasingly dehydrated. The water in Hak's two-quart canteen had disappeared within the first two days. JD had consumed most of that precious liquid. At least in the cool of the lava tube, perspiration was not contributing to fluid loss.

❦   ❦   ❦

Though JD had never been popular with his staff of law enforcement specialists (JD had developed no lasting friendships throughout his park service career), by Monday concern for his whereabouts was growing at park headquarters. He was known to be a control freak who kept his staff on a short leash. It was unlike him to disappear unannounced. He had not signed out for vacation time, yet he had not reported to work on Sunday. Here it was Monday morning and there still was no Jefferson Davis Pickett at the office. The familiar sounds of JD fondling his mace and firearm were absent, if not missed.

Archie Boggs paid a quick visit to JD's house. He found the TV blaring and scraps of southern culinary delicacies molding on a table next to half-empty cans of RC Cola and beer. JD was still not responding to radio calls. Archie decided it was time to do a little road patrolling in search of his boss. If an official investigation into JD's whereabouts didn't start soon, Kamph might get curious.

Archie drove west on Highway 11, toward the Kona coast. This stretch of road had seen more than its share of accidents over the years. On several occasions, speeding out of control cars had plunged off into the rough roadside 'a'ā lava, coming to rest out of sight to all but the most vigilant searchers. Archie cruised slowly down 11, to a point a bit beyond the park boundary. He reversed and drove back up to the park entrance booth. He found nothing of interest…just the normal amount of new roadside trash thrown from the passing vehicles of Big Island residents. Through some twisted logic, these folks kept their home property immaculate, while considering the rest of the island to be their personal garbage dump.

Next Archie drove slowly down the Chain of Craters road to the barricades where visitors continued to marvel at the edge of active lava. A car could easily be hidden in thick rainforest just off the roadway. Again, he found no clue of JD's whereabouts, just the jackstraw parked cars of tourists at the Hilina Pali road intersection.

Backtracking, Archie slowed as he approached the intersection. He considered driving straight past. Hardly anyone used this road, other than the park biologist when he wanted to visit Kīpuka Nēnē, a primary nesting area for that native Hawaiian goose.

Archie stopped to consider his options. He used this opportunity to write two parking tickets, as he convinced himself that his search for JD should be thorough. There were no other roads to cruise, except the continuation of the Chain of Craters, behind him, beyond the lava river. That could be checked later, by driving down Highway 11 to Keaʻau, then right to Pāhoa and looping back toward the park along the south coast.

Ten minutes and two miles down the Hilina Pali road, Archie found JD's car. It was face-to-face with a tan Toyota Land Cruiser. Archie recognized this position as a symbolic, though usually ineffective, standoff ploy that JD liked to practice. Both vehicles were locked. Their hoods were the temperature of the day's cool air. There were no signs of a scuffle…no signs of anything amiss.

Archie radioed the park dispatcher and had one of his men bring a set of keys for JD's car. Inside, they found a radio-beacon receiver. Archie clicked it to ON. Readout indicated an incoming signal within spitting distance. A quick check under the rear of the Toyota revealed the signal sender magnetically attached right where JD always placed them.

JD had been following the Land Cruiser for some reason. Archie began to suspect foul play.

His take-charge-in-the-field decision was to enter the locked Toyota, an easy task for any properly trained law enforcement specialist, with or without a key. Registration papers in the glove box indicated that the vehicle belonged to Mr. Gregory Hakonē of Hilo. The only other item of interest, of substantial interest in fact, was about fifty pounds of shrink-wrapped pakalōlō bricks, hidden under a disgustingly dirty blanket in the luggage area. Foul play was now the most likely theory of the day.

Archie had the Toyota towed back to park headquarters. He would contact the Big Island police later, at his convenience. The park was Archie's jurisdiction, not theirs. The pakalōlō bricks went into an evidence vault for safekeeping at park headquarters. Another patrol car was dispatched with an extra driver to retrieve JD's vehicle. Since none of the other park officers had been trained in tracking, their cumulative efforts discovered no signs of JD, and whoever had driven the Toyota, leading away from the scene of parking.

By early afternoon, Archie and the rest of the park cops gathered back at their office. They drank a lot of coffee and talked about a plan to search for JD. None of them seemed to be in a great hurry. No immediate action was taken.

Archie clearly spoke for the group when he closed their meeting with "Fellas, let's think on it for awhile."

CHAPTER 44

ERUPTION MARCHES EAST

Tuesday morning. December 28.

The HVO staff was starting to believe that they had a non-threatening and scientifically interesting eruption to monitor. It was also a tourist's delight. Pele was entertaining scientists and park visitors alike.

Andy was at the tourist window, surreptitiously admiring the nēnē of a well endowed, ah, fraulein, judging by the guttural sound of the words coming through the glass. Suddenly, hundreds of small earthquakes began to record on the seismograms. Fraulein began to wave her extended index fingers back and forth in imitation of the moving seismograph pens. Andy was treated to some interesting body jiggles. His mind snapped back to magma, from its temporary lapse into flesh. He shouted down the hall.

"Ben! Get your butt up here, pronto!"

Ben's head appeared through the door of his dark windowless office. He squinted, blinked, and rubbed his eyes to adjust to a normal level of lighting as he walked toward the seismographs. He watched the pens flicker and flap, writing code-like signatures of earthquake shaking on the paper charts. He continued to watch, visually comparing the tracings of the six growing records. In the back of his mind, he created a map that showed the field locations of each of the six seismometer instruments. He was cranking through some mental calculation, cracking the codes. He smiled and called others to the window, including The Don.

"Well, friends, I know exactly what's happening. The eruption has decided to move down-rift, to the east. If you have any doubts, just take a gander toward the eruption site."

Ben himself was so sure of his conclusion that he didn't bother to look up.

All other pairs of eyes stared toward Āhua, where the curtain of fire had been performing since the eruption began. At first, the scene appeared unchanged. But within five minutes, nodding heads and murmured phrases confirmed that the curtain was on the move.

Like a powerful underground fluid wedge, magma was splitting the volcano open down-rift, to the east. The leading edge of the curtain of fire followed shadow-like, in lock step, close behind the tip of the opening crack. The HVO crew now had more to do. They needed to closely track the migration of the erupting lava, especially if eruption seemed destined to leave the park and enter the inhabited part of the Puna District. The Don jumped in to take charge.

"I'm going to order on-demand helicopter flights. A Bell Jet Ranger out of Hilo will be on standby for HVO until further notice. Damn the congressionally mandated Continuing Resolution and the USGS-imposed lid on the rate of HVO spending. Maybe Congress and bureaucratic bean counters at headquarters can wait, but we can't. Only an idiot might think that Kīlauea will march to the cadence of a Continuing Resolution.

"Andy and Rob, I want one or both of you on every chopper flight. Be in the air whenever you think it's worthwhile. Some of the rest of you can ride along as space and your in-office duties permit. I'll stay here at HVO and periodically brief Kamph and Fuzzy Chee about eruption antics."

By Tuesday nightfall, the migrating fissure and its closely following quarter-mile-long curtain of fire had marched past Puʻu Huluhulu, a tree-and-fern covered prehistoric cinder cone, had moved past Makaopuhi, a thousand-foot-deep pit crater, and had arrived abreast of somewhat smaller Nāpau Crater. These places were all in remote undeveloped parts of the park. The good news was that people and property were not threatened. The bad news was that tourists could no longer dip their tools in active lava.

Adjacent ground along the way was veneered with a new layer of glistening black glassy basalt, as though a huge Barber Green asphalt machine had passed by. Vegetation paid the supreme price. About two more miles of the Chain of Craters road were buried and burned. A complete photographic record was collected, from the safety and convenience of the helicopter cabin. Ground access was virtually impossible, and certainly dangerous.

A live-in staff of The Don, Andy, Rob, and Ben reoccupied HVO and the cots. Andy discovered the metal frame of one cot bent, as though it had been overloaded, and wondered out loud what had happened since he had last used it. With a slight twinkle in his eye, The Don said he had no idea.

By Wednesday nightfall, the curtain of fire was about three miles outside the park, on the move at a pretty steady six-miles-a-day pace. Eruption was now within dense uninhabited rainforest of the Puna District.

Late that afternoon, looking back uprift from the helicopter, Rob saw and photographed a black strip of devastation, a stripe of rough hot lava branded right across an otherwise lush green landscape and extending all the way back to where eruption had begun five days earlier. Rob was reminded of a mutant skunk. The worrisome thing was that the growing stripe showed no signs of stopping before it moved into inhabited parts of Puna.

Thursday. Migration of the curtain of fire was continuing eastward about a quarter of a mile each hour. Though no more than a leisurely human saunter on foot, how fast the lava arrived didn't matter to immobile objects in its path. Destruction by burning and burial were on the menu...death, too, for any living creature that moved too slowly.

With no active river of lava to enjoy, tourist visitation dropped way off where the eruption had first begun. The number of parking citations issued each day by Archie Boggs and his crew had dropped way off, too.

Viewing the eruption from the sky was a whole different story. Fixed-wing tourist flights were propeller to tail, when weather permitted...staying safely above the frequent HVO chopper activity.

The whereabouts of J. D. Pickett was still a mystery. Boggs and his boys were working that case...slowly.

CHAPTER 45

HIPPIES IN HARM'S WAY

From its beginning, Hak's partners tracked the progress of the unfolding eruption through frequent reports they watched on a large-screen TV in their hui office. Big Island radio and TV stations couldn't get enough of the story.

At about noon of day five, Hak's pakalōlō plantation was transformed from lush green weed, beneath its arborescent camouflage, to a rough swath of scorching-hot new basalt. Later that afternoon, the hui partners saw their crop being destroyed through footage beamed out by Hilo's ABC affiliate. They watched in mesmerized disappointment.

"What a shame that nobody was close enough to enjoy the free fumes of secondhand smoke," they joked, a bit philosophically.

"But, hey, not to worry. We've got inventory in the Koa'e to carry us through this setback. There's plenty more rainforest out there to put under cultivation once this eruption settles down."

They *were* worried about Hak, though. They hadn't seen him since the day eruption began, the day of their most recent Operation Pakalōlō Transfer. It wasn't unusual to go several days without contact, but something seemed not quite right. Hak should be around the hui office when his plantation was threatened by eruption.

On day five, Andy was watching and photographing the moving curtain of fire from his aerial perch. A brisk trade wind was blowing. Wilbur was keeping the helicopter just upwind of the erupting lava and about seven hundred feet above the ground. At that height, Andy had no inkling that anything other than natural rainforest vegetation was being destroyed as Hak's crop went up in smoke just below him.

But Andy recognized humans when he saw them, and now he was surprised and shocked to see two people just down-rift from the leading edge of the migrating fountain. He grabbed his binoculars for a closer look. He was almost certain that no one lived out here. These were two young-looking haoles. They were moving slowly about, bent in the posture of garden work within an area of what looked like thinned vegetation. Andy nudged Wilbur, who nodded in recognition of seeing the people down below.

"Jesus, Wilbur. Those two are naked as newborn babies."

Wilbur piloted the chopper down about a hundred feet closer to the ground to give Andy a better look.

"One is very female and definitely not a baby. They both have hippie length hair. I don't think they have any idea that an eruption is moving straight for them."

Andy was the lone HVO observer in the air today. Somehow, he would have to warn these two threatened souls. Hovering low enough to shout and gesticulate to them would put the chopper too close to erupting lava. Helicopter, Wilbur, and Andy himself would be at risk. That was not about to happen.

"We've got to try to save those poor unaware jerks. See if you can find a spot that's open enough for a landing, or maybe just a place where you can hover low so I can safely drop to the ground."

Wilbur, if anyone, could find a landing spot. He had put down in much more hostile places than this…in jungly rainforest with the added challenge of people trying to shoot him out of the air. He quickly scanned the area for an opening. Time was short if Andy was going to get to the threatened nudists before their skin burn was from more than the sun.

"I see a promising-looking break in vegetation a couple hundred yards north, upwind of where the lava fountain is headed. Let's give it a try."

As Wilbur headed for that relatively tree-free spot and started to descend slowly into it, Andy keyed his two-way radio.

"HVO, this is Andy. HVO, this is Andy."

A brief pause ensued, followed by The Don's voice.

"Andy, this is HVO. What's up?"

"The eruption is still in undeveloped rainforest, advancing slowly to the east. Believe it or not, Wilbur and I just IDed two people down there, exactly in harm's way. They don't seem to be aware of the approaching danger. We're going to try to land nearby. I've got to try to get them out of there. There's no time for a ground-based rescue."

"Okay, understood. But no heroics. I want you alive and back here at HVO by day's end."

"Couldn't agree more. We'll be out of radio contact as soon as we drop below our line of sight to the HVO radio antenna. I'll call back ASAP."

With sidling back and forth, and breaking off a few in-the-way branches by putting weight on them with the chopper's skids, Wilbur created an open space just wide enough for his machine to drop to ground level. He hovered at the top of a thick green carpet of grass and fern.

"I can't tell if the earth is solid and flat under that ground cover. You'll have to hang off the skid and drop the rest of the way. It's probably no more than a big step for you. As long as the weather holds like this, and it should, I can hover here for as much time as you need. Get your butt going if you plan to get to those folks in time to be of any help."

Andy nodded in agreement. He grabbed a vicious-looking curved-blade cane knife from his backpack, gave Wilbur a friendly tap on the shoulder, opened the passenger-side door, and lowered himself to the ground. The chopper lurched a bit as the weight of his two-hundred-pound muscular body was transferred from helicopter to earth. He headed south, toward the clueless two, cane knife swinging savagely enough to create a passageway.

CHAPTER 46

THE GIRL OF HIS DREAMS

As eruption approached their little garden and homestead, Josh and Valerie, naked as usual, were working their land, trying to weed out enough unwanted plants to promote faster pakalōlō growth. They were also harvesting some crop. Tomorrow would be a Pāhoa day, and they needed barter for shopping. They had just smoked joints. Their senses were at less than full alert.

They had also just had another argument, something that was occurring with increasing frequency. Well, maybe argument was too strong a word, but recently Valerie had begun to be concerned, if not alarmed, at Josh's waning interest in anything but being on a pakalōlō high in his favorite hammock.

Their relationship had started with interesting discussions about contrasting lifestyles, life values, and what each of them hoped to move on to. But now Josh couldn't, or wouldn't concentrate beyond smoking another joint and dozing. Major planning for him seemed to be scheduling their next trip to Pāhoa.

Since taking up residence in the Puna rainforest, Valerie had thought through her situation long and deeply enough to know that she still wanted some sort of "conventional" life back in mainstream, or maybe in robust sidestream society. By contrast, the most profound statement she could squeeze out of Josh these days had something to do with Mr. Hermes and a pendulum that was stuck way out on its swing to the left. A friendship that had started as soul mates on a common path was now two minds headed in widely divergent directions. The net result of today's "argument" was that they were working in opposite ends of their garden.

In the bent-over posture of gardeners pulling weeds, they were quite unaware of any pending danger. The smells and sounds of approaching eruption were carried away from them, on the wings of the trade wind. The sight of eruption was screened from view by rainforest vegetation. Without looking up or giving it much thought, they heard the noise of a helicopter as just one more tourist flight, probably heading up to Kīlauea Caldera from the Hilo airport.

Josh was working near the west end of the garden; Valerie was at the east end. Suddenly, one of those hated feral pigs came running toward Josh, from the west. Porky pua'a streaked and squealed past Josh, disappearing into rainforest near Valerie.

"Well fine," he thought in his state of diminished awareness. "I won't have to chase the mangy bugger away."

Before Josh could refocus his efforts on uprooting undesirable plants, here came another pig, and then another and another and another. Josh grinned and started to talk to himself.

"Like wow, man. Am I in one of those pig drives of good old Chickasaw County? I bet Valerie has never seen hundreds of hogs being herded down a country road to a railhead for shipment to slaughter. She's one of those city people who thinks milk comes from a carton, instead of a cow."

Josh paused his slow and somewhat slurred speech long enough to grin and then giggle. In his condition, just about anything would have seemed funny. He was a classic pakalōlō laugher.

"I'll bet a Texas cattle-drive cowboy would fall right out of his saddle at the sight of an Iowa pigboy on the move. But, hey, that's what life was like back home."

This wasn't back home. This was Hawai'i. Something was weird. Weirdness increased as the occasional mongoose joined pigs scurrying across his homestead. Josh went into a fit of giggling.

"Man, next I'll probably see Bambi come sprinting out of the forest."

Driven by curiosity, a mumbling, jovial Josh sauntered toward the source of the stampeding animals, the west edge of their garden. His was the slow and uneven pace of drug-hazed consciousness.

He was soon greeted by the sound of cracking rock and the sight of erupting lava burning its way through the rainforest, toward him. In his stupor, Josh was mesmerized, hypnotized, and paralyzed long enough for the propagating fissure to open right between his feet. The leading edge of the curtain of fire was not far behind. He looked straight down in fascination. He saw red.

"Whoa. If it ain't Bambi, it's a remake of one of mom and dad's favorite Bible stories. They'd be pleased to know that I'm living through Hawai'i's version of the parting of the Red Sea."

Josh continued to see red. But instead of salty water he was gazing into a sea of molten rock, rising up through the crack opening between his outspread feet. He barely had time to shout "Valerie, Valerie, what's happening?!" before being engulfed in lava.

It was the curtains for Josh. The growing curtain of fire lifted his akimbo body, spinning it like some bizarre human pinwheel. He tumbled back to earth, a charred corpse being encased in solidifying basalt. Joshua had met his Jericho. He lost the battle as the curtain of fire splashed down on him. The fleshy parts of his body were vaporized.

Though they knew not what had just happened, back in Iowa Amos and Rebecca got the wish of having their sinful son roast and burn, though the process happened on earth and may never have moved on to hell. After all, Josh wasn't a bad enough person to deserve hell. He was just a bit confused and misguided. He had been unwilling to live by any of the several literal translations of the many Bibles that filled the bookshelves back on the family farm.

He was a once living and now dead example that extreme lifestyles may not be good for one's health. He had ridden his pendulum too far. Had he lived through this volcanic inferno, his philosophy might have been "By all means, enjoy the things you like best. But enjoy these in moderation."

Valerie watched in stunned horror as Josh disappeared beneath the splashing curtain of molten rock. In a New York minute, her companion of the past several months was gone forever. She screamed, sat down in a lotus position, hung her head, and began to cry convulsively in confusion over what to do. Her entire body was trembling, as was the ground beneath her.

She peeked toward where Josh had disappeared, hoping that the past couple of minutes had been an unreal nightmare. She wished that Josh would be there looking at her with a silly pakalōlō-induced grin across his face. Instead, she saw that the erupting crack was a scant hundred feet away and approaching at the pace of a slow human walk. She felt too lethargic and dispirited to act quickly. Running would tear her bare feet to shreds. Her situation seemed hopeless.

"Goodbye, mother and dad. I love you. Thanks for being so understanding...for letting me try to find my own direction in life. But I seem to have..."

Before she could finish the thought, she felt herself being lifted by a pair of strong hands.

"Up you go, my friend. Sorry to handle you like a piece of luggage, but there's no time for formalities. We've got to get out of here. Pronto!"

Andy slung Valerie over his broad shoulders, as gently as possible, into the classic position of a battlefield rescue. He moved quickly, upwind and away from the approaching lava maelstrom.

He had arrived with maybe thirty seconds to spare. Without the protection provided by a covering of clothing, the naked female's skin had been bombarded with intense radiation of heat from the nearby lava. Her skin would have blistered if he hadn't snatched her when he did. Andy himself had felt an uncomfortable tingly burning sensation on his exposed face and hands when he bent to scoop her up.

As he walked further from the lava, Andy smelled the distinctive odor of singed hair, hers. Her hair might look unusually frizzy for a while, but there would be no blisters. Was she conscious?

"Where's your friend?"

The reply came slowly, in phrases that dribbled out between sobs.

"He's gone...dead...buried by the lava...Oh, god, what have we done?...We should have been more alert...We should have known enough to get out of the way...Why did we have to fight this morning?...I'll never see Josh again, to tell him I'm sorry."

Andy listened to her pangs of remorse tinged with guilt, as he kept moving toward the chopper. He was well beyond any danger from the lava. His load was as limp and about the same weight as a hundred-pound bag of rice. She was also a non-stop crying machine. Soon, her sounds were drowned out by those of the hovering Jet Ranger.

Wilbur was steady as a rock at the controls. He had the chopper positioned just above the open patch of grass and ferns. Andy approached the front of the chopper and made eye contact with Wilbur. Wilbur nodded in recognition. Andy walked as close as possible to the passenger-side skid. He lifted his limp load from his shoulders and boosted her toward the door of the back seat.

"Grab the skid and try to pull yourself up into the chopper!"

She responded slowly. Andy helped by pushing up on one sweet-looking pair of buttocks. The distraction pulled his mind briefly away from the seriousness of their present situation. The view, as she slipped into the rear cabin, was one to remember. "*Buenas nalgas*" he whispered to himself.

"Move over to the other side of the seat!"

Space for him now available, Andy quickly and easily entered the chopper. He tapped a signal on the right shoulder of a concentrating Wilbur, and up they moved, slowly, between tree branches spaced just wide enough for passage. An unexpected wind gust blew them into a small ʻōhiʻa branch. The main rotor functioned successfully as a weed whacker. Once above tree line, Wilbur twisted the throttle to pour on the power. They moved up and away to the north.

The next thing Valerie knew, a man's shirt was being wrapped around her naked body.

"Here. Put my shirt on. You might appreciate the warmth and modesty. Besides, the folks at the Hilo airport will wonder what Wilbur and I are up to this time if you arrive naked."

Valerie did appreciate some body covering in the presence of unfamiliar men. She was still wrestling with emotional hurt and confusion about what was happening. Then, a pungent odor helped snap her back to relatively rational if not mundane thinking. It was as though strong smelling salts suddenly pulled her from semi-consciousness.

Her savior's shirt carried the not-unpleasant smell of male sweat generated by physical, rather than mental stress. She knew the difference, harking back to her days of dating preppies. The bare-chested man beside her, the source of the sweaty shirt, looked like a Greek god. Was she dreaming or was this real? He was talking to the pilot.

"Take us to the red private-aviation hangar at Hilo airport. My car should still be there. It'll be dark soon. The eruption just keeps marching slowly down-rift. The good folks of Puna should be safe through another night without our aerial eyes."

Andy grabbed his radio and called the office. "HVO, this in Andy. HVO, this is Andy."

The Don answered: "Good to hear your voice, Andy. How'd you do?"

"We managed to save one, a young woman. By the time I got to her on foot, there was no sign of her friend. She says he was buried by lava. I'll see that she's taken care of. We'll have to try to ID her friend later, when she feels like talking. We're headed into Hilo now. I should be back at HVO within an hour."

"Okay. We'll talk more then. Good job, by both you and Wilbur. Tell that chopper jockey that I owe him a steak dinner with all the trimmings at the Volcano House. Mai tais are on him."

"Will do. Over and out."

As they flew over Keaʻau, Andy put a comforting arm around the lady beside him and managed to get a conversation going. He learned that this lovely and frightened young woman was named Valerie. She was twenty-three years old and on her own in Hawai'i, now that her friend Josh was dead. Her father and mother lived in New York City. She missed them.

Valerie shuddered and nestled closely into the protection of Andy's arm and the warmth of his body. She didn't say so, but his curly chest hair tickled her nose in a pleasant way.

Though it hardly seemed like the appropriate time or place, Andy couldn't keep himself from thinking, "Could this be the lady I'm searching for? *Ojalá*, she's beautiful…short, built, and with long blonde hair."

Once they had landed, Valerie objected not at all when Andy suggested that she stay with him until she decided how to put the pieces of her life back together. He dropped her off at his house in Volcano on the way back to HVO. He introduced her to his claw-foot bathtub, a reasonably well-stocked pantry and refrigerator, and a closet with plenty of clean dry clothes, albeit in sizes and styles for a male body. Andy was back at HVO by late afternoon, feeling anxious to return home as soon as possible.

CHAPTER 47

ERUPTION BACKTRACKS WEST

Friday morning, December 31...New Years Eve Day.
Eruption continued. The propagating crack and its following curtain of fire were now within one mile of Highway 13, the main connecting route between Pāhoa and the south coast of Kīlauea. What so far had been a spectacular and interesting scientific experiment (except for Josh, Hak, and JD) seemed destined to adopt a more human dimension within a few hours. Tragedy in the form of destroyed homes might soon be added to the eruption mix.

Rob was the sole HVO observer in the helicopter. As usual, Wilbur was the pilot. They were hovering several hundred feet above the ground, looking west immediately upwind of the curtain of fire. Rob reported frequently by radio to The Don at HVO. The Don relayed information about as frequently by telephone to Fuzzy Chee, who in turn briefed appropriate officials in the Puna District.

It would have been faster, easier, and perhaps more logical for Rob to report directly to Puna officials on the ground near the threatened area. But that way, Chee wouldn't be in the flow of information, to gather the notoriety and credit he craved. With eruption entirely outside the park, Kamph was out of the need-to-know loop.

A plan for the evacuation of people living along the east rift zone was in place. Police and fire sirens, supplemented by bullhorns beamed from low-flying helicopters, if needed, would trigger evacuation.

Rob was on the radio, talking to The Don.

"The curtain of fire remains about the same size as it's always been. It keeps migrating down-rift at the pace of a slow walk. I estimate it will intersect the highway a little after noon."

"I'll let Chee know about the timing, so the Puna folks can be prepared to stop traffic on 13."

Sharp turbulence suddenly buffeted the chopper. Wilbur decided to reposition. Both Rob and Wilbur knew what squirrelly winds had done to a helicopter during an eruption of Mauna Loa that had threatened Hilo in the early 1970s. Over the years, that accident had become labeled the "candy crash" in reference to the bonbon appearance of the lava-coated machine as it disappeared into the maw of a lava river. Rob and Wilbur didn't want to repeat that tasty fate.

Rob remained silent as Wilbur maneuvered. He turned clockwise toward the east, and flew down-rift to the highway. He then spun back west for a straight-on look at the action. Incredibly, there was no action. Both Rob and Wilbur rubbed their eyes in disbelief.

"Crap, Wilbur. What's happening?"

Rob thumbed the transmit key of his radio. He spoke without the usual call-up signal.

"You folks at HVO aren't going to believe this, but the eruption has stopped within the past couple of minutes. There's no more live lava visible at the surface. Tons of steam and sulfurous fume are still billowing from the fissure, where it was last active, but that orange molten stuff is nowhere to be seen. I don't know what the hell's going on."

The Don was listening to Rob's message from a spot in front of the tourist window. He watched as a flurry of small earthquakes began to record on the seismographs.

"Keep reporting from down there. I'll get back to you soon."

The Don ran down the hall to Ben's office, grabbed him by the arm, and pulled him to the seismographs, repeating Rob's most recent message on the way. Ben watched the pens flapping back and forth for several minutes, scribing their records of tremor and small earthquakes. He quickly ran through a mental calculation, just as he had when the down-rift migration of eruption had begun three days earlier.

"Holy tsunami!! The earthquake action is migrating right back up the rift, toward Āhua, where it all began. I'm guessing that a wave of underground magma pressure is pushing back up the rift. Whatever it is, it's traveling a lot faster up-rift than the curtain of fire migrated down-rift.

"Keep looking out the window, toward Āhua, while I watch these seismic records."

By now, the rest of the HVO staff had gathered. A minute or two of palpably charged silence passed as eyes kept focused on their targets. Ben spoke first.

"Okay. The instrument near Heiheiahulu is receiving the signals from earthquakes first right now. That's a couple of miles back up-rift from where Rob said the curtain of fire died out."

In the background, Rob's voice was still reporting that eruption was finished…all pau in Hawaiian palaver.

A few minutes of pregnant silence followed.

"Now the shaking is originating near the instrument closest to Nāpau, even further up-rift."

By this time, the rest of the HVO crew could anticipate Ben's next statement.

"The station nearest Āhua is now recording the seismic action first and most powerfully. Maybe something is about to happen there."

Ben continued to watch the seismic records as The Don and staff kept their eyes focused in the direction of Āhua. The Don suddenly shouted.

"Holy Martha!!" This was instantly followed by "Excuse me dear" as an aside. "Ben, look up. There's eruption again near Āhua."

All watched as a new curtain of fire appeared near Āhua. The scene was unexpected, hypnotic, and puzzling. The Don immediately sent Andy, Bruce, and Jeb down to see what was happening on the ground.

CHAPTER 48

JD FRIES AND HAK DIES

Hak and JD were weak with dehydration. According to the Rolex, which was their only contact with the pace of life outside their dark underground prison, today was Friday…exactly one week since they had become trapped. It was now four days, going on five, since their last drink, and that final slurp had been JD's. Lack of solid food was less of a problem. Both had plenty of flesh to burn to keep the body fed. They passed most of that week in gloomy silence, trying to conserve what little energy they had.

To make their prison as livable as possible, they had agreed to some semblance of housekeeping. The privy was at the far end of the lava tube, where the collapsed roof sealed off further passage. For the first couple of days of captivity, solid waste was piling and stinking up their poorly ventilated cell. After that, though, about as much waste came out as new food went in and the raunchy smell of crap abated. Like solid waste, the volume of expelled bodily liquid also shrank to a dribble in a couple of days. But what came out was so concentrated that their air smelled like a poorly ventilated old Parisian pissoir along the Champs Elysées.

There was no kitchen, but this didn't stop them from audibly fantasizing over their favorite foods, above the rumbling of empty stomachs. In fact, food words frequently slipped involuntarily into their vocabularies. JD mostly ranted about moon pies and RC Cola. Hak raved about cone sushi, poi, and ice-cold beer. The only solid food they could consume was pakalōlō from some of Hak's lava tube cache. It helped make their stomachs feel fed, and it dulled the pain of slow death. It also robbed them of what little saliva their liquid-starved bodies could produce.

The bedroom sleeping surface was the relatively smooth pāhoehoe floor of the tube. They spent most of their time asleep, or trying to be that unconscious, as a way to pass the hours.

As time wore on, they began to accept the idea that the lava tube would be their tomb. An urge to relive the past generated conversation. They discovered that both had grown up in poverty…and that that was about all they had in common.

JD's parents had encouraged intolerance and strong-arm tactics to overcome money and intelligence deficiencies. The family motto, defined by practice rather than any written word, was something like, "if you don't have it, but want it, take it." JD had copied the example of his parents during childhood and beyond, and look where it got him. Who knows what he might have grown into, with different role models in a kinder and gentler environment? There was a fundamental lack of gray matter, though, whatever the living environment might have been.

Hak knew that his parents and maybe even all six of his siblings were still on Oʻahu, probably struggling to keep life flowing. The parents, especially Lillie, had tried to teach the children a work ethic embedded in respect for others. For reasons he never understood, Hak had rebelled. Though surrounded by love and support, he had been driven by some inner rage to be a mean guy. Yet, try as he might to always be that tough dude, for the past several weeks he had been having increasingly frequent kind thoughts about family, especially about his mother. Maybe he should have gotten back in touch and shared some of his wealth with her.

Hak and JD were talking about life again, as the Rolex moved further into Friday morning. Both were lying flat, on their backs, staring into the darkness as they chewed on a few more pakalōlō leaves. Their minds were dulled. They were almost too weak to care about much anymore. Words spilled out without much rhyme or reason, like water from an upset glass.

"Ya know, Hak, I had a good run at life, takin' lots a pleasures along the way. I surely didn't want it ta end like this, but goin' out painlessly, stoned, ain't so bad."

PAUSE

"I've had a good run, too. But I wish I could go way back in time and do something to make my mother proud of me. She was a steel pillar of goodness, which I didn't recognize or appreciate as a kid. She was safe landfall in a wild Pacific typhoon, and I ignored her."

They lay in silence for a couple of minutes, frazzled and starved brains trying to process what they had just said. Surprisingly, the one with less gray matter piped up first.

"Hominy grits, bubba. You're sure one soft pussy of a person for a fella in the illegal drug business."

PAUSE

"Well, luau pig to you, scar face. For someone who's supposed to enforce the laws of our land, you're nothing more than one hell of an outlaw. If we get out of this mess, let's trade jobs. You can be the badass drug king, without any special training needed to play the part. And I'll be a cop, but one who actually enforces the laws. I'll get you, too, man, and put you right where you should be."

Silence hit again, until they simultaneously realized that JD was right now where Hak said he should be. They giggled together, in an effort to ignore their hopeless situation.

"Holy pork rinds, Hak man. Somebody done beat ya ta the punch. I wonder who that other cop is?"

Just then, the ground shook and the earth opened. Even in their weakened state, their bodies could feel the same kind of tingling that had occurred a week earlier when the crack had closed enough to trap them. Rocks once again came tumbling down the crack onto the lava tube floor. Could the new shaking mean even more closing?

The tumbling stopped. They stood up, approached the crack, and were amazed to discover that upward passage looked once again possible. In their weakened condition the climb out would be a substantial effort, but given enough time they might escape to the surface. They began a laborious ascent.

Still the stronger of the two, JD was in the lead. Progress was painfully slow. He was barely able to squeeze between still-close walls, one handhold to the next, rocky step by rocky step on ledges protruding from the walls of the crack. Partway up, he looked down at Hak, an evil grin decorating his face. The old Pickett family motto kicked in.

"Well, so long sucka. Who needs ya? I've changed my mind 'bout takin' ya in."

With those words, he stomped on Hak's lead hand, breaking fingers in an audible crunch. Hak grabbed for the hurt hand with his good one, falling back down the crack several feet for lack of support. Bowling balls of basalt, purposely dislodged by JD, came tumbling down, smashing Hak's right shoulder, but more important, obstructing the newly widened passageway. Hak was once again trapped underground. He backed a few feet into the tube to avoid any additional falling boulders. Mentally nursing his pains, he could hear JD's slow upward progress above.

Then new sounds pierced the atmosphere. They came as an unusual combination of hissing, crackling, and clinking. Hak was baffled. The hissing reminded him of the bubbling off of carbonation from a glass of his favorite beer, or of a slowly leaking tire. The other sounds were more like breaking glass, the rather gentle breaking of millions of thin glass shards.

At first these sounds were barely audible. Within a minute they were louder and more persistent. The next sound was a scream and some dialogue from JD.

"Holy 'possum crap. Why's this happnin' ta me? I'm damn near home free."

A few more seconds of silence broken only by the hiss and tinkle…then.

"No!! Hominy grits, no! Not this way!! Aaaaagh!"

That was the last Hak heard from JD. He peeked up the crack and could see a faint orange glow. He could also feel a pulse of heat push against his face, whooshing down the crack like a sudden surge from the opened door of a blast furnace.

Hak now knew exactly what was happening. A lava flow had spilled into the crack, all over JD. The distinctive odor of burned human flesh tickled his nostrils.

"He must be toast. Good riddance to the jerk. He's my last experience with a lū'au pig, Pele style. Guess I'll be next."

Hak backed away from the crack. He saw no reason to hurry his hot demise. He waited, but searing heat never came. Fluid lava had solidified to solid rock before it flowed down to the level of the tube. Above, the crack was now completely sealed with a plug of new basalt. Hak was solidly trapped in his vault. The residue of J. D. Pickett was nothing more than an unusual fossil in that plug.

Within a day, Hak died of dehydration. Heartbreak may also have contributed at the end. He expired thinking about his family and what his life might have been if…if only he hadn't been so angry, mean, and selfish. He thought about his mother a lot. She had borne seven children and worked her fingers to the bone to raise them as best she could, never complaining.

During his last hour, Hak kept repeating, "I'm sorry mother, so sorry. I hope the other kids are pleasing you." Though invisible in the darkness, droplets streaming through the scruffy beard of his unshaven cheeks were proof of his spilled tears.

Very near the end, eyes closed, flat on his back and strength rapidly failing, he remembered again Lillie teaching her children as much as she could about their Hawaiian heritage. She was so proud of that, even though the family bloodlines were mixed. One of her many lessons for the kids had been about how ancient Hawaiians often buried their dead in lava tubes, especially in tubes with difficult access to discourage later intruders, unwelcome grave robbers.

"Lillie, my sweet mother, here I am, about to lie down one last time, in a tube that may never be discovered. My Hawaiian heritage, passed so lovingly on from you, will be safe forever."

Hak moved from the floor of the tube to one of the side benches. He lay back, using a brick of pakalōlō for a pillow.

"This will give whoever might discover my body plenty to speculate about. Talk about an unusual funerary headrest."

He died humming the family song about pulu and hāpuʻu, with a mental image of his mother and siblings clearly in focus. As befit his father's lifelong behavior, dad lurked silently in the background of that image. Mother had always been the strong one, a true Hawaiian matriarch.

CHAPTER 49

THE WATER HAMMER HYPOTHESIS

As JD was being toasted and enveloped by lava in the Koa'e fissure, the HVO crew sent by The Don was surveying the eruption situation at the surface. By the time they arrived near the new outbreak, a crack and its following curtain of fire were migrating westward from the eruption's original starting point of a week earlier. New crack and curtain had already advanced across the Hilina Pali road and were moving westward at the pace of a brisk jog.

Andy parked the Ford as close to the action as he considered safe. He, Bruce, and Jeb hurried to stay abreast of the eruption, being careful to stay upwind and upslope of the source of molten rock and its pungent volcanic fumes.

Crack and eruption were aimed directly at the base of one of the tallest palis of the Koa'e. They soon linked in with the pali, prying that preexisting crack open even wider. The music of accordion tectonics was in its pull-on-the-box expansion mode. Simultaneously, and for the first time in the recorded history of Kīlauea, newly erupted lava was oozing down against the face of a Koa'e pali, spilling into and filling the gaping crack even as it grew wider.

Andy, Jeb, and Bruce trotted along, watching this action play out. They collected a sample of the new lava for study back in the lab. They took a ton of photos, especially of lava spilling into the crack. At one point, Andy and Jeb thought they heard the scream of a human voice coming from the crack. The eerie sound lasted only a few seconds. They looked at each other and then at Bruce. Andy spoke.

"Hey, Bruce. Did you hear that? It sounded like some guy in distress."

They all stood motionless and listened, hearing nothing like a human voice.

"I didn't hear anything unusual. You guys are getting mystical on me."

They watched as lava continued to spill into the crack. Eventually, all agreed that Andy and Jeb may have heard the sounds of heated air streaming and screaming through the crack, like music-creating breath forcibly expelled between a whistler's lips. Andy had another idea, too.

"I think Pele was whistling in admiration of my hunky body."

Within a half hour of their arrival, the HVO crew watched as eruption ceased so abruptly that it seemed as if the valve to a magma-spewing faucet had been ratcheted shut. At 11:30 the eruption was over, all pau. Andy radioed a brief summary of what they had seen to HVO. They jogged to the Ford and drove back to the office.

The Don called the staff together around the conference table. They were trying to understand what had happened, and why. No one had ever before seen eruption migrate up-rift. They speculated that magma migrating down-rift had encountered some impenetrable underground blockage, which subsequently sent a surge of fluid pressure back up to the magma source beneath Āhua. This scenario wasn't a scientifically defensible explanation, but it would give the group something to think on for the time being.

Frank, ever the jack-of-all-trades handyman, chimed in to suggest that what had happened reminded him of the water hammer of home plumbing infamy. He stood while the rest remained seated and puzzled around their conference table. He put on the most serious expression possible for an unshaven grease-smeared visage.

"Look at it this way. The eruptive fissure sealed itself shut at the surface with all of the new lava that erupted from Āhua on down the rift to where the action stopped. So, a pressure surge, which was created when magma that was moving down-rift was halted dead in its tracks, was trapped underground in a sort of natural pipe."

Frank scratched his nearly bald head and thought about what to say next. The rest of the HVO staff was watching and waiting for this old self-taught journeyman plumber to continue. He looped his thumbs around the vertical supports of his suspenders, in mock professorial stance.

"Now, when the pressure pulse got back up to where the eruption first started, it cracked new ground around the magma-filled balloon. Remember it was the bursting of that balloon that caused eruption to start in the first place."

He stopped, scratched again, and decorated his face with the faintest of smiles. He was enjoying himself. Here he was explaining what had happened, while the four college-educated men seated there in front of him seemed clueless.

"Well, that balloon and the surge that hit it had just enough oomph left to push renewed eruption a ways westward, into the Koa'e. That last push finally deflated our magical balloon, and here we are back to nice quiet times, balloon flat as a pissed-out bladder."

He briskly shook his head down-and-up once to indicate self-satisfaction and being finished. His facial expression suddenly changed to total relaxation mode. He still had the floor and his colleagues' attention.

"Did I ever tell you folks about the time I cranked the hot-water faucet shut just as my bathtub was filling up, only to hear the loud metallic bang of a water hammer followed by the sound of a gushing burst pipe under the house? God, what a mess! I charged outside in my birthday suit to look for the main shutoff valve. My neighbor, spinster Wright, was out tending her garden. She started screaming her head off when she saw my privates flapping in the breeze. I always thought it was interesting that she simply stared at me, rather than retreating to the modesty of her house."

The Don jumped up and took charge, to avoid subjecting everyone to a long string of home-spun homilies of the sort that Frank liked to tell when allowed to occupy center stage.

Frank sat down, took a greasy rag out of his hip pocket, and started reflexively rubbing his already dirty hands with it. Everyone else was speechless…and confused.

"Frank's story, though interesting right on down to the finish, contains more than one loose end. For the time being, let's consider the water hammer hypothesis as a possible explanation of what happened. It's about as believable as many other geologic tales I've heard over the many years of my career."

He looked Allan squarely in the eyes.

"We geologists hate to admit it, but we're almost as infamous as geophysicists for describing a complete picture when most pieces of the puzzle are missing. We'll all have plenty of time and chances to try to tie up some of Frank's loose ends later…if spinster Wright doesn't get to one or more of them first."

Most of the staff laughed at The Don's attempt to lighten the mood.

Meanwhile, tremor and earthquakes had disappeared simultaneously with the last of the curtain of fire.

"Go home. Enjoy the weekend. With a little luck, life here at HVO will revert back to a quiet routine for the foreseeable future. And may we all have a Happy New Year. Hauʻoli Makahili Hou!"

CHAPTER 50

WEDDING PLANS

Following the staff debriefing, Andy was anxious to get home for the possibility of a bit of de briefing of his own design. After spending last night together, he and Valerie were well on their way to becoming more than two strangers thrown together by a volcanic disaster. And with only his clothes available for body coverings, both were wearing his briefs.

※   ※   ※

   Yesterday when he got home from HVO, he had found Valerie asleep on the couch. She was wearing a pair of his blue jeans and a Kīlauea-Volcano-emblazoned tee-shirt. She lay on her side, facing out. Sleeping or awake, her facial expression carried an enchanting smile…a hint of Mona Lisan mystery. The lovely blonde hair that he had seen hanging to her hips when he snatched her from the grasp of eruption was in a halo-like mass, bunched around her head. A few frizzed ends still carried the signature of a singe. The image of Kīlauea on the tee-shirt looked like it was draped over a two-humped camel…not stretched over a balloon-like pocket of magma, which was part of the shirt's image.

   As he watched her sleeping, Valerie's beauty continued to grow on Andy. She was the epitome of his ideal female. Now, he wanted to know if there was a brain inside that lovely head, rather than the relative vacuum attributed to so many blondes. If sufficient gray matter was present, this could be the steady sensible lady that he was looking for, to replace his life of too much partying and female variety.

He moved quietly about the house until he found a paperback novel by Stephen Greenleaf, his favorite author. He sat where he could watch Valerie asleep on the couch, and read about Private Investigator John Marshall Tanner solving yet another mystery in the San Francisco Bay Area, the beloved hometown place he planned to return to once his stint at HVO was finished.

A half hour into the plot, with the cast of good guys and bad guys well established, his sleeping beauty stirred. When she opened her eyes, the first thing she saw was the man who had saved her life earlier that day. They smiled at each other in mutual curiosity and physical admiration. They began a long conversation of explanations and getting-to-know-you.

Valerie started. She understood that Andy must wonder what she and Josh had been doing in such a remote part of the rainforest. She told her story chronologically. The part up to cohabitation with Josh was a retell of her first conversation with Josh.

"Josh and I were both drifting. Each of us hated our lifestyle at home. Each of us had decided to look somewhere else for what we wanted. We met in Pāhoa by accident."

Valerie paused and shed a few tears as her mind slipped back to when she and Josh had first talked…their sharing deeply personal life stories over a cold drink, and then slinking out the back door of the café to start an incredible adventure together.

"We came from totally different backgrounds. We were unhappy at home for different reasons. But we were compatible enough to try to sort things out together. This worked for a while.

"We decided to live off the land. We knew we could do that here on the Big Island. By setting up a primitive home in the rainforest we had plenty of quiet time, time to talk with none of the distractions of a hectic mainstream life. We had time to think about and plan for the future. We grew enough pakalōlō to supply ourselves with smokes and provide a medium of barter that's readily accepted for food and drink in Pāhoa. What a bunch of friendly and open-minded people in that town!

"We talked a lot about how and when we would get back into the flow of society. All along I planned to go back home…you know, to a modified version of the home I fled. Josh never seemed sure about going back, though. Unlike me, he had left the family nest under a dark and stormy cloud of bad feelings.

His parents disowned him. Mine always loved me. I want to get in touch with them soon, to let them know I'm okay."

"You can phone from here any time you want."

"Recently, Josh seemed to be losing the spirit and will to live. He only wanted to smoke pakalōlō and sleep. While I was making a plan to get back into some kind of life that would include my parents, Josh was becoming an introverted zombie. He didn't want to talk about the future any more.

"Now that he's gone, I guess none of this matters. Someone should try to locate his parents and sisters, though, and let them know what's happened. All I know is that his last name is Brown and that he's from a part of Iowa where they grow corn and raise pigs."

"I'll talk with the Big Island police about locating the family. They'll probably handle this as a missing-person case. It could be a challenge with only Brown, corn, pigs, and somewhere in Iowa as leads."

Valerie finished by emphasizing her growing urge of wanting to get back into a relatively mainstream lifestyle…just so it wasn't in her still-hated New York City financial scene.

"I think I'm more suited to coastal California living."

Andy's pulse suddenly surged. He grinned and began his half of the who-am-I session. He was almost shouting. "I was born and raised on the mid-Peninsula, about halfway between San Francisco and San Jose. And I'm moving back there soon."

He thought he saw some additional twinkle in Valerie's eyes at this mention of his life's geography. That's what he had hoped for. He continued.

"It's hard to beat that area for its Mediterranean climate, laid-back lifestyle, a variety of opportunities for outdoor recreation, and all the intellectual stimulation anyone could want! Hey, I don't mean to sound like a chamber of commerce, but the reason so many people live around San Francisco Bay are the things I just mentioned. The only part I've never liked about life there is the crowding. But I grew up in a town with larger than average hilly lots. That offers plenty of privacy from the throngs and madding crowds. My dad and mother still live in the old family house, right next door to Stanford."

Andy went on to describe his growing up there, through his graduation from Stanford. He downplayed his bacchanalian times, and emphasized the inspiration gained from David Johnston, and how that role model had put him on the path of studying volcanoes. He explained that being on the HVO staff was his first volcano assignment since finishing college. He was effusive about how challenging, exciting, and unusual the work was.

Valerie listened quietly and with elevated interest. She was worldly enough to know plenty about the mid-Peninsula lifestyle, especially when lived from such an advantaged base as Los Altos Hills. She smiled inwardly, knowing that Andy must have skipped the parts about wild parties and multiple girlfriends. Her smile was also in recognition that this guy appealed to her because of his past…and because of his uniquely interesting job. He was a handsome hunk to look at, too.

By the time they finished talking, the clock said eleven. Both were exhausted…Andy from the recent long and frantic days of surveying and then following the progress of eruption once it started…Valerie from her near-death ordeal earlier that very day.

Andy was on twenty-four-hour call. But unless some unexpected eruption twist triggered a nighttime call, he didn't have to report to HVO until tomorrow morning at six o'clock. Rob was to be the geologic eyes in the helicopter flight scheduled to depart Hilo airport tomorrow at dawn.

With unspoken asking and consent, Valerie and Andy slipped into bed together, naked. Valerie's back was molded tightly to Andy's front in the posture of nested spoons. Their bodies were held together as one by Andy's strong arms. Though there was plenty of interest in consensual physical play banging around in each one's mind as consciousness morphed into slumber, an overpowering awareness said that sex now would only diminish the significance of a new and strengthening bond.

"Besides," Andy was thinking, "tomorrow is another day with Valerie in my house. Still, I can't believe I'm not trying to jump this beautiful lady right now. For the first time in my life, I'm not moving in for quick physical gratification. Maybe there's hope for me to grow into a giver rather than a taker."

He pulled Valerie a little closer and slept the sleep of a truly satisfied guy.

When Andy awoke on Friday morning, Valerie was still asleep. He unraveled their intertwined bodies without waking her. He got dressed, gulped a glass of passion-guava juice, ate a half-papaya flavored with nectar he squeezed from a fresh lime, and headed off to HVO. He left Valerie a note suggesting that they go to Hilo tomorrow and buy her some clothes…if he could get away from his eruption duty long enough.

He had an unexpected and welcome surprise coming with regard to eruption that Friday. It stopped before noon; HVO once again became a rather quiet place of routine work. No more tremor was recorded that day. A few small earthquakes occurred, but nothing beyond the normal amount of background shaking for a volcano like Kīlauea.

The staff was quickly immersed in the throes of winding down from the preceding hectic weeks…looking for their version of what professional counselors call closure. Conversations focused on what they had done for Christmas and what they planned to do tonight to celebrate New Year's Eve. Shoptalk was kept to a minimum.

Late that afternoon, when The Don called everyone to the conference table, he laid out a plan for studying the effects of the recent eruption. There was mapping to do, samples of the new lava to collect, and damage to assess. Much of the Chain of Craters road was covered with Pele's asphalt or broken by gaping fissures. Ditto for a short stretch of the Hilina Pali road. The Park Service would appreciate a damage assessment with a geologic perspective from HVO. Work assignments were agreed upon and everyone went home for a quiet personal-time weekend…finally.

When he opened the door of his little house on stilts that Friday afternoon, Andy was surprised to find Valerie up, cleaning the place. She walked to the door to greet him. They shared a quiet hug.

"How're you feeling?"

"Pretty good. I called home this morning. Mother and dad are relieved to know that I'm safe. I told them about how you saved me and are helping me get back to a normal life, whatever normal may mean now. I also mentioned that you're a pretty neat guy."

That comment made Andy smile like a teenage kid who had just scored his first kiss.

"I could almost *hear* smiles of approval when I told them about your Los Altos Hills and Stanford background."

"I'm glad they feel that way."

"I've been thinking a lot about what happened yesterday out there on the volcano…and also what happened here with you last night. I feel terrible about Josh's fate. At the same time, I think I finally see what I want for the rest of my life. I did a little practicing today to find out if I still know how to live in a real home."

With those words, Valerie looked up into Andy's eyes, wearing an expression that dovetailed with what he was thinking. At least, that's what Andy saw.

They took a step back from each other. Valerie was barely covered with a creative and sexy combination of his clothes. His Speedo swimming trunks hung loosely on her slender body. One tug on a tightly tied, jerry-rigged drawstring would expose all. Above, she wore only a blue cotton shirt, unbuttoned. Shirttails were tied around her waist. Deep cleavage between mounds of flesh peeked out of the open shirt.

"Wow! You look like a Hawaiian version of the classic French maid."

Andy switched his tone of voice to friendly sarcasm.

"What other happy surprises has madam prepared for me today?"

Smiling coyly, Valerie walked to the refrigerator and fetched Andy an ice-cold beer. She pointed to the kitchen sink.

As he nodded his head with the first gulp of the refreshing liquid, he noticed that the usual disorganized pile of dirty dishes was not there.

"Ummh. How remarkable for my house. Dishes are clean and stacked orderly in their cabinets."

Valerie watched with bemused expression as Andy walked across the small kitchen and peeked into the bedroom.

"And what have we here? The normal pile of dirty clothes is nowhere to be seen. My shirts and pants are washed, pressed, and hanging in the closet. Socks, briefs, and handkerchiefs are clean and neatly arranged in dresser drawers. I must be at the wrong address."

Next, Andy looked in the bathroom, with Valerie a few steps behind. Mildew was gone from shower tiles, and that was a true, though probably pretty temporary, accomplishment in Volcano's humid climate. The claw-foot bathtub was clean, but then that was the one piece of furniture that Andy cared for regularly, simply because it gave him so much pleasure.

He moved into the small living room. Valerie shadowed his progress. Books were back on shelves, arranged by author. His small but growing collection of Stephen Greenleaf mysteries was sorted, left to right, by date of publication. Records and tapes were back on shelves, sorted by artists. Magazines were racked, rather than strewn across the couch and adjacent floor.

Andy looked straight up. My God! Valerie had even removed that extensive network of cobwebs that had always decorated the ceiling. He and Valerie smiled at each other. They were both relishing the game being played.

Andy had a semi-fiendish grin across his face as he walked toward the oven. He looked at Valerie with a "gotcha" expression and opened the door. Months' worth of burned drippings from pre-prepared frozen meals and pizza were gone.

Not to be bested, he walked over to the couch, dropped to his knees and looked beneath. Throwing a puzzled look up at Valerie, he repeated this kind of inspection for his bed. There was not one creeping fuzzy to be seen under those pieces of furniture. The game was finished.

They approached each other with seriously happy expressions. They wrapped arms around each other, and then leaned back enough to look into eyes only inches apart.

"Jeez, Valerie, thanks for all the work you've done. But, ah, I want an equal partner, a lover, a friend…not the world's most efficient maid."

"I want those things, too, Andy. As a bonus, I'm happy to clean *our* house for a long, long time. Of course, there're lots of other things I want to do in our house, too."

"You've got a deal."

In unison they said, "Okay, then" and fell into a bout of kissing, caressing, and talking that lasted until growling stomachs announced dinnertime.

Valerie covered herself with an ankle-length raincoat. They drove to the Volcano Store and bought fixings for a New Year's Eve meal. Hidden behind rows of sake, they found a dust-covered bottle of Korbel Champagne. Andy recognized the label as one of California's so-so own.

"This stuff isn't great, but it's palatable and bubbly. Tonight, it can be our reminder of where we hope to eventually set up housekeeping."

They drove back home, where they ate, talked, and listened to music. They managed to stay awake until midnight, at which moment they sipped a glass of the Korbel and shouted Happy New Year! They started 1983 with a bang. The little house on stilts shook in a long and steady rhythm, though not from Pele's volcanic tremors. Then, they got out of bed and began making plans for their wedding.

CHAPTER 51

ALL QUIET ON THE VOLCANO FRONT

The first workweek of 1983 was pleasantly boring at HVO. Kīlauea was in a languorous between-eruptions quiet mode. Without the demands that come with eruption, Monday's routine chores were back to being top priority. Howard changed the paper on the rotating drums at the tourist window, and delivered the records of the past twenty-four hours to Ben's office. Then he got back to milling out that new instrument for Allan.

Frank was fiddling with the WWII Jeep. He wanted to change the windshield wipers from vacuum to electrically driven. More than once in the past, a driver's visibility had been totally obliterated by rain when the little four-cylinder engine was so stressed climbing a hill that no excess vacuum was available to power the wiper blades. He had just recently got his hands on a couple of small electric motors as surplus from the Army on Oʻahu. They would look pretty ugly mounted at the top of the windshield, but they'd probably do the job.

Jeb, Bruce, and Jane were entering data from the leveling survey into yet another computer program for redundancy that would minimize the chances for data loss. There were always the hand-written numbers in the field books, too, but eventually HVO's humid and caustic environment fed by the fuming nearby caldera would render these illegible.

Andy, Rob, and Ben were huddled in Rob's office, discussing ideas for writing research papers about the eruption. There had been many rift zone eruptions during past years, but none that had migrated more than halfway to the sea, only to turn around and march back up-rift for a final burst where it had all begun. They should get some valuable mileage from this oddity for their professional résumés.

First thing that morning, Allan had thrown a batch of strange-looking gear into the Ford and headed to the Puna District. He was going to probe for anomalous geophysical signals in the area where the eruption had stopped and surged back to its starting point. No one doubted that Allan would find some puzzling geophysical signature in that area. What that meant, of course, would be subject to the usual multiple interpretations. But at least the behavior of the eruption was a real event. That would help put limits on Allan's otherwise free-wheeling imagination.

Kabana was frantically poring over the HVO budget. With the Continuing Resolution still in effect, the observatory was now horribly overspent with regard to the rules passed down from USGS headquarters. However, Kabana could make expenditures appear spread out in time, even if they all occurred in less than a week. Once again he was wondering why he had to play this silly game. But play he would rather than risk losing his job; he had less than a decade to retirement.

Jane was typing a memo for The Don's signature, an aptly phrased strong recommendation for a one-time monetary award for the entire staff in recognition of a job well done leading up to and during the eruption. Rob was singled out for exceptional service under fire. This memo would have to go through multiple levels of approvals back at headquarters, but past experience showed that eventually the awards would be forthcoming. In addition to some highly deserved extra cash for the entire staff, The Don would achieve his objective of garnering praise, rather than punishment, following Rob's recent head butting with the USGS safety officer.

While the typing of this mischievous ploy was underway, The Don was once again on the phone with headquarters, for the Monday morning round of briefings. It seemed that the principal national news story from the eruption focused on the destruction of marijuana gardens by Kīlauea's lava flows. USGS bureaucrats at headquarters wanted details of how this had happened, so they could knowledgeably brief the Hawaiian congressional delegation about such a substantial accomplishment of their outpost on the Big Island.

The Don answered all of their questions to the best of his knowledge, with a relatively straight face and steady voice, trying to paint the kind of picture his listeners wanted. The truth, of course, was that HVO had not and could not have targeted those illegal gardens for extinction due to eruption. "Oh well," The Don was thinking to himself. "Just two more years of this nonsense before the liberation that will come with retirement."

That Friday, Andy was the last to leave. Out of habit, he strolled to the tourist window on his way to the exit door. He smiled at the fact that he no longer spent hours watching for lovely women at this window; he now had a very special lady of his own. Any "extra" office time was spent on the phone with her, discussing wedding arrangements. They planned to tie the knot on May 10, at Andy's house in Volcano. Valerie was waiting at home right now, so why was he standing here musing over fleeting thoughts?

As Andy turned away from the window, his peripheral vision picked up the unmistakable flapping of seismograph pens. He spun back toward the instruments. All six pens were swishing back and forth in unison. Volcanic tremor was being recorded. Was Pele seriously restless...or just teasing? The pens reverted to tracing straight lines in less than a minute. Andy turned and walked away, not looking back as he spoke with his X factor.

"Hey Pele, are you trying to keep me here? Are you jealous? Well, I won't let you lure me away from my real love this weekend. Sit tight at least until Monday."

Had he turned to look back one more time, he would have seen the rippling record of Pele getting the last word in their conversation.

CHAPTER 52

PELE MAKES PLANS

She turned to sit up in her bed, smiling over the success of recent endeavors. Her long flaming-red tresses were particularly lovely today. A yawn and simultaneous stretch sent shivers through her volcano home.

"I've accomplished so much during the past two weeks. I applied a new layer of protective covering to part of the windward side of my volcano home. Other parts of this side need recovering, too, but that will have to wait until I've rested a bit."

Rapid weathering caused by persistent hot and wet conditions there called for frequent maintenance repairs. She wanted her volcano home to always look young and active. She hated the aged look that comes with thick vegetation and the works of humans.

Her smile widened.

"As a spin off, I've also succeeded where Big Island and national park police have failed for years. Those bilious bickering backbiting babies! My home-improvement project destroyed gardens of pakalōlō, buried a despicable ranger, and entombed an evil grower in a subterranean prison. I'm sorry that young and foolish pakalōlō fan was killed, too; it's not my fault he was so numbed out that he couldn't flee."

She sought a comfortable position in her warm fluid-filled bed, ready to fall back to sleep after the hectic and tiring time She had spent spewing new lava over her volcano. The bed's filling sloshed and shook, but the overall feel was a bit flat. She reminded herself to add more fluid soon. Her last pre-sleep roll sent a second quiver throughout her house. Now She was properly positioned for another rest. She would work again on the deteriorating windward side of her house in a couple of months, if sufficient home-improvement material was available by then.

EPILOGUE

The bodies of Hak and J. D. Pickett were never recovered. Speculation was that they were buried somewhere in the new lava flow, having been overtaken by a surge of molten rock as officer J. D. Pickett was trying to subdue and arrest drug-runner Hak.

Hilo's south-side chapter of Rotary International was shocked to learn that one of their own had gone astray. They agreed to a one-year fund-raising binge for the Big Island Brotherhood of Law Enforcement Officers. They were sure that more and better-equipped cops held the answer to snuffing out crime.

Once informed of her son's disappearance, Lillie organized a memorial service. She and the rest of the Hakonē family recalled the good times, though these were few when it came to Hak's involvement in their family life. They sang Hawaiian songs in the native tongue.

JD had no living relatives, at least none willing to step forward and be identified as such. Somewhat curiously, the in-house Park Service scuttlebutt that spontaneously followed JD's disappearance and presumed death created the image of a truly mean, vindictive, intolerant, and morally bankrupt person. Stories originated in every park where JD had worked. It seems that JD's coworkers had been afraid to talk about him while he was alive.

Within a couple of months, the bricks of pakalōlō that had been discovered in Hak's Toyota disappeared from the park's evidence vault. No attempts were made to recover them. Their disappearance coincided with the early retirement of Archie Boggs. Archie moved to Loreto in Baja California, where he lived lavishly.

The Don, in the person of Jack Richards, retired in early 1985. He and Martha built a dream house on their piece of the southwest rift zone of Mauna Loa. From the makai lānai, they often watched the changing moods of the vast

Pacific Ocean. Many evenings, mai tai in hand, they pretended to see a green flash at the moment of sunset in the west. Through the power of suggestion, many of their mainland visitors swore that the green flash was real. The sun set on the lives of Jack and Martha Richards within days of each other, following an extremely fulfilling and satisfying marriage. They left this earth before renewed eruption on Mauna Loa's rift zone could threaten their home. They had played the odds of being missed by the next eruption of Mauna Loa, and they won.

Frank, Howard, Kabana, Liz, Bruce, Jeb, and Jane...lifetime residents of the Big Island...spent all their working years at HVO and retired when rules of the Federal Civil Service System allowed. Theirs were hard acts to follow. But replacements recruited from the Big Island workforce successfully carried on the HVO tradition of world-class volcano studies.

Ben eventually found a satisfactory way to balance family life with his passion for chasing volcanoes. The USGS permitted him to work half time at HVO, and hired another seismologist to round out the staff.

Shortly after the Christmas Eve eruption of 1982, Allan quietly resigned from HVO and the USGS. He moved back to the mainland. Colleagues heard nothing from him for several years. Then ads for Springs Geophysical Surveys began to appear in earth science magazines and trade journals. It seems that Allan and some of his Rube Goldberg instrumentation, most especially the gadget that Howard machined for him back in 1982, had become highly successful at discovering low-grade, high-volume gold deposits in Nevada. All evidence pointed to one and only one interpretation. Allan had become very wealthy.

Rob had a long, productive, and illustrious career with the USGS. In 1988, he transferred to the Vancouver, Washington, office from which he studied volcanoes of the Cascade Range for a couple of decades. Then, he returned to HVO to fill the role of The Don until his retirement.

Andy and Valerie were married, as planned, on May 10, 1983. Delighted parents from New York City and Los Altos Hills gathered on the Big Island two days earlier to get acquainted by celebrating Mother's Day together. The wedding party consisted of the two sets of parents, Andy's friends Liz and Rob, and a preacher...period. The little house on stilts could hold no more people, even if the happy couple had wanted additional guests.

Three years later, Andy transferred to the USGS office in Menlo Park, California. His father, still a real estate broker, found his son and daughter-in-law a cute two-bedroom fixer-upper in Los Altos Hills. It was a steal at only three quarters of a million dollars. Dad bankrolled the purchase and threw in a late wedding present by gifting them with his usual six percent sales commission.

Andy discovered that the high-pressure competitive atmosphere permeating the USGS office in Menlo Park was not to his liking. Many of his colleagues there seemed to like pushing coworkers back as much as the thorny frontiers of science. Andy left the USGS when he landed a job teaching geology at Foothills Community College, within biking distance of his home. Valerie studied landscape design at Foothills. Credentials in hand, she became a one-person company creating landscape plans for trophy homes of the mid-Peninsula area. In 1990, Andy and Valerie produced a son, who later would attend nearby Stanford as a fourth-generation Clark on The Farm. As an entry in Valerie's diary said: "This fourth-generation Clark on The Farm may be part of a family tradition, but at least our kid isn't an Ivy League preppie."

Early in 1983, following a short snooze, Pele began an extensive resurfacing job on the weathered windward side of her volcano home. She burned and buried many buildings in the process. These were simply unwelcome blemishes on an otherwise uniform finish. Her work of adding a new coat of lava was still underway three years into the twenty-first century.

In 1996, She briefly visited a volcano called Lōʻihi, that new abode that She had earlier heard was under construction. Her visit coincided with a substantial addition to the foundation. She was impressed with the quality of workmanship and traditional Hawaiian design. Use of a mix of lava types added a dimension of interest not apparent in some of her earlier homes. This growing volcano was still three thousand feet beneath the sea.

She genuinely enjoyed the developing neighborhood. At only twenty miles from Halemaʻumaʻu, a home at Lōʻihi would be close to old Kīlauea friends. But, it seemed obvious that her need for an active-crater home, comfortably above sea level, was many millennia away.

Until then, She would stay at Kīlauea and find new ways to confuse and confound that non-stop cadre of probing and snooping scientists at HVO. From time to time, She would permit them to accomplish a few of what they somewhat arrogantly called "fundamental breakthroughs" and "cutting-edge discoveries" under such titles as "How Volcanoes Really Work." Otherwise, they might become discouraged to the point of despair. But She would *never* reveal her innermost secrets about Hawaiian volcanoes. These She would keep beyond the ken of mortals, assuring a permanent place for her in Hawaiian culture.

GLOSSARY OF HAWAIIAN WORDS

'A'ā	Rough rubbly surfaced lava
'Ahi	Tuna fish, especially the yellow-fin variety
Āhua	Swell, mound
Akamai	Smart, clever
'apapane	A Hawaiian honeycreeper (*Himatione sanguinea*)
Haole	A white person or foreigner
Hāpu'u	A tree fern (*Cibotium splendens*)
Hau'oli Makahiki Hou	Happy New Year
Hui	Partnership, firm
Huluhulu	Hairy
Iki	Small, little
Kahuna	Priest, minister
Kama'āina	Native born
Kapu	Taboo, forbidden
Kea	White
Keiki	Child, baby
Kīpuka	"Island" of older lava surrounded by younger lava
Loa	Long
Lua	Crater, toilet
Makai	Seaward
Manu	Bird
Mauna	Mountain
Mele Kalikimaka	Merry Christmas
Nēnē	Hawaiian goose (*Branta sandvicensis*)
Nūpepa	Newspaper
'Ōhelo	Shrub of the cranberry family (*Vaccinium reticulatum*)
'Ōhi'a lehua	The tree *Metrosideros collina*

Pāhoehoe	Smooth-surfaced lava
Pakalōlō	Marijuana
Pali	Cliff
Pau	Finished, over
Pohā	Cape gooseberry (*Physalis peruviana*)
Poi	Pasty Hawaiian staple food, made from taro corms
Pua'a	Pig
Pulu	Soft glossy wool at the base of tree-fern leaf stalks
Pūpū	Snack, hors d'oeuvre
Pu'u	Hill
Ulu	Growing
Wahine	Woman

The HVO Logo

0-595-30224-6

Printed in the United States
95085LV00004B/146/A